TWISTED ROOTS

TWISTED ROOTS

a light into the darkness

shelly goodman wright

TATE PUBLISHING
AND ENTERPRISES, LLC

Twisted Roots
Copyright © 2012 by *Shelly Goodman Wright*. All rights reserved.
No part of this publication may be reproduced, stored in a retrieval system or transmitted in any way by any means, electronic, mechanical, photocopy, recording or otherwise without the prior permission of the author except as provided by USA copyright law.

Scripture quotations, unless otherwise indicated, are taken from the *Holy Bible, King James Version* ®, Cambridge, 1769. Used by permission. All rights reserved.

Scripture quotations marked "NIV" are taken from the *Holy Bible, New International Version* ®, Copyright © 1973, 1978, 1984 by International Bible Society. Used by permission of Zondervan Publishing House. All rights reserved.

This novel is a work of fiction. Names, descriptions, entities, and incidents included in the story are products of the author's imagination. Any resemblance to actual persons, events, and entities is entirely coincidental.

The opinions expressed by the author are not necessarily those of Tate Publishing, LLC.

Published by Tate Publishing & Enterprises, LLC
127 E. Trade Center Terrace | Mustang, Oklahoma 73064 USA
1.888.361.9473 | www.tatepublishing.com

Tate Publishing is committed to excellence in the publishing industry. The company reflects the philosophy established by the founders, based on Psalm 68:11,
"The Lord gave the word and great was the company of those who published it."

Book design copyright © 2012 by Tate Publishing, LLC. All rights reserved.
Cover design by Erin DeMoss
Interior design by Sarah Kirchen

Published in the United States of America
ISBN: 978-1-61862-210-5
1. Fiction / Christian / Romance
2. Fiction / Romance / Fantasy
12.03.20

This book is dedicated to all those who have encouraged me to pursue this dream of publication and to my Savior, Jesus Christ, through whom all things are possible.

Acknowledgments

I'd like to acknowledge those who read my first manuscript years ago and encouraged me to continue. Thanks to Michelle, Tami and Tammy, my sister Susanne, Laura, Carol, Gloria, Tiffany, Cat, Danielle, Sangita, Eileen, The Colorado Springs Fiction Writers, and Brook, who has read everything I've ever written. To my beloved friend, Christy, and Grandma Goodman. I miss you! My wonderful editor, Amber Losson, and a special thanks to my wonderful husband, Tim, and my three beautiful daughters, whom I thank God for every day.

Table of Contents

Prologue 11

The Deal 17

One More Night 31

Destination Nowhere 37

First Impressions 53

Ghosts in the Wind 63

A Lazy Saturday Morning 73

Stranger in the Clearing 83

I'm Not a Little Girl 93

Lovely Garden 101

The Picnic 109

Prince Charming Syndrome 115

And Then He Was Gone 121

Well, Hello 133

To Dream or Not to Dream 143

Trail of Tears 157

Interrupted 171

Two Empty Pails 183

Warning	195
A Vision of Things to Come	203
All Dressed Up	213
Enchanted Ball	227
Lights Out	247
A New World	255
A House Full of Boys	275
The Bonfire	287
My New Secret	307
Molly Returns	319
Into the Dark of Darkest Places	327
Seth's Rise to Power	337
The Diversion	347
To Kill or Not to Kill	355
New Beginnings	371
Epilogue	379

Prologue

A little girl watched her father pace back and forth along the sandy shore.

She yawned and stretched up her arms toward the starry sky. "Can I go back to bed now?"

He turned to face the fair-skinned child and proceeded to watch her twist a piece of her dishwater-blonde hair into a curl, but it only fell straight back down to the middle of her chest.

"Mother said I'm supposed to be well rested for tomorrow, for the party." The six year old then placed her hand on her hip and pressed her feet into the cool sand.

Samuel frowned. "You hate your mother's parties." He put both hands in his pants pockets and stared into her green eyes. "I hate your mother's parties, especially this one."

Jessica didn't like the parties any more than he did, but this party was different. It was for her. The thought of her mother planning anything for her—it was a new start and a chance for her mother to love on her. At least that's what she hoped.

"But this party is different, Daddy." Her hands moved off her hip and slid straight down her sides. "She's planning it for me."

Samuel kept still as her green eyes pierced through him. But it was too much for him to endure, and he changed his focus to the mansion on the hill.

"*Different* isn't the word I would use." His hands moved up through his hair, and then he dragged them down along his face. "I have no choice."

"What?" Jessica asked.

He continued to mumble words, but nothing she understood. So Jessica plopped down on the sand and watched the water move closer each time it spilled out while her father continued to talk to himself.

The sound the ocean made was one of Jessica's favorite sounds, that and the sounds that came from the piano every time she pushed down on the ivory keys. And although she despised her mother for making her take lessons in the first place, it was the one thing she did right and beautiful, the only thing her mother praised her for.

"Jessie." Her father turned toward her and pulled her to her feet. "I don't agree with your mother on a lot of things, and if it hadn't been for you, I would have left a long time ago."

The little girl's eyes began to water.

"No, no. I'm not going to leave you." He wiped her tears with the bottom of his shirt. "Of course I wouldn't purposely leave you. I love you more than the entire sky, more than my own life. It's been just you and me since you were born. But what your mother has planned…I just can't sit back and watch." He hugged his daughter. "I want to tell you something now, something you should know just in case. I need you to listen closely and don't forget. I'm not sure how much time I have." His mouth closed shut, and he scratched the stubble on his chin. "What I mean to say is I might not always be…"

He stopped again and shook his head at the sky. He then pointed out a vivid star high above them in the moonless sky. "There are magical places that exist in this world, Jess, places that the Master Architect created to balance good and evil. The time will come when you will leave this house and enter into another life that awaits you, a life you deserve and one with greater purpose. You don't know how special you really are."

"But I don't want to leave you." The little girl's body trembled. "I'll be better around Mother. I'll be extra quiet so I don't give her headaches, and then she won't be mad at you. It's my fault. It's always because of me."

The corners of Samuel's mouth fell. "It's not your fault. It's never been your fault, and I don't want you to ever think that." He pulled his daughter into a tight embrace.

"If I go, you'll come too, right?" she asked.

"It's not that simple, Jess," he replied and stroked her long hair. It was then that an idea popped into Samuel's head. "Maybe it is that simple to return. I'd have to face the consequences, but she'd be safe…"

Jessica pulled away from his frozen hold and broke his train of thought. He then kneeled down in front of her.

"Did I ever tell you about the angels who watch over us?"

The little girl shook her head from side to side and rubbed her red eyes with her fists. He had talked about angels and fantastical creatures the little girl assumed were make believe, but not that they were watching her. She looked around to see if one was watching.

Her father reached out for her hands and took them into his. "You are not alone in this world, my sweet Jessica. There are angels who watch over us all the time. Some watch us from above while others walk among us to help shield us from the evil that lives in and among us too. In our worst times, we are not alone. All you have to do is believe, and help will come." He stroked the inside of her palm and smiled. "Just in case something happens and I'm not around, I wanted you to know that."

A large wave crashed onto the shore and spattered toward them. The salty fish air inundated Jessica's nose at the same time cold, bubbly wetness covered her ankles. A chill ran up through her as the water retreated and pulled the sand out from under her tiny feet. She squeezed her father's hand tight and held her breath for a moment and then let it out slowly.

The next wave crashed, louder this time.

Samuel pulled a piece of folded paper out of his pocket and handed it to his daughter.

"Put it in your pocket. Hide it somewhere safe. I pray it will help you remember what I told you."

The little girl hesitated and then looked at the folded square in her palm.

"I'm sorry, Jessica," he said and looked past her.

Jessica didn't have to turn around to know a person was behind her. The smell of her strong perfume was enough of a clue. The little girl then slipped the paper into her night robe and turned to face her mother's bitter, cerulean eyes.

No one spoke as the three walked back up through the dirt path, between the cliffs, toward the house and entered through the kitchen door.

"Jessica," Evelyn said while she strummed her fingers against the granite countertop, "go back to bed. You need your rest for tomorrow."

Jessica hesitated, and the hair on her arms reached for the ceiling. She looked over at her father. "I'll see you tomorrow morning," she said.

Her father grinned and nodded.

She then turned toward her mother, whose eyes sent tiny shards of ice through her soul and she felt incredibly cold. "Good night, Mother."

The little girl quivered and then ran up toward her room. Once inside, she pushed the door almost closed, leaving a slight crack to hear the argument she knew was coming. Her father, who never raised his voice above a normal tone, was loud and moved up the stairs. She shut the door all the way but kept her ear flat against the wood.

"I should have done this a long time ago," he said with a nervous chuckle. "You'll never be able to find her, not ever."

"You will not take her anywhere." Her mother followed him into the master suite and slammed the door behind her.

Unable to hear them clearly through the shut door, Jessica stepped out into the hallway and made her way toward the suite. She could see the shadows pass in front of the light, which filtered out through the bottom of the door. She was close enough to touch it when the sound stopped. She placed her ear against the door, and the door opened just enough for her to see in.

Jessica watched her father move from the closet to the dresser. He placed his clothes in a black suitcase on the bed. Her mother sat at the mirror and brushed her hair calmly. A third figure brushed past the girl's eyes, and she gasped in horror. Both hands moved over her mouth to muffle the sound, and she shut her eyes tightly. Her chest pounded in her ears, and she couldn't breathe.

A strong, pungent smell took over Jessica's senses and covered the tip of her tongue with the bitter taste of blood. She heard her mother's calm voice over the madness in her mind.

"I told you, dear Samuel. No one gets in my way."

The Deal

Seth walked into the room with the usual expression spread across his face, the one that said, "I own you."

He did own me, like a slave sold to pay off an owner's debt. My mother, the debtor, was selling my soul into marriage for future endeavors, one that ensured power and influence in the political realm. If it were not for my father's life on the line, I would leave. But where could I go where they couldn't find me? Where could I hide? I'd much rather see my father wake up and point out my mother as his assailant and Seth as the coconspirator. Then we would leave this place to live a beautiful life, one like the fairytale endings he once told me about.

"Hello?" Seth stared at me, irritated by my lack of acknowledgement of his presence.

My eyes met his, and I bit down on my teeth.

"Good morning to you too." He moved toward the foot of my bed.

"You could knock when you enter my room," I said to him, and then I tossed the quilt off of me to reveal the blue, tattered sweats I had worn to bed. He shook his head in disapproval and continued toward the small bistro table I kept by the window for reading.

As far as fairy tales were concerned, Seth fit the physical profile with his soft, blond hair; tall, confident stature, and ice-blue eyes, but he was no prince.

"Don't start with me." He snapped his fingers, and the maid appeared with a tray of food.

She set it down on the table and hurried out of the room.

"I wanted to surprise you," he said.

"Big surprise." I sneered and moved to the edge of the bed, where I put on my slippers and then followed the scent of food.

My stomach growled at me. I couldn't remember the last time I had eaten.

Yesterday and most of the night, I had been in my father's room and hadn't touched one morsel of food. I was worried. The doctor said pneumonia was the cause of the liquid in his lungs and to keep his head elevated. Since my father had been in a coma for almost thirteen years, he couldn't do it himself. I stayed with him until he became stabilized for fear that he would die alone. It was close to four in the morning when his breathing became steady and I headed to bed. Food had been the last thing on my mind.

I sat at the table, where a plain, one-egg, white omelet laughed at me. Of course he got the plump, cheese-and-pepper omelet.

So not fair.

I sighed and gazed out toward the promise of another day with the glow of dawn just about to streak the sky. The faint light touched the tips of the ocean waves, which resembled white clouds as they rolled onto the shore. It was calm, serene, and peaceful, and I wished I was outside with my feet dug into the wet sand and not where I was. My mind raced around plans to leave, but nothing ever seemed to work out. Even in my daydreams, I ended up dead.

Seth moved behind my chair and bent down until his lips touched the tip of my ear. "You know what would really make my day better?"

My stomach cramped as lava formed in my stomach. What would be his request today? The last one ended up with me on the floor, my knees torn up from being tossed against the marble-tiled floor, all for a slap I rendered across his face when his hand wandered into my blouse.

"Agree to marry me now, willingly. I really dislike using your mother's persuasion. I know I'll make you happy, even if you don't believe it now." He kissed my ear and whispered, "You know you belong to me."

I jolted up from my seat. "I belong to no one."

Seth grabbed me and spun me around to face him. His breath was hot, and his face developed red blotches across his cheeks.

I had wondered before if Seth was on medication for his mood swings. I'd say there was a ninety percent chance my guess was right, and I was pretty sure he didn't take the pills that day.

How much longer can I endure this? Forever? Until my dad is at peace or until he kills me with his bare hands.

"I bet if I gave the same offer to Rose..." Seth said as he loosened his grip on my arms and slid his hands down to touch my outer thigh.

The words that should have stayed in my head exploded like Krakatau.

"Then go find the maid. Better yet, why don't you marry her? Why do you think I told Mother to hire her in the first place?" I looked down at his feet, afraid to see his face, but I couldn't stop the words. "I know you've been with her. She's told me. I was hoping she'd be pregnant by now and then you'd have to marry her. You'd have to leave. This isn't the life I want." As the words came out, my stomach cramped harder. *Why don't I stop talking? Why do I keep digging myself further into his anger? He could go right into father's room and pull it. There would be no way for me to stop him. Then Father would be dead and I killed him. I must be really stupid.*

Seth's cold hands were quick to wrap around my throat before I spoke or thought another word. He pressed on my vocal cords with this thumbs. I coughed at first, but as he lifted me in the air, my toes could barely touch the ground and I could no longer breathe.

That was it, or so I thought. My feet came back down and touched the ground before he pulled my body tight to his. He placed his lips back at my ear.

"You keep in mind everything I have done for you, your mother, and especially your father. He'd be dead if it wasn't for me, and how quickly I can take it all away." He released my neck from his grasp and then sat in front of his breakfast as though nothing had happened.

I coughed and rubbed my throat. My body felt numb as I sat back down in the padded chair. Seth straightened his tie and then spread out the newspaper. How fast he changed from hot to cold, and quicker than usual.

He reached out for the cup filled with coffee and looked at me. "Rose," he called as he lifted the coffee to his lips.

The maid entered seconds later.

Did she hear his threats behind the closed door? Would she be concerned for my safety? Would she run to my mother to tell her what she witnessed?

"Yes, sir?" She smiled and batted her eyelashes at him.

No, probably not.

Seth looked up at her and winked. "Miss Jessica requires some water. She seems to be choking."

They both laughed before she sauntered out the door to fetch the water.

Rose was young and naïve, and if she could land Seth, she'd be set for life. I tried my best to nudge her, encourage her to go after him, but his only interest in any of the young woman who worked in the house was always short lived. It wouldn't be long before he had his fill of her and then tossed her out too. But they did serve a purpose. It bought me time, time alone and time with my dad.

I picked at the bland, tasteless eggs.

"You're getting too skinny eating that crap your mother plans for you. Here." He slid his omelet over while he scanned the black-and-white print.

The smell of the sautéed mushrooms and peppers made my stomach rumble.

I pushed the plate across the table and back in front of Seth. I didn't want to accept his abstract apologies, no matter what outburst it might create. However, he didn't say anything to me. His lips mouthed the words he read, but no sound came out. He flipped over to the next page.

I then stared at the food. *Come on. Just one bite.*

I can wait until he leaves.

"Ha!" Seth slammed the paper down on top of the table.

I closed my eyes and waited for him to strike me or choke me again, but instead, laughter filled the room. Not a normal laugh either, but one that made the hair on my arms stand up. One of my eyes popped open first to see Seth's head tilted down toward the paper. I opened the other and relaxed. This outburst wasn't about me for once.

"That'll show him for getting into my affairs. Missing? He's not missing. I know exactly where they buried the body." Seth folded up the paper and looked into my wide eyes. "Not the only body missing either." He flicked the paper with his index finger. "I hope no one else tries to derail my plans. I've got people all over the world. No one can escape me."

My eyes widened, and I could feel my pulse serge. "You've killed people?"

"Of course not. I'm soon to be a governor and then president someday. I could never associate with people like that. I just have very loyal followers, and I'm not responsible for their actions, especially when others try to go against me. "

Was this just another threat to scare me, to threaten my life? Of course I was scared of him, all the time in fact, but my mouth didn't seem to care. "Your father is a governor, not you, and how does that make you president?"

"It's just a matter of time, my love." He winked with a smile.

I cringed. I hated when he called me that.

"This is his fourth stroke, one foot in the grave, and it won't be long before the state hands over the title to me for doing the job in his place." His eyes twinkled. "At age twenty-six, I will be the youngest governor in history."

The thought of him in that kind of power sent chills down my back. "But your father will recover, like he has before."

"He won't recover this time." He wadded the paper into a ball and tossed it in the small trash can next to my bed. "Besides, the people will elect me. Why else do you think I pushed through the recent stimulus? Not because I care about jobs, lowering taxes, or the general welfare of California. It was to secure my father's position. My staff assures me that things are moving in the right direction, and the polls are strong in my favor."

He had told me once that he wanted to be president over the whole world. He was fourteen at the time, and I had laughed so hard, I'd had to wipe the tears from my cheek. Moments later, the tears of laugher were tears of pain as he had struck me for the first time. It was then I knew his true nature, and even now, I shudder to think others will praise him and follow him in his quest. The role of governor was his first step, that is, if it went his way. Would they really allow a twenty-six year old to be in office?

"Let's go back to our first topic, shall we?" Seth said as he glanced at his watch. "Our official engagement is coming soon. Why your mother said she wouldn't let you marry until you were twenty-one is beyond me. And a year engagement seems odd in this day and age, but I agreed to it and have waited patiently."

He hadn't known it was a deal between my mother and I to delay the wedding. I would then agree to the marriage and she would keep my father alive. Although it wouldn't stop me from trying to reason with her.

"She has her reasons," I said.

Although Seth was five years older and had a knack for being a puppet politician, I allowed him to think he was smarter than me—most of the time.

Seth snickered. "Your mother hasn't been much of a mother, but she does have her uses." His tongue swept over his lips. "I'll be proposing publically, as you already know, and I don't expect to be let down."

The usual outright defiance didn't get me very far. *Maybe I should try something different.* If he were to call it off, no deal would be broken, and I would be free and clear.

I mustered up all the acting I had in me.

"I don't deserve someone like you. You could have any girl you wanted, probably even some Jamaican model who would adore and worship you. I'm just a plain, normal person, unattractive, dull. Do you really want someone like me?"

By his unmoved expression, I knew my words didn't change anything. I sighed in defeat. "Why me?"

He leaned back in his chair and stared at my face. "You don't see what I see. Your mother says things that aren't true, and you believe them. You look more like her every day. The curves, hips, the way you tilt your head when you think I'm crazy." He chuckled, watching me change my position. "Almost identical, well, except for the dirty-blonde hair you got from your father's side. Jess, you are beautiful, even if you don't see it."

I hated he knew my moves and looks. Even if it was pointless, I wasn't ready to give up just yet.

"Wouldn't you rather have someone who adores you, who will want to be your wife?" The words came out almost sweet, caring, as if I wanted only the best for him.

He moved forward and took his eyes off me and looked toward the Palisades Verde cliffs. "You will, even if it takes years. You'll see." He then put on his gloves. A corner of his mouth went up, and he chuckled.

It was no use, but I had to say it.

"I don't love you. I never have, and I never will."

Seth pushed his chair away from the table, and it smashed hard against the wall. "You will not disappoint or embarrass me. You will act exactly how you've been told to and wear what I say is appropriate." He looked me up and down. "And I will be burning all the rest. Then you'll have no choice in what you wear."

I swallowed hard at what he considered appropriate clothing. "Seth, I'll never accept—"

"Oh, but you will accept." He slammed his fists against the table. He paused and took in a long breath while he removed his fist off the table to look at his watch again. "I'm late. You might like to know that I can be generous. I'm giving away some of Father's antiques to a charity auction this morning. You'd like it. It's to help the bastard children."

I cringed at his word choice. "You mean orphans," I sighed in defeat.

"See? You'll be great at that sort of crap, leaving me to the more important stuff. And then, once I've acquired a position at the United Nations…"

He stopped, but his stare felt hot against my face. I didn't look away from him, nor did I reply, even though I wanted to scream.

"Anyway, the press will be there at seven sharp, so I'd better go." He moved behind me and kissed the top of my head before I could dodge it. "I'll be back later to finish our discussion. I have a feeling you'll be a bit more receptive then."

Seth walked out, and I heard the maid giggle as he shut the door behind him. No doubt he had a few more minutes before he'd leave.

"Please let her get pregnant," I mumbled, and then I inhaled his untouched breakfast before I headed back to bed.

The low click-clack of her stilettos woke me before she entered.

"Sleep well, did you?" Her voice seared through me like a hot iron. "It must be nice to be a nineteen-year-old with not a care in the world and to sleep away the entire morning. Are you sick?"

"I was up late." I sat up against the pillows. "Enjoy your time at the spa, or did you go shopping with money that's not yours?"

"Yes. I know where you were last night." Her jaw clicked back and forth. "The liquid is filling up in his lungs again. The doctor said we should pull the feeding tube."

"You can't let him starve to death!" I shouted.

"Well, that's completely up to you, now isn't it?"

It was the same old routine. *What will it be this time, another party? Dinner at the club, where I pretend to be a loving daughter? Or will it be a piano recital for her friends to show off how talented I am and how it's all because of her? Her trained seal, preforming tricks?*

"So what do you want?" I reached for an escape from the words soon to spew from her lips: my iPod. My fingers reached for the top of the nightstand, but it was gone.

My mother's straight, blonde hair hardly moved along her thin face as she tapped her foot in a steady rhythm against the marble floor. Her painted-on eyebrows rose up at the same time her acrylic nails struck something silver and shinny in the palm of her hand.

"We need to talk." She shook the device in her hand before she placed it in her front pocket.

I murmured and rolled my eyes before I collapsed back down on the mattress. I pulled the covers up to my chin.

"Jessica, why does everything have to be so dramatic with you?" She rubbed her temples with her long, boney fingers. "For once, could you just do what's being asked of you without me having to"—she paused to stare at me—"use persuasion?"

This is it. Payment is due, and I'm the unlucky pawn. I know what Seth meant earlier about being more receptive later.

She crossed the front of my bed without so much of a nod in my direction.

"You know, Jessica, I didn't want you. When I found out you were going to be a girl, I wanted to get an abortion. Your father"—she looked out the window—"threatened to leave me if I went through with it. Divorce is something we do not do in this family. Your father didn't have a problem using threats against me to get what he wanted."

I watched her stare out the window. It was clear that she never wanted me. I had known that from an early age, but I hadn't known she'd wanted an abortion or that my father had fought for my life, like I was fighting for his.

"I wanted a boy, a boy just like Seth. He's not only extremely attractive, but he can take command over a room filled with arrogant slobs and make them listen to his ideas." Her voice purred. "Well, at least they'll think they're his ideas." She paused for me to interject, but I didn't.

"Seth will make a good son-in-law, and you have the opportunity to make me proud of you and pay me back for giving you life," she said.

I let go of everything else she said and focused only on her last statement to rebut.

"But, Mother—"

She turned away from the window. "You will marry him. He has gone to great lengths for us: this house, the equipment to keep your father alive. You owe it to him. You owe it to me. Do you know what potential Seth has?"

Why does she think I even care about Seth's potential?

"Can you even imagine what power that has, to become an influential leader of men? No longer will people point their finger at me and say, 'Poor Evelyn, up to her eyeballs in debt. She's just a big disappointment to her ancestral tree." Her fingers squeezed the white lace curtains, and the rod fell to the ground. She took in a deep breath. "I'll show them, I'll be the most powerful ruler yet. Together, Seth and I will make this world see things my way." She walked toward me with the curtain still in her hands. She then threw it down at the foot of my bed. "You will not take that from me."

"Seth is very handsome, just like his father used to be. You should be on your knees, thanking me for arranging this union."

"I was only six, Mother," I said. "I'm an adult now."

"Yes, well, be glad I did. Forcing the two of you together like I did was brilliant. Seth fell in love with you just like he did with any of his possessions." She picked up my brush and combed it through her hair. "His father helped some too, telling him all the time how beautiful you are and how other men will chase after you when you're older. That used to get him so mad that he'd punch a hole in the wall and swear he'd kill anyone if they touched you." She laughed and looked at my reflection in the mirror. "You remember how he felt about his things?"

I did. Even now, they sat in a box, untouched by anyone. They were his. They would always be his and no one else's. If he could, he'd put me in that box and lock it tight. My throat and chest burned.

"You don't even know what's it's like in the real world. You barely leave the house, and you spend all your time with a dying man in a small little room."

"Don't say that. He's not dying."

"You need me, Jessica. You couldn't make it a day without me. And whether you know it or not, you need Seth too."

She was right and wrong. This was wrong and unfair, but I couldn't make it on my own. I had no experiences in the outside world. It was only through books, self-teaching, and an occasional glimpse of television that I knew another world existed outside this house. I wanted those experiences but was afraid of what might happen to my dad if I left for even a minute.

"You won't get a better offer," she said and set the brush down.

"But I don't love him. I don't even want to get married to anyone ever."

"You will."

"I won't."

"Of course you will marry. Every woman does. I'm just making sure you marry the right man. You'll even want a little boy someday to carry on for you. You're forcing my hand, Jessica, to do something drastic, something I really don't want to do."

Of course you do. You wanted him dead years ago. "I don't want to bring any child into this crappy world. Maybe we can work something else out. I could get a job," I said.

My mother's lips tightened. The look reminded me of the day she pushed the wheelchair into the house after the attack. I was told in advance that he couldn't walk, speak, or even blink his eyes. I waited on the bottom step of the staircase to see him. My mother's face was crumpled up as she struggled to push the wheelchair over the threshold.

Things didn't go the way she planned then, and I was resisting her plan.

"There is a small piece of paper in my pocket, and all I have to do is sign it and the doctor will stop the—"

"Fine," I blurted out before she could say the words.

I just could not bear to hear the words vibrate in her throat as if she were singing for joy. "You can leave now." I choked back the mass stuck at the back of my tonsils. "You got what you wanted."

"You're giving me your word that you'll marry—"

"Yes!"

My mother wore an upturned smile of victory as she reached into her pocket to pull out my iPod. She tossed it at me.

"Really, you'll thank me one day. You'll see. Everything I've done, I've done for you." She walked through the open door and took the brass knob into her fist. "It's a mother's love that will do whatever it takes to see their child happy, even when they don't appreciate it."

Who does she think she's talking to?

I was unmoved by her words. Her gloat changed and her lips disappeared as she pulled the door shut.

My mother, Evelyn August, got what she wanted, at least for now. This was just one more step toward her goal.

It took me a few minutes to break the stare at the door. I wondered if she was on the other side of it with her ears pressed hard against the wood. She would love to hear me break down, and nothing would please her more than to hear my pain, but I kept silent and still until the sound of her shoes faded down the corridor. I might not have given her the pleasure to hear me sob, but she won nevertheless.

I slipped on my robe and headed to my father's room.

"Hi, Dad." I walked through the door, over to the only window in the room, and pulled open the shades. "I'm sorry I haven't come by before now." I noticed the sun had dipped down into the kaleidoscope of colors. I felt bad for depriving him from feeling the sunlight on his face.

I turned around and leaned against the window ledge, and right away noticed the scenic pictures I had torn out of a calendar and had put up along his walls were missing.

She threw them away. "Don't worry, Dad. I'll find them. I always do, and in their normal, obvious place." *The trash next to the bed.*

I shook my head and pushed off the window ledge. I walked over to bin next to the bed, but they weren't there. I looked around the hospital-like room, but there was no sign of the photos.

My eyes followed the wires and tubes wrapped around the bar of the bed to the life-support machine.

"Sorry, Dad. I guess this time she really did—" I gasped.

Stacks of papers were under his left hand and pressed against his chest. It was then I noticed the absences of the normal hum and beeping sounds of the machines.

I was frozen, unable to move.

"Is he?" Seth's voice came from somewhere behind me.

"Please. Not now, Seth." I walked to the chair and sat next to my father's bed. I took my father's ice-cold hand into mine.

I heard the door click shut before I spoke. "It won't be long before he brings Mother." I stroked the inside of his palm. "What am I going to do without you?" I cried, tasting the salty tears on my lips. "You were my only hope for escaping this place. I can't do it alone. I'm...I'm afraid if I leave, he will find me. I'm not strong enough to go out alone." I sobbed harder, clinching his hand in mine. "Daddy, Daddy, please don't leave me here."

I felt rotten. I felt selfish for crying for myself. I felt envious of his death and wished it was me. The tears fell all around my face. I brought his hand up to wipe the tears on my cheeks and tried to remember what it was like before he was hurt, specifically the stories he'd read to me about princesses and happily ever afters.

"Tell me one last story, Daddy, like when I was little. Tell me that there is a fairy tale ending for me. Tell me you're in a better place now and that you're happy. Send me a sign, any kind of sign. Tell me what to do."

The clack of my mother's shoes moved down the hall and toward the small room. She entered with the doctor at her side. He lingered at the doorway while my mother enjoyed her moment.

"I've sent Seth home for now. There are many things to be done in the next few days, so go to your room and let the doctor attend to the body," she said and waved the doctor in.

That's all he was to her—a body. *I hate you, I hope you get what you deserve someday, and I hope I'm the one to give it to you.* I got up to leave and passed the doctor in the doorway.

"Oh, and Jessica?"

I paused with my back toward her and my hand on the doorknob.

"Remember, you gave me your word."

Although I felt numb the little voice in my head whispered, *Don't let on. They'll watch me like a hawk. They want me to be scared, so I'll act scared while I plan the escape. I have to leave, I have to take a chance or suffer in this prison the rest of my life. I have no choice but to be strong.*

"My word," I said as an unexpected smile formed on my face.

One More Night

In my room, I fell onto the mattress. My eyes shut, and I saw my father's cold, blue face etched inside the lids. My pulse quickened and my eyes flew open.

I didn't want to remember him that way.

I looked around the room for another image to take its place, but everything was blurry through the fresh tears. I searched for the young photo of my father, the only photo in the entire house of him smiling. It was missing from the room. The once-happy and carefree man with wild brown hair which was longer than mine was now only a dirty outline of a frame against the white wall.

I believed he would wake up someday and tell me how much he loved me for taking care of him and for not giving up. Then with my mother and Seth in jail, they could no longer torment me. But that day would never come, and if I didn't leave soon, I was already dead.

I wrapped the comforter tightly around me and lay back down. Sleep soon swept over me and tossed me into a white dream. Soft music played as I reclined my head back against my arms. The peaceful world I wished would let me stay was interrupted by a black cloud. It drifted into my world, and with one flicker of light, followed by a sizzle, my peace was gone and I was back to reality.

I glanced over at the clock that read two thirty-two in the morning. I tossed my legs over the side of the bed and stumbled to the window. The moon peeked in and out of the growing clusters of clouds. I could hear the sound of the waves crashing hard against the shoreline. A fierce wind bent over the surrounding palm trees and created an eerie, hollow sound, like air blown through an empty log.

A light sparkled below on the sand. An object grew brighter in the darkness. It held my stare for several minutes and taunted me. The light danced along the surface of the sand like a ballerina lost in a musical recital.

Nonsense. I laughed and rubbed my eyes. *It's just the trees, an illusion.*

The tide moved closer toward the object. The sea would soon take possession of it if I didn't move fast enough.

I changed clothes and climbed out the open window. After I climbed down a few emergency ladders and then to the dirt path down along the cliff, it wasn't long before my feet felt the sand on the beach. The object was still bright next to the darkened ground when I picked it up. I shook off the sand, and it turned dull.

"How did you make that little light?" I said to the rectangular piece of folded-up card stock. "How very strange." I looked at the weathered postcard before I unfolded it in my hands.

On the front of it was a picture of a parade or festival, with families lined up along the street. I flipped over the card to see in big black letters across the top, "Welcome to Folkston." A metallic, oblong sticker read "City of Folkston, Georgia," and along the bottom read, "The Gateway to the Okefenokee Swamp."

The words my father said to me so long ago echoed in my mind: "*The time will come when you will leave this house and emerge into another life that awaits you, a life you deserve, a life with a greater purpose.*"

I remembered something else too, something I'd forgotten so long ago, a piece of paper my father had given me on the last night of his normal life. I never read it, and I doubted I could find it now.

Maybe he's telling me now. There is nothing left for her to hold over me, accept death. The small and scared child cried out, *But I don't know how to be on my own. I'd never make it. And even if I did leave, he'd find me. He'd find me and I'd be dead. He'd find me and kill anyone who helped me.*

The salt of my tears burned the corners of my dry lips. I was afraid to leave, but I was even more afraid to stay. I screamed at the roaring sea. "Is this all the help I deserve? If this is your way of proving to me you exist…" I paced back and forth while I kicked at the sand. A thought entered into my head, one that if I walked out into the ocean and let the undertow drag me out, no one would ever find my body. It was a coward's way out but my fear of drowning would prevent that as well.

If I stayed, my mother would continue to dictate my every move, and I'd be scared every day that my husband would kill me for anything he disliked. I was in a swirling pit of endless darkness, a hole that would go on forever, and the only future ahead for me was here.

There was no other way, and I had only one choice that gave me a chance at life.

"Death would be better than this." I looked at the postcard again. "She wouldn't go anywhere near a swamp."

A vision of her getting her limited-edition heels stuck in the mud brought a smile through my tears.

The next morning, I grabbed the hidden key to my father's office and entered. Bookshelves lined the walls and just about covered them completely, except for the wall behind my father's desk. A book on every subject, about every place, including every imaginary story ever written, was all contained in this one room, and I'd read them all. There was a stack of journals my father kept in an oversized, beat-up, wooden trunk locked with an old-fashioned golden key that dangled out of the lock. Years ago, I had looked inside, but on the pages were unreadable markings and sketches.

"Hello, Chief," I said to the painting that hung on the wall behind the desk and in-between two wooden crosses.

I moved around to the leather chair behind the desk and touched the geographical book in the middle of my father's desk. It lay open on top of the oak desk. Because it was the last book my father touched, I'd left it alone.

I blew off the dust and ran my hand across the page. I sneezed, and the pages flipped in a flurry. After a few seconds, the pages stopped.

Geez, I didn't sneeze that hard. How strange.

"The Okefenokee Swamp?" I read and then looked closer at the handwritten bookmark on top of the page. I read the words on it out loud.

"'There is a time for everything, and a season for every activity under heaven: a time to be born and a time to die, a time to plant and a time to uproot, a time to kill and a time to heal, a time to tear down and a time to build, a time to weep and a time to laugh, a time to mourn and a time to dance, a time to scatter stones and a time to gather them, a time to embrace and a time to refrain, a time to search and a time to give up, a time to keep and a time to throw away, a time to tear and a time to mend, a time to be silent and a time to speak, a time to love and a time to hate, a time for war and a time for peace.' Ecclesiastes three, one through eight. Dad, are you trying to tell me something?"

I couldn't help but doubt my previous thoughts on the whole God thing. Maybe there were angels watching us.

But if they do exist, where have they been? Stick to what I know, and it's not angels. I suppose an afterlife of some sort could be possible. A soul that continues to live after the body is gone.

My father was trying to help me escape. At least I wanted to believe it.

I took the bookmark and placed it in my pocket alongside the postcard.

"Well, Chief, it's time to leave this jail house. I might not make it out alive, but I have to try." If I didn't know better, I would have thought the chief smiled at me. "I guess I'd better find out about my new adventure." I pulled the book into my lap and started to read.

The day was just about over when I exited my father's office and peered into the kitchen just in time to see the cook exit out the back door.

My stomach growled, and with no one else around, I raided the refrigerator. Carrots, celery, a jar of green olives, and a container full of hummus were not helpful.

"Yuck."

My mother came in through the door. "What are you doing?"

I shut the door. "Nothing."

"Where were you?"

I turned to face her. "I've been here all day."

My mother no doubt spent most of the day out of the house making funeral arrangements. She didn't care where I was.

"Oh, well, Seth said he came by, and when he didn't find you, he thought you might have gone with me. I was concerned, although I knew you were here, somewhere."

I rolled my eyes at her. *Yeah, that's why you locked all the doors from the outside just in case I tried to leave.*

"I am surprised at you. I thought you'd want to help make the arrangements."

"I want nothing to do with the plethora of flowers, the lavish funeral home, the bronze casket, or the media spectacle you've planned." None of it was for my father. "Besides, my day was better spent reading."

"Fine. Whatever." She rubbed her temples and then tossed a garment bag at me. "Go try this on. The funeral is tomorrow at noon. I can have Eleanor come over in the early morning if the dress needs to be pinned."

I held the bag but didn't move fast enough for her.

"Now," she barked.

Instead of telling her to shove it, instead of igniting more threats, I walked past her and up the stairs to my room.

Soon, I won't be here for you to kick around. Soon, I'll be gone, and you'll never find me. At least I hoped not.

Destination Nowhere

My mother barged into my room. "It's going to be a lovely day." She crossed the room to the window and threw open the new curtains. "The sun is brightly shining down on us today." She turned toward me and laced her fingers together. "So let's not be late."

My mother saw that I was already dressed. She smiled as I put on the final additions to my face. I wanted to look nice today for my father, not for her or the freak show already gathering at the front gate.

"Good girl. I want you downstairs when you are finished. Seth is here and waiting for you."

Brilliant. Seth will keep her occupied.

Anytime the three of us were in public, I became invisible. That would work to my benefit today.

I finished the last touches on my hair while my mother watched me. She stared at me and waited for some sort of remark.

What? No argument today? No protest? I imagined the words in her head.

A low sigh moved out of her parted lips, and she walked out of the room.

There wasn't anything for me to protest, because I was leaving and never coming back.

The white limo pulled up to the curb of the funeral home. The camera lights flashed against the dark, tinted windows, and both

Seth and my mother laughed. They lifted up their champagne glasses and clinked them before swallowing the last drop of liquid.

A toast of victory. I hope they enjoy this moment, since it's about to be their last victory over me.

"We're ready, driver," my mother said as she pinched her cheeks.

"Yes, ma'am," he answered and made his way to the outside of her door.

The door opened, and the camera flashes blinded me. I pulled over the black veil attached to the hat I wore to shield my face. Until then, except for my mother's cocktail party friends, my face was not well known, and I wanted to keep it that way. There would be no recent photos of me that I knew of to send to every police station across the US. That would get me some chance of not being recognized.

I dodged away from the media and escaped out the opposite side of the car. I could hear the questions fired at Seth the moment he stepped out of the car. My mother stood at his side, and neither one looked for me.

"How's your father doing?" one reporter asked.

"He's strong and encouraged by all your support. I deeply appreciate the cards, love, and prayers said for my family," Seth answered.

Like he would ever pray. He's got them all fooled.

"The people know how much you've helped your father, and they really admire you for your commitment to not only him, but to the people of California," another spoke out. "But they want to know if things take a turn for the worse, are you going to accept his seat?"

Seth turned toward the man and put on his best fake expression of grief. "I hope that day never comes. My father is a great man, and he will overcome his cancer like before. If God decides to take him, I will do what I can to continue his work and help others."

He then wiped tears from his eyes, and the crowd let out a sweet sigh.

"Fraud," I whispered and moved around the outside of the crowd.

I crossed over to the front of the parlor to find a man standing guard at the door. He wasn't allowing anyone in.

I'm the daughter of the deceased. Of course he'd let me enter without permission from my mother. But just as I was about to step out to reason with the man, a woman approached with a small child dancing behind her. "Restrooms?" she asked. He turned and pointed, giving me the perfect opportunity to slide behind him, through the red double doors where my father's casket was.

The parlor was lined with stained glass windows on both sides with sunlight radiating through them. Angels, I assumed, were painted on the glass, and they watched me as I walked down the bright red carpet to the shiny coffin.

My hand reached out to touch it. "I'm going to do it. I'm leaving tonight on a train, and I'm not coming back." I felt a jab into my heart, and it ached. "I hope you are in a better place. Maybe I'll see you again someday." I couldn't bear to look at the box anymore, and the tears streamed down my face. An angel on the glass with outstretched arms looked right at me.

"I want to believe it like he did. I do, but how can I, after everything we've been through? You haven't been there for me, ever," I said to the angel, who just stared at me. "I've always tried to do the right thing, to put my father's needs before mine. I sacrificed having friends, going to a regular school, and for what? He's dead."

Don't lose it. I pulled a tissue out of my pocket and wiped the tears away. "Show me, Dad. Make me believe."

The doors squeaked open, and I darted out the back door of the building before people began to enter. There was just enough time to get to the train station, buy my ticket, and get back to my seat before Seth entered with the bereaved wife.

My mother would have made a spectacular actress.

Finally, they were both down the aisle. My mother sat to my right, and Seth sat to my left.

Seth propped his hand behind my chair and touched my shoulders.

I hoped he didn't notice that I was breathing harder than usual.

"I delayed your mother so you could have more time to say good-bye. I hope you used the time wisely."

"Yes, I did," I said calmly. "Thank you."

The reception went on forever. It seemed like it would never end. I looked at my watch a million times, but it only made me more nervous. Even if the party ended at midnight, the last train boarded at one-thirty. There was plenty of time.

I watched my mother sway around the room and down drink after drink. After a while, it was all I could take before I approached her.

"I'm heading up to bed," I said as she spilled champagne on the floor.

"Why don't you play something?" she slurred.

"No. I don't feel like playing, Mother. I'm tired." I looked over at the piano, and I did long to play it. It would be the only thing I would miss in this house, the only comfort I'd ever known.

"Oh, Evey." Another drunk put his arm around my mother's waist and twirled her away from me. "Let's dance."

"Don't forget to say good night to Seth," she called out as she was whisked into another room.

Seth was equally drunk and hanging all over a blonde girl with a rather large chest. I looked down at mine, and I still didn't get it. Why me? I had neither the perfect figure nor large breasts.

Regardless, I could safely assume that neither would be looking for me tonight and possibly not until late afternoon. It gave me time to get far away before they discovered me missing.

I ran upstairs and began to get ready.

My idea was to make it look like an abduction. I tossed my possessions around the room and ripped open a feather pillow. The fluff fell on everything in the room. I knocked over a lamp, the chairs, and the table by the window. I tore my jacket using the tip of the bed post, and left a piece of it to dangle down the side of the bed.

"Not bad," I said, looking around at the mess I created.

I shoved some clothes into a backpack along with a stash of cash I had saved, and then I noticed that the music had stopped.

"Party is over." I looked at my watch, which read one o'clock.

It's now or never.

I put my hand down on the window ledge to climb out, and I felt a poke.

"Ouch." My finger started to bleed. It wasn't a huge cut, but it was enough blood to give me an idea.

The blood trickled out of my finger as I squeezed it along the window ledge and onto the floor. I then grabbed the bag and went out the window.

Once I got down to the ground, I took one last look at the house, and my knees knocked together. An excitement went off inside me, a feeling of valor and adventure, and then the more familiar feeling washed over me.

How will I eat? Where will I live? I'll have to find a job, but who will hire someone with no experience? Worrying about those things seemed small until the last thought, the one that was there to begin with but I had been afraid to admit to. *Seth will find you and kill you.*

I would rather be dead than stay, I told myself. *It's time to go catch a train.*

I walked away from the house and didn't look back.

For nearly twenty-five minutes, it was just me in the darkness before the glow of the lights from the station grew brighter, and then I heard a voice. "All aboard."

I hurried toward the man, and then panic stopped me. I hid in the shadow of the building. I could see the man and a handful of people who gathered near him. The same voice of doubt went over all the reasons to stay, like a CD stuck on the same song.

"Ticket please," he said to each of them, and in turn, they handed him a ticket. He punched it with a shiny tool, and then the passengers stepped up onto the train.

Simple enough, and I have my ticket in my pocket. Will I live under a bridge? Steal food to eat? "You're stalling, Jess," I said, rubbing both hands together.

My body trembled like I was cold, but I wasn't. Actually, I felt hot, uncomfortably hot and faint.

No one would have been in my room yet. It's possible that I could make myself love him. He was attractive.

"Last call," the man shouted in my direction.

Tears streamed down my face as I felt defeated once again. I couldn't do it. I was weak and helpless, just like my mother said. I hoped my father wasn't watching. I hoped that I was right all along not to believe in ghosts or spirits, because if he was watching, I couldn't bear the disappointment he must be feeling.

I turned away from the train to go home, and as I put both hands in my pockets, I felt the postcard. I pulled it out and carefully unfolded it to let my eyes see it once more before I tossed it toward the trash bin. It didn't sparkle, it didn't come to life and tell me I was coward. It was just a worthless postcard that meant nothing. I flung it toward the trash, the wind caught it, and it blew right toward the conductor. I chased after it until it landed in front of him. "Ticket please." The man smiled.

I looked up, surprised to be standing before him. I handed him my ticket and then boarded the train. On the train, the worry faded. I was still scared, but the overpowering paralyzing fear was gone for the time being.

Thanks, Dad.

The one good thing about departure at one-thirty in the morning was vacant seats. I was able to have an entire row to myself.

I can't believe I'm really doing this.

I watched the train pull out, and as it picked up speed, the lights turned into a blur of colors. I pulled down the shade and stared at the seat in front of me while my mind continued with its protest.

It's not too late. I can still go back. I'm not really going to some hick town after the life I've lived with cooks and servants? I shook my head. *I was a servant, a servant to Seth, to mother. And look at how many years I took care of father, and all the things I gave up to care for him.*

I couldn't shut off my thoughts. All the reasons to go back, all the reasons to run swirled around like water circling the drain of a tub. The motion of the train calmed me some, and the arguing became less and less. I shut my eyes, and before long, the battle stopped and I fell asleep.

The warmth of the sun on my face woke me. I must have been asleep for hours and in the same position, because my body did not want to move.

"Excuse me." Someone spoke, the first voice I'd heard since the ticket man.

I stretched out of the fetal position and sat up. I yawned a little too loudly and blushed at the tall redhead trying to get my attention.

"I'm sorry to wake you. Um…well, all the seats are taken and…" The young man smiled and stuck out his hand in my direction. "My name is Mark."

I looked around at the full train car. "Oh. You need a place to sit." I scooted next to the window.

The man dropped his hand down to his luggage and lifted it up into the overhead compartment. He bumped his head as he sat.

"Long legs. I guess not many tall people ride on trains," he said as he rubbed his forehead.

"I suppose not."

"I'm sorry for waking you. You looked quite peaceful, rather angelic."

"No. It's okay." I glanced at my watch, which read close to seven thirty, and sighed. *Still a long way to go.* I pulled open the shade and allowed the light to warm my face, and my mind began to argue again.

"I'm not going back."

"Sorry. Did you say something?" He turned his body toward me.

"Just talking to myself. Sorry," I added.

"Oh. I do that sometimes too." He paused for a long moment. "So, where are you headed?"

The first thought to pop into my head was the story of Little Red Riding Hood. "My grandmother's house." I smiled as I remembered how my dad read the part of the wolf with a low growl in his voice.

"I'm on my way to New Orleans. I'm a youth leader, and we're taking the kids there." He pointed to kids who sat across the aisle and those in front of us. All wore bright yellow shirts that read TEAM GOD. "We're going to help clean up the neighborhoods after the hurricane."

Perfect!

Mark continued to talk about his mission. He wasn't anything like Seth. He was helping because he cared about people, not because of what he could get out of it. The more he talked about his calling to aid others, the more I felt at ease. I was in awe of the good work he did for others, up until he mentioned God. That's when I grew less interested and stared out the window.

The redhead stopped talking for some time, and I felt bad for the silent treatment. He hadn't done anything but be nice to me, and it wasn't his fault I blamed God for what happened to me or to my father.

I wiggled in my seat at the uncomfortable silence now between us. "I'm sorry. My father believed in God, but I just don't. You've been really nice to me, and I'd like to talk about something else if you don't mind."

"I'm sorry too, and I've done nothing but talk at you the entire ride. So tell me about yourself. What is your favorite thing to do? What are your fears?" He laughed. "Tell me everything."

I laughed too. "I like to play the piano. I hate water unless I can drink it or if it's only a few inches deep, and I love the smell of roses."

"Why do you hate water?"

"When I was about five, I went out into the ocean and the water pulled the sand from under my feet. I was already waist deep, so it knocked me off balance. The current dragged me out, and I thought I was going to die."

"That must have been scary."

We talked for the remainder of the trip, and as each topic changed, I wanted to tell him more than I should, but the warning was playing in the back of my mind.

If I tell him too much, I put his life in endanger. Seth will not be merciful to anyone in his way.

So I kept on with the charade, the fake person I wished I was.

The conductor walked through the train. "Waycross, Georgia. Thirty-minute stop."

"That's where I get off. We are picking up some donations from a sister church before our final stop. Can I at least buy you a soda? Any kind you like."

"Sure." I smiled. It was my stop too, but it was better not to let on. "I could use a stretch and a decent bathroom break."

"Yeah. Not too pleasant, are they?" He stood up to grab his bags. "Where did you say you were going?"

"I know it's the next stop, but I forget the name. My grandparents are picking me up," I lied. I stood up, slinging my backpack over my right shoulder, and followed Mark down the aisle and out the exit.

"Oh no. There's our bus to the church." He lifted his wrist to read his watch. "I guess they don't want to waste any time."

"I'm fine. Thank you though. You don't want to miss your bus." The soggy, humid air hit me for the first time, and I coughed. "I'll take a rain check on the Coke."

"Thanks for keeping me company." He winked before he turned to holler at the kids still exiting the train. "Okay. Let's get a move on it," he commanded. He turned toward me one last time. "Well, maybe we'll run into each other someday."

"That would be nice." I waved to him until he turned and sprinted for the bus.

The sweat began to form on my skin, and I smelled rather stale from the trip. There was at least an hour before the bus to Folkston would arrive, so I headed for the bathroom to freshen up.

The train station was a long, one-level building with a gravel parking lot. The green bathroom sign caught my attention, so I headed in that direction. I was not quite there before I smelled the stench.

"Ugh."

I pinched my nose and pushed the door open. Fecal matter covered the walls, and I let the door shut to stop the smell from escaping. "Gross." I said and turned to leave, but the urge to go and having no other options prompted me to turn right back around and enter the stench with only one goal—to pee and exit without touching anything. I was quick and flushed the toilet by lifting up my foot to use the bottom of my shoe, which was dirty anyway, and left in a hurry. I pulled out a bottle of hand sanitizer I thankfully remembered was in my bag.

I headed back to wait for the bus. A man in a black coat, who wore dark sunglasses, was headed in my direction. He didn't say a word but grabbed my pack and knocked me into a steel pole.

Everything went dark.

My head hurt and throbbed against the top of my skull, and for a moment, I forgot what happened.

Oh yeah. My pack, clothes, bus ticket, cash, and everything I possessed is gone. Now what do I do?

That was the least of my problems as opened my eyes. I was in a jail cell. The door wasn't locked shut, but the familiar stench of scotch filled the air. Seth's favorite drink.

Seth is here to drag me back, but I won't let him. I'll fight. Then when he kills me, it won't be in vain. There will be witnesses, and they'll put him in jail.

"Hey, look. The girl's awake. Now, what's a pretty thing like you doing in here?" Across from the cell I was in, two men sat on a wooden bench, handcuffed together.

"You two, pipe down," a woman commanded.

"But she's awake now," one of them said. "Aren't you, sweetheart?"

"I bet she's a runaway," the other man slurred. "My daughter has run away ten times, but we always manage to drag her back. She puts up such a fuss." He laughed.

"Shut up. I wasn't talking to you, moron," the first man said.

But the second man paid no attention and continued. "They just need someone to break their spirit, and eventually, they give in."

They're not going to break my spirit. I'm stronger than that. I have to be. I needed to get out of there fast. I put my palms down on the side of the cot and pushed up.

Twisted Roots | 47

"Oh no you don't." A young woman sat on the edge of the cot and forced me back down. "You've got a pretty good lump on your head, young lady." She handed me an ice pack and some aspirin. "Are you allergic to anything?"

I shook my head. "Thanks," I said and noticed her pink tube socks and black sneakers.

"You were robbed. Do you remember anything? Did you see anyone?" she asked and patted at her flower sundress.

"Um…" I couldn't help but notice this woman was a bit off. "Some guy took my backpack and knocked me against a pole. He wore a black coat and shades, but that's all I remember."

"How do we contact your parents?" she asked.

"I don't have any. Besides, I'm twenty, almost twenty-one," I stuttered, and I saw that my fingers were trembling.

I wasn't any good at lying, but I had to tell her something so she'd believe there was no one to call and not comb through any missing persons reports. I wouldn't have put it past Seth to file one.

"My father died when I was five, and my mother died shortly after. I've been in and out of orphanages most of my life. When I turned eighteen, they gave me some money and told me to leave, and I've been on my own ever since. So you see, there isn't anyone to call."

She nodded as though she believed me, so I continued. "I've got a job lined up in Florida, and if I miss my interview…"

"Okay, dear." She got up and stared over me. "After the doc gives you the okay, you can go."

"You don't understand. I can't stay here. You don't want to be responsible if I don't get the job," I pleaded to the odd woman.

"You just give me the phone number, honey, and I'll give them a call to explain." She laid me back down on the cot and covered me up. "See. No worries."

"I don't have the number," I said.

"Sorry, but that's the rules. You've got a serious head injury. It wouldn't be right to let you go off and then something happens to you. Then it would be my fault. I could lose my job, and not many people are willing to hire someone like me." The woman shuffled toward the two men.

If I run out of here, she wouldn't be able to catch me.

She released one of the men from the cuffs. I sat up and was ready to run.

"Now go sleep it off," she said and pointed to the vacant cell next to the one I was in. "And you…" I heard her say as I slipped out the station doors.

That was easier than I thought it would be. "Now to hitch a ride." I looked at the sun in the sky. "East."

Off I went in the opposite direction of the sun's path and down the road.

Hours passed by, and there was not one car. I began to wonder if I had missed a "road closed" sign or something, although at that point, it didn't matter if I had or not. I was not going back.

The night was coming, and the weather was changing rapidly. The clouds were falling in around me, and there was dampness in the air. I breathed in the wet particles and watched the dry road begin to reflect the intermittent sunlight soon to vanish.

Another hour or more went by, and my feet were soaked and sloshing around inside my shoes as I entered the canopy. The green, wet moss covered the branches of the trees and pulled them down to the ground. The same fungus also covered the trunks of the trees like gum. My heart beat fast in the dim and gloomy surroundings, but at least that meant the swamp was close.

The chatter of birds filled my ears. Some sang with a sweet and steady melody, and some were high-pitched screeches, and together, they created a musical harmony. I liked those noises. I didn't like the rustling sound that moved along the bushes at the edge of the road. I tried to ignore it, watching only from the corner of my eyes until the silhouette of an animal stopped on a path between two large trees. I stopped too and muffled my breath with my hands.

It's a wolf, I thought at first as I noticed the long snout and pointed ears, but his body was smaller than a wolf. It didn't growl or even look in my direction; it just stood there as though it was fixated on something on the tops of the trees.

I removed my hands from my lips and walked backward with tiny steps. A run in with a wild dog would be just as bad as a wolf.

The animal turned its face to me and blinked its orange eyes in my direction and then let out a growl.

I turned and leaped forward into a run and ran as fast as my legs would take me down the wet road. I ran as long as I could before I looked back to see nothing was chasing me. I stopped and bent down with my hands on my knees, huffing and puffing.

The chatter of the birds grew louder, and the buzzing, hissing sounds of the cicadas hurt my ears.

What am I doing here? I'm not ready to die. I shouldn't have left. I should have made a better plan.

I stood erect and covered my ears to muffle the noise, which got louder as I continued my journey down the road.

I tilted my face toward the sky. "I need you, Dad." The light drizzle accumulated on my nose and dripped off my face. "If there is an angel watching over me, I need help now. I don't know where to go from here."

The mist turned into a downpour, and the swamp became instantly silent.

That's just about the answer I would get. *Geez. Thanks.*

I scurried under a large tree for cover. "Fine. I'll do it without your help. I got this far, didn't I?" I'm not sure who I was trying to convince, but it felt good to say it out loud.

The farther into the trees I went, the drier I stayed, which was good; however, I lost track of the road, and the sun was just about gone.

I moved in the dark, knowing at any moment the small twigs bending under my feet could turn into a waist-deep bog. Even with my hands straight out in front, the branches whacked at my face. A million things kept going through my mind, mostly comparing death here to death by Seth later, and neither appealed to me.

I was in an unknown place, with bugs and animals at every turn, blinking their eyes at me. I was sure to be something's dinner soon.

"Just get it over with," I called out.

Once again, a light appeared, and much like the one at the beach, it danced in the distances.

The postcard.

I reached into my pocket, but it was no longer there.

"I've come too far not to follow." I combed through the bushes to find a path lit up by the light. "Here I come," I said, feeling a little more confident I was heading where I was suppose to go.

I followed it over fallen logs; I weaved in and out of trees and jumped over bushes. My enthusiasm and energy level were wearing off.

"Where are you leading me?"

The light didn't reply.

"Is it really you, Dad? Are you taking me somewhere special? Or am I just a fool?"

The light sped up, and if I wanted to keep up, I'd have to as well, so I did. The faster pace made me clumsy, and I tripped repeatedly over branches, the mud, and my own feet. I reached a large, flat rock, and imagined for a moment I was looking at a plush bed. I leaned my body against it. I just needed to rest.

The light will wait for me.

"Just a few minutes," I said to the light and climbed onto the rock. "Just a moment of rest"—I laid my head down and closed my eyes—"and then I'll follow."

I drifted off into another dream away from the wetness. I floated on a cloud in a summer sky. The warm rays of the sun bounced off the white cotton fluff. But my body was too heavy for the cloud, and I began to seep through it. Down, down, down I fell until I woke up to face new surroundings.

Five people in an unfamiliar room stared at me.

First Impressions

"Leave that child alone."

The voice came from the shadows, where a rocker sat next to the fireplace. A dog lay next to her feet and barely moved as she stood up from the chair and reached for a lantern on top of the mantelpiece. I noticed a wooden cross on the wall above.

Just like the crosses in my father's office.

The round silhouette of the woman waddled toward me. The bottom of her tattered dress brushed against her cocoa skin. She plopped down on the corner of my bed. Her long, black, wavy hair, bound with a piece of tied cloth, dangled along the side of her face.

"How do ya feel, honey?" She placed her hand on my cheek and smiled.

"I'm fine," I said and tried to sit up to see the other figures in the room.

I moved too quickly, and white static flew around the room, like sparks from a fire, and I felt nauseated.

"Mmmhmm." She pushed me back down and placed a wet cloth on my forehead. "No fever. That's good, but you do have a nasty bump."

"I fell." I sighed.

"Well, you go on and get some sleep. It's nearly two a.m." She stood up and looked down on me. "You've had a long journey. Get some sleep, child. We'll talk in the morning."

How does she know how far I've come?

I watched the woman walk back to her chair and between the many beds. She turned down the lantern and then set it back on the mantel.

"Oh, and the outhouse is just outside the back door to your right if you need to use it before morning. Just make sure to light the lantern by the back door and take it with you. Lots of critters roam around at night, and it's black as coffee out there."

She sat down in the rocking chair.

Outhouse! Did she just say outhouse? "Yes, ma'am," I answered.

"Miss Mabel. Everyone calls me Miss Mabel. Not sure why. They just always have. Now, for the rest of you young'uns, time for bed." She yawned as the other four in the room jumped into their beds. "It's a good thing tomorrow is Saturday."

How did I end up here, and where did the light take me?

The sugar-sweet woman and the blazing fire made me think of Hansel and Gretel.

Maybe she'll fatten me up and then they'll devour me.

Of course, that was silly. I looked up at the cross, barely able to see it.

Okay, Dad, show me.

The room went quiet except for the occasional crackle from the fire. I wondered if the woman had called my mother and if she was on her way here.

How else would she know how far I've come?

I yawned. The warmth of the bed embraced my body like a glove. I thought about leaving. *I should leave in the morning before they all rise.*

The heaviness of my eyelids finally had their way. I'd sleep, at least for a few hours, and then I could leave. A few hours wouldn't make much of a difference, and they'll all be sound asleep. My mouth opened wide and my eyes watered as I stretched down into soft covers.

The morning light was brilliant and burned through my eyelids. I pulled the covers over my head and flipped over to the other side of the mattress. I was sure my mother would once again barge into my room with some sort of request.

"I think she's awake." A small child's voice rang in my ears, and I remembered the train, the police station, being lost in the swamp, and the old woman.

Oh no. I didn't leave.

Then I thought about what the woman said about my long journey. I swallowed hard before I opened my eyes.

The woman, Miss Mabel, left the kitchen and strolled toward me. Whatever she was cooking smelled delicious, and my stomach rumbled. My mother would never let me eat something that smelled that good.

"Good mornin'." The woman smiled. "Sleep well, I hope?"

"Yes, ma'am, I did. Thank you."

"Miss Mabel," she corrected.

"Yes, Miss Mabel," I answered back.

"There's a bag under your bed. It contains things a young woman might need, including clothes that should be about your size. There is already a tub of warm water prepared for you in the washroom." She headed back toward the kitchen and then looked over her shoulder. "Go on now. We don't have all day."

It was on the tip of my tongue to ask if anyone was coming for me, but then I might give away more than I should.

Maybe I can sneak out the bathroom window.

A little blonde girl skipped toward me, and the black dog followed behind her, licking at her fingers.

"May, I need you to set the table," Miss Mabel said, and the little girl huffed and changed her direction. The dog followed her and then passed her to go out the back door.

No one else was in the room besides the three of us, and all the beds were neatly made up except mine.

Did I image more people in the room than there were?

I picked out a few items from the bag along with a change of clothes and headed for the only room with a lock.

There are no windows in here. Great.

I went ahead and bathed and then got dressed. There was no hairdryer or curling iron, not even an electrical outlet.

Ugh, I've stepped into a Little House on the Prairie *novel.*

However, no electricity meant no phone. No phone meant she couldn't have called anyone. A sense of relief fell over me, but there was still the matter of a fake story. This woman wouldn't be as easy to fool as the police station lady.

I placed my hand on the knob to leave the washroom, and a bubble moved up into my chest. I took two deep breaths and then emerged from the washroom, and two more bodies stood in the room.

Miss Mabel waited for me outside of the washroom door and took my arm as I exited.

"This is May." Miss Mabel pointed to the young girl with the long blonde curls.

"You're pretty." The little girl bounced over to me and took my other hand. "We're going to be great friends, even better friends than me and old Scraps."

"Scraps is the old hound dog. Just showed up one day, and May feeds it all of our leftovers. He comes and goes as he pleases," Miss Mabel said.

I nodded and smiled at the little girl. "I'm Jessica," I said as I noticed the blue twinkle in her eyes. *Darn, I didn't use the fake name.*

"This one is Joseph," Miss Mabel said and pulled the thin, fragile boy by the arm.

His dark brown eyes shifted to the ground, and his black hair fell to cover his face. "Hey." Joseph's voice crackled.

Miss Mabel let go of him, and he walked out the front door, letting the screen door slam shut behind him.

"I'm Josephine." A girl who looked similar to Joseph in size and age stepped up and took my hand into hers. "Excuse me, please, Jessica."

I nodded.

"Joseph and Josephine are twins," Miss Mabel said, as she watched Josephine chase after him. "Just because he's fifteen, he thinks he's all grown. Sometimes that boy gets on my last nerve. It's a good thing I'm a Christian." She shook her head and then scanned the room.

May tugged on her dress. "Remember, he was taking the blankets to the orphanage and then over to the—"

"Oh yes. That's right. Thanks, May," Miss Mabel said. "I suppose you'll meet him eventually. Have to forgive us old folks, we sometimes can't remember from one moment to the next." She laughed and put her arm around my shoulders. "I bet you're hungry." She led me into the small kitchen at the back of the square room.

A black, wood-burning stove sat in the corner of the kitchen. It had a long pipe that went out through the top of the roof. The red-hot coals were visible through the middle of the glass window and warmed the space nicely. I sat down on a thin-wire chair across from the stove and put my hands on the square table with a beige-tile top. Above the table hung a picture of a white, colonial-style house surrounded by a lush garden and angel statues. A silver plaque attached to the bottom of the frame. I read it aloud, "As for me and my household, we will serve the Lord."

"Amen," Miss Mabel said while she set a plate of food in front of me. "Now that you've said prayer, you may eat."

"I didn't say a prayer. I was just reading the—"

"Now, I'm sure you'd rather eat than argue with an old woman." She smiled and slid the plate closer to me.

The food smelled amazing, and I was starving, so I nodded and grabbed the fork. *What difference does it make?* I planned on leaving, so what good would it have done to bring up my unsure feelings about God? *However, it would be rude not to eat this.* I smiled before I gulped down the delicious, greasy food.

Oh, my mother would kill me. But father would have liked her.

Halfway from a clean plate, Miss Mabel sat down across from me with a white lily teapot and two matching cups.

"Tea?" she asked and poured the hot liquid into her cup.

I quickly chewed the bacon and swallowed. "Yes, please."

"So, Jessica," she began, "how did you end up so far from the road?"

My stomach started to flutter, and I panicked.

"I'm an orphan. I've been on my own for quite some time. I heard about a job." I paused, looking up into her face. She was not buying it.

"A good friend said her father's cousin, who works for the Okefenokee Swamp, is looking for help in their gift shop."

"That's not what I asked you." The old woman picked up her cup and sipped the tea.

"I was on my way there when I was robbed. A man took my money, clothes, and my bus ticket. I tried to hitch a ride, but no cars came by." There was no point to lie about that. "It started to rain really hard, and the only way to stay somewhat dry was to stay under the big trees. I guess I got turned around and could no longer see the road." I was there all over again, and my heart raced, chasing after the little light. Or was the light my imagination? Was all of this my imagination?

I didn't tell her about the light. *She'll think I'm crazy and drive me to some hospital, and then they'll find me for sure.*

"Interesting. And no one told you to come here?"

Yes. My father's dead spirit led me here. That would go over well. But do I really believe that's what happened and how I ended up here? No…well maybe a small part of me does.

"No ma— Miss Mabel," I answered her.

She took another slip of her tea and then set the cup down on the tile.

"Well, if it's work you're looking for, I sure can use a couple more hands around here for plantin' and then for harvest time. I can't pay you, but I can offer you room and board and you can stay as long as you like," she said. "We might not have much, but we always have plenty." She stood up and walked over to the sink.

I nodded even though what she said sounded odd, and I smirked. I wanted to say in return, "Thank you for hospitality, but I'll be leaving now." However, the only part that came out was, "Thank you."

"No need for thanks, but it is appreciated." She beamed and reached for my empty plate. I tried to help clean up, but May bounced in and tugged on my shirt.

"Go on, you two. I got this," Miss Mabel said as she placed the dishes in the deep sink of soapy water.

"Let's go outside." May tugged again and then ran out the front door.

I followed.

I gazed out at the barren field in front of the little shack and toward the tall, deep-green trees with branches that hung down to the ground and surrounded the property. A thin gravel road disappeared into the thickest part of the wooded area. On the right side of the house, there was a stream covered with purple water lilies. A slight pungent smell came and went in the air, as did the smell of the lilies.

May sat down on a long swing that hung in the middle of the porch and gestured toward me to sit next to her. The porch was almost bigger than the shack. May began to chatter the moment I sat next to her. She talked a mile a minute, and I caught bits and pieces of her words as I debated whether I should take Miss Mabel up on her offer. The house was perfectly hidden by trees, and my mother would never think to find me in a swamp, although not having electricity and running water was not how I had planned to start my new life.

"Hey, there's Hunter. He's back early." May interrupted her monologue on the dangers of the swamp and pointed out toward the road. "You'll like him. He's nice like you."

I recognized Joseph first as he came around from the side of the shack. He ran down the gravel road and toward the guy May called Hunter, and he was walking toward the house. As they met, Hunter, who was a good head taller than Joseph, ruffled his long hair with his hand. They both stopped for a moment and looked toward the house. Both sets of eyes were on me, and my heart pounded. I turned my head away so they wouldn't know I was watching.

"They're going to race. But I'm faster than both of them," May said, which prompted me to look back at them.

They were standing next to each other for a moment and then took off running toward us. Hunter, wearing torn, tight-fitted jeans was faster than Joseph. His hair jetted back behind him, exposing his cheerful, carefree smile and perfectly tanned skin. As he ran, his feet firmly met the ground and gave him even more power behind his well-formed legs. His muscular arms moved along the side of his body in consistent swings. When Hunter realized Joseph was far behind, he stopped and turned toward him. Joseph wasn't happy about losing.

"Come on," Hunter said to Joseph, laughing. He didn't struggle to catch his breath as he kicked up the dirt on the road toward Joseph. "You're not giving me much of a challenge."

Joseph ran faster and tackled him. I cringed and looked away before seeing their bodies hit the gravel. After a moment, I searched for them, but they were gone from sight. However, I could hear them laughing around the other side of the house.

"Did you hear anything I just said?" May giggled.

I shook my head, embarrassed that I hadn't.

"It's okay," she said. "They are silly sometimes and fun to watch. It really is the only time Joseph seems happy these days. I don't think he likes being left with all the girls."

"May," Miss Mabel called from inside.

She stood up quickly. "I'll be right back. Don't go anywhere without me," she said and entered through the screen door.

The thought to run did occur to me. *If I do leave it should be when everyone is asleep.* I agreed and stood up to stretch while I walked to the edge of the porch. Roses lined the outside of the porch and climbed up the white lattice. They were white roses; however, a brilliant red outlined each delicate petal, something I had never seen before. I breathed in the sweet perfume and reached down to touch one of the soft petals.

"Watch your fingers. They can be sharp," someone said as I heard the screech of the screen door open.

I turned around.

"Although they are beautiful to look at, they produce thorns bigger than the average rose." The tan-skinned boy blinked his thick, black eyelashes.

"Oh," I said, startled by his shirtless chest.

I tried to keep my focus on his light blue eyes and away from his uncovered chest, which made my skin feel hot all over. Seth worked out and had a nice build and all, but this felt different.

Dizzy. I can't breathe. Please don't pass out.

I held my breath so I wouldn't smell the alluring musk coming from his skin and hoped the loud thunder in my ears would stop.

Don't speak, it will just come out stupid.

I gripped the railing behind me and shifted my gaze to my feet. *What the heck is wrong with me?*

"Sorry I wasn't here this morning to greet you. Properly, I mean. I guess since I found you, technically, I met you first."

Great, his first impression of me was being covered in filth.

I looked up as he chuckled and watched him wrap a bandana around his hand.

"What were you doing out there anyway? And how did you get so far from the road?"

The way he asked sounded suspicious, the same way that Miss Mabel had asked if someone had told me to come here.

"I…I just got lost is all." The tone in my voice was unsteady.

"I guess we'll know soon enough." He tucked the remaining cloth under the folds. "Who would have guessed a little girl would be out in the middle of the swamp in a rain storm?" He chuckled and met my eyes. "It's a good thing we needed firewood last night."

I felt my heart stop. I was not a little girl and not much younger than he had to be. I wanted to tell him my age, but then he jumped over the railing, vaulting himself with one arm to clear the roses. His muscles rippled and rendered me speechless.

"I'm Hunter, by the way." He plucked one of the roses and used a pocketknife to trim off the thorns. He extended his hand with the rose in it to me.

I took the rose and stared at his face. He was beautiful. He lifted one eyebrow and waited for me to say something, but I stayed frozen.

Hello, he's waiting for me to say my name. All I could do was stare into his eyes.

"Okay. Well, I've got chores to do." He shook his head with a smirk. "Have a good day, whatever your name is." He turned and started to whistle as he walked toward the tree line.

"Jessica," I called out with my entire body leaned forward against the railing.

He turned around. "See ya later, Jess." He picked up an ax from the ground and hoisted it up onto his shoulder, as if it weighted nothing, and disappeared into the trees.

The static in the air was back and danced before me, just like all the times my mother or Seth had burst into my room and made me sit up fast, causing the fireflies to appear—only this was more pleasing.

What is that? I felt pins and needles stabbing me all over, although I didn't mind. "I'm definitely staying."

Ghosts in the Wind

Miss Mabel was right; there was a lot of work to do, and with Hunter gone during the daytime, the four of us worked the soil and planted seeds in the garden behind the house. Time moved faster in the swamp, as two months felt more like two weeks. Soon, the harvesting would start, and she would need me for that as well. I loved the new family, and the thoughts of leaving there had left me for weeks. But one night, the fear of Seth came into that room. It came in the wind and paraded in the shadows outside the window. The wind howled through the cracks in the door and created a long screeching sound. I was able to make out the tree branches that scraped against the window back and forth, but I shuddered and pulled the covers close to my body at the unfamiliar shadows that danced in disguise. No moon peeked through the canopy and left the night in complete blindness.

A dark silhouette paused where my gaze stopped, and it did not look like a tree branch. I yanked the covers over my head, feeling the rush of blood flowing throughout my body, and my mother's small but irritating voice echoed in the back of my mind: *"You're being way too dramatic, Jessica."*

I looked over toward Hunter, and he was deep asleep. Although I hadn't seen much of him except for Sundays, when the pastor would come out and give a sermon, his mere presence calmed my spirit of dread. I felt safe with him near. But something else was at work, something even he couldn't help with—my bladder—which meant I'd have to go outside and brave the absolute darkness in the wind and rain and creatures and whatever else might be out there. I thought about making a loud noise to wake him. If he knew I had to go, he would walk me out. But if I did, I would wake everyone else up as well.

I tried to hold it, but it was no use, so I sat up and stepped into my boots and then made my way for the back door.

Nothing is going to hurt me. I've been there and back before plenty of times without him following.

The darkness wasn't the reason my hands trembled. It was the fear of what might be in the dark—an unexpected person, just past my sight, waiting for the right moment to seize me. I pictured my mouth covered and not being able to call out for help as he dragged my body across the swamp.

Seth knows how to get rid of a body.

I shook the image and turned to light the lantern on the edge of the kitchen counter.

The wind continued to shriek a high-pitched, whistling sound that pierced through my ears. I held onto the back porch door tightly so it wouldn't blow off or slam shut. Once shut, I stayed close to the house, as it protected me from the full force of the wind and slanting rain. At the edge of the house, I turned to leave the shelter of the eaves and made a run for it. The wind instantly blew out the light inside the lantern and left me in the pitch-black night. Nothing was visible, including the outhouse.

My hair whipped at my eyes and made it harder to see. I stumbled in the dark for what seemed like more than a few minutes with my hands outstretched in front of me until the feel of the familiar handle on the outhouse gave me some comfort. The wind did not let up at my victory but wrestled against me as I struggled to get the door shut. One pull with all my might and a lot of luck, and I shut the door and locked the metal hinge to keep it closed.

I plopped down to take care of business and closed my eyes. In my heightened state of observing everything around me, I did not want to deal with whatever might be in there with me, taking refuge while the storm raged out of control. Just the thought of little, hairy creatures with eight legs dangling over my head, webs in each corner of the ceiling, and the eyes of insects looking in my direction made my skin crawl. I should be grateful for the hissing and whistling of the storm. It was all I could hear and not anything scurrying about.

Bam! Bam! Bam!

A bang at the back of outhouse made me jump, and I pulled on my undergarments. Another thump rattled the structure. I placed my hand reluctantly against the wall, where the sound came from. No longer afraid of the insects around me, I opened my eyes and placed my ear alongside my hand. I felt another thump against my cheek and it jolted me back. Not to waste any time, I turned around and fumbled to get the lock undone. It took me a moment, but as soon as the door flung open, I ran fast, as fast as my legs would go, and I didn't look back. There was a feeling that someone was running after me, and if there was, I was too scared to look for sure. The feeling moved around in front of me, so I turned around to go in the opposite direction.

Panicked and confused at where I ended up, I called out. "Where are you, shack?"

I stopped running and extended my arms straight out to try and feel my way.

I need to calm down.

I took deep breaths as my heart beat in my throat. Finally, the tips of my fingers felt the porch railing and I let out a big huff of air.

I climbed up under the railing and sat on the swing. No one seemed to be following me, or they would have caught me. I laughed and placed my head in my hands. The shadows chasing me where gone, if they had existed at all.

No more liquids late at night for me.

A strong gust of wind swept over the patio and chilled me down to my bones. I went inside and back into my warm bed.

"Now don't I feel silly," I said to myself and looked over at Miss Mabel, sleeping in her rocker.

Miss Mabel wore an old, crocheted blanket draped across her shoulders. The blanket contained different fall colors woven throughout: brown, gold, amber, and many different shades of the same base colors. Beautiful as it was, it was also falling apart, with loose, broken yarn dangling from it.

I continued to watch her. It calmed me.

She shifted in her seat before she noticed that the fire was only burning embers. She bent down to add another log to the red-hot coals, which caught instantly and filled the room with light. She turned to glance around the room and then pushed herself up on the arm of the chair. She stood up and walked through the path between the beds, making sure everyone was under their blankets. On her final round, she returned to her chair. She yawned and began to rock back and forth as she hummed a lovely tune. Soon, my eyelids felt heavy and I drifted off to sleep.

Dreams had been scarce since my arrival in the swamp, and I was thankful for that since most were not pleasant, but the ghosts of my past loomed in the familiar sounds of the winds and brought me somewhere new: lost in the swamp.

I was in a dream, and I knew it, feeling the soggy ground under my bare feet. I noticed the moon was full and everything around me was shimmery, like walking in a reflection through water. I took a step farther into the placid world and felt a hard, prickly object wrap around my ankle and pulled me down into the soil up to my knees. I struggled to free my legs with my arms, but it wasn't working. I reached out for the moss-covered vines, which hung down from the treetops, but it only teased the tips of my finger. The air around me smelled like rotten eggs and I gagged.

Finally, after much wiggling, I was able to yank one leg out and then the other. A line of glittery light filtered in through the canopy of cypress, maple, and pine in a star-like pattern and it blinded me for a moment. Then a silhouette of a man appeared in the middle of the light directly in front of me.

Instantly, I wanted to be near the figure. I desired it more than anything else in the world, even more than a real family or being rid of Seth for good. I was drawn to it like a magnet to a fridge. I sped up, but the ground wasn't going to give up so easily and continued to tug at my legs until I was waist deep in the thick, tarlike chasm and couldn't move any farther. There was something other than the prickly object at my feet. It was smooth, soft against my skin, and swirled up and down my calf. I looked down to see the creature, and the ground changed before my eyes. The muck hardened around my waist, like ice forms on top of a lake, and then it turned into black glass.

The creature below moved around and through my legs. The serpent was long and narrow and touched my skin, sending a pleasing shockwave up my body. I felt almost hypnotized by it, leaving me with a desire to join the creature at my feet.

A strong sour smell drew my attention above my head. A giant hand reached down through the thick, gray mist. The smell was familiar and brought me sorrow followed by pain. I reached out even though my senses told me not to. But at least I could pull myself out of the mess and out of the dream—I hoped.

The bright light flared up, and I turned to face it. A smile broke through the silhouette and filled me with its love.

"Are you waiting for me?" I called out and reached my hand forward.

He didn't respond but continued to blind me with his smile.

The serpent tied my legs together and began to pull harder. I looked around for something immediate to grasp before the creature could pull me down into its den. The giant extended his hand to only inches from my face. I strained to see the face of the person who was my only option. I screamed.

"Jessie."

I felt Hunter's hand on my face as he gently and quietly woke me.

"Bad dream?" he asked in a whisper, sweeping away the hair stuck to my cheek.

I nodded, breathing in the woody pine smell that lingered on him from stacking firewood, which relaxed my tense body.

"Scoot over," Hunter said, sitting on the edge of my bed with his own blankets tightly wrapped around himself. He propped his pillow against the headboard and sat up straight.

I felt the rhythm of my heart speed up, which had nothing to do with the dream.

"Some night," he said. "I'll have to inspect for damage in the morning. Hope it's not too bad." He paused. "When May can't sleep, I tell her stories." He chuckled. "Puts her to sleep every time."

"I know. But I can never hear what you're saying."

"I don't want to wake anyone else in the room, so I'm especially quiet. The trick is to speak directly into the ear. So…"

His arm went around my shoulders, and I leaned toward him, letting one ear rest near his heart, just like I saw May do, and the other ear ready to listen.

Please stop shivering, I demanded my body. *Don't get the wrong idea about this. Remember, he does this with May all the time. He treats me the same as a six year old.* I sighed inside.

"Let's see," he said, and the air from his mouth tickled my ear. "How do you feel about history?"

"Sure," I said, trying to contain my racing heart.

Hunter's voice was soothing, comforting, and when he spoke, his tone caressed my soul and I felt safe and serene. I longed for everything about him in a way I didn't fully understand; nothing like the contempt I felt for Seth or the looming pit of darkness I felt before I left.

But I can't stay here forever.

"How about the Cherokee Indians who live in this very spot?" he asked.

"Lived," I corrected.

"Oh yeah. Lived…many years ago."

His hand shifted from my shoulder to rest on my arm, sending my entire body into a quiver.

"Cold?" He pulled up the blanket over my exposed arm and placed his hand on top of the quilt.

Are there such things as fairy tales? Father wanted me to believe each one had some truth to it. I could relate to Cinderella the most, with my mother as the wicked stepmother. Could this new life be my glass slipper? Could Hunter be my prince charming? Ridiculous, I thought as Hunter began his story.

"The Cherokee Indians lived on this land for hundreds of years before the Puritans came here to settle. They were peaceful people, living out their lives according to centuries of beliefs and customs handed down from generation to generation. The women spent their days doing domestic things: cleaning, preparing meals, sewing clothes, and making baskets out of the river cane that grew abundantly along the riverside and still does. The men were the providers and protectors of the tribe. They not only hunted and were the protectors of the tribe, but they also trained up the young boys to be men. But their lives would soon change as the white folk entered their world."

Hunter paused with a big yawn, and the wind continued to whistle through the cracks in the walls.

"At first, it was a good thing. The first white people wanted to help the Cherokee. They brought with them medicine and food, taught them to read and how to govern, and in turn, they taught the white man a few things as well. Eventually, the tribe embraced their friendship, and as time went on, they began to share their God with the Cherokee and soon won them over."

"But didn't they have their own god? Didn't they believe that god existed in all living things?" I asked, remembering a book I had read on Indian beliefs.

"They believed in one creator at one point, bits and pieces of an even older belief. So really, they transitioned back to the original belief. We were all created by the same God, and we all come from the seed of Adam."

"Oh." I squirmed uncomfortably at the new turn of religion. "Go on."

"Times changed when gold was found in the swamp, and the white man wanted the land for themselves. They felt the Indians had no right to it, so they began suggesting to government officials the land was too good for the Native Americans and that the white people deserved it more. Some didn't wait on the government and raided the land. Many on both sides died." Hunter yawned again. "Eventually, the Cherokee were forced off their land to the new land no one wanted. The path to the barren and dry land is known as the Trail of Tears." Hunter stroked his hand along the outside of the blanket, where my arm laid underneath. "Jessie?" he said in a faint whisper.

"Yes?"

"Shouldn't you be asleep by now?" He chuckled, softly stroking my arm, sending a minor quake throughout my body.

"I'm not tired." A knot rose up in my throat. "Your story isn't over. It can't be." It was so sad. *Those poor people.*

"I'll stop for now and continue it another time. You really should get some sleep." He squeezed my arm gently and sent another wave of sensations throughout my body.

It's late, and who am I kidding? Why would this person want anything to do with me anyway, even if he did see me as a woman? No. I need to see him the same way he sees me, like a sibling. It's a safe and less-complicated feeling. No one would get hurt or stop my departure when the time comes.

It's easy to convince a logical mind. Not so easy to convince my illogical heart.

The haunted howls and screams, the ghosts in the wind, were gone, and they left the little shack quiet once more. Only the rhythm of my heartbeat echoed between my ears as I watched Hunter return to his bed.

"Good night, Jessica," he whispered in the dark.

A Lazy Saturday Morning

The bright sunshine streamed in through the windows, followed by the humid and sticky air lingering in the room. I wondered for a moment if the whole encounter with Hunter the night before was just something I had dreamed up. But even with an imagination like mine, I couldn't have come up with story about the Indians on my own.

I sat up in bed to see Hunter and Miss Mable in the kitchen. As I watched them, they worked around each other like two dancers, never getting in the other's way yet contributing to what the other one was doing at the same time. I then looked around the room to notice the others still slept, so I grabbed the opportunity to use the washroom before May. She liked to splash the water right out of the tub, leaving me inches of leftover water, which was gross, but I didn't complain.

Once in the washroom, I wasted no time and climbed into the warm tub. My mother would consider this very unsanitary, the five of us sharing bath water. I leaned my head against the side of the tub and tried to focus on something other than my mother, but her voice was beating along the walls of my skull.

"Do you have any idea what you've put me through, what Seth and his father have done for us? You owe me your life."

I stepped out of the tub and dried off. As I dressed, I thought about the dream the night before and the thing I had screamed at. But it was no use. It was like the fog rolling in from the ocean and covering everything in its path, leaving me with the eerie feeling of anxiety of things not yet revealed.

"Jess!" a small voice pleaded at the door.

I opened the door to see May standing there. "Sorry. I didn't know I was taking so long. It's all yours," I said, stepping out.

May rushed passed me and shook her tiny, impatient face at me before she closed the door behind her. I went into the kitchen.

The aroma from the kitchen made me look over Miss Mabel's shoulders to see what was in the cast-iron pan. A whiff of the applewood bacon overpowered my sense of politeness, and I reached out to snag a piece of cooked bacon. Quick as a humming bird, Miss Mabel whirled around with the spatula and tapped my hand.

"Not yet, my dear. Why don't you check the mailbox for me? I don't think I've checked it in a while. I'm so absentminded these days." She paused. "That is, if the mailbox is still there." She winked and spun around to scold Hunter, whose eyes were on me. Her eyes narrowed at him. "Boy, you are going to burn those eggs!"

Hunter snickered and, with a big smile, turned his attention back to his work.

"Sure. I'll go check," I said.

"May," Miss Mabel called, keeping her eyes on Hunter, "go with her, please."

May bounded out of the washroom, already bathed and dressed and wrapping her wet hair up into bun. "Where are we going?"

"The mailbox," I answered.

Hunter turned around to face Miss Mabel, folding his arms against his chest. "What did I do?"

"Last night?" Miss Mabel asked.

What about last night?

May pulled my hand out the door. "Race you," she said, darting off toward the mailbox, leaving me in her dust.

I stood just outside the door to hear this answer, but no one spoke.

May stopped almost half way down the road and called back to me. "Come on!" She whined and puffed air.

I ran to catch up to her. "What was that about? Was Hunter in trouble for something?"

The little girl shrugged her shoulders and then focused on her own agenda. "Ready…set…"

"How about we just walk?" I giggled at the hyper child who couldn't be still for a moment.

"Fine," she said in a pout.

We walked about a mile to the mailbox. There was quite a bit of damage from the storm all around us. Branches from the trees were snapped off and lying all across the ground like matchsticks. I was grateful to be walking on top of the branches instead of wading through the oozing mud that would have sucked our feet into the sludge, possibly making us lose one or both of our shoes.

I came across a wide and thick mud puddle. The sun reflected off it and created a glassy, mirror-like appearance. Below the surface, a long, round object wiggled. I grabbed a broken tree limb and dipped the broken end into the pool of mud. My pulse raced.

This is like the dream.

I dug the stick around until the creature was looped around it. I pulled it up slowly, not letting it escape. It was big, long, black, and round. I couldn't believe my eyes. An earthworm four times as big as an average worm and covered in a thick, tar-like mud.

"What are you doing?" May asked. "Are you listening to me?"

I let out a nervous laugh and placed the worm back down into its new home away from the puddle.

"Sorry, May. I guess I wasn't. Doesn't that worm seem a bit larger than it should be?"

"I heard Miss Mabel say that everything is different here than in the real world. The worms are great for the garden. She calls them natural gardeners."

"You mean like how we plant seeds one day and the next day it's an inch tall?" That was strange, but Miss Mabel did say the soil there was richer than in most parts of the country. I guessed that could be true. It took at least three weeks before I saw the first sprout of a rose bush emerge in the garden back home.

"Oh look. We're here." May pointed to the mailbox. "You know, I think it's going to be a lovely day."

I pulled down the rusty handle to peek inside. "Nothing in here."

"It's not like we get real mail anyway," May said with a stutter and looked away from my eyes toward the ground. Her hands went behind her back.

"What you do mean no real mail?"

"I'm not supposed to tell." She squirmed.

"What, that you don't get mail? I'm not surprised, being way out here."

The little girl shrugged her shoulders. "Don't tell I told you… or about the other thing."

"But you didn't tell me anything, May." I placed my hand on my hip. "Okay. I won't tell," I said, thinking maybe she'd read too many fairy tales. I wondered if she had ever been away from the swamp.

"Thanks." She smiled.

"Well, I guess we'd better head back. I'll race you this time."

May loved to race, and I was anxious to get back to find out why Hunter was in trouble.

"Go!" May said.

I took off faster than May for the first time; however, only a quarter into the race, she passed me. I laughed and then began to choke on the air. I stopped to catch my breath, watching bits of water kicking up in the air behind May's feet.

The smell of breakfast loomed in the air and caused my stomach to growl loudly.

A sound came from behind me, just past the trees that outlined the road, and I held my breath. Standing perfectly still and quiet, I listened for the sound. Again it came, moving closer.

I snapped my head around to look behind me and on to the brush on the side of the road.

If it hadn't been for the dream, I would have just continued on my way, chalking it up to the sound of some kind of wildlife making its way to the warmth of the pebble road.

Another crunching sound came from the same area, sounding more like footsteps breaking the branches beneath their feet. I remembered the unfamiliar shadow I had seen outside the window last night and the feeling of someone chasing me. The sound changed direction and faded back into the thick of the trees.

Someone grabbed my arm, and I jumped, falling onto the ground.

"Why did you stop?" May looked down at me with a puzzled expression.

"I...I needed to rest," I said, pushing my body off the ground.

I couldn't tell her the truth, and I felt horrible about it. She had her secrets and I had mine, although in all fairness, her secrets were more of a game. At least I thought so.

I took hold of her little hand, and we ran toward the shack. By the time we got back, Miss Mabel and Hunter were back to talking about breakfast and I had missed the entire conversation.

Shoot! I stomped my foot on the ground. Miss Mabel looked up at me. "There wasn't any mail today," I said and continued to go through the screen door.

Hunter noticed my flushed face and looked somewhat concerned. May told him about my earthworm, and they both laughed.

"Well you'd better get yourself some food. I could hear that rumblin' all the way from the road. Don't' worry. It's worm free." She laughed, handed me a plate, and kissed my cheek before she sat at the kitchen table.

Everyone else bowed their heads for prayer, and I headed for the front porch swing and away from the praying.

I walked through the screen door and sat on the swing. I curled my legs underneath me and placed my plate on my knees. I looked out into the wilderness.

How long can I stay here? How long before the evil finds me? Or has he already found me? "Shut up," I said to myself.

I scooped up some food on the fork and shoved it into my mouth. Scrambled eggs cooked in the bacon grease topped with cheese, along with grits and a biscuit still hot from the stove. It tasted so good and I gathered up another bite.

I had a vision of my mother standing before me, shaking her boney finger at me. *Can you imagine how many calories and fat grams you're consuming? Are you trying to embarrass me? You're trying to ensure that Seth won't want to marry you? I can't be expected to take care of you the rest of your life, Jessica. You have obligations, and certain things are expected from you!*

I shook my head and snarled at the vision.

"What were you just thinking about?" Hunter asked as he walked through the screen door and sat next to me.

I didn't answer and gestured at my mouth full of food.

"At least you're enjoying the breakfast."

"It's very good," I answered, hoping nothing in my mouth fell out.

"I'm glad you like it. You know, when you came here, you were a bit underweight."

I swallowed hard. "So what you're saying is that I'm fat?" I had noticed a few days back the jeans I came here with were not as loose as they had been. Hunter might have been the one talking to me, however, my mother's voice called me fat.

He laughed. "Far from it. Didn't you eat where you came from?"

I didn't answer. It was hard not to cry, and I bit the outside of my lip and stayed quiet. *What? Get a hold of yourself. It's silly to cry.*

"You're not going to talk about your past. That's fine. I'll find out eventually." He looked out toward the trees and chuckled. "I know people."

I couldn't help but laugh at the way he clicked his tongue against the inside of his cheek. It was quite charming. I just wished I wasn't so clumsy around him as I watched the fork of food fall into my lap.

"You know that we get sixty inches of rainfall each year?" He changed the subject as I brushed the food off my shirt and back on the plate.

"The Okefenokee Swamp is pretty big. It's the largest swamp in Northern America, with over two hundred different types of birds."

"I bet May has names for all of them too," I said, surprised my words came out naturally, without carefully thinking out my reply.

He chuckled. "It's possible. She loves all of God's creatures, but she especially loves birds."

"I think they love her too."

"God created all the birds and all the animals. He created the world and all the stars in the sky. He created all things uniquely and for a purpose. Most people, though, wouldn't see the swamp as anything more than a mud pit."

He looked over in my direction again.

"That's exactly what I thought before coming here."

My mother would see it that way too.

"So you did come here on purpose." He grinned.

"I've read about a lot of places." I shoveled more food into my big mouth.

What I didn't read about was it being a magical swamp. Nothing else explained the way the plants grew, why the sun always seemed to shine on just the right spots, or how the storm winds barely touched the garden. I felt as though I had stepped into an episode of *The Twilight Zone*. It wasn't really a magical swamp, but it was easier to pretend, and I was getting quite good at pretending.

"The really dark areas creep me out, but the garden is beautiful," I added. "Peaceful."

"Not so peaceful where you came from?" he asked.

"No, it wasn't," I answered and looked down at my plate.

"And where was that?"

"Oh, all over. This home, that home," I said and traced my fork around my empty plate.

"Here. Let me take that for you," he said as he got up.

The sweetest, brightest smile I had ever seen was on his face. Hypnotic. I stared into his eyes, which took on a turquoise hue. My stomach felt like it had a thousand buzzing beetles bouncing around inside and traveling into my ears. I heard nothing else as they swarmed. He inched closer. I couldn't look away. My breath moved quicker, and I could feel the pulsating blood flowing through me.

"Jess!"

I heard May's voice and jerked my head toward the sound, pulling me out of the trance, and then back at Hunter. His eyes still watching my face, he winked and then took my plate.

Stupid, Jess. Really stupid. From now on, avoid eye contact.

I replayed over in my mind what he said and what I said like a tape recorder.

Did I give too much away? Why should I be worried that he might not think I was an orphan? Silly. Of course, an orphan would have had a miserable life being in and out of homes with different families. How miserable would that have been? I sighed.

I envied the orphan and wished I was her.

Hunter, in an almost singing voice, called to May, "She's out on the porch!"

And seconds later, May was on the porch, holding a book in her hand.

Hunter was back a second later with a sketchbook. He sat down on the top step of the porch, leaning his back against the railing, facing me. Of course, then I wouldn't be able to see what he was drawing. I wondered if that was his intention.

Joseph didn't seem happy as he stormed out of the screen door. He shot an angry look in my direction before he stormed passed Hunter.

"Joseph, come on!" Hunter called to him in a playful way and reached out for his leg. He kicked Hunter's hand off his leg and kept walking until he disappeared into the trees. Hunter sighed and shook his head as he flipped open his book. Josephine came out with Miss Mabel, carrying bundles of bright-colored balls of yarn. Miss Mabel was teaching her to knit. Josephine looked over at me with an approving grin before sitting down to her task.

I began to read the book to May, Miss Mabel and Josephine began to knit, and Hunter began to sketch.

This was a typical Saturday, except for Hunter's new desire to stay with us. Normally, he was off the porch and out some distance from the house, tossing a ball with Joseph or wrestling with him in the tall, yellow grass.

I understood why Joseph stomped off. Hunter wasn't spending any time with him, and I think he blamed me for it.

Joseph's issue didn't stop us from enjoying our lazy Saturday afternoon. Saturdays I had known before were filled with avoiding Seth, arguments with my mother, and compromising for the sake of my father's life. I wondered if my father saw me now or if he was just rotting away in that fancy coffin buried beneath the earth. I felt bad thinking it, but I was glad for the events which led me to this interesting family. I was also glad Hunter sat a few feet in front of me.

I read for hours. May listened with her head resting on my lap until she reached boredom. She then grabbed the book out of my hands and ran.

"Let's go explore," May said.

I laughed louder than I meant to and Hunter looked over at me and closed his tablet. I stood to chase her, but the smell of lunch stewed in the air.

Wow. Is it really noon?

Stranger in the Clearing

May and I started out for our adventure. It was frequently just the two of us on these little escapades through the marsh. Hunter had come a few times, but it seemed to upset both Joseph and May. Joseph had never said more than two words to me since I'd arrived, and he purposely avoided me by studying my movements and going in the opposite direction. May, I think, wanted me all to herself.

Combing through the marsh was not Josephine's idea of fun. She stayed behind with Miss Mabel, determined to complete her knitted blanket. Time and again, I watched her pull out the long strands, letting her work unravel, and then grumble and toss down her needles. Then, moments later, she was picking them back up and starting again. I admired that quality about her. She didn't give up and vowed to have a completed project by the time May and I returned.

"I think today we should look for unicorns," May teased with a wink, stepping down from the porch.

"Don't go too far in this time, May," Miss Mabel said in her singsong voice, "ya hear me?"

"Yes, Miss Mabel," she said before she took off in a run, leaving me in her wake.

"Hey," I called after her, but she was already weaving in and out of the trees.

May and I ran fast against the peat moss, which felt similar to stepping on squishy sponges. The moss had absorbed the rain from the night before and was squirting out as our feet came down hard on top of them. The little twigs covering the ground kicked up in the air and landed back softly on the earth behind

May's feet. The trees were so thick and vast in that part of the forest that when May got even a few steps in front of me, she disappeared into the darkness of the canopy. May knew her way around the swamp, but I knew there were other dangerous things living in there, things that could eat up a little six-year-old in one bite. There was one dangerous creature I wasn't particularly fond of: the cottonmouth snake.

We saw quite a few cottonmouths on our little jaunts. Their greenish gray-and-black-striped skin easily camouflaged against the trees and bushes. One snake I encountered on my first trip into the swamp with May was completely camouflaged in moss. I barely noticed it as it slithered past my feet. The last snake I saw was inches away from me as I leaned against a tree. Its body was curled up on top of a low branch, and it inched itself closer and closer toward me. I was afraid to run. The snake was in a perfect position to strike. Then something bizarre happened. The snake changed its mind and slowly wound its body in the opposite direction while slithering and flicking its tongue. I remember thinking, *It must have found a better prey.*

The next encounter, I might not be so lucky.

May and I continued to wander deeper and deeper into the thickest part of the forest. The chirping sounds of birds were distant and hollow. Two black beetles flew over head and landed on a tree stump a few feet in front of me. They circled each other before fluttering their wings to create a high-pitched resonance that vibrated the lining in my ear.

Staying behind May, I continued to followed her down the path covered in vines. The path grew thicker and harder to walk through. Vines streamed across from tree to tree covered in a lush, dark-green, wet moss that hung close to the ground, blocking out most of the sun, like a heavy blanket covering all the windows in a house. I didn't see the sky, only slender lines of light keeping us from going completely blind in the shadows. The ground felt springy beneath my feet, like walking on top of a wet mattresses.

Why are we continuing to move forward in this creepy area? I thought about those movies where I've yelled at the people, "Don't go in there!" The thought of unusually enormous, hairy spiders dangling from a massive web came to mind.

Darn Seth for making me watch those types of movies.

"May," I called in a shaky voice, "do you think we are going too far?"

May scampered ahead. She had not heard me.

A new type of vegetation and life I had not seen before stirred in the most mysterious part of the swamp yet. A thin layer of white fog floated close to the ground. I wondered if May knew where we were as she hopped from plant to amphibian to bugs and then to birds very excitedly. I assumed the answer was no.

"May," I called louder.

I watched a blue heron land on a boulder. Determined to get May's attention, he squawked at her until she noticed him. She moved over to him, taking soft, careful steps. And then I heard her whisper as she talked to the bird. The bird stood two feet tall with blue-gray, supple feathers and an elongated, tapered, orange bill. His neck curved like a question mark, and his eyes were similar to a dartboard, with the bull's eye perfectly centered. The bird twisted its neck to look at me and then blinked twice.

"Shh," May said and motioned for me to come to her. She placed one finger against her lips and squatted down, eye to eye with the heron. She watched the bird with such stillness I could hardly believe it was May. I leaned against a tree, close enough to the bird to make her happy and I stared up through the tall trees, still not being able to see the color of the sky. The sharp smell of a lit match carried in the air and jolted my senses. I felt an uneasiness creeping up and the urgent need to run in the direction we had come from. I shifted my eyes in a different direction, but the feeling surrounded me and squeezed out the air.

There I go again, thinking someone is watching us. Just breath slowly, in through my nose and out my mouth, just like my mother's yoga instructor said.

A swoosh of air spun around and weaved in and out of the trees. A low moaning sounded off in the distance, and the hair on my arms and the back of my neck stiffened. The bird took off and flew inches above my head in a flurry.

"Someone is coming," May said with a snap in her tone, and she stood to her feet.

Cicadas, which we heard mostly at night, began to buzz and clack.

"I think we should go back to the house," I said and took a few steps back in the direction we had come from. "We've been out here a while, and it's getting darker in here."

May looked over at me and nodded her head in agreement.

We started back the way we had come, only that time, we ran, jumping over decaying logs and thick foliage and weaving in and out of the trees. Finally, ahead of May was a break in the trees. Although it didn't look like the passage we had come through, I looked forward to seeing the sunlight. May broke through it first, and I watched her disappear into the narrow, bright opening between two oak trees.

Behind her, I ran through the two trees and into a bright-yellow field, passing May by a few feet. Everything looked blurry, and I turned my back toward the blinding light. I blinked my eyes over and over, letting the natural tears wash over my irises. Finally able to see, I noticed that May stood petrified, staring past me into the light, and I turned around to see what she was seeing.

Three young men were standing in the middle of an opening where the sun shined in between two tree lines dripped with black moss. It was hot, and the yellow-bladed grass was so dry it sounded like paper being crumpled as it swayed back and forth in the light breeze. The light then faded from a blazing brightness to a gray dimness in a matter of seconds. The breeze turned to a strong gust and bent the long blades of grass closer to the ground.

I've never seen any area of the swamp so dry. *This is very odd.*

I focused my attention back on the strangers.

The one in the middle moved his head to face the man on his left, who wore a black hood, and spoke to him only we were too far to hear any words. He then turned his head to the man on his right and placed his hand on his chest. His hair was fire red, wavy, and flowed past his shoulders. He rocked back and forth, heel to toe, and glared in my direction.

The dark-haired, unfamiliar person turned toward May and me and meandered his way toward us. As he did, the condition around us changed again. The air around me felt serene and inviting, with a light breeze blowing across the landscape. I smelled the sweet water lilies somewhere nearby. But the only noise I heard was the sound of the dry grass. No birds, insects, or other such creatures made a noise.

Just your imagination.

May moved forward, taking my hand into hers. She squeezed hard. I didn't feel scared. *Intrigued* would be a better word. His movement toward us was graceful and confident as he came closer. I didn't tear my eyes off of him.

"Hello, May," the young man called out.

So, he wasn't a stranger after all.

His voice echoed in my ears, and I wanted him to continue to speak. His tone was calming and somewhat familiar.

I've felt this way before. Yes. Someone with no interest in me. Who was it?

I glanced down at May, and I barely remembered who she was. All I knew, all I wanted was to touch the person moving toward me. My feet wanted to sprint toward him, but May was like a rock anchoring me down. She glared at him until he shifted his eyes off of me to her. May shut her eyes forcefully and looked away.

"Who is your beautiful woman friend?" he asked.

She did not reply.

The stranger stretched out his hand to me and then stopped. He was quite a distance from us, and I couldn't see his face clearly. I took a few steps toward him, but May tugged on my arm to stay back. I stopped, but I didn't want to. I wanted to get closer to him. The urge to move forward at any cost, including leaving May behind, grew stronger.

"Don't look into his eyes," she whispered. "Don't trust your feelings."

The stranger glanced at her as if he could hear her soft words and smiled. It didn't matter what she said; I still wanted to reach out and touch him. I felt like I was caught up watching a spinning pinwheel, so mesmerized by how he moved and spoke. I could get lost in the illusion.

"It's okay. He's not going to harm us," I said in a whisper.

He moved forward again, and May stepped out in front of me, planting her feet firmly on the ground. She crossed her arms over her chest. The dark-haired one chuckled, and it echoed along the meadow as he continued to travel toward us. I focused on his face for any sign of familiarity.

Why I am I not afraid?

My curiosity was unhinged, and if May wasn't standing solid in front of me, I might have sprinted forward.

Instead, May leaned back on me, pushing me with her body. I looked down at her, breaking the stare with the stranger. Blood rushed to my brain, and the ground stirred around me. I swallowed the uneasy mass back down and got down on my knees to face May, who was trembling. May turned her eyes toward the trees with a pleading look.

The crunch of the grass beneath the stranger's feet stopped, and I could see his black shoes only inches from us. When I looked up, I began to wheeze. My heart pounded, and the blood in my head rushed to my face. I felt the air around me become thick as it moved into my throat with each breath. His black hair danced around his strong, stout face, and his eyes were deep brown with sharp, auburn specks, which fascinated me. He was beautiful.

Just like Hunter.

He held me in a trance, and I didn't want to escape from it as his hand reached out to touch mine. His eyes stayed locked on mine, and he brought my hand up to his lips. He kissed the top of my hand so gently that it felt more like the touch of the breeze. My face burned, and a tingling shot out all over my body.

Please, don't you faint.

The outsider broke his gaze with me as he looked past me toward the forest behind us. A big smirk formed from one side of his mouth, and he released my hand, which came crashing down to my side. If it hadn't been for May, I would have gone crashing down on the hard ground.

"Hunter, so good to see you after all these years," he said with sarcasm in his tone.

"Is it?" I heard a cynical tone reply behind me.

No. That can't be my Hunter.

I turned around to see Hunter stepping out of the trees. He was out of breath and gasping for air. He bent down for a moment, placing his hands on his knees. After a moment, he stood tall, taking a stance similar to what May was doing in front of me. He shone, standing there surround by the grayness that continued to swallow the daylight. His expression was so different from his carefree self that I knew. Hunter stood there with his chin up and no smile on his face. Instead, his lips were a thin line and his jaw clinched.

Just waiting?

The stranger walked backward toward the other two guys, who were pacing back and forth like lions in a cage. They appeared agitated by the new events, and it gave me the impression they were ready for a fight, especially the redhead, who growled loudly.

Hunter looked down at May, and she beamed, no longer shaking against me. Hunter's eyes moved to mine, piercing right through me like little daggers. I felt like a child who had done something wrong and was being scolded for it. First, a feeling of guilt washed over me. But why? Then anger rose, and I narrowed my eyes back at him. *I'm not a child, I'm not your little sister to be told what to do,* I wanted to yell out loud. *How can he not see me?* I sighed and thought about what the stranger said. He had said I was a beautiful woman, and I liked it.

Hunter shook his head at whatever thought he was having and focused back to the stranger. He walked past May and me, moving closer to the three figures.

"Aren't you a little farther north than you should be?" Hunter asked, only it sounded more like a statement of fact than a question. One corner of the stranger's lip curled up, and his eyebrows pushed together as though he were trying to read in a poorly lit room. "Really?" the stranger asked, as if something amusing had just been revealed. He looked at me and then back to Hunter.

Hunter didn't reply but narrowed his eyes on the stranger.

"We have every right to go where we please," the stranger said, holding his arms up to the sky. "If you have a problem with that, you know who to take it up with." He raised both hands up toward the sky.

"You didn't answer me," Hunter pressed.

The redhead snickered and flipped his hair back with a quick whip of his neck. The hooded stranger, still looking down, wrung his hands in a frantic circle, over and over.

"Well, if you must know, we were retrieving a new family member. It's lovely that so many are willing to join our cause. Lots of souls to recruit," the stranger continued as he put his arm around the hooded boy. "Say hello to my friend Charles." The stranger held up the hooded boy's face.

I couldn't see anything from where I was.

The stranger, changing his tone, twisted his body around to look past Hunter and right at me. "And you are?"

"She's no concern of yours." Hunter moved to block his view of me. "May, take her straight home," he said with no emotion.

She nodded and took my hand.

"Wait," I said, looking down at May, feeling irritated.

"Please, Jess. Please," May whispered, stroking my hand and pleading with her eyes.

"So you speak for her as well?" the stranger asked. "You know you can't ha—"

"I think it's time you go back to where you came from," Hunter replied with his lips barely open and the muscles in his jaw extending his chin forward, "and leave us be."

The stranger smiled, pleased at himself for Hunter's reply.

"Please, Jess." May whimpered again, tugging on my hand.

"Okay," I spat out, but I didn't move.

There was more to this conversation than just words, and the two men stared at each other.

May forcefully pulled on me to leave. I started to walk across the grassy field. Everything fell into slow motion, the crackling of the yellow grass bending beneath my feet, the air on my face lifting the strands of my hair up as if they were weightless. Then the smell of violets filled every breath I took. It was delightful.

May and I stepped to the edge of the meadow, and everything was back to normal.

I smiled and took in a deep breath. "Did you feel that?" I whispered to May.

"Feel what? We need to go," she answered.

Well, whatever it was, I felt great.

"There's no need to be so impolite," the stranger said. "Well, it was nice to almost meet you," he called out. I looked back, and the stranger winked at me. "Another time, perhaps?"

A snarl came from Hunter's lips. He looked ready to squeeze the life out of the stranger. May pulled on me until we were out of the meadow completely and back into another array of trees.

As we moved farther away, the voices became mumbled. I heard the tone of the stranger's voice when he yelled, but never Hunter's. I wanted to go back, but May kept pulling me farther and farther away from the men.

Why am I being forced to leave?

Irritation gnawed at me, and I entertained the idea of meeting the stranger in secret. After all, I wasn't in any danger, and I didn't belong to anyone—not yet, anyway.

I'm Not a Little Girl

The time it took to get back to the shack from the open field where we left Hunter and the strangers, seemed to take forever. I stayed with May until we finally reached the familiar surroundings of the shack. As we approached, I knew why May hesitated forward, but I pressed on anyway.

How did he beat us back?

An argument coming from the shack between Miss Mable and Hunter could be heard down the road. The sharpness shocked me at first. They were both loud, louder than I had ever heard them. Even with the stranger, Hunter never raised his voice above a normal speaking tone, even though he had been agitated by Joseph before. The sound was not only loud but stern and serious, with both trying to talk over the other. I quickened my steps, not able to make out any actual words.

"Hey, I think I see something in the bushes." May hesitated to continue toward the house.

"There is nothing there. We need to get home," I said, and I was willing to let her stand there alone. I wanted to hear the conversation going on in the shack.

And then, just like that, May sprinted for the house, being loud and obnoxious.

"Race you to the kitchen. I'm winning," she called back to me, stopping me in my tracks.

No point now. They know I'm here.

Another secret was being kept from me. I accepted the magical garden, I accepted living in this world which time forgot, but I didn't want to accept the secret of the stranger.

And I have my secrets, which are way worse. What right do I have to be mad about it? But I was.

Twisted Roots | 93

"Hush now. It will all work out," I heard Miss Mabel say to Hunter with some command in her voice.

Through the window, I could see Hunter sitting backward on one of the kitchen chairs, his legs straddling the back of it. Miss Mable leaned down to kiss Hunter on his cheek and rubbed his arm briskly back and forth at the same time May and I entered the room.

"Well I bet you three are pretty hungry," Miss Mable said and then grabbed plates that were wrapped in foil from the oven and set them on the table.

Hunter glared in my direction with bewilderment in his eyes and then back at Miss Mabel before he skulked out of the room, placing his hands in his pockets, his face drawn down toward the floor.

I sat down at the table, but I didn't eat. I looked at Miss Mabel with all these questions in my mind, the most pressing being: *What is wrong with Hunter, and why is he looking at me that way?*

I pushed around the food with my finger while May gobbled up hers. With no words, May got up, washed her dish, and disappeared out the back door.

May, silent? She hasn't been silent since the first day Miss Mabel introduced us.

I looked at the food still sitting on my plate and picked up the fork. I twirled the noodles around it with no real intention on taking a bite.

So who is this stranger in the clearing? I let my memory comb over him. *He called me a beautiful woman. How did he know just what I wanted to hear?* A warm, tingling feeling fluttered up, and I was no longer angry at those around me. *Is he still standing in the warmth of the sun? Maybe he is waiting for me.* I couldn't help it. I wanted to see him again, even if the others didn't approve. I wanted to be near him. *May did say, "Don't trust your feelings." But she is only six! She knows nothing of a woman's heart.*

I got up, forcefully pushing my chair against the wall. I scraped my plate into the bowl on the porch out back for Scraps and washed my plate and placed it back in the dark brown cupboard. Night was coming, so I lit the kerosene lamp that hung next to the back door before I picked a book from Miss Mabel's collection and headed for the long swing on the front porch..

"Oh," I said, startled, and my mood changed instantly.

Hunter rocked in Miss Mabel's chair, his face toward the setting sun. I stood at the doorway, watching the sun disappear. It was hot, even without the rays of the sun. Crickets and cicadas filled the air with their songs. The soft strum of the cricket's legs rubbing together and the sharp rattling of the cicadas were a beautiful combination. It was nothing like the night when I had been lost and scared in the swamp and the sounds had been deafening.

The creaking of the rocking chair, back and forth, added to the orchestra recital.

I turned to go back inside.

"Don't go," he said, still rocking back and forth, not moving his head.

The resonance in his voice compelled me to stay. I hung the lantern on the farthest hook from him and sat on the swing, curling one leg under the other and placing the book on my lap.

The music in the air softened, and my thoughts of the stranger changed to Hunter. His silhouette, even in the growing darkness, was handsome. His long face and stern jaw didn't move. He seemed to be in deep thought, I assumed going over the events of the day. He arched his back, bringing his face into his hands and resting his elbows on his knees. He stayed like that for several minutes.

Could the stranger really cause him this much grief? I wanted to ask, but what would I ask? Everything that came to mind was in favor of the stranger. I wanted to defend someone I didn't even know. It was so illogical.

Hunter took in a deep breath, stretching his arms up. He stood up without a word and looked over at me. From the light of the lantern flickering across his face, he forged a smile, sighed, and then walked out into the dark, moonless night. I watched him until he completely disappeared.

Go after him. The stranger is out there too.

My mind felt like a horse race, all my thoughts lined up behind a gate, all jittery in their stalls, not wanting to be confined to such a small space. Then the race began, and they all took off. The first one out of the gate was my mother as she clawed her way past everyone, followed by the life I'd left, snickering at my current situation; then gliding by was the stranger, dark and mysterious, and then, out of nowhere, it was Hunter ahead by a mile. It was a silly thought, childlike, I know; however, it described my mind perfectly.

Hours had passed since Hunter had stepped off the porch, and I sat with my unopened book in my lap. I laid my head down on the swing pillow. Sleep took over.

I woke to a strange sound in the distance. I got up, rubbed my eyes, and walked into the trees, not thinking about the dangers of the swamp at night. I then found myself somewhere I had been before—the opening in the swamp where I had seen the three strangers. At least, I thought it was the same, but when I looked closer, it seemed different. The ground was covered in a dark brown, stiff grass instead of the yellow, dry grass. My bare feet sank into each step, the indentions filling up with water. A burnt, decaying log sat in the center of the clearing. There was an outline of a dark, masculine shape sitting on one end of the it.

"Hunter," I whispered.

A long chuckle followed my words. My heart raced. I knew who it was, and it was not Hunter.

The figure gestured for me to come closer. Everything invited me to move forward: the air swirling around me, the rustling of leaves coming from the trees, the smell of a sweet and luscious bouquet of flora. Just knowing the stranger was there was enough for me to continue walking. I didn't feel like a child in his presence.

I walked about halfway before the atmosphere changed. It went foggy and damp, but the air felt dry in my throat. A strong wind came up and raged against the limbs, tossing them around like a rampant storm approaching. The smell no longer sweet but bitter and hot, burning my nostrils with every breath.

I continued forward, but the solid ground no longer existed. It was like walking on a thin piece of flexible glass covering a void. Movement behind the glass stopped me in my tracks as I bent down to take a closer look. I jumped back as a hand reached up and struck the glass with such a force it wobbled beneath me. The force should have cracked the glass, but it didn't.

I looked up at the figure near the log. It stood up, barely touching the grass as it strolled toward me. In my heart and mind, I wanted to turn around and run back to the shack, but my foot went up, and then the next, moving me forward. I was moving without my consent, and it frightened me.

Wake up, wake up. I'm dreaming. This isn't real. Wake up.

A song came from behind me. Miss Mabel's voice rang out behind the thick-footed trees. Her melody grew louder, and I saw a white glow coming from behind the tree line.

"Raise me up, Lord. Raise me up into your light. I will cast out the devil from your holy place. Raise me up, Lord. Raise me up," she sang.

Another hand with long, red fingernails reached up and clawed at the glass. It was the same color my mother use to wear, fire red.

How can this be happening? Why am I not waking up?

The figure stared into my enlarged, frightened eyes, and continually moved toward me. The old voice in my head, the logical voice, was telling me to back up, turn around, and run. My body was not responding. A part of me, the part that believed the stranger in the clearing was the figure moving toward me, wanted to be near him. If I could just see his face clearly and know it was him, my imagination would stop playing tricks on me.

No, I'd just wake up. I closed my eyes and pinched the underside of my arm really hard.

I opened my eyes to see the dark figure gliding along the glass-like surface. I pinched several more times until a purple circle formed, but the figure's long, skeleton-like fingers with long, white fingernails extended out toward me.

I couldn't breathe. I tried to step backward, but something below grabbed my foot. I looked down, the glass was gone, and hands pulled me down, down into the black nothingness and burned like fire all over my body. I heard another sound behind me.

"Shh." I felt someone's hands on my face.

Confused, I flipped quickly on my back to look up. It was still dark, and the lantern no longer burned.

"Sorry," Hunter whispered.

"It was dream," I said. "Just a dream." I breathed in deeply through my mouth and then out through my nose.

Hunter pulled at the hair around my face, looping his finger around the loose strands and my head rested on his thigh.

"Yep. Just a dream," he said.

"What time is it?"

"I'm not sure." He laughed nervously, tossing fragments of my hair around his finger. "But it must be pretty late."

There in the darkness, I couldn't see his face, although I looked up at him. The nervous panic, the clumsiness I felt around him, stayed quiet and calm.

"Where did you go when you left earlier?" I stared up into the darkness that should have been his face.

He let out a heavy sigh. "Uh…well, I can't be giving away all my secret hiding places."

"What happened in the swamp today? Who were those guys?"

"The dark-haired one who spoke to you, we don't quite see eye to eye on things. We were once"—his fingers stopped moving as he took a long pause—"friends long ago, but he chose a different path. He's…"—Hunter swallowed hard—"not to be trusted. He's dangerous."

"I didn't feel in danger."

"He's not what he seems, Jess," he shot back at me, and then he lifted me up in his arms. "It's late. You should be in bed."

"I can walk, you know," I said. "I'm not a little girl."

He bent down to release me, but my hold around his neck tightened. Hunter chuckled and carried me into the room. A faint light shimmered in the far corner of the kitchen, lighting up his face, and I recklessly looked up at him.

"I know you're not a little girl," he said, letting out a soft puff of air.

The tingles started at my feet and worked their way up to my face. I felt the room spin around me. Nothing else existed in the room as he laid me down in my squeaky bed, and then he knelt down beside it.

"I'm sorry for being a bully earlier today. I didn't mean to." He paused for a moment. "But really, it is for the best." He changed back to his scolding tone.

Is he talking about me or the stranger? Either way, Hunter has his reasons, whether I agree with him or not.

Watching him reach over and touch my hand and feeling the fluttering inside, I could have easily given into his demands if I knew he felt something more for me.

"Well," he said, still touching my hand, "sleep well." He lingered a moment longer before he stood up and headed over to his bed.

"Good night," I said, but I didn't want him to go. *What if the dream comes back?*

I yawned loudly but not on purpose. Feeling the emotional heaviness of the day, my eyelids closed easily. *Will Hunter see me differently? Does he already?* I also wondered if the stranger was out there waiting for me.

Lovely Garden

I had been right about one thing: Hunter treated me differently. The little sister thing got worse, much worse. He rarely left the property, May no longer took me out into the swamp, I was no longer asked to get the mail, and it felt like every move I made was being carefully watched.

Thoughts of the stranger had begun to fade into distant memory. The good thing about all this was the work that kept us all busy and less time to think about him. Time felt unimportant except for when harvest time came. Then we worked hard to gather it all before it rotted on the vines, on the trees, or in the soil.

Miss Mabel's garden was tremendous and located in the middle of a large, open field behind the shack. It stretched from the banks of river, which curved behind the west side of shack, to the north, like a long, slithering snake, to timberline on the east side. All kinds of things grew in the garden: squash, carrots, cabbage, onions, potatoes, tomatoes, a few peach trees, apple trees, and more. If I were to guess, I would say the garden was about as big as two baseball fields back to back. Miss Mable had said because of the warm climate, food grew all year long, but I had other ideas about that—none that made logical sense, of course. What she said reminded me of what Hunter told me about the Cherokee. Their reasons for not wanting to relocate and leave this land: they had known the land would supply their basic needs of food and fresh water. I witnessed the fresh water stream overflow from the banks of the river every few days or so and water the tender plants. We had planted some seeds in raised beds and farther away from the river so they wouldn't drown, but for the most part, nature did its thing with little help from us.

The few people who knew of the shack would come out to buy food or barter for items we needed other than what we had grown.

One of our jobs was to collect the produce for the customers. Hunter, May, and I would run through the garden, picking it fresh off the vine or digging it out of the dirt to see who could get done first and then grab another list if there were any left.

The game, in the beginning, used to include Joseph, but as Hunter hovered over me more and more, Joseph stayed clear of us. He also pulled Josephine in the same direction. She looked sad sometimes, but Joseph had a way of making her feel guilty, and she would give in to his demands. An apologetic exchange had become a normal routine between the two of us; I apologized for being the cause and she for her brother's behavior toward me.

"Ready…set…"—May sprinted off—"Go."

I ran after her, followed by Hunter, who pulled my shirt back so he could run ahead of me. I twirled in a circle, laughing, before finding my balance again.

"Hey, cheater," I called to him.

He looked back and snickered. The awkward moments—the fast-beating heart, the fluttering—I hoped were a thing of the past, as I tried to convince my heart I loved him like a brother. At least I wanted to believe that to make things easier, even though it was untrue.

"What?" he asked innocently as he rounded the first corner and disappeared.

The garden was divided into four long rows and twenty sections. The row along the river was where the heaviest-drinking vegetables grew: celery, artichokes, tomatoes, and squash. The farthest row from the river, where the raised beds sat, was mostly herbs, garlic, and onions. Everything else grew in the middle.

I went to the opposite side of May, who went for the herbs first. It didn't matter what you collected first, just that you got your basket filled with the list of items and back to the shack before the others. I rounded out the corner to collect squash and carrots. May flew around the corner before I could made it to the next section, her basket almost full.

"How did you do that?" I asked her, confused as she reached down and pulled squash off the vine and then tossed it into her basket. She winked at me, and off she went like a flash of light. May would usually win. I guess it was all that energy she contained. It's too bad Miss Mabel couldn't put that in a bottle. She'd make millions.

I sat on the brown, damp grass and looked out at the small, slow-flowing river. I watched the water push a twig through the shallow rocks. The sun danced on top of the liquid, reflecting beads of twinkling light. My eyes shifted to the trees past the river. The light struggled to penetrate the canopy there. My thoughts wandered, for the first time in weeks, to the stranger.

Is he still out there somewhere? Has he thought about me at all?

"Everything okay?" a voice asked. When I looked up, all I saw was a dark shadow outline. My heart jumped and caused me to gasp. I shaded my eyes from the glare of the sun. It was just Hunter, and he looked worried.

"I'm fine, but May beat us."

"Doesn't she always?"

"Did you finish?" I asked, looking at his full basket.

"Yep." He offered his hand to pull me up. "Let's finish yours."

"No thanks," I said, but it didn't do any good to protest.

Really, I can do it alone. I've done everything on my own, and I don't need your help. I don't need anyone's help, I wanted to say but didn't.

"So…Jess." He scratched his head. "Do you play an instrument?"

It's an easy enough question. But why was he asking? Did he find out something about my past?

"I've taken many years of piano lessons," I answered after my long pause.

"Do you enjoy it?"

"Yes."

"What do you like about it?"

"I can go all over the world when I play."

At the mention of the piano, I could hear the music begin to play in my head. A whirlwind of emotions flooded inside. The last song I played had been for my father, along his arm with my fingertips. If I didn't stop the music inside, I would explode into tears and ruin everything. Would they kick me out if they knew my real past?

"Jess?" he asked.

Focus on another thought. The places the music has taken me. I've been to lots of places I've read about.

"I've imagined being all over Europe," I said, swallowing down the emotion and dabbing the corner of my eyes with my index finger without him seeing. "High tea with the Queen of England, dancing in the Trevi Fountain. I've explored the Australian Outback, wandering through the desolate prairies with a kangaroo as my trusty sidekick. I've even found myself in an enchanted forest, dancing to the faraway sound of the keys. It's my escape from the world and into one that is just as lovely as the music is." I spoke fast, and it chased my sorrow back into the vault of forgotten memories. I stared into the bright-blue sky and sighed. It worked.

Hunter was quiet. I replayed the words over in my head, and it sounded ridiculous. I looked down at my basket. "Sounds sort of silly saying it out loud," I said, feeling the shaky tone vibrate in my throat.

"I don't think it sounds silly at all. You have a great imagination," he said.

"I'm sure some of it comes from the books I've read too, so I won't take too much credit in the imagination part," I said, bending down to add another item to my basket.

"I hope to hear you play someday. Have you been to any of the places you've dreamed about?"

"Only through the voice of the authors, although some authors are better than others at describing what they see." I paused. "Those who can really bring you into the story, those who have a gift of pulling you out of reality and into theirs. But I do hope to see for myself someday," I answered. The answer reminded me I hadn't planned to stay here forever, there were other places I wanted to go and experience. Seth and the wrath he'd bring to the others if he found me here screamed out as a reminder of my selfishness. *But I don't want to leave.*

"It's not quite the same." He chuckled.

"So where have you been?"

"Oh, I've been to quite a few places," he answered without details and with a chuckle in his tone.

"Have you ever composed a song?" he asked.

"No," I answered

That had been something my mother pushed, but I rebelled simply to defy her. Even if I had wanted to, there hadn't been time between my homeschooled lessons, arguments with my mother and Seth, and the time I had wanted to spend with my father.

"I bet you miss playing." He sighed and kneeled down to add another vegetable in my basket. "It's too bad we don't have a piano here."

I hadn't thought that much about it. My old world and new world didn't have much in common, even the parts I liked. When I played, it was an escape out of my miserable life, away from my mother, away from Seth; and in the music, my father danced with me. There, I had been living in one of those compositions, one that took me to an enchanted world and my father could be there with me. I smiled, checking over my list. "Done."

"Let's head back to the house," Hunter said.

"So do you play an instrument?" I asked.

"The river cane flute."

I gave him a puzzled look.

"It's a lot like a flute. The first one was made by the Cherokee. River cane grows wild here and looks like a long bamboo stick."

"Is Cherokee Indian in your genealogy?"

"You could say that." He laughed. "I guess I talk about them a lot, don't I?"

"I…" Causally looking up into his face, and then I forgot what I was going to say. I could feel my face getting hot. *Oh my gosh. Just look down and head for the house! Just go!* my mind screamed. I didn't want to be his sister. I wanted him to see me as a woman, not a silly little girl, which was exactly how I was acting. "I guess we'd better get back," I said, covering for my lapse in memory and tearing my eyes from his handsome face.

Hunter and I entered the shack moments later with our baskets. Three ladies stood in front of us, two with welcoming grins on their faces, and the other looked me up and down with disapproval. She then looked at Hunter and batted her thick lashes at him.

May tugged at my shirt and mumbled something. I was too busy watching the young woman move closer to Hunter.

"Good morning, darling," she said lacing her arm around his. "It's been so long, why haven't you been out to see me?"

"That's right, you haven't met our newest family member." Miss Mabel came behind us with a serving tray of snacks and tea cups and then set them down on the kitchen table.

I felt warm inside that she called me family. Although this hadn't been the type of family I had dreamed of, one with a mother and a father, but it was the love and comfort I had so longed for.

Miss Mabel reached out for my hand and then pulled me to her side. "Jessica, this is Miss Caroline, Miss Betsy, and the skinny, tall, red head is Molly. She's about the same age as you."

"Really?" Molly looked down at my feet and moved up until her eyes met mine. "You look much younger."

"Oh, you're just a dear thing." Miss Caroline bounced forward toward me and pulled me into her round, soft body, her cheek against my chest.

I wiggled my hands free to return the hug and could only make it around to her waist. My mother would have been disgusted by her size, but for me and the way she hugged me, I could feel the heart of a loving and wonderful person.

If only Hunter would hug me close like this, I'd be able to tell how he feels. I saw Hunter watching us with an approving smile on his face. Molly noticed too and then whispered into his ear. Whatever she had said made her smile but had no effect on Hunter. *Could they be dating? She did call him darling.*

Miss Betsy stood behind Miss Caroline and cleared her throat.

"Oh yes." Miss Caroline released my body only to take my hands into hers. "Isn't she a pretty girl?

"You're embarrassing her," Miss Betsy whispered while tugging her back.

"I just love your straight hair. No matter how much I try or how gray I get, curls, curls, curls. It's just not natural for a—"

"Jessica, you'll have to forgive Miss Carol." Miss Betsy reached out to shake my hand and then bent down to my ear. "She's a little high strung for a sixty year old. I'm hoping when she hits seventy, she'll finely act her age."

"I heard that." Miss Caroline folded her arms against her chest, and yet she didn't look mad at her comment. "Don't forget, we are the same age, my dear and oldest friend."

"Yes, I am your oldest friend." She spun around, and her floppy straw hat covered in flowers flew back, and I caught it. Her black hair barely moved along her long, thin face as she turned back toward me and I handed her the hat. As she adjusted it back on her head she faced Miss Caroline again.

She sure doesn't move like a sixty-year old. Wow.

Miss Betsy paused with a puzzled look on her face, and then laughed. "What on earth was I saying?"

Everyone in the room laughed.

"Hello, Miss Caroline, Miss Betsy, " Hunter interjected in-between his laugher. He set his basket down, and walked away from Molly and hugged both of the women. "It's been awhile since last time I saw you both."

"Yes, I know, but we have some folks visiting tomorrow, some prospective parents, and we just wanted to make sure we make a good impression," Miss Caroline answered. "We know we will with Miss Mabel's special garden food." She smiled, looking at me. "Miss Mabel said you were an orphan."

"Yes ma'am." I said and looked down, feeling guilty for the lie.

"We hope to have four adoptions tomorrow," Miss Betsy added and clasped her hand together..

Molly stepped around to stand next to Hunter again. I tried to ignore it.

"Well that's just wonderful. Praise God," Miss Mabel added. "And I'm glad we can help. It's just about lunchtime, and you know that I won't let you leave until you've eaten and have some of my very fresh, just-baked peach pie."

"You don't have to ask me twice. I'm not afraid of more padding," Miss Caroline said, patting her stomach. "We'd love to after we get all these goodies into the car."

Miss Mabel nodded and grabbed a handful of crocheted blankets and followed the ladies out to the car. Hunter, Molly, May, and I followed behind, carrying out our boxes of produce.

Joseph and Josephine were already outside, loading other needed items into the car.

"You really have a lovely garden, Miss Mabel," I heard Miss Betsy say as they turned to go back inside the little shack.

"It's just another gift from God and I've been blessed to tend it," she answered and then winked in my direction.

It's something all right, but what I think falls more into the strange and unusual category—not God.

The Picnic

We all entered into the shack, and May went right for the kitchen and plopped her bottom on top of the table.

Molly leaned toward Hunter's ear. "I found the most beautiful spot to have a picnic. How about we take our lunch there?" she asked, with her eyes meeting mine.

Why would I care? I thought, turning my eyes in May's direction, wondering if she heard what Molly said.

"That sounds nice," he said loudly.

"What sounds nice?" May asked Hunter.

I couldn't help but chuckle when Molly winced.

"Molly found a nice picnic spot," Hunter repeated.

"I want to go this time!" May propelled herself off the table and jolted toward Hunter.

"Of course you can, and Jess is coming too," he said, looking directly at me while putting his arm around May's shoulders.

Molly's eyes narrowed. I wasn't scared of her, because I knew if it came down to it, I could take her, but there was something in her look that chilled me to the bone.

She's just staking her claim and making sure I know it.

Seth talked about how other women wanted him and were upset when he told them his heart belonged to another and I should be grateful he wanted me. However, it didn't stop him from sleeping with whomever he chose, and I more than encouraged it. Even with girls panting after him, I had no desire for Seth Worthington.

But I do care for… not that I have a right to. I'm the one stepping on boundaries.

"It's okay, I'm not much in the mood for a picnic." I faked a smile at Molly. "I'll keep Josephine company," I said, knowing

Joseph wouldn't allow her to go even if she wanted to. I turned to go back into the shack.

There you go, Molly.

After all, I didn't have any right to come between her and Hunter, if that's what he wanted. I was nothing more than a sister, and it didn't matter how I acted or what I said. Things stayed the same between us.

"Nope. You're not getting out of it ," he said.

"No, really. I've—" I tried to say, but he darted in front of me, not allowing me to leave.

His eyes pleaded with me. "I'll drag you," he teased, looking deeper into my eyes.

My knees wobbled while the burning sensation traveled up my legs.

He only wants me to come so he can keep watch over me, nothing more. "Fine," I spat. "How far are we going?" I turned my back on him and looked over at Molly.

"Not far," she said flatly, looking directly at Hunter, not at me. She was clearly irritated.

May and I gathered some food from Miss Mabel and placed it in a basket. We then headed out into the swamp. Molly hooked her arm around Hunter's as she led the way. May and I trailed behind.

"I don't think she likes me much," I said to May.

"Oh, she's just wants Hunter to herself. She doesn't want me here either. They've gone on lots of picnic and never once have I been allowed to come." She smiled. "So I'm glad Hunter made you come, so I could come too." She laced her arm into mine, like Molly had to Hunter.

We both laughed hard.

Hunter noticed how far back we were and made Molly stop until we caught up. "What are you two laughing about?" He smiled, grabbing my free hand.

I liked it, the touch of his strong hand surrounding mine, but pretended I didn't and tried to pull it away. He enjoyed the challenge and held it tighter. I shot him a look that apparently amused him, and he laughed.

"Just girl stuff." May giggled, watching him play tug-of-war with me.

Molly didn't like it and changed the topic back to her. "Remember the last picnic?"

She babbled on about the many adventures she and Hunter have had. Mostly, she had the damsel-in-distress thing down to an art form. In every story, she was in some sort of peril and Hunter came in to save her.

At first, I thought, *How pathetic,* but then I wondered if it really worked.

We got to the spot, a patch of green, long-bladed grass next to a free-flowing stream. The blue swamp irises towered over the water, reflected down on it and followed along the edges of the calm water. White water lilies spread out over the water and stayed pushed to the sides of riverbank. A large oak tree sat at the edge of the stream, shading both the water and the patch of grass. The perfume of the flowers saturated the air.

"Here we are," Molly sang, proud of herself.

May and I spread out the large blanket we had brought, and Molly flipped out the small one she had, one big enough for two. Hunter plopped down on our blanket, right in the middle. May jumped on him immediately.

"Get off." She giggled, beating her little fist against his chest.

Molly cleared her throat loudly. "There's plenty of room over here," Hunter said, noticing she was sitting alone.

"I'm fine," she said, clearing her throat with a low grunt.

"I'll come and sit with you." May jumped up, leaving Hunter and me alone.

We ate lunch under the old oak tree and listened to May talk about anything and everything that came to her mind. Molly put her hand on her head, so similar to my mother when she faked a migraine. I felt a surge of anger toward Molly and then pushed it back to the vault, where I kept my darkest secrets. I tried to close the door, on the thoughts of pushing her head under the water, but it wouldn't budge.

I focused on the sounds coming from the stream. The flow of water created a smooth, steady sound with an occasional *plop* sound, which was either something jumping in the water or the water hitting a rock in a new way. I lay back, cupping my hands to hold my head and looked up into the blue sky through the tree branches. I examined each of the tiny, shimmering strands of spider webs stretching from branch to branch in a circle pattern. *How do they know?* I wondered with amazement at the details.

Hunter turned his head and was watching me. I didn't acknowledge it, but my heart, on the other hand, thumped loudly in my ears. I hoped he couldn't hear it.

"What are you thinking about?" he asked, shifting his head closer to mine and turning to looking up at the same sky.

May continued to speak to Molly, and Molly pretended not to hear. My thoughts of drowning Molly were probably not good for conversation, and I couldn't very well tell him my other thought, of my heart jumping right out of my chest. So I went with a third thought.

"The sounds of the stream cascading down, flowing through the rocks and around the vegetation, the different sounds of the birds chirping high in the canopy, the wind softly blowing through the trees, the clicking and scraping of the branches; it's all like a mini orchestra," I answered.

"So should we applaud?" he asked, trying to be funny.

"Maybe we should," I said in the same tone.

Hunter continued to ask me questions. Some I answered. Some I changed the subject.

I looked over at Molly and May. Molly fumed, and both her hands were rubbing her head. I almost felt sorry for her since

May had been doing a lot of talking, possibly the most I'd ever heard from her.

"It's getting late," Molly called.

"Yes, I think you're right, Molly." Hunter sighed.

He stood up and offered his hand to me. I took it, and he pulled me up to him, so close I thought he would surely hear my quickened breath. I cautiously looked up at him. The sunlight bounced off his blue eyes and twinkled like when the sun hits the top the ocean waves. I gasped at their beauty.

"Hunter. Hunter," Molly said in a painful cry.

He turned slowly from me, still holding my hands.

"Hunter," she cried out again.

"Go," I said in a whisper, feeling out of breath.

May came right to my side and helped me pack up our stuff.

Molly was pretending to have twisted her ankle and asked Hunter to carry her back. He picked her up while Molly wrapped her arms tightly around his neck and then buried her head against his chest. Her slim, smiling face glared at me. I couldn't watch.

"May, I bet I can beat you back to the shack," I called. May would never pass up a good challenge, and I was counting on that.

"See you back at the house," May called to both Hunter and Molly as she took off and I followed suit.

We found Miss Betsy, Miss Caroline, and Miss Mabel sitting out on the porch.

"There you are," Miss Betsy called out. "Where are Molly and Hunter?"

"We're here." I heard Hunter's voice behind us.

I quickly turned around to see him standing there with Molly in his hands. "Wow. I'm impressed," I said, bending over, huffing in air.

"You're easily impressed," he said back, not breathing nearly as hard as I was.

I blushed at his comment. *Now why did I say that?*

"Molly, now what happened?" Miss Caroline asked, putting her arm out as Hunter put her down on her feet.

"Oh. I just twisted my ankle. It's nothing. See. I can walk now," she said. "Thank you, Hunter," she said as she hugged him tightly and planted a light kiss that lingered on his cheek.

"Any time," he said, opening the car door for her to get in. "See you in a few days."

"I can't wait," Molly said before he closed the door.

I didn't wait for the car to vanish before I went inside. I picked up the book I was reading and sat out on the back porch step. Scraps curled up next to me and I petted him with my free hand.

I didn't want to think about how Molly kissed Hunter's cheek or the way he said, "Any time." I didn't want to feel anything for him. It had been a lovely day, and the picnic was nice. I'm not sure that Molly would have said the same. Everything in me wanted to push out these feelings.

There are no fairy tales, no princes, no love that lasts forever. I need to get my head together and start planning my future, make the plans to leave here and not come back. But if a prince does exist, could it be Hunter? Is he mine to have? No. Fairy tales do not exist.

Prince Charming Syndrome

"Everyone up," Hunter called from the back door.

I peeked out from my blankets, but no one jumped up at this request.

"We have orders to fill." His eyes caught mine for a moment, and then he looked down. "Ten minutes," he called out and then left the room.

Did I do something wrong?

May whined, pulling off the covers, and then stretched while she sat up on the edge of the bed. Miss Mabel wanted to plant a new vegetable. Someone had traded a bag of fresh produce for two big bags of corn kernels.

A picture came to my mind from *Little House on the Prairie*. I had read all the books and remembered the stories Laura told about Pa tilling the field for the wheat. I could picture the dusty field, the wind whipping it all around as he led the oxen forward, pulling the sharp, metal blade along the ground that dug deep beneath the surface. I could see the dirty sweat dripping down Pa's face. It made me laugh. Nothing seemed to thrill me more than being covered in dirt at the end of the day.

Well, that wasn't entirely true. Feeling Hunter's hand wrapped around mine yesterday had given me another sort of thrill, one I didn't want to feel.

Everyone else followed May's lead, and soon, we were all dressed, fed, and bagging up the food we collected—all of us except Hunter.

"Where's Hunter at?" May asked Miss Mabel.

"He's doing something else today," she answered. "You just worry about getting your own work done."

"Yes, Miss Mabel," she answered and then shrugged her shoulders at me.

It was like May knew what I was thinking. Or maybe it was because I kept looking at the back door, waiting for him to enter so I could ask him why he looked away from me. It wasn't like I got in the way of him and his precious Molly. He was the one begging me to go.

We worked all morning doing various chores along with pickling some of the vegetables that were over ripe. Josephine baked pies while Joseph sat off in a corner by himself, slicing up the different kinds of fruit for her to use. Miss Mabel was in and out of the shack, washing clothes and the bed linens.

"Jessie," Miss Mabel called from outside.

I packed up the last bag for an order and folded the top down so the flying bugs couldn't get to it. I walked through the screen door to see Miss Mabel standing at the front edge of the garden. She motioned for me to come to her. Hunter came walking down the center aisle of the garden, covered in dirt, and stood in front of Miss Mabel. He bent down to dust off his jeans, and dirt flew everywhere.

I walked briskly over to them.

"You and Hunter are going to plant the corn," Miss Mabel said as she patted me on the back and started walking toward the house. "I've got so much to do today. Help me, Lord," she prayed out loud, her words fading into silence as she disappeared into the house.

Hunter and I stood there, silent, for a moment. His eyes seemed to be everywhere except on me. He took out his water bottle and drank the last bit of water he had, letting the water dribble off his chin. He then wiped his chin and grabbed the two sacks of corn, tossing both over his shoulder with one hand like they were pillows. I stared at him for a moment. I didn't know how much they weighed, but they weren't pillows. He chuckled as if he knew what I was thinking.

"Come on. It's this way," he said dryly. "Let's get to work."

We walked through the garden on the largest path going down the middle. The aroma of apples, peaches, tomatoes, and all the other produce played with my nose. My stomach rumbled.

"Here." He tossed me the apple.

I took a bite, chewing slowly to soften the loud crunching sounds in the silence between us. He looked straight ahead like I wasn't even there.

Maybe I did do something. Molly was not happy with me. This is getting way too complicated. I thought about her little trick. *Maybe I should fake a sprained ankle.* I shook my head. *But if I did, I'd be no better than her. Stay focused on the next plan, the one to leave here.*

My thoughts were beginning to get on my nerves. I knew the plan; I also felt obligated to help these people who had been so kind to me. Once I thought it was safe, I would get job, a place to live, and then travel. I would go to college maybe, but I didn't have to decide on that yet. I'd have to have money, and that would take some time.

I don't want to leave. My passive voice spoke softly. *It's not safe to leave just yet. Seth and my mother could still be looking for me.*

"You okay, Jess?" Hunter asked.

"Oh yeah…just fine," I answered, lying.

I wasn't any good at hiding how I felt. My mother had been able to read me like an open book. Thankfully, Seth wasn't as good, and I was able to trick him all the time. I had the feeling Hunter could see right through me, only he didn't press me hard when the topic got uncomfortable. He'd just let it alone. Could he see the fear on my face? I was scared of Seth, more as each day passed. I knew the more he looked for me and couldn't find me, the angrier and the more unpredictable he would become. I swallowed the dark, deep secret inside.

He hasn't found me yet.

"What's your favorite color?" Hunter asked out of nowhere, breaking the silence.

I gathered my thoughts back to the present. *Favorite color?* He nudged me at my long pause.

"I don't know. Blue, I guess."

"Why?"

Why does anyone have a favorite color? I didn't know, but I needed to give him an answer. *Blue…blue…how does it make me feel?* "There's a saying that the sky's the limit, meaning there is no limit, and the sky is blue." *Wow, and I came up with that in less than a minute.*

"Huh. Wouldn't have guessed that one." He laughed.

"Okay, okay. So what's yours then?" I snickered too.

"Hazel," he said immediately.

"And why?" I asked in the same manner.

He stopped and looked into my eyes and smiled.

I blushed, turning my eyes away. *Stop it. Don't read more into it.*

We continued down the center path to its end, and then he stopped and pointed.

"There it is," Hunter said.

The field was another twenty yards or so from the edge of the garden, and the stream snaked away from the square patch of land. It wasn't as big as the garden but was impressive all the same. It was already plowed, to my amazement.

Who could have done all that work? When, and without me seeing?

Hunter was only gone for a few hours. There was no way he could have done it alone. I put my hand up to shield my eyes from the bright sun and looked for any signs of workers and multiple tractors, but if they had been here, they hadn't left any evidences.

It was easier not to think about it and even easier to assume workers came and went.

"Wow," I exclaimed.

"Race you." Hunter leaped out in front of me, first running backward.

I couldn't help but laugh as I took off after him. He reminded me of May. The difference was I wasn't going to let him win, and since he was carrying the seeds, I would assuredly win. Of course, I was already wrong about that, as he was way out in front of me.

I didn't see the log. *Smack!*

A very small cry escaped my lips, and Hunter turned. He dropped the bags, darting toward me, and caught me flying through the air. Our arms wrapped around each other in a full-body hug, and we rolled in the soft, blond grass. Coming to a halt, he was on top, straddling my body. I wasn't hurt at all. Maybe later a purplish blotch would show up on my shins from where the log came into contact with. I was more surprised at how he caught me and how fast he was.

Hunter looked deep into my eyes, but I vowed not to get all swoopy. No silly little girl moment.

"Are you okay? Do you feel any pain?" he asked softly, looking me over.

I felt something, but it wasn't pain. I shook my head, swallowing hard, feeling my chest rise and fall as the air swooshed in and out.

Where is May when I need her?

He moved to my side, lying in the grass, his hand propped up his head toward me. He pulled back a strand of my hair and retrieved a piece of straw. I could only imagine what I looked like, since he also was covered in straw. I pulled straw out of his hair too.

"Well, at least we are both a mess," I teased, sitting up and tossing my hair around to get the grass out.

"That's okay by me," he said with a chuckle, "but if Miss Mabel finds we haven't planted the corn by dusk, we will also starve together."

I laughed, getting up to my feet first. I offered my hand to help him, and he took it. We walked over to the field side by side, my hand in his. Something did change; the damsel-in-distress thing had worked like a charm. Molly had it right all along. I liked the way it felt to be rescued and the concern on his face for me. With my hand securely in his, two separate parts felt like one.

Dangerously, I was starting to buy into the Prince Charming syndrome.

And Then He Was Gone

It had been two months since the incident in the clearing, and things were much the same with planting, packing, and pickling.

Hunter continued to probe me for more information and kept me engaged in conversations about me from my favorite flowers to the best book I had read, and he listened intently. I had never talked so much in my entire life, and I loved being listened to. But it got increasingly harder to leave out the parts of my life I was hiding.

"Jessie," Hunter whispered in my ear.

I gasped and sat up in bed. "What time is it?" I flipped over on my side, pulling the covers over my eyes. "It's still dark."

"Sorry. Didn't mean to startle you, but I want to show you something," he continued to whisper. "I'll meet you outside." He stood up straight and then walked out the back door.

I pushed off the covers and quickly changed into a t-shirt and jeans before meeting him just outside the back door. When I came out, he was sitting next to Scraps, scratching him behind the ear. Hunter looked up at me and reached his hand out for mine and then lightly took it into his. Lightning shot through my hand and traveled throughout my body as he stood up, gazing at my flushed face.

A girl moment—and I let myself enjoy it.

We walked through the garden with no conversation. I took in a deep breath of the dew and let it fill my nose. I loved the smell of a fresh, clean, new day. The sun leisurely rose with just a hint of light, tossing red and orange colors into the thin, wispy clouds lingering above. The ground held on to the dark shadows not revealed by light as I hung on to Hunter's arm for support over the unseen ground.

He led me to the edge of the established garden, looking out toward the corn. I hadn't been out there since we planted the corn weeks before. The cornstalks were taller than Hunter, and he was about six feet tall.

How can that be? It couldn't have grown that fast.

I stood there, not sure what to say. Here was more proof I had somehow slipped into a world that didn't exist in reality. How much longer could I go on pretending and making excuses for what I saw? I was beginning to think God did exist and this was His garden. *How much longer would I deny His existence?* The thought scared me because then I would have to accept He allowed me to suffer—and allowed my father to suffer. I tightened my grip on Hunter's arm. *No, I don't believe it.*

We stood there as the sun broke through the thick trees, the streams of light filtering through. Each stream glistened down on the field, catching each leaf and reflecting the light. The sky was a light blue, only with hints of red and orange fading into nothing, as had the clouds. The air was calm and unusually quiet. It was like an oil painting coming to life. I loosened my grip on his arm as the fear left me.

Master Architect ran through my mind. *More like Master Painter.* I shook my head. *Either I believe it or not, make a choice.*

"The corn will be ready in about ten to fifteen days, and then we'll harvest" Hunter said, looking out over the fruits of our labor.

"It's the most beautiful thing I have ever seen." For the first time in my life, I felt proud of something I helped do.

"Well, I wouldn't say the most beautiful," he commented and turned me to face him.

A light red glow appeared on his cheeks. *Is he blushing?* I felt a burning sensation ascended into my chest. *Beautiful? Is he saying I'm beautiful? No. My mother is the beautiful one.*

Men just looked in her direction and followed. Even Seth worshiped my mother. I paled in comparison to her, and she never let me forget it.

I couldn't breathe from the way he looked at me. My heart moved fast. My hands and feet quivered. Hunter pulled out a small box from his shirt pocket. It was wrapped in shiny, pastel green paper. On top of the wrapping was a rose carved out of wood. I had seen him working on something a few days before and had watched the long shavings fall to the ground.

"I wanted to give you this before I left. Happy birthday!" He smiled.

Birthday? How does he know my birth date?

"How did you—?" I glanced around. *Have I been found? If either Mother or Seth were here, I would know it.*

"Open it." He placed the box in my hand, his hand lingering on mine.

I looked at the rose first.

"That's really not the present." He laughed. "Just something I whittled."

Just that little rose would have been the perfect gift, something he had made with his own two hands for me.

The box was perfectly wrapped, so I carefully peeled back the paper without ripping it. *Did he just say, "Before I leave"? Where is he going, and why does he sound like he's not coming back?* It was silly to think he would never leave the house again, but he had never been gone for more than a day. *Why couldn't he give me this when he got back?* I stared at the box and fiddled with it in my shaky hands.

Hunter touched my chin and raised my face to meet his. "You'll have plenty of things to do to keep you busy without me pestering you." He moved his eyes from me, and his body stiffened. "Just make sure you don't get lost in the swamp." His jaw tightened.

I didn't say anything, holding the unwrapped present in my hands. I couldn't imagine even one day without him, seeing his smile or hearing him laugh. He was someone whom I had longed for my whole life, and if friendship was all there was, I wanted it. My emotions were trying to betray me. I felt an ocean of tears swelling up behind my eyes. I needed my mind to override them, to tell me once again how I didn't belong here, and Hunter wasn't mine to have, but it just stayed silent.

I tore my fingers into the rest of the paper, ripping it to shreds. A black, hinged box was underneath. I opened the box to find a golden locket. "It's beautiful," I whispered, looking down into the box. Tears streamed down my face. I fought back the sentiment of tears while I gazed at the locket and screamed in my head to get a grip.

The locket was heart shaped with a cross in the middle. The outline of the heart was surrounded by vines with thorns around it. It looked very old and worn. "Is this a family heirloom?" I asked and rubbed my nose.

"Passed down from generation to generation," he said as I pulled the locket out of the box, "made by my great grandfather for his daughter."

"I can't take this," I said, wiping the tears from my cheeks.

"He gave it to her when he went off to war, to keep her safe. Open it."

I opened the locket, and there was a tiny inscription written inside.

Hunter spoke, not looking at the locket. He knew it by heart. "'Our Father who art in heaven, Hallowed be thy name. Thy kingdom come, thy will be done in earth, as it is in heaven. Give us this day our daily bread. And forgive us our debts, as we forgive our debtors. And lead us not into temptation, but deliver us from evil: For thine is the kingdom, and the power, and the glory, forever. Amen.'"

Hunter lifted my head up to meet his eyes. "It's the Lord's Prayer." He took the locket out of my hands and placed it around my neck. "It will keep you safe," he continued.

"Are you going to war?"

Hunter chuckled. "I have another gift, only this one is from Miss Mabel. I did, however, bookmark a few things for you to read."

He pulled a book out of his pocket and placed it in my hands.

"The Holy Bible," I said, forming a half smile in the corner of my mouth. Miss Mabel knew me too well, having Hunter give me this. However, I felt sadness, dwelling on his words about leaving and giving me a locket that meant a lot to him.

"Thank you." I paused. "When are you leaving?" I asked, holding down the emotions in my throat while I slid the locket along the chain.

He pulled me into a long hug. It reminded me of the day he had caught me in the air and we tumbled down onto the grass. It seemed so long ago.

"I'm sorry. I didn't mean to worry you. It really isn't anything you should be worried about," he said, but his tight grip said otherwise. "We'd better head back to the house. I bet I'm already in trouble for keeping you out here to myself."

I could have stayed there forever in his arms. Maybe he wished for the same, but then he moved his hands to my arms and rubbed them before taking my hand and leading me to the house.

He sighed when we reached the back door. "Ready for your next surprise?" He smiled and then gestured for me to enter first.

As soon as I opened the door, I heard, "Surprise!" May, Josephine, and Miss Mabel shouted and started to sing "Happy Birthday."

But how did they find out? What else do they know about me? The fear of someone unexpected in the room came back, and I scanned the room from top to bottom to find no such person. I only saw a small, white cake covered with candy roses, a handful of gifts, and happy faces beaming at me. This was far from the birthday my mother had planned—the birthday I never wanted to happen and a gift of a ring I would have been forced to accept. Even with my father gone, the only way out of it was to leave. Leave or be killed.

I could almost feel Seth's anger in the air surrounding me. *And mother's too. Please don't let him find me.*

A small cake, homemade gifts, and happy smiles all around were a perfect surprise.

"Don't just stand there, make a wish and blow out the candles, silly goose." May clapped excitedly.

What could I possibly wish for? Everything I need and want is right in this room. Why do I care if the place is haunted, magical, or whatever?

As I looked around at my unique family, my eyes stopped at Hunter, who lingered next to the back door. The light streamed in behind him. He looked angelic with the light filtering in, and his blue eyes sparkled. I felt the Bible in my hand and gripped it to my chest. I closed my eyes, made my wish, and blew out the candles. I looked back at Hunter, but he was gone.

A few days passed, and still no Hunter.

I helped Miss Mabel stock the pantry, and she asked me if I started the book she had given me.

"No, not yet."

"Why are you afraid to read it?"

"I'm not afraid to read it. I'm not afraid to read any book. It's just stories."

"I know of someone who was afraid"—she paused—"afraid of what God wanted him to do."

Miss Mabel was going to tell me another story. I loved her stories. Some had been about her life, but most had been about the stories in the Bible. I treated the Bible stories more or less as fictional stories, just as the one she was about to tell me.

"Now, Jonah was an ordinary man. God told him to go tell the people about Him. Jonah knew the people were doing terrible things, and he didn't think they would listen. So instead of going where God told him to go, he ran in the opposite direction. Do you know why Jonah tried to run away from God?" she asked.

"He didn't think it would do any good to talk to the people?"

"He didn't want to hear God's plan. He was scared to listen. He didn't have the faith to believe God would make a way for him. So God put him in the belly of a fish to think about it. We don't have to be scared of God. If we listen closely, we don't have to spend time in the darkness of the fish. Do you understand what I'm saying?"

"I'm not sure." I giggled, wondering if age was causing her mind to slip.

"There is someone else not of this world who lives in darkness. He wants our souls and is the king of liars. He feeds on our doubts and fears. He did with Jonah at first. Then Jonah began to pray and sing praises to the Lord, lifting away the fear. The fish spit out Jonah, and when he went to the town, the people turned away from sin and praised God." She stepped down from the stool and then sat down on top of it. "Nothing much has changed in the world since time began. People only do what they want to do, what feels good, and not what they are supposed to do. They would rather believe in themselves, their control, than have faith in a creator. I think it takes more faith to believe we were fish, sprouted feet and walked onto the land." She chuckled and shook her head. "You've got to have some sort of faith to believe you're here, don't you? Some of the things that go on here can't seem normal to you, and yet you continue to stay with us."

I stopped shelving the cans and stared into her milk-chocolate eyes. Her acknowledging the swamp was unusual, and I waited for her to continue. Her eyebrows went up as her serious expression wiped off her face.

"What were we just talking about?" she asked, wiping the beads of sweat on her forehead.

"I think you were trying to get me to read my book." I grinned at her.

"That's all I'm trying to say. Whew! It's hot."

We both laughed. At least I knew I wasn't crazy, and she was right about one thing—I had faith I was in a safe place no matter what else happened around me.

"I'll get you some lemonade."

More days had passed, and still no Hunter. The rest of us kept busy with weeding, replanting, and tilling the soil in the garden. May spent her free time chatting at me, but it didn't fill the void I felt inside.

"Time for lunch," May called.

Everyone ate while we sat on the front porch. Josephine left and came back with a checkerboard and spread it out on the wood floor. Joseph immediately sat on the opposite side of her and made the first move. May held her favorite doll and carried it over to the long swing next to me. Miss Mabel hummed as she started a new blanket, one of many she wanted to make before the coolness in the air came back. I looked over at the empty space where Hunter would have sat.

Off in the distance, the sound of a rumbling storm approached. The clouds were lined up in the distance, dark blue and filled with fluid. Lightning flashed along the clouds, like flipping on and off a light switch. The air smelled damp and clean. A nice rain would have been good for all the new little plants and for the seeds we had planted.

I ran my fingers over the cover of the black book I held in my hand. I couldn't help but be curious of its contents, and I wanted to prove to Miss Mabel that I wasn't afraid to read it.

The cover was soft except for the raised letters on the bottom right hand corner. "Jessica." I looked over at Miss Mabel.

I didn't know much about religion or God. My mother wouldn't hear of it, even when it came up in my history lessons. "Skip over it," I heard her tell my history tutor. She believed it was all a lie and only the weak-minded fools believed in it because they couldn't think for themselves. Not only was this the belief of my mother but also of those around her, including Seth and his father. They had believed everything happened by chance and not *created* by a superior being. The big bang theory had been one Seth tried to explain to me in detail, but I didn't care either way, and if there was a God, He didn't care too much about me. However, the idea that mankind started out in the sea and then sprouted legs seemed more fantastical. If it were true, why wouldn't it still be happening?

There was another point I didn't believe for one second. Miss Mabel and Hunter were not weak fools who didn't think for themselves. Actually, I believed the opposite. They were confident and stronger than anyone I knew. So why was I hesitating to open the book they both wanted me to read? And a read my father would have approved of.

I paused, staring at the cover. *It's just a* book, *and one my mother would despise me reading.*

An even better reason to read it.

Okay, Dad, stop pushing. I took a deep breath and opened the book. I felt the air swish around me. The storm moved closer.

My pulse quickened when I noticed the letter from Hunter:

> Jessie, I have bookmarked scriptures and passages to help guide you along. Although the Bible can be read from beginning to end, I feel certain parts will give you a better understanding.

Jess, I know you have felt all alone, and I know you have never felt someone truly love you, but there is one who loves you so much, beyond what you could even imagine.

One more thing before you begin reading. Pray for guidance and understanding. Think about this scripture from the book of Matthew, chapter seven, verses seven and eight:

"Ask, and it shall be given you; seek, and ye shall find; knock, and it shall be opened unto you: For every one that asketh receiveth; and he that seeketh findeth; and to him that knocketh it shall be opened."

With much love, Hunter

I lingered on the signoff as I twirled the locket in my fingers. I could have lingered longer and thought about what it could have meant, but I didn't dare to let myself. *He might not come back.*

I focused back on the letter. I had never prayed before, and I felt silly doing it. It didn't feel natural.

I closed my eyes. *Dear God, please help me to understand why they want me to read this book. Amen.*

My first assignment was the book of Romans, chapter one verse one, and I read for hours, only taking a break for a quick stretch and a run to the outhouse.

I read the last paragraph out loud.

> "Now to him that is of power to establish you according to my gospel, and the preaching of God's Son, according to the revelation of the mystery, which was kept secret since the world began, but now is made manifest, and by the scriptures of the prophets, according to the commandment of the everlasting God, made known to all nations for the obedience of faith: To God only wise, be glory through God's Son forever. Amen."

As I finished reading, I heard a pleasing sigh, but no one was there. The rain was lightly falling, making little splashing plops as it hit the ground.

Questions about what I read filled me, but I understood most of what it said. It flowed just like any other book I had read. I stood up and stretched my stiff body while I walked into the shack. Everyone was sleeping except for Miss Mabel, who sat at the kitchen table. She pulled out two plates of food from the oven and set them down on the table.

"Come sit and eat some supper." She smiled. "Would you like to pray?"

I was panicked, and the locket felt heavy against my chest. I pulled it out and read the inscription.

She smiled and said, "Amen."

"Do you have any questions about what you read?" she asked.

I had one particular question burning over and over, and it seemed important.

"What is the mystery of God?"

"In Old Testament times, before God sent his only Son to earth, the only way people could be cleansed of their sins was to offer up sacrifices to God. I imagine it wasn't an easy thing to do. The Bible spoke of a Savior that would one day come and be the final sacrifice. By His death all sins, past, present, and future could be forgiven by believing in the name of God's Son and asking Him to dwell in our soul." The mystery is revealed when we ask the Son to dwell in us." She paused. "Did I answer your question?"

"God dwells inside us?"

"It's like a bottle floating in the ocean. The bottle is filled with the ocean water, and it's tossed among the waves. The Son is the water inside the bottle, and it never changes, although the outside, which is us, can be calm or turbulent. You keep reading. It will all make sense. Don't expect to understand all at once. His spirit starts out like a small light in the darkness of our soul, and as we grow in God, the light becomes brighter." She patted my hand as I took my last bite. "Well, you'd better skedaddle off to bed now. I'll clean up," she said, taking my plate.

I kissed her cheek and changed for bed.

The night seemed to go on forever with so many things dancing around inside my mind. The air felt hot and sticky, and I tasted the saltiness of my skin on my lips. I tossed off the sheets and headed for the washroom. I wrapped my hair up in a knot and then cupped my hands into the pitcher of water and brought it up to my face. The water felt good as I rinsed the sweat from my face and the back of my neck. I lifted my head, and I caught a glimpse of someone moving behind me, something dark and hooded. I quickly turned to look behind me. No one was there.

I climbed back into bed quickly, pulling the sheet over my head. I closed my eyes and tried not to think about what I had probably just imagined. I forced my thoughts on Hunter, trying to remember every detail of our last moment together. He hinted he thought I was beautiful, and in his note to me, he wrote, "With much love."

I missed him more than I cared to admit.

Well, Hello

It was like before, only I didn't remember falling into a dream. Lying on my side on the bed, I felt his hands pulling back my hair, soothing me, comforting me. I felt his nose touching the base of my neck and his hot breath cascading down my back. My pulse quickened. A thin layer of sheet separated our bodies with his legs pressed up against mine. His hand moved slowly from my hair and began to trace the contour of my side, down my shoulder to my waist, where he stopped. Shivers of excitement and guilt filled me all at the same time.

This isn't right. Push him away.

I should have pushed him away, but I didn't want to.

He kissed the back of my neck, and it seared my skin. In shock, I opened my eyes. Hunter stood in front of me. Radiant light surrounded him in the dark, and his eyes burned. His lips pulled together tightly, and his jaw grinded back and forth.

"What the—?" I sat up and looked behind me. No one was there, just a wadded-up white sheet. I looked back to where Hunter stood. No one was there either.

I lay back down, my heart pounding. *Just a dream.* But my mind wouldn't let it be, and I didn't want to go back to sleep. I saw May moving around in the early morning light. "Good morning, May," I said, which woke the rest.

Everyone looked over at me. " Sorry," I said and jumped up to grab the pails. "I'll fill the tub and make breakfast while you guys get dressed."

No one argued with me as I ran back and forth with the pails of water until the tub was half full. Miss Mabel had already put the large pans of water on the stove, and they were bubbling over by the time I finished. I then poured the hot water into the cold water.

Joseph ran into the washroom, almost knocking me down. "I hope you can cook," he said before closing the door.

I ignored his comment and went to work in the kitchen. Miss Mabel jumped in to help, but she let me do most of the work. I hummed as I worked and tasted the food as I went along. I surprised myself on how well it all turned out, and everyone cleaned their plates, even Joseph.

"It's not like French Toast is hard to make," he said as he washed his plate and set it on the counter.

"Don't listen to him. It is really good, Jessie, thank you," Josephine added.

"There's not much to be done today, Jessie," Miss Mabel said, looking at May, and then May shook her head. "Would you like to go exploring in the swamp today? I told May she can if you go with her."

I looked over at May, and she forced a smile.

Shouldn't she be happy to take me out after all these weeks? May loved combing all over the swamp and making new friends.

"But if you would rather read, or we could…" May said.

Miss Mabel cut her off mid-sentence with one look.

"No, I don't mind. My back is stiff from sitting too long yesterday and after breakfast, I think a nice long walk is a good idea," I said, looking at May.

I had other reasons for wanting to explore the swamp, reasons I dared not say out loud.

"See. I told ya," Miss Mabel said as she put her arm around May's shoulders and kissed her head.

May smiled, although I felt that she didn't really want to go, and that wasn't like her.

Miss Mable and Hunter had not been the only ones who wanted me to know who God was. May wanted me to believe; she said it would give me strength to fight against evil. So her suggesting I stay and continue to read made sense.

She is scared of the stranger. I watched her squirm away from Miss Mable. She sucked in her bottom lip and stomped toward the front door.

I fiddled with the chain around my neck and thought of Hunter. *Could he be out there?* And then I thought of the other—the stranger.

Move on with the plan. There is no reason for you to stay now. All these people want to do is change you anyway, a voice said.

I quickly twisted my waist to look behind me, where the voice had come from, but no one was there. I looked at May, who stared out the door.

"Did you hear something?" I asked her, hearing the beats of my heart thump against my eardrum.

May's face turned slightly as she put her hands in her pockets. "It will be a good day to be in the swamp," she answered.

I wasn't sure if she purposefully ignored my question or if she hadn't heard me.

"Get dressed, Jessie," Miss Mabel said. "I'll pack you two some sandwiches."

A little adventure sounded good. I didn't want to think about the plan. I couldn't leave. *If he did come back, how would he find me? No. I need to stay busy and not think about it.*

Wandering in the Okefenokee Swamp had been a different experience every time we went into it. If I hadn't been a logical person, I would say it changed every time we stepped past the surrounding trees and past the small stream. However, I couldn't tell which direction was north, south, east, or west, and most of the time, it was May guiding us back to the shack. Ending up in new parts of the vast swamp was quite possible.

We walked most of the morning along the stream. May showed me where a family of toads lived, and she introduced me as though they could understand. I just played along and said, "It's nice to meet you," and then we continued on with our journey.

"Did you know the name *Okefenokee* means *land of the trembling earth*?" May said, balancing her steps across a decaying tree.

"I did not know that," I said, following her lead and putting out my arms like airplane wings.

"The Cherokee gave it that name because of how the land constantly changed. I could walk by a huge, tall tree, and it would quiver as I passed." She jumped off the log and then pointed to an opening where the sun shined bright.

I laughed inside. *Now she's talking about the Cherokee. I should look for the book they read. It's got to be in the little shack, somewhere.*

"Wow. That's impressive information," I exclaimed, and then I heard her stomach cry out.

We both laughed and headed for the sunny patch of yellow flowers.

The sun hung high above us as we ate. The morning had been perfect with blue skies above. We ate the sandwiches and drank the lemonade Miss Mabel packed for us. With full stomachs, we both fell on our backs and looked up into the sky. There were light, fluffy clouds dancing in the sky. I thought about Hunter again, wishing he could be there with us. I thought about the last picnic we all went on. The day had been just as nice. May had been lying between Hunter and me…

"New game," May had said, stretching her arms up behind her head. "We all look up at the clouds and describe what shape we see. Whoever calls out the best shape wins."

May could make a game out of just about anything. Hunter and I played along until she got bored and left to see what the twins were up to.

Hunter and I had continued on without her.

"No way," I said, laughing.

"It's a dragon. Look." He moved into the space where May had been and brushed up against my side. "There is the pointed-arrow tail, his snout, and his wings." Hunter had traced the empty sky.

It had looked like a dragon after he pointed it out, but I hadn't given in to him.

"Well, I still think it looks like a ship." I took his hand and outlined my ship. "There is the anchor, the bow, the stern, and the sail."

His fingers closed in around mine, and then he brought them both down to rest on top of his chest.

"You win." He had sighed peacefully and looked over at me.

Luckily, May had interrupted us with a new game to play. Leave it to May to break up the awkward moments. I couldn't tell for sure if it had been on purpose or just May wanting all the attention on her. But with Hunter gone, she had me all to herself as we finished up lunch. She then stuffed the last orange wedge in her mouth and smiled.

I bet she misses him too.

May's focused changed to a bridge that crossed over a creek to a thick set of moss-covered trees. I packed up our trash and stood up. May continued to stare. I looked again, but there was nothing or no one there, and yet her body shivered.

"Come on," she said with a flat tone and snatched the handle on the basket. "Let's go across the bridge."

"I don't know. It looks pretty dark," I said, "Let's go in another direction."

But May headed to the bridge without a reply, and I followed. She crossed over the old wooden bridge. Wet moss covered the bottom, so she placed one foot carefully over the other. She looked back at me and then away before disappearing into the trees and vines.

"May," I called, following her steps.

I stepped past the bridge, but May was nowhere to be seen.

"May," I called louder, realizing I had been there before. The clearing, the one I knew well, the one we had stumbled on twice before and once in my dreams.

The sky began to darken as I stood there, frozen. The tops of the trees covered over the sky, blocking out the sun, the ground no longer yellow blades of grass but dull and shadowed. The presence of something or someone approached.

I felt uneasy. *This is not possible.*

A familiar voice came from behind me, and I turned to face him.

"Hello again," he said in a low, soft voice, while his dark brown eyes sparkled at me.

The uneasy feeling swept past me, and I felt strangely comforted.

"We haven't met…properly," he continued. "My name is Davior." He reached for my hand and brought it up to his face. He caressed his lips on the top of my hand and then lingered, sending shockwaves through my body.

"Davior? That's an interesting name," I said, feeling my voice tremble.

"It's pronounced *Davior*, like *Savior*. My mother was quite the religious woman." He then said, in almost a whisper, "Too bad the joke was on her."

"What do you mean?" I asked with the same tone.

He removed his lips from my hand. "I don't believe you've told me your name."

"Jessica." The feeling I had the first time we met resurfaced.

"So, Jessica, what brings you to Georgia?" he asked.

A weird but wonderful feeling came over me. I felt like I was in a thick fog and I couldn't see anything but the man in front of me, as if I had been looking for him and he for me. We were happy to finally be together. But there was something else in the fog, something I chose not to see. I began to tell him the story I told everyone else.

"No, no, no." He stopped me in a soft, gentle voice, shaking his head. His hands cradled my face to meet his eyes. They glistened a soft gold; I didn't see the brown anymore. I felt mesmerized, like a baby staring at bright and colorful object. I heard a growl coming from the edge of the trees, and Davior looked away, smiling. I felt dizzy, my legs unstable. He caught me before I fell to the ground and then carried me over to a dead log. The log looked familiar.

How am I going to answer him? I can't tell him the truth! I hung on to him for support and took shallow breaths.

"Better?" he asked, setting me down.

"Yes," I whispered, confused about what had happened.

"So," he continued, "you were about to tell me about yourself."

I had it in my mind to continue with the story I had started with. But my tongue betrayed me. His arm went around my shoulders. I thought of the dream for a second, the one with the hooded monster in it. *Is he the monster?*

"I would like to be your friend, Jessica, if you want me to be. I'm not here to judge you."

His voice was so familiar, smooth, and easy to believe, like someone else I knew.

"The world is full of people judging other people, those who think they are better than everyone else because they don't do this or that. The real truth is that no one is perfect. Everyone has their own ideas about what is right or wrong. So who is right? How can we judge anyone? Shouldn't we just embrace who we are and have the things we want without feeling guilty, without judgment?"

That sounded like a world in confusion. *I might not believe in God, but if there were no rules…* I thought about what my mother could do, what Seth could do, what they would have done to me. Davior frowned as if he'd read my mind and didn't like it.

"You want to know the answer, Jessica?" He looked up as he talked loudly. "Religion! Religion is what causes wars, hate, jealously, anger, and death. Religion is what people fight for and about. God is just myth, a fairy tale. You have to get what you can out of this life because that's all we have. Here and now." He paused and moved to my ear. "And to pay back those who have hurt us."

You know you want to tell him. I turned to look behind me, but no one was there.

Where is that voice coming from? It can't be mine, or can it? Oh, I'm losing my mind.

Davior stared into my eyes, and I started speaking. The words rambled out one after another, and I lost my ability to filter what I had been hiding all these months.

I started from the beginning, telling Davior about everything. From my father's death to my mother and her unrelenting need for power and about Seth. I couldn't stop until it was all out, and I felt terrible. *I don't know how, but he did something to me.* It was like having a stomach flu, knowing I needed to throw up and not wanting to, but no matter what, I couldn't hold it back.

"Even better than I thought," he whispered to himself, his hand tapping the side of his face. He sat there quiet, staring blankly forward, before addressing me again. "You did what you had to do. Any smart person would have done the same." He arched his back and then laughed. "I think I like this Seth person. Well, except for his obsession with you, of course," Davior said, turning toward me to look into my eyes again. "Tell me more about him."

I couldn't stop myself, so I told him about the conversation we had about the man in the paper who went missing and how he wasn't the only one.

"Oh, I do like this one." He stood up and clasped his hand together.

Is he being serious?

No longer charmed by him, I felt uncomfortable sitting next to him. The log started to feel warm beneath me, and I wanted to run. He took my hands and pulled me up quickly to stand in front of him. He smiled softly and touched my cheek with the back of his hand. It felt cool against my warm skin.

"You are an exceptionally attractive woman." He sighed, his eyes drawn to my lips. "Pity." He paused. "It looks as though our time is up, but I am delighted for our time together," he said, pointing to the edge of the meadow, where May stood next to the bridge.

He wrapped his arms around my waist and tugged me to his body, his lips at my ear. "Until next time," he whispered then kissed my cheek. He let go of his hold, turned, and walked in the opposite direction of the bridge.

I stared after him as he left. *Why don't I want him to go?* I wanted to be with him. I wanted him to hold me in his arms longer. But I felt scared too.

May didn't say anything on the way back. I felt guilty for not looking for her or even thinking about her while I sat there with him. *Where did she go? When did she notice I wasn't with her? How could I forget she was with me?* Tears swelled up in the corners of my eyes, and I felt nauseated. I was glad she was okay and just upset with me. *I'll make it up to her,* I thought as we walked back to the shack.

I hadn't talked much at dinner, and instead of sitting out on the porch with everyone, I heated up water and drew a bath. As I lay in the warm water, I thought about every word I had told Davior. Would he tell the others about me and that I was putting them in danger by staying?

"How could I tell him everything? I'm so stupid," I said and then sunk my head down under the water. I watched the air bubbles from my breath rise to the surface.

You better leave and leave now. I breathed in water as I gasped and sat up in the tub. I choked continuously until Jospehine knocked at the door.

"Are you all right in there?" she asked.

"I'm fine," I choked out. "I should remember not to inhale while under water." I tried my best to sound normal. What would I tell her anyway. "Oh, I'm just hearing voices in my head that aren't mine," I whispered to myself.

"Okay then," she said. "We're turning in, so make sure to put out the lantern when you're done."

"Sure, thanks, Joe." I answered.

Maybe the voice was mine, a voice of reason, and not my heart. But why would it sound more like someone telling me what to think than me just thinking it?

Or I'm just mental.

I finished my bath and crawled into bed. I stared out the window, wondering if I would see him again. The thought excited and terrified me at the same time.

To Dream or Not to Dream

The evening air felt the same as the night before, searing through the front open window and out the back screen door. Beads of sweat formed along my forehead and under the back of my hair. I wore the lightest nightgown I owned—a long, white, flowing, spaghetti strap cotton dress—but I was still hot. I looked around the room.

How is it everyone else can sleep in this heat?

A scratching noise came from the back door.

Scraps.

I got up and tossed some leftovers in a bowl we kept by the door. I opened the door, but he wasn't there. I turned to go back inside, setting the bowl on the counter, and then I heard a rustling sound coming from bushes outside.

"Scraps…Scraps…come here, boy."

I exited the back door and headed toward the bushes. I heard a whimper moving away from me. I climbed past the bushes and through the trees with my arms in front of me. Every step I took crackled under my bare feet, some branches stabbing my feet as I moved forward. To feel dry ground in the swamp or to hear a waterless branch snap was very unusual.

I looked up to see a crescent moon mid-sky, it's light pouring down and through the trees. A fuzzy orange ring surrounded the blurred moon.

A shadow moved ahead, but it wasn't Scraps.

His back faced me, and his head looked up into the expansive universe. He wore a black, hooded, leather jacket, and his long, black hair blew around his shoulders, unrestricted. I stopped in the spotlight of the moon as darkness fell around me. He turned leisurely, exposing his identity.

Davior.

His eyes caught the last of the moonlight and reflected it to me. His smile comforted me.

"You are astonishing," he said, not holding back his words as he stepped forward. "I can understand why Seth won't let you go." He continued forward, changing the subject as he looked above. "I love the night, the dark shadow of mystery, the best part of the day."

I then remembered why I was out there and unattended.

"Did you see a black dog go past you?" I asked, trying not to catch his eyes this time but still looking in his direction.

Davior raised his hand, and a dog appeared, coming through the brush, and sat next to his feet. "This one?" he asked.

The dog's hair appeared to be a deeper black and badly matted. His eyes contained a yellow secretion in the corners, and he revealed his teeth at me. He not only looked rabid but acted like he wanted to taste my blood. Davior moved close enough to hold my hand up to his face, and the dog stayed. He stroked my hand against his face, which sent the hair on my arms straight up, and I forgot about the dog.

"I'm sorry, but I couldn't wait to see you again," he confessed as he dismissed the dog and it scampered into the trees. "Please forgive me for the hour," he said and then kissed my hand.

"I wasn't sleeping," I said breathlessly.

"Of course you weren't. You were thinking about me," he said arrogantly.

I had, both scary thoughts and otherwise, but the scary thoughts were fading.

"Shall we?"

He held his arm out for me to take, which I did, and we walked through the moonlit trees.

"So was I right?" he pressed.

"Yes, but…" I hesitated.

"But?" he repeated with a hint of irritation.

"I'm a little afraid of you," I spat out quickly.

He laughed. "I'm not the one you should be afraid of." He grinned. "But that's not all of it. I feel like you are holding something back from me, Jessica, something you want to tell me."

I went silent. *What is he talking about? I told him everything. Everything but the light.* Somehow, I was able to leave that out.

He pulled me into his embrace and stared into my eyes. I suddenly felt another shiver run down my spine and out my feet. Davior's entire body felt cool against mine. My blood pulsed through my body, and I struggled to breathe. His lips were close to mine.

No, no, no, no. This isn't what I wanted. Not him.

My hand rose up against his chest, and I gently pushed.

Another low growl came out through the trees.

Davior's eyes burned amber as I pushed against him with more force. But his eyes weakened my effort. I couldn't escape his eyes. I was dizzy, and his hot breath on my face made it impossible to breath. His hands moved up my body to my face as he tilted my head up and exposed my neck. His lips moved to kiss the base of my throat. I swallowed hard, closing my eyes, not able to move.

Then, all at once, everything went black.

The next thing I knew, I sat up, gasping for air as though I had been under water. I was back in the shack in my bed.

How did I end up back here? Was it a dream? It couldn't have been.

I looked around the room, and no one was there. All the furniture was gone: pictures, my bag under the bed; everything had vanished. I ran to the back door. The garden was gone. There was nothing there. The ground was gone. I looked down at the nightgown I wore, and it had pieces of grass and leaves attached to it.

This isn't right. I tried to stay calm. I would wake up eventually. *Right?* However, it didn't stop the feeling, the very real feeling, I was there, and this was all real. I reached for the Bible under my pillow, but it was gone as well. I reached for the locket hanging off my neck and held it between my fingers.

Hunter said it would keep me safe.

I bravely went toward the front porch. I was not surprised to see Davior standing past the steps with three others.

"Seth?" I whispered in shock.

My knees felt weak. Seth didn't look up, but I knew it was him. He reminded me of the stranger I had seen standing next to Davior when I first saw him, the stranger whose face I couldn't see. Seth kept his head down, staring at the ground. His body moved anxiously, and he murmured something over and over.

"How? What?" I didn't know what to ask. I stared, confused.

"Don't worry, my love," Davior said calmly as he put his arm around Seth. "I have great plans for him and for you. But you need to come with me now."

"What are you talking about? What plans?" I shook my head, holding on to the screen door.

This isn't what I wanted. This isn't what I wanted.

My head spun, and I felt sick to my stomach.

He's dangerous.

I closed my eyes and thought about Hunter as I held the locket tightly in the palm of my hand. I remembered some of the words.

"Our Father, who is in heaven…"

"He doesn't care about you or for you… Not like I do. He doesn't even really know you, Jessica. In his eyes, you're just like a sister, a little sister and someone to take care of," he said in a mocking tone, "and nothing more."

He changed his tone again with a deep sigh, now sounding sincere. "I see you for who you really are, a beautiful, strong-willed woman, willing to go to any length to get what you want, and I can help you get it."

I couldn't remember any more of the words inscribed in my locket. *Don't open your eyes.* I thought about opening the locket, but it was too dark in the shack anyway. No chance on risking it.

"You don't even know if he'll return for you. I personally think he's left you for good," Davior continued his speech.

Another stronger, deeper growl came from somewhere behind Davior, and I opened my eyes to see. If it was his dog waiting for the command to attack me, I wanted to see it coming. I would fight as long as I could. Davior turned to face the sound.

I didn't know if Hunter was coming back. He hadn't said; however, I felt he didn't want to go. The words Davior said about Hunter seeing me as a sister rang in my mind.

He doesn't even know who you are, Davior's voice sounded in my head, and then out loud. "What if he knew you were here only to take advantage, telling your lies?" His tone changed as he spat out my own words like daggers to my heart. The things I told him, the things I couldn't help but tell him, were weapons against me.

"The reason he wants you to read this"—he held up my Bible in his hands—"is to change you, to make you more acceptable in his world, but, Jessica, don't be deceived. He is just as flawed, with indecent thoughts like everyone else. He's human with human envy." He said *human* in a loud, booming voice, twisting up his lips in an odd sort of way.

No, I thought. *No one here is trying to change me. They believe in something bigger than themselves, and they want me to feel it too, that's all.* I started thinking about the story of David in the lion's den. Although face to face with hungry lions, not one had eaten David. I pressed the locket against my chest with my hand over it.

Davior went from a prince to a lion and he was losing me fast, and he didn't like it. "Why would a God who loves his people allow horrible and detestable things to happen? Think about it, Jessica. Think about what your mother tried to do to you. Think about all the bad things she did. Remember what she did to your father, what she took from you. You can seek out revenge for your father without guilt. I'll help you do it, Jessica," Davior said.

I swallowed hard and fell to the ground. The smell of iron caught my senses and I guarded my eyes, which began to water.

The surroundings changed around me, like being caught up in a twister, and then it stopped, leaving me on the floor of my old room. The sound of the waves crashed in the background while the voices of two people arguing grew louder.

"Remember, Jessica," I heard Davior's voice as a whisper, floating through the air.

Confused, I followed the arguing down the dark hallway. The people in the picture frames hanging along the wall were moving. *That's not possible, I have to be dreaming,* I thought as they watched and whispered, pointed and giggled as I made my way down the long stretch of wooden floor. The floor creaked and moaned until I reached the end of the hall to the crack in the door, the door to my parents' room. I peeked in to see my father packing.

"When I'm done, I'm packing Jessie up and we are leaving. You don't love her. You've never loved her. This plan you have for her is completely insane, Evelyn. I will not allow it."

"And where will you go, Samuel?" My mother laughed.

"I know of a place, somewhere she'll be safe and you won't be able to get your hands on her," my father said, slamming the suitcase shut and pulling it off the bed.

"No. You are wrong about that," I heard my mother say in her smooth, calm voice. "Jessica will not be going anywhere."

A shadow passed the door, like before in my dreams. A lump formed in my throat, and I couldn't swallow.

Davior's voice filled the hall. "It wasn't a stranger, Jessica. Look and see for yourself."

I kept my eyes on the stranger, and he was right. "Seth's father?"

He came up behind my father with a knife in his hand, and jabbed it into his back.

I screamed, "Stop it! Stop it!" but no one heard me. I dropped to my knees, watching the blood spilling over the light, round rug and trickling toward me. The rug vanished into thin air, and I heard Davior's voice again.

"Do you see, Jessica?" Davior asked calmly. The hall faded, and I was on the porch of the shack on my knees. Davior moved closer to the steps. "Don't you want revenge?" He paused. "If you stay here, the only resolution you'll get is to just forgive them, let it go. Can you do that, Jessica? Can you just forgive them for what they did? Your father didn't deserve to suffer all those years, just lying there day after day with no purpose to his life." He paused. "And he did it all for you."

Davior is right. How can I just forgive them? I just stared at him, tears running down my face. *I always knew the truth, but what good did it do to remember? What can I do about it now? No. I just want to move forward. Can I do that now?*

"Come with me and you can be a part of something amazing by my side. You don't have to become something else; you can be who you are. Great authority has been given to me, Jessica. I can do things that will amaze you. We'll seek justice together," Davior said as his hand reached out toward me.

I didn't move, but my eyes moved to Seth, who continued to move anxiously, with his head down, staring at his shoes. I heard Hunter's voice echoing stronger and louder in the depth of my mind.

He lies.

"What about Seth? What are your plans for him?" I asked with hesitation.

"You know better than anyone, this was all your mother's doing. He was just a pawn like you. I'm sure we can come to some kind of arrangement that we can all agree to."

I stood up and took two steps backward into the house. It shook with tremendous jolts. It felt like an earthquake, and things fell down around me. The old wooden floorboards started coming up and flexed up and down, creating a thunderous, clamoring. Every other plank wiggled loose and flew out the door. Through the open spaces below, hands were reaching out for me. I looked up, and Seth was staring right at me. His eyes were swollen and blood red, and his fists were clenched. His breath came fast and furious, like a wild animal getting ready to attack. *I believe, I believe.* I closed my eyes and thought about the Lord's Prayer again. The words came easier to me the second time, and I said it over and over again, clutching the locket with both hands. I could feel the room spinning and the swish of hair against my face. Suddenly, everything stopped. My eyes flew open, and Miss Mabel's face smiled at me.

I hugged her tightly.

"Must have been some dream you were having." She pulled me tighter to her and let me stay there until I let go. She smiled and winked. "Breakfast is on the table. The rest of us will be out in the cornfield. It's time to harvest."

If it was a dream—and how could I not believe it was—had I really seen Seth's father try to kill my father? Did my mother plan it? Was my father going to take me away somewhere, away from her? I doubled over with my hands wrapped around my stomach. I wanted to throw up, but I swallowed it back down.

I forced myself out of bed. My nightgown covered in dirt, leaves, and grass.

Am I still in the dream? Oh please, no.

I got dressed and headed down to the cornfield and stood at the edge of the garden. It was an incredible sight. The stalks were taller than the house. I could hear everyone working out in the field, but I couldn't see anyone.

I heard Miss Mable and the two girls laughing. I heard another voice too. *Hunter is back.* I started to run, excited to see his face. I didn't care what my mind thought. Then I stopped.

He doesn't even know you. You are a liar, Davior's voice whispered into my mind over and over again.

I felt his presence, his spirit, near me, even though I couldn't see him. A gust blew over the cornfield and moved toward me. An eerie rustling sound swept over the ground. Light-yellow strands of grass tossed up in the air and encircled me.

I'm full of lies. Am I ready to tell everyone who I really am, how my mother was planning this life for me that I didn't want, how she treated my father—everything. There was something I had to do first. I had to stop lying to myself. Miss Mabel had been right all along; I was afraid of God, and it was time to stop being afraid.

The wind stopped, and the grass fell down around me. I took slow steps backward as I heard the voices in the cornfield getting louder.

You don't belong here. Davior's haunting whispers floated in the still air. My chest felt like someone had grabbed it and was twisting it tighter and tighter until I couldn't breathe. I couldn't stay there, not like that. I had to do something, and fast, before they saw me.

Run…run…run! Davior's voice screamed.

I ran. My first thoughts were not of revenge like Davior wanted. They were all about me and what I had done, the lies I told to those I should have trusted. I thought about the pages in that little black book, the one I felt so intimidated by, the pages that told me how to find peace. I wanted peace. I also needed to forgive and be forgiven. For so long, I carried the burden, and I couldn't do it alone anymore. I had known who could give me peace and forgiveness, but it was easier to deny it.

I'm done denying.

I ran in to the house, where I grabbed my Bible and went out the front door. I ran through the cypress trees and as far from the house as I could before collapsing on the hard ground. I was in a field surrounded by oak trees covered in dark green moss. The moss hung down to the ground, pulling the limbs with it. Above, a bright-blue, cloudless sky looked down on me.

Davior's voice filled my head with doubts, making my head hurt and my eyes burn. I let the thoughts of hate and revenge consume me and then let each one go. Every thought of forgiveness caused the voice to get angrier and louder. Tears flowed uncontrollably down my round face and on to the ground. I rose up to my knees, clenching my hands together, and looked up in the sky. I cried out to God to forgive me and for strength to forgive.

A swoosh of air swirled around me, lifting me off the ground. White and red flower petals blew all around, gently caressing my exposed skin. I could smell the sweet floral scent filling the air. All the pain I felt pulled out of me and into the swirling wind, along with the fragments of the forest. As the air retreated back into the sky, I landed gently on the ground.

Then the sky began to darken. *Davior is coming*. I didn't know how I would act or who was with him, but I had faith everything would be okay.

Out of the woods, Davior and three others glided toward me.

I stood there with my feet planted firmly on the ground with my hands to my hips. Davior laughed and smiled lovingly at me.

"I love that you are so stubborn," he said, motioning the three to stay as he moved closer to me. "Why don't you just make it easy on yourself, Jessica, and come with me now? Someone might get hurt if I have to do things the not-so-pleasant way."

I avoided direct eye contact. He found it amusing. "I'm not the only one who can control you. It makes no difference to me how we do this."

I clutched my Bible in my hands. He saw it and stopped moving toward me.

"I know you love books, so I have a new book for you, one that won't judge you." He spoke softly. "My love."

I scoffed at his word choice.

He tried to catch my eyes as he held the book out to me. I reached to take it, but he pulled it back to his side.

"First things first though. Toss that book over by the tree," Davior said, glaring at my Bible.

I thought about it, tapping the book against my thigh, but I didn't toss it. I held my ground and focused, this time letting his eyes meet mine. His eyes were similar to a thunderstorm, and they flashed and twirled, but they didn't have the same power as before.

I smirked at him. Davior was losing his composed and elegant temperament.

I remembered part of my assigned reading about Lucifer and his desire for souls. All that was good in the world would be gone. I saw it so clearly now. Whatever cult that Davior had joined now had Seth as a new recruit. I felt guilty.

How else would he have gotten involved if it hadn't been for me? But, Seth had fit right into it like a glove. For him to join them wouldn't have taken much convincing.

But there was something else about Davior, the way he looked, sad almost, that I defied him.

Is there a chance for him to change, for him to turn around and ask God for forgiveness?

"If it's the book you want, I'm sure I can get you one."

He chuckled, and I heard him whisper under his breath, "Never."

He waited for me to get rid of the book. It bothered him to be near it. So, I tossed the book to the tree. Davior's eyes softened, and he regained control of himself. He once again extended the book to me, only I didn't try to take it this time. Still looking in my eyes, I could see his frustration. Quickly, he reached out and grabbed my arm, hard. He was stronger than I, and it hurt when he crushed me to his body. He put his cool hands on both cheeks, our foreheads and noses touching as he continued to stare into my eyes. I felt slightly dizzy from the pain in my arm and my constricted chest. His lips moved inches from my lips, his sulfur breath on my face. I wiggled to free up one arm, but I was no match for him. He chuckled at my effort to push him away.

"So stubborn...you're mine," he whispered softly.

I closed my eyes, feeling helpless. I tightened my lips together and expected to feel his lips on mine. His arms pulled me closer to him. In a flash, his body was ripped from me, and my eyes opened.

Hunter lifted Davior into the air with a loud roar and then threw him across the field. Davior smacked against a tree and tumbled to the ground. Hunter, panting furiously, took off in a run toward Davior. The other three strangers with Davior started to run toward Hunter. Just as I thought Hunter needed help to fight them all, Davior screamed at them.

"No! Stay where you are. This is between us." He stood up, brushing off the grass and straightening his jacket. "Seth," Davior called loudly.

Seth walked out of the trees and stood next to Davior, his head down as he approached them.

"Hunter, have you met Jessica's fiancé?" Davior asked, putting his arm around him.

I didn't like the way Seth snapped his head up at the sound of Hunter's name. Seth pushed Davior's arm off him, looking even more dangerous than I had ever seen. He glared at Hunter with a half smirk on his lips.

The fast pulse in my throat moved into my head and pounded. "Do you not know me better than that, brother?" Hunter asked through his teeth.

Davior looked surprised.

Brother? Is that the connection? I thought. *Why he feels so familiar but so different?*

"Jessica has never accepted any proposal, so she is free of any claim he might think he has over her," Hunter said, staring back at Seth. "But as for your request that had nothing to do with your new convert, she has clearly made her decision."

"This isn't over, Hunter," Davior said and then motioned for the two other men to come to him as they prepared to fight.

Seth smiled, still not releasing his glare at Hunter.

Six tall, slender figures appeared all around the edges of the field. I could only see their silhouettes, no faces, since they were standing among the shadows.

Davior laughed, looking around. "So that's how it's going to be?" he sang. "I'll be watching and waiting." He pointed his finger at me.

"She'll be well protected, I assure you," Hunter replied.

"Like I said, this isn't over!" he whispered, showing his teeth and losing control. "Do you hear me? This isn't over," he screamed out to the silhouettes, who didn't move.

Another high-pitched sound came out of Davior's mouth.

Trail of Tears

I woke again from the twisted dreams—or not dreams. I wasn't sure. But I was sure someone's arm rested on my shoulder, and I heard a heartbeat in my ear. My cheek moved up and down with the rise and fall of someone's chest. But whose chest? Whoever it was held me tightly, and my knees were curled up close to my hips. Another arm looped under my calf. A warm cheek rested on top of my head.

I thought for a moment about my options. I could throw open my eyes and just face my situation. The last thing I remembered was Hunter attacking Davior, but who won? For all I knew, I still could be in the clearing. I needed a weapon before moving, something sharp, but nothing was near enough to grasp.

Just do it, already.

My hand went for the unknown arm with a gentle and precise touch at the wrist and moved it off my shoulder. I opened my eyes and realized I was on Miss Mabel's porch.

That's good, but it doesn't mean I'm in the clear yet.

My eyes scouted out for a weapon just in case. The metal chair next to the small table could inflict some pain and get me far enough away. Even in a dream, if that's what this was, I would not go down without a fight. The unknown person shifted just enough to loosen the hold under my knees and enough for me to slide my legs off the swing and firmly onto the ground.

One…two…three.

I pushed off the swing, my knees bent as the swing moved backward. My bottom lifted from the swing, and I went for the chair, my weapon. I felt pretty confident I'd make it, and then an arm wrapped around my waist and pulled me back. The swing moved forward and knocked both of us to the ground in one big *thud!* Keeping my focus, I crawled to the chair. I pulled myself up, and grasping it firmly at the top, I whirled it around, knocking the other person down the front porch stairs. I admired my skills and ran for the door.

Not so helpless after all.

"Jess…"

I stopped cold. The voice sent a wave of panic through me.

"Wow. She got you good." Joseph laughed, walking out the door, passing me, and down the steps.

I turned slowly, swallowing hard, and tears formed in my eyes.

"Would you like me to take her out for you?" Joseph sneered, offering his hand to help him up.

"I'm fine," Hunter said, taking his hand and getting to his feet. "It's my fault." He looked at me, apologizing.

Why should he apologize to me? I'm the one who should have made sure who I was swinging at. Once again, my well-thought-out plan missed a step and hurt someone I care about.

"Whatever," Joseph said. "Look. We got a lot of work to do. Where is the axe?"

The two exchanged conversation, but the voices were drowned out by my own thoughts. Hunter then approached me while Joseph headed out past the trees.

"Hi," he said, slapping the dirt off his shirt, avoiding eye contact with me.

"I'm so sorry. I thought maybe…then, when you grabbed me, I panicked…then…" A tear flowed down my cheek.

His face lifted up. "Hey." He raised up his hand to wipe off the tear. "I'm totally fine. Not a scratch."

He was right too. Nothing showed on him except for the brown dirt on his clothes.

"I tried to put you into your own bed, but you have quite a firm grip. I sat out here to wait until you woke up, but after a while, I fell asleep too."

My cheeks felt hot thinking about being in his arms and holding to his firm, muscular frame, listening to the sturdy, secure rhythm of his heart, breathing in the very breath he exhaled in an intoxicating aroma, all, of course, things I didn't remember but desperately wished I could.

Not fair.

"Time for breakfast," May hollered, pulling me out of my fantasy.

"It's morning? You mean another new day?" I asked, smelling ham and eggs filtering out through the screen door.

"You've been asleep for a while." He snickered, stretching his arms behind him, and then shuffled past me.

My stomach confirmed it by the pangs of hunger. "I guess so," I whispered to myself, but my mind was filled with questions and thoughts. *Does that mean this was all a dream? But if it was, when did Hunter get back from wherever he was? Is Davior Hunter's brother? My* stomach interrupted the echoes of questions as I followed Hunter through the door to the kitchen.

Hunter finished his breakfast and slipped out the back door. It wasn't until his fourth trip out I noticed he was carrying pails of water. "The tub is filled with fresh warm water. " He flashed his eyes at me for a moment and then quickly back down to the floor. His feet hesitated, rocking slightly like he was going to go back outside, like he still had something more to say to me.

"Thank you," I said, watching his feet shuffle a few steps.

A heavy sigh escaped his lips as he nodded his head in my direction before he hurried out the door.

I tried not to think about what happened or about Davior as I sat in the bath water. Instead I thought about the melody of the ivory keys. How I missed the sound of each stroke, the soft touch of each key pressing down to form a harmonious array of reverberation full of life. Music use to be my world, my world of escape, and for the first time in a long while, I needed that comfort.

My thoughts strayed to Davior, seeing him all alone in the dark meadow. He looked sad, and it bothered me. He looked so much like Hunter.

My torn feeling made perfect sense now. But it was Hunter I wanted, no matter how he saw me.

The water began to feel cool, a sign I had been in the water too long, and I still hadn't washed the leaves out of my hair. I dipped my head below the water and scrubbed out the grime. I sat up to see the water a rusty brown color, with bits of leaves and grass floating on top. I dressed and opened the door to an awaiting Joseph.

"Sorry. I—" I started to say.

"Save it," he said hastily, with a bucket in his hands. "I'm the lucky one who gets to empty the tub out twice."

"I can do it," I said to him, reaching out for the bucket, but he moved it before I could touch it.

"Don't worry about him," Hunter quickly spoke from the table, standing from his chair. "It's good for him. Besides, we have our own work to do."

"Are we working together today?" I asked.

"Everyone is, and we have lots to do before lunch." He paused and then reached out his hand toward me. "Ready?"

I wanted to ask him so many questions, but my lips didn't move. I stared at his hand, and a flash of Davior's hand crossed my mind. I flinched and looked at Hunter's face. For the first time, I saw a boy nervously fidgeting with his feet and hands. I waited too long to take it, and he moved his hand into his pocket. I bit down on the outside of my lip.

Why did I hesitate?

He looked away from me. "Okay. Well, everyone is out in the cornfield, so whenever you're ready," he said, and he turned and walked out the door.

Go after him, dork! I let out a nervous laugh. *Don't make more out of it. Why do the thoughts in my mind always contradict each other? I do believe Hunter was blushing…*

Walking down to the cornfield, May and Josephine jumped over to me with a bear hug, waking me from the zombie-like walk.

"We were told not to say anything at breakfast…but I knew you wouldn't give in to him. I knew it." May laughed and clapped her hands.

Well, that was one question answered.

"Miss Mabel and Hunter thought it was best to let you absorb what happened and not overwhelm you all at once," Josephine added.

"That was probably a good idea, although, until just now, I thought I might still be in a dream." I smiled.

"No, it wasn't a dream. None of it was." Josephine then whispered, "You'll tell me everything later?"

"Sure," I said as Miss Mabel approached us, Hunter tagging along behind her.

"Yes, we are all very happy that you are still with us, Jessie." She hugged me again.

"Not all of us," Joseph said from behind me and passed all of us.

Hunter glared at him but said nothing.

"Never mind that boy. He's got his own problems. Anyway, I knew you would make the right choice." She glanced over at Hunter, who avoided her look, and back at me. "Well, are you ready to harvest, or would you like to rest today? You've been through quite a lot," she said.

"No. I want to help," I said quickly, looking in the direction Joseph went. I'd make sure to go to the opposite side.

"Now don't go worrying about that boy. I think when you become a teenager, you just lose your mind. Aliens come down and take over your body or something." Miss Mabel stared after him too, watching him kicking up the dirt path as he walked. "He'll come around. Don't you worry." She smiled again.

Joseph turned around toward us, as everyone besides me had taken their eyes off him. His eyes glowed amber and I gasped. But it wasn't him I was seeing. I recalled something in the dream, or *not* dream—a flash of memory. And Seth was in it, My body trembled. There was another reason to be afraid—he knew where I was.

"I think she should rest. She looks a little flushed." Hunter's voice broke through my vision.

"No. I'm fine," I said quickly and moved closer to Miss Mabel.

Miss Mabel divided out the work. First, she told Josephine to find Joseph and then to start at the north side of the field, plucking the corn husks as high as they could reach. She gave her two wooden baskets to fill.

"By the time you have these filled, it will be close to lunchtime. You can bring them up to the house when they are full."

Josephine nodded and dashed off to find Joseph.

"May, you and I are going to start here in the middle and work outward. Hunter, you and Jessie can start at the south end. Some of those husks are really high over there, so you might have to put Jessie up on your shoulders to reach them." She handed us both a basket.

On his shoulders?

My father hoisted me up on his shoulders once. I remembered looking down, feeling petrified he would drop me. There had been nothing to grab onto if I started to wobble. I panicked. My father panicked too, as I clawed at his head and he couldn't see. We both fell to the ground. The funny thing was, I wasn't afraid of heights. Me climbing out onto a window ledge overlooking cliffs and sitting for hours dispelled that theory. But climbing out onto the ledge, I was in complete control over every step, and my hands knew where I could grab.

Hunter, not really noticing I was panicky, grabbed my hand not waiting for me to accept and dragged me toward the field. I should have been extremely happy, he was back. But my only thoughts were nervous thoughts about being hoisted up on his shoulders.

Hunter held a tight grip on my hand as we walked. Occasionally, he would look over at me, his mouth open like he was going to say something, and then turn his head to look forward. I would have given anything to know what he was thinking or what he wanted to say.

Finally at the field, we saw the corn husks high on the stalk along the southern end. I could see why Miss Mabel sent us there with her directions. I could easily reach the corn if I were on his shoulders, *or if I had a ladder.* I liked that idea better. Hunter stared at me, trying to read my expression.

"So which would you prefer? I can lift you up, or I can bend down," which he did, "and you can put your legs around my shoulders."

All that has happened, all that I've been through, and I'm scared of him dropping me. How silly. I was stalling while I paced in front of him.

He didn't budge but looked up at me with glittery eyes and a brilliant smile.

"Okay," I said, unsure, taking a deep breath. "Stay."

I placed one leg on his shoulder carefully and held the first hand he offered to help me balance and then the other. He held them tight as he stood up. I let out a deep breath, as if I had been holding it the entire time he was hoisting me up.

"Are you okay?" He laughed.

"Uh huh." I locked my legs behind his back. I was hunched over, tightly griping his hands.

"Ready to let go of my hands?" he asked.

Well, I knew the answer to that: *Duh. No.*

"You know I'll catch you if you fall."

I guess I needed him to tell me that. If he could catch me in the air, being yards from me, he could do that. I felt a little better about the whole thing.

"Okay," I said, closing my eyes.

I let one hand go and then the other. I balanced and sat up tall. I opened my eyes. I felt pretty secure, and my lingering worries faded. I could see over the tall stalks, along with the little stream and tall trees off in the distance. Hunter's hand rested on one of my knees. *He is not going to let me fall, and even if I do fall, it's not like falling out a window of a three-story house.* I braved to glance down and realized how ridiculous I was being.

Hunter bent down slowly and released one of his hands to grab the basket. He hoisted it up to me, and I grabbed the sharp sheers out of it and began to cut the husks off the stalks and dropped them into the basket.

"So I probably could guess that you have quite a few questions for me," he said with a smug tone.

Of course, I had lots of them, but most of them I wasn't going to ask while I was perched up on his shoulders. I wouldn't want to upset him; besides, I wanted to see his face and read his expressions. *Go for the simple yes-or-no questions.*

I dropped a husk into the basket. "Well…" I said, feeling a little more confident up there in my own world.

"Is Davior your brother?"

He hesitated. "Yes." He sighed.

Okay. One down. I had more questions about that, but again, I wanted the face-to-face conversation.

"Oh." I continued. "Where did you go?"

"I didn't go anywhere."

I felt him shake his head, which made me wobbly.

"Oops. Sorry." He laughed.

"That doesn't make sense." I paused. "If I wasn't dreaming…"

"I promise to explain that one later." He rubbed his hand against my knee.

"Okay," I said, feeling a little frustrated. "How did you know my real age?"

"Pastor James," he said.

I felt a lump in my stomach. *Why did I ask that? Should I ask him how much he knows? No more secrets, remember.* There was a time and place for that, and it wasn't now. *So what do we talk about?* The silence made me uncomfortable, and I wished May were there. I scrambled for something, anything to say. Then I remembered I wanted to hear more about the Native Americans. That was good, and not about either one of us—neutral territory.

"You never finished the story about the Cherokee." I dropped another husk in the basket.

"Good call."

I could hear relief in his tone.

"Let's see. Where did I did leave off?" he teased.

"The Trail of Tears," I answered quickly.

The story continued where he had left off, with the Cherokee being forced to relocate to territories in the west. The Cherokee Nation had divided. There had been half who wanted to stay and fight for their land, and the rest, who wanted the peaceful solution of relocating.

Hunter explained there had been many promises made to the Cherokee if they left peacefully. They would own land that no one could take from them and could have their own government without interference.

"Those were empty promises," he said with disgust and then described the land as barren and dry.

"Many died from not being able to survive on the land," Hunter said.

"So what happened to those who stayed and fought?" I asked.

"The president ordered they be rounded up and forced out."

"That's horrible."

"Many died in the battles, both the Cherokee and the soldiers. Those who survived were arrested and escorted to Oklahoma. Along the way, many more of us died."

"You mean your ancestors," I corrected and then snickered. "You couldn't have been there."

Hunter became quiet.

How could I laugh at such a tragedy? I knew he didn't mean "us" to mean himself. That would be unreasonable.

"Yes," he finally said, "I mean my ancestors. All of them died."

They couldn't have all died, or else he wouldn't be here, I thought but kept it to myself.

"On the Trail of Tears, four thousand to five thousand Cherokee lost their lives," he concluded.

He heard me sniffle and he rubbed my leg.

"It's a sad story." I tried to hide the sadness in my throat.

"There is another part of the story, one that is more folklore about what really happened on the Trail of Tears. Would you like to hear that as well?" he asked, as if he wasn't sure he should tell it.

"Is it happier?"

"Yes, it is. I'm pretty sure you'll like it." I dropped another corn husk in the basket.

"All right then, but I'm warning you, no tears," I said, no longer thinking about anything else but the Cherokee.

He chuckled and took a quick breath. "The story goes, God looked down and saw this great injustice, and He wept with them. His heart was burdened for those who fought so hard to keep their land. Seeing them chained and bound and hearing their cries to have mercy on them, He decided to save them. God put all the people under a deep sleep. The Cherokee were awakened by an angel, the great warrior. He told the people how God wept for them and heard their cries. He wanted to undo the injustice that had been done to them by giving them another option. The people decided, each for themselves, and the angel left. The next day, those who had chosen to follow God appeared to die on the trail. God had put them into a deep sleep until the soldiers had gone. It is said that God woke them and would give them a chance to fight against the evil of this world in a great battle that wouldn't take place for centuries."

"So God made them immortal?" I asked.

"Yes, but it wasn't like the fountain of youth. They would still age, only at a slower rate. God designed it that way so the people could live normal lives and blend in with the rest of the world. Making them immortal was not a punishment, but a reward, allowing them to experience all of God's wondrous creations, including marriage and families."

"But wouldn't people around them begin to notice they didn't age the same?"

"There is a lot you can do to make it look like you're aging, but you're right; at some point, they would have to disappear or stage their own death."

"You sure have thought about this folklore a lot to know that."

Hunter was once again silent.

I clipped off another corn and held it to my nose. I had expected the smell to be sweet, but it was earthier, like the smell of the soil.

"So they live among us?" I asked.

"Some, but God also built them a great fortress in the land they loved. A place kept secret and protected from even the worst evil. In the end, it would also be the place they would all gather, in the last days of man, to prepare for battle. Until then, some are scattered around the world. Some living normal lives, and some devoted to God alone."

Wow, that is some story.

I thought about the land they had loved and it was in the swamp. I thought about all the mysteries surrounding the shack and how it was hidden, almost like a secret place. I wondered for a second if the story could be true.

That's just crazy. It's just a story.

Hunter continued. "But there were some who would choose a different path—the path of Lucifer. They too would fight in the great war. They would fight against God. They would fight against their own tribe," Hunter concluded as I dropped another corn husk into the basket. Then the basket fell out of Hunter's hands.

"Well, that must mean we are done for the day. Two baskets, right?" Hunter asked.

"Yep," I answered. Still thinking about the story, I asked, "But why would they choose a different path when they just saw what God could do? And what is the great w—?"

Suddenly, without warning, Hunter lifted me off his shoulders and twisted me around to face him. He brought me down slowly, my hair falling around my face and showering down on his. My arms rested on his shoulders. He held his gaze to mine, and my toes touched the ground. He leaned in closer, stroking my hair back and then cradling my face. My heart was burning, my pulse racing.

"Hey, are you guys—? Oops." May blushed and ran back around toward the house.

Hunter quickly looked away, toward May. The expression on his face was both agitated and relieved.

We heard May call out from a distance, "Lunchtime. Better not be late." She giggled.

Hunter released his grip on me and grabbed the baskets and continued to answer my questions. "It's just like Adam and Eve. They were deceived by Lucifer. He convinced them that his power was stronger."

I had read that story as part of my reading assignment. Eve thought she could become godlike if she ate from the forbidden tree. Of course, she did it. It was about power, and she wasn't going down alone, which was why she then gave it to Adam.

I thought about how Davior tried to convince me to follow him.

"I guess I could see how wanting that kind of power could be temping," I said, and my thoughts went to my mother. "Although, I wouldn't have cared about the power."

"But Lucifer uses our desires, our downfalls, our sin and uses it for his benefit. For you, it wouldn't be power, but he could use other things." He spoke with tightness in his tone.

"What about the great war?"

"I think it's time you read Revelation, the last book in the Bible," he answered. "It's all in there."

We were at the back door.

I pulled him back before he entered the room and glared at him. "Later. You promised to tell me where you went."

"I Promise."

Interrupted

We worked only half the day collecting produce. Pastor James was coming out for a lunch visit to practice his upcoming sermon. Since Miss Mable never left the shack, from my observation, he would come out once a month or so. I would disappear into the garden with a book in hand on those days. I tried to be polite about it, but he looked for me, disappointed each time I hid. I think he just wanted to share his message about God with me, but I had not been receptive. I liked Pastor James the moment we met. He wasn't like the preachers I'd seen on the television, shouting about fire, hell, and damnation.

Pastor James and Hunter shared a special type of relationship. They acted more like brothers when they talked and played chess. They were actually quite amusing to watch, as each one accused the other of cheating. They were more entertaining than any television show. But I could tell it had been all in good fun as they laughed and teased each other. By the end of the game, Hunter would be the winner just about every time.

"I don't know how to play," I said as Hunter and I entered the house with our baskets of corn.

"I can teach you," he said, setting his basket on top of the kitchen table. Then he reached for mine.

"I think Pastor James looks forward to your game. Maybe next time."

We booth looked around the empty shack.

"Food's out here. Come on and eat," Miss Mabel called from the front porch.

Just above the little house, a patch of crystal-blue sky hung. The sun felt warm on my skin, but not blazing, and a slight breeze blew over the roses and perfumed the air with their sweet fragrance. May and the twins sat on the porch steps while Miss

Mabel sat in her rocker. Pastor James watched us from the small table with the chess pieces already ready for play. He smiled big at both of us.

I was almost sure Hunter would have kissed me if May hadn't interrupted.

You've spent too much time here. It's time to leave. I froze at the sound of the voice, only this time, I didn't turn to see if anyone was behind me. I then swallowed hard and ignored it.

Hunter noticed Pastor James's lingering eyes on me too. Pastor James looked up at Hunter for a moment, and an entire conversation in silence exchanged between them. Hunter then casually slid his arm to my waist, guiding me to the large folding table laid out with country fried chicken and all the trimmings.

I liked the feeling of his arm brushing my back, sliding along the curve of my waist and then letting his fingers dangle just past my hip. Tiny little pins poked inside my cheeks, and a warm wave of giddiness became an embarrassing grin everyone would see.

I quickly broke free of his touch to sit in my usual seat on the swing. Hunter followed, and instead of taking his seat across from Pastor James, he sat next to me. Pastor James stared at Hunter and then chuckled.

My mind swirled around all the events that had led me to that moment, and I thought about Davior and the bad choices he'd made. He could have been there with us, living a happy life, and not in misery, separated from his brother. I felt sorry for him. But he did try to take me.

*He didn't want me. He want*ed *my soul.*

I was still unsure what was a dream and what was real. But I did know a few things. Davior was Hunter's brother, he was involved in some kind of cult, that he wanted me to join. Whether Seth was really there, I wasn't sure. I could have been tricked. I wished Miss Mabel owned a television, because if Seth was missing, it would be broadcasted all over the news; my mother would make sure of that. However, I could sneak a listen to the radio later.

If he is missing, if Davior recruited him, it would be my fault. Remember how his eyes lit up when I told him about Seth?

After Pastor James ate, he began his sermon. He talked about God's freedom for his people, the freedom to choose. It seemed a very relevant topic for my run in with Davior and the story about the Cherokee. He read from Galatians chapter five and then set the book down on the porch.

"We, as believers, are free from the old laws. People are so busy worrying about what everyone else is doing or not doing, we miss what God has called us to do, which is to serve Him." Pastor James said, pointing toward the sky.

He continued by giving examples of real-life events going on around the world. Some I could relate to. My mother wanted the same sort of power that my great-great-grandmother had as a ruler of a small England village in the early eighteen-hundreds. To have that type of power was the most important thing to her. But that wasn't the only thing my mother focused on; she cared about what other people were doing or saying or having. Seth held similar views. He wanted what his father had. Actually, he wanted to become his father, taking all his influence, the power he obtained through his work.

"God's Son healed a blind man. All the people knew he was blind from birth, and then suddenly, he could see. The people should have seen a miracle, but instead, the priests condemned the action. They said it was against the law to heal on the Sabbath. They then questioned whether or not the man was truly blind. They did not want to accept the miracle performed in front of their eyes. They had missed the point entirely." Pastor James leaned on the railing, a bit out of breath. "So, in conclusion, don't worry about what everyone else is doing or not doing. Do not envy what others have and focus on what God has called you to do. Don't get caught up in set rules that man created. Remember that you have been set free by our Savior," Pastor James finished. He looked over at me and winked. Then he caught Hunter's eyes.

"Okay, okay." He laughed, softening the tension. "So, Jess,"—he snickered—"Miss Mabel tells me you've crossed over to our side."

I stared at him for a moment. I wasn't sure what he meant by that. Davior's less frightful eyes stared back through the pastor's eyes, and it startled me. *They both have the same brown eyes, the same amber specks.* Hunter touched the locket around my neck, and I understood what he meant.

"Oh, yes. Well…" I had asked God to forgive me and stopped denying what I already knew. He existed. I didn't know exactly what came next. *Unless I did it wrong.* I squirmed, feeling uneasy by his question.

He chucked softly and then smiled. "It's okay. You don't have to know how to explain it. It's between you and God only. I still don't know all the answers, and I made a decision at eight years old, which was an eternity ago. When God touches us, he knows where we are in life, and that is where he starts. Don't expect too much from yourself or think that there is some miraculous instant change."

That was a relief.

"Just remember that once you are forgiven, you are always forgiven." He paused. "Would you like to be baptized? I can do it in a shallow creek around here."

"I thought only babies got baptized."

"God's Son was baptized as an adult by his cousin, John." He looked over at Hunter. "I thought you were going to have her read the Gospels."

Hunter smiled sheepishly. "It's been a busy few weeks."

"Well then, we'll finish this conversation later, after you have read them, Jessie," he said, smiling. But he was so formal, as if he didn't want to step on any boundaries. "You know, it's been months since I played a good game of chess." He looked over at Hunter.

"Bring it on." Hunter grinned, but before he got up, he kissed my cheek.

I blushed. I heard Pastor James mutter something like, "You lucky dog," but I couldn't be sure, and my thoughts struggled against it.

He kisses May's cheek too.

The rest of the afternoon consisted of the boys playing chess—except for Joseph, who went off on his own again. Miss Mabel crocheting while humming something upbeat and rocking back and forth, and me and the girls playing games May wanted to play. My eyes casually wandered to the porch on several occasions to watch Hunter, and each time, I noticed I wasn't the only one stealing a peek. I quickly turned so the upturned corners of my mouth and the slight redness in my face didn't give away my secret, the one about how I felt about him.

As twilight drew near, May curled up in my lap and listened to me read *Peter Rabbit*. Josephine picked up her latest crochet project and slumped down next to us. Miss Mabel had slipped inside to prepare supper while the two boys continued with their game.

"Checkmate," Pastor James said softly, like he wasn't sure, as we all looked at him. And then, he said, "Checkmate! I can't believe I beat you. Thanks, Jessie." He smiled, noticing my shocked look.

I guess I wasn't the only one who noticed where Hunter's eyes were.

Embarrassed, I fumbled with the book, and it slipped out of my hands and onto the floor. That didn't help, and now all eyes were on me, all but Hunter's. He looked down at the spine of the book.

Is he embarrassed too?

A logical purpose for him watching me could be Davior. With May always wanting to head out deep in the swamp, he could have been watching us just to make sure we didn't break the rules. We were not supposed to go out there alone for a while, and with

Seth out there, I was relieved to know May couldn't go exploring either. Seth didn't like little kids.

Pastor James rose out of his chair and pulled Hunter into a hug and then looked at his watch. "Oh my. I'd better get going."

"Not before you eat, you don't," Miss Mabel hollered from the kitchen.

"Really, Miss Mabel. I'm supposed to let the choir in for practice. I'll still be a few minutes late, but they'll forgive me." He put the chess pieces in his bag. He hugged May and Josephine. "Tell Joseph to come see me," he whispered to her. Then his eyes met Hunter's. "Maybe next time we'll have a real game," he teased him with a playful slug to the shoulder.

"Enjoy your only victory while you can," he teased back.

Pastor James moved toward me last. He looked at Hunter while he pulled me into a hug. Hunter's brow went up.

"Thanks again," Pastor James whispered into my ear.

"Well, I won't keep the choir waiting, so here you go. You can eat it on the way." Miss Mabel handed him some food in a bag.

"You're the best!" he said, hugging her, and then he kissed her cheek.

"Now get," she said with a slight push.

He ran out with one last wave before getting in his truck. The baskets of corn in the back rattled back and forth as he went down the road, and he was gone.

A cool breeze swept over the porch while the sunlight dimmed, and I could no longer see the words on the paper.

"Time for bed," I said to May, closing the book.

After tucking May into bed, which she insisted on, I strolled back outside and stood at the edge of the porch. My head tilted to look up at the stars, which seemed to sparkle at me. There were so many without the moon outshining them. The crickets strummed a soft and steady chirp while the frogs in the distant bog made their own kinds of music. Together, the sounds blended into a harmonious array, drowning out my fears of what lurked beyond my sight, and what waited for me.

The air carried a combination of wood smells as it blew over the trees before lifting the strands of hair along my face. I wanted to block out everything except for the peacefulness of the moment, although it was not an easy task with so much to think about, worry about, and be happy about. There also lingered all the questions I wanted answers to.

But now would not be the time.

I felt him approach me from behind, maneuvering his hands around my waist from both sides and then locking his fingers together, just under my ribs, and pulling me into his faultless frame. His warm skin touched the coolness of my arm, sending my heart pounding like never before and louder than the cicadas in July. I stayed perfectly still, afraid that if I moved, he'd come to his senses and release his hold on me. His cheek rested against my hair as we both looked out into the night. Our bodies moved as one with each breath, and his heart thrashed with mine.

All thoughts of Hunter caring about me like a sister was quickly dissolving.

I'm getting in too deep. Stick to the plan. Things were going to get even more complicated. *What about Seth? What about Davior?* To add Hunter to this equation was so wrong. I couldn't do that to him. He deserved better than me.

Hunter released one of his hands to grab one of mine, and he twirled me around to face him. I stared up at him, forgetting the thoughts running through my head and letting myself get lost in his gaze. I didn't care about anything else, breathing in his musk. My body tingled all over, from the tips of my toes to the top of my head. His body trembled slightly as he traced my cheekbone with the back of his hand. Closing my eyes to delight in the moment, he moved my face up to his.

"What are you thinking?" His voice was so quiet he was barely able to speak as his nose touched mine.

"I need to remember to breathe," I whispered back with a dry laugh. "What are you thinking?" I opened my eyes to look at his, swallowing down the lump in my throat.

"Uh…" he said, his eyes burning through my soul. "I guess I asked for that." His eyes shifted to examine every part of my face. "I'm thinking that I want to kiss you, but I don't know that I should," he said then altered his focus. "This is all so new to me." He trailed off as if he was no longer talking to me.

"It's new to me too." I timidly looked down at his blue-checkered shirt.

He pulled me closer into his embrace, and my arms moved to circle around his neck. The movement felt natural, like I had done it so many times before, like he already belonged to me. As much as I tried to reason, as much as I wanted to resist, I was completely powerless under his charm.

His satin lips brushed against my forehead and moved down my cheek, which felt hot. I closed my eyes, waiting, waiting for the kiss I wanted more than anything I could think of.

Then he stopped sharply and his body stiffened.

"What's wrong?" I asked, but I felt it too. Something intangible waited in the darkness.

My heart pounded differently, frightened, thinking it might be Davior and Seth. Hunter's body tensed again, and he shifted his jaw back and forth. He nodded his head a few times, staring out, and then I felt him relax and place his head on top of mine once again.

"I'd better get you to bed. We have plans to be up early tomorrow," he said softly, trying to cover the irritation I heard in his voice.

No, no, I thought, the feeling of disappointment washing over me. "But I'm not tired."

"Jessica, please."

My mother insisted on calling me Jessica every time she called my name, which was why I preferred to be called Jess or Jessie. Hearing Hunter say my full name, I couldn't help but nod and comply. I dropped my arms quickly, in sort of a pout, and walked into the shack. I grabbed my nightclothes and changed. Hunter stood at the door, looking out, until he heard me crawl into the squeaky bed.

He walked over and kneeled down at the bed. "Promise me you won't leave the house tonight and will go right to sleep. It's not safe for you to be out of this house right now."

I didn't say anything, but in the darkness, he must have imagined me nodding my head like a good little girl. He kissed my forehead slowly, softly.

"Sleep well."

He pulled the sheet over me, tucking it in around me, and then walked over to Miss Mabel. He hunched over, putting both hands on the arm of the chair, leaning into her ear. I couldn't hear anything, not even a whisper. Hunter then stood up and walked out the front door while Miss Mabel followed.

I wasn't going to stay—of course not. It had all happened because of me, and I had no idea what Seth was capable of if he was part of this cult.

If anyone here gets hurt because of me... I tumbled through the brush behind them into the black, stricken night. *See. I'm making things worse for everyone and being sneaky about it. What if Seth has been watching me? He would rip Hunter apart for getting that close to me. And what would have happened if he saw him kiss me?* I shut out the voice and continued to follow.

With no moon and no shadows to follow, I relied on the swishing sound the branches made against each other when passed. And it worked well until the voice repeated again and again with the same message: *It's your fault.* Lost with mysterious trees looming overhead and not able to make out where I was, the race inside my chest began. It beat hard against my lungs, cutting down the flow of air.

"Great. Just great." I spun around to go back the way I came and then spun around again. "Oh no."

I felt a swoosh of air pass overhead and move forward between the brush in front of me. With nowhere else to go, I followed with my pulse thumping in my throat. Whispers of voices in the night became recognizable once again as I stumbled at the edge of the meadow. A greenish glow with no visible sign of a source filled the meadow.

"We've made a deal. It's already done. He won't be letting her go easily, nor will I," Davior said.

"Oh, and you are going to just let him have her?" Hunter spoke.

"One thing you know, my brother, is how my mind works. You tell me."

"At some point, he'll realize you've used him. What would stop him from killing you then?"

"We don't fall under the same rules you do. You know that. Besides, once he see's the whole picture, Jessica will not be as important. However, a deal had to be made in order for him to come. The plan is already set in motion, and my only requirement is that I give you fair warning." He paused. "Consider yourself warned."

"She's protected here, on this land."

"She's only protected if she stays inside that joke you call a house. You won't be able to keep her caged in that filthy shack for long. "

"I don't plan on keeping her caged. Apparently, that's your plan," Hunter spat. "And as long as she is with me, she'll be safe."

"Yeah, well, good luck with that. At least I'm not afraid to say how I f—"

"I'm still bound by honor and respect, unlike you, Davior. Do you even know what that means anymore, or have you let your mind get so twisted into evil that you can't see past your own selfish desires? Have you forgotten where you came from?"

"Your time here is done, Davior," Miss Mabel added in her soft, loving voice.

I moved in a little closer to peek through the branches.

"She will be miserable here. At some point, she'll miss the things she's become accustomed to, and she'll disappear; she'll leave here like she did her last home. It will be then that I'll make her an offer she won't be able to refuse," Davior voiced.

"Your little mind tricks are worthless on me, so just give it up. You don't know her as well as you like to think you do."

"We won't be giving her up easily, Hunter. It wasn't a fair fight." Davior's tone raised.

"I did everything you asked, and it's now over. She's clearly made her choice."

"Well, I see things differently. It's good then that I'm not bound to your rules of the game."

"Why her?" The two tall shadows paced in front of each other. "I'm sure you can find plenty of others to fill your—"

"Brother, why do you ask questions that you already know the answer to?" Davior replied.

The tallest figure stopped and paused for a moment and then lunged at the other. Both fell to the ground, and they tumbled close to where I stood, hitting the bush I cowered behind. I tried to hold my breath so they wouldn't hear me breathing hard. But they were too busy. One shadow threw the other off and then jumped on top of the other. I didn't know who to root for until Miss Mabel stepped in. She stood in front of the tallest shadow and put her arm on his shoulder before he lunged again.

"That's quite enough," Miss Mabel spoke, her hands stretching out between the two boys.

"She is not a trophy or some pawn to get what you want!" Hunter stated in a loud, booming voice.

"Hunter, I said that's enough," Miss Mabel said. "She is safe here with us. They cannot touch her anywhere within our border." She paused a moment. "There is another option to consider." She pulled Hunter's face close to hers and whispered something I couldn't hear.

Hunter stepped back away from Davior.

"Yes, dear brother, she is safe…for now. But no matter where you take her," Davior said, " we'll find her, and she'll be ours forever." He grabbed his jacket and then left through the other side of the clearing.

I realized I knew this area and my way back. But if I wanted to beat them to the shack, I had to hurry.

Davior is in alliance with Seth. This is not good. This is so not good. He won't give up easily or without a fight. He'll call out the entire police force and call in every favor from all his attorney friends, all those other "friends." I'm putting everyone I care about in danger. I'm so stupid.

I ran up the steps and then tiptoed to my bed. No one moved. I didn't have time to pull the covers over me, as Miss. Mabel and Hunter entered through the back door. I lay very still.

Crap! I'm caught!

Hunter headed toward me, and I closed my eyes tightly. His warm hand touched my cool cheek, and he pulled back his hand quickly. I then felt the warmth of the blanket contouring over my body. Hunter sat on the edge of the mattress and placed his hand back on my face, already feeling warmer. I shifted slightly, leaning into his hand, pretending to be asleep. He bent over and kissed my cheek, holding his lips there for only a moment before he left for his own bed.

Besides the secret meeting and the still, small voice of reason echoing in the catacombs of my mind, telling me to leave, the day proved to be amazing. Hunter vowed to protect me, to not let me out of his sight, but before that, before we were interrupted, he intended to kiss me.

Two Empty Pails

The morning light filtered into the room. I didn't hesitate getting out bed at the anticipation of the special trip Hunter schemed. Making a run for the washroom, I grabbed my blue sundress with spaghetti straps and got dressed.

Ready to go, I noticed a round, floppy hat with blue flowers tossed on my bed. *Cute,* I thought, placing the hat on my head. It reminded me of the hat Audrey Hepburn wore in *Breakfast at Tiffany's* as she was about to go to visit Sally Tomato, the mobster.

The secret meeting in the night hadn't changed the plans for the day. I watched Hunter and Josephine prepare breakfast while Miss Mabel and May packed lunches. I couldn't help but wonder if this little trip was putting the others in danger.

"Can I help?" I asked.

The old woman pointed to the bamboo basket in the corner next to the door and then continued to slather the bread with egg salad. I grabbed the basket and began to pile in the items set out. Only a moment passed before I noticed his eyes on me. My cheeks turned hot, but I didn't glance up and kept packing.

The voice I didn't want to hear whispered in my ear. *I told you this would happen, you silly girl. You should leave now. Save the people you love. You didn't help your father…*

"I am going mad." I tapped the side of my head with the palm of my hand, stopping the male voice instantly.

"Did you say something, dear?" Miss Mabel asked.

I shook my head and continued to pack as a vague memory of my grandmother talking to an empty chair came and went. I was very young. My father had told me it was my mother's doing. She drove her insane.

Did I get out in time or did my mother drive me mad? I worried as I packed the last item in the basket and then wiped off the table.

"I'll take that." Hunter grabbed the towel from me.

"Hey, I wasn't done."

"I guess you'll have to come get it back." He twirled the cloth over his head.

I laughed at the challenge, letting everything else in my thoughts fade away as I went for the cloth.

"You two, out of my kitchen," Miss Mabel said, taking the towel out of Hunter's hand. "You" She pointed at Hunter. "Go fetch me more wood." She sighed. "Kids today."

We finished eating breakfast, and Miss Mabel handed out gear for us to carry to our secret destination that was only secret to me.

Heading out, Hunter led the way, carrying more than his fair share. I walked closely behind him with May on my right side, chatting away. I didn't hear one word she said. I watched Hunter glower at the landscape surrounding us. May didn't notice and kept talking.

We walked for at least a mile, crossing small streams and going through meadows and around a few bogs until we came along a river. The water flowed swiftly, tossing the water up and over rocks along the banks.

There was no visible bridge, and yet I asked, "We're crossing over it, right?"

My fear of rushing water welled up inside me.

I stopped and watched everyone move closer to the water. Hunter ran ahead down to the shore, where an elongated wooden boat, which looked ancient, bobbed up and down against a post. Everyone except me climbed into the boat as Hunter untied it. I stepped back. I imagined myself slipping on the wet grass on my way down, splashing into the water, and then being dragged facedown along the bottom of the river. *No thanks.*

"Come on, Jess," May said.

"Give me a break," Joseph said.

Hunter, with one foot in the boat and one on land, tried to keep the boat from sailing off without me and smiled.

"Trust me," he said, outstretching his hand toward me.

I felt silly standing there, not able to move and all eyes on me. Of everything that should scare me, water shouldn't be one of them.

"Leave her if she doesn't want to get in the boat," Joseph said. "Someone will find her way out here."

Hunter shook his head at Joseph but kept his eyes on me. Miss Mabel, however, lifted her hand and smacked Joseph on the back of his head.

"Ouch," he said, climbing out of the boat. "Fine. I'll take matters into my own hands." Joseph moved inches from me. "Get in the boat."

He reached out for my arm, but I pulled it away before his hand touched me. Hunter tied the boat to the post and sprinted over toward us.

"This is ridiculous," Joseph said, walking past me, away from the boat. "I'll see you all later," he said.

"I'm sorry," I said to Hunter, feeling bad Joseph walked off. He hated me, he made sure I knew it, and he hated me the most when Hunter's attention was on me. I pouted, "I don't know how to swim."

"I won't let anything happen to you," he said, staring after Joseph. "Besides"—his hand took mine—"there is no swimming required."

He stepped into in the boat, lugging me behind him. "Trust me."

How pathetic, I thought, looking at the water rush around the boat. There were much worse ways to die. I pictured Seth's blood-red eyes pulsing at me.

"If I fall out of the boat…" I said, lifting the heavy rocks of my feet into the boat.

He laughed, stroking the top of my hand before I plopped down on the hard wood plank that stretched across the craft. "I'm insulted that you feel like you have to tell me to save you," he said, pushing off the shore.

Okay, so it was a silly thing to say, but it didn't change the firm grip I maintained on the edge of the boat or from removing my eyes from the white-capped water bubbling up ahead.

We traveled along, letting the stream take us. May pointed out and named each tree, bush, fish, bird, just about everything she saw. Hunter guided the boat while scanning the waters ahead and the shoreline of trees.

"Look." May laughed and pointed over toward a sand cove. "What a bunch of lazy crocs."

They casually looked over and then closed their eyes and continued to soak up the hot sun beating down on their bodies.

"Is that smell coming from them?" I asked, pinching my nose.

"No. It's too strong to be them, although I would guess they don't smell like roses," Miss Mabel said. "No. It's the bog just over that ridge." She pointed north, the same direction the breeze moved from. "The water doesn't move much, so the vegetation rots and creates a foul gas. Keeps people away from that part of the swamp."

With a smell like that, I wouldn't go near it.

We continued to float down the river until Hunter pointed out the wooden dock ahead. Hunter steered the boat toward the matchstick platform, touching the bow to the wood. We all got out and entered a large red and green meadow. The red were big, ripe strawberries, which covered most of the area.

"Let's eat first. I'm starving," May said.

Miss Mabel spread out the big blanket along the grass, and May clapped, her lips red from devouring a juicy strawberry.

Everyone sat on the blanket and ate lunch.

After taking my last bite, I let my body fall back onto the ground to look up at the sky. The aqua color speckled with white, fluffy clouds showed no signs of danger or darkness. I relaxed, soaking in the warmth of the sun.

Hunter fell back next to me. "So, what should we talk about?"

I shifted sideways, onto my elbow, catching a glimpse of Miss Mabel, May, and Josephine grabbing pails and heading away from us. I looked at Hunter, still gazing up at the cotton-ball clouds.

The questions I promised to keep vaulted up swam around in a giant vortex, bouncing off the walls of my skull. I gulped, clearing a way for the words to come out.

Am I ready to hear the answers? Am I ready to accept the illogical?

"So, you didn't leave?" I asked, and Hunter stayed silent. "You promised," I reminded him.

"No, I didn't leave."

"How is that possible? You were gone for days."

"Before you came, I used to take May exploring into the swamp. I taught her everything she knows about it from the time she was old enough to walk. She is very independent, as I'm sure you already know. After a while, I started letting her trail ahead of me, giving her some freedom. Of course, the whole time, my eyes never left her. I was always close enough to intervene if danger was near. Eventually, she caught on and knew I was there, but she continued to play the game. When you came along, she wanted to be the one to share with you, teach you, and show you what she loved most of all. She begged me not to tag along, and I agreed, but just as I had done before, I stayed in the shadows."

"Every time?" I asked.

If he had been there when I told Davior my life story, he would have known everything, and yet they continued to let me stay.

"The swamp is a dangerous place if you don't know what to look for. I've lived here long enough to spot danger or areas that are not meant for humans. Even May can wander in places she shouldn't be," he said, answering my question. "The day you saw

Davior started out just like any other, with May begging you to go exploring with her. I followed until I saw someone cloaked in a black coat also watching. When he noticed me, he went in the opposite direction of you both. I decided to follow him until I realized I was being led away from you on purpose. I ran toward where I had last seen you and followed my senses. Before I stepped through the clearing, I knew it was Davior. I also knew that he was using his mind games on you by the way you looked at him." He turned on his side and met my gaze. "I wanted to kill him."

"Why would you want to kill your own brother?"

"You have to understand, Jess, that Lucifer is very strong in this world. Not stronger than God, of course, but he has a way of finding our weakness and twisting it for his enjoyment. Davior chose that same deceitful way, and he found something he could twist. He's not my brother in the same way he once was."

He could tell I didn't understand. Maybe he wished he would have given me more time to read my Bible. He lay back, fixing his eyes on the clouds again.

"Seeing him there in the clearing, staring at you the way he was—I'd never experienced that type of emotion before. Davior was trying to take you away from us. I couldn't allow that to happen. He knows what is going on inside my head. He knows what I'm thinking and feeling, and I him."

"He can read thoughts?" I asked.

"Don't worry," he said at my surprised tone, "he can only read mine, but he can influence, or a better word, he can *push* thoughts and feelings into your head as though they are your own. We both can."

"So you were talking when I couldn't hear," I said, though as more of a thought to myself, relieved he couldn't hear my thoughts.

"Something we were born with. I've heard it's common for twins to have a portion of the ability. My older brother can communicate with all of us in the same way, only we can't read his thoughts. That is only something Davior and I can do. It was fun when we were young, before…before things changed."

"Davior is your twin?"

"Yes."

Twins! I thought. *Well, that makes sense, the reason I felt attracted to him at first.* I could see it then in his jaw, body, and facial expressions.

"We were best friends long ago, shared just about everything."

"I'm so sorry." The brief feeling of sadness I'd had for Davior previously grew more.

"Anyway, of course he is attracted to you. I couldn't blame him for that." A crackle vibrated in his tone. "You are quite a young woman. I'm sorry for not seeing that before. People's ages are subjective in my world."

What did he mean by subjective? You're age is your age, right?

He took my hand and brought it to his lips and then kissed the top of it. The little tingles moved all over my body, the kind when my hand falls asleep, causing my heart to beat uncontrollably.

I cleared my throat unintentionally.

"Oops. Sorry." He smiled before continuing. "He challenged me. And in our culture, you have no choice to but to accept a challenge, whether you want to or not. Davior knows I believe in upholding our traditions and honor, so even though in my head, I wanted to deny what he wanted, in the end, he knew what I would have to say."

"What was he challenging you for?" I asked.

He stroked his thumb against the top of my hand. "You."

The word fell out of his mouth and danced around inside my head.

"The rules would be simple. You had to believe that I was gone and that Davior would get alone time with you. I'd be allowed to watch in the shadows to make sure you were safe and that he didn't cheat by pushing your thoughts. Miss Mabel thought it would be better if she kept watch, but I knew Davior. I knew he would try every trick he knew. At least I had the upper hand in knowing his thoughts." He paused. "But even more than that, I couldn't just leave you."

The tingling moved into my cheeks, and I turned my face from him so he wouldn't notice.

"I have to admit it wasn't as easy as I thought it would be, seeing you and not able to be near you or talk to you. Of course, Davior knew that. He played into the dark side of my soul I didn't know was there. Apparently, he didn't either, but was all too thrilled about twisting it for his enjoyment.

"Anyway," he continued, "the time wouldn't begin right away, which was why he stayed away for a few of days. If I had pushed your thoughts, which I would never do, it would have worn off. Typically, it only lasts a day or so, but I've never done it to anyone. I've only done it with animals and only so they wouldn't hurt a human."

I thought about the snake in the swamp that almost had me for lunch.

"Davior accused me of using this power on you, so he claimed he needed time for my influence to fade. He called it a fair fight, but he knows nothing of the word." I saw him from the corner of my eye turn toward me. "I've never used it on any person," he stated again and squeezed my hand.

As I turned toward him, our eyes locked.

"I'd never do that to you."

"I remember how I felt. How he made me tell him things I didn't want anyone to know," I said feeling guilty I kept the secrets in the first place, "it was like an intruder inside my head telling me what to do."

Like the male voice I keep hearing.

Don't share that. You'll end up like Grandmother.

I bit the outside of my lip and shook my head at my thoughts, but Hunter didn't notice and went on.

"I think he prolonged it to torture me. His mind is warped, and he's adopted a new set of moral values." His thoughts drifted away for a moment and then back. "He got his time, and you refused him in the greatest way possible. I've never felt so relieved. But then, when I thought you were safe, sleeping in your bed, I didn't realize how much of you had gotten down into his soul. He was going to try again. When I finally got to you and saw you holding your ground, you really surprised me."

Hunter pushed himself off the ground and on to his feet and then offered his hand to pull me up.

"When I saw you, down on your knees,"—tears swelled in his eyes—"and then to see you react to him the way you did, well… impressive and very mature."

Hunter's light-blue eyes twinkled at me, as he pulled a stray strand of hair from my bottom lip.

"Of course, he knew I was watching when he went in to kiss you. He knew I wasn't going to allow it, provoking me to fight him," he said. "Although, if you had made a different choice in the end, I…"

"Would have had to let me go," I whispered, "which is why everyone seemed so happy after it happened."

Hunter put both hands on my face. "You and you alone make choices for your life, and none of us can choose for you; not your mother and definitely not *Seth*." He spit out his name like poison.

Those last words started to work in my mind, the mention of my mother, who, to my knowledge, was thousands of miles away.

He pulled me up to his face, and every thought faded back into the shadows.

"Of course I'm happy about the path you did choose," he said, speaking in a calm, low voice. "Some things in this life are really bad, and I'm sorry that Davior unlocked your memory. You've gone through so much in such a short period of time and have carried such a heavy burden. He needed to use whatever he could to persuade you to follow the malevolent path of revenge, hate, and power, all of which now consumes him."

"Like Pastor James was talking about yesterday," I added.

"You were listening." He chuckled.

"So it's done then. He got his chance and lost," I said, knowing the answer from being sneaky last night, but I hoped to get more information.

A heavy sigh escaped his lips. "No, there is more to it than that, but he can't touch you now like he could before. You can now see him for who he really is. You are now one of God's children and cannot be pulled from Him by anyone. However, he can still try to deceive you, play on your fears, your sin, and even love."

"Love?"

"Yes. Love can be twisted and used as a gateway for evil, which is why you need to continue to read your Bible. It will help you be stronger mentally and make it harder for you to be temped. When you know God, evil ways are easier to spot and you can fight against it. But, unfortunately, things are never as black and white as we would like them to be. There is one other factor. They can physically hurt you or kill you, but I'll do what I need to do to keep you out of their reach."

But who's going to keep you safe? It was my fault Davior found Seth, and although I'm sure he was an easy recruit, I wanted to know what he'd promised him. Seth wouldn't have joined unless it benefited his plans. *He'll come after everyone, their deaths will be my fault.*

My eyes shifted back and forth.

Hunter saw the panic on my face and frowned. "What's wrong?"

"Seth. That's my fault. All the things I told Davior about him. He wouldn't have found him, and he wouldn't be—"

Hunter pulled me into his chest, stifling my shaking body, his hand stroking my hair. "It's not your fault, Jess. They would have found Seth without you."

I pulled my body away.

"I don't understand. Found him for what purpose?"

"I know you don't understand, but understand that it's nothing you could have prevented."

"You shouldn't say things that aren't true to comfort me," I said, turning my back to him.

I knew it was my fault. Even though I couldn't stand Seth, I just made things worse, a hundred times worse. *A demon-worshiping cult! Just great! I thought everyone was in danger before, and now…what have I unleashed?*

"Jessica."

His use of my full name took on another meaning.

"I wouldn't lie to you," he said. "I don't think I could even if I tried," he said as he moved his hand gently down my arms until he found my hands. "Seth is…well, important, for things to move forward. They would have found him sooner or later, regardless of what you told them. The only thing you did was make it a little easier in their search." His lips met my ear as he whispered, "Please don't be mad at me. I don't think I can bear it."

"Now you're talking about more than one person—you mean the cult he's in? I don't understand how or why, if I hadn't talked about him," I answered in a low whisper, leaning into his chest. His arms moved around me. I wasn't mad at him. I was mad at me.

Important? What does that mean?

A conversation began to fill the air around us, and four people surrounded us, looking at our two empty pails.

Warning

Joseph had not returned after stomping off near the river, and no one seemed to be worried about him.

"Should we go look for him?" I asked with the thought of Seth and Davior potentially out there wanting to hurt anyone associated with me, possibly rallying more recruits for their club.

"Oh, he'll be back in his own time. He just needs some time to himself to gain some proper perspective." Miss Mabel swished the water over the strawberries in the colander. "Better get started on these if they are to be ready for the ladies to pick up. Lots of pies to bake for the orphanage bake sale."

"Don't forget the crocheted blankets you made and the one Josephine has almost finished," I added.

"She did finish." She handed me the bowl of clean fruit. "I have to say she did a wonderful job on it, too."

Josephine smiled at her. "I only finished one, but next time, I'll have three done," she said.

"You'd have three done if you weren't such a perfectionist," Miss Mabel said and winked at me.

We laughed as I took the bowl from her to the table outside, where Hunter waited for me.

Hunter sat at the small table, chuckling at our conversation.

"We've got work to do," I said, placing the bowl between us.

"I'm ready," Hunter showed me his knife and then furnished one for me.

I could already smell the first batch of the buttery dough, prepared by Josephine and May, cooking in the coal oven.

"How much did you read last night?" Hunter asked.

"I read all of Matthew, Mark, and Luke and almost finished John." I sliced the juicy strawberry in my hand, the liquid running through my already-sticky, red-tinted fingers, but heard no reply to my answer and looked up at a scowling face.

"What? I found it interesting how similar the chapters were, but from a different perspective. Really, I didn't realize how late it had gotten."

"That explains why you keep yawning." He looked back down at his fingers.

"I'm surprised you didn't notice."

He squirmed in his seat at my tease, but his tone went flat. "Just remember not to leave the front porch without me.

"Ready for more?" May bounced through the swinging door, letting it slam shut behind her.

"Sure," I said, taking the bowl from her, not looking at Hunter.

"What's wrong?" May asked.

"Nothing," I said. "Here. You can take these." I handed her the sliced ones.

"Okay." She took the bowl and went back inside.

"I'm sorry," he finally said. "I guess I'm mad at myself for falling asleep before knowing you were safely in bed. It won't happen again."

"I promise not to leave the porch without you knowing. I don't want to be responsible for you not getting enough sleep. I'm not a baby. You don't have to watch me all the time," I said, although I loved that he was so protective over me. However, watching me all the time, he was bound to see me do some not-so-lady-like actions—like biting my nails. My mother said it was like putting filth in my mouth. "So getting back to what we were talking about, the chapters I read," I said, slicing a strawberry in half.

"Yes." He cleared his throat. "They are all very similar and told from different points of view." He plopped a sliced strawberry into the bowl, still not looking in my direction. "Each one had a gift of recalling certain events that stood out for them, which is why it isn't exactly the same. No two people who witness the same event will recall the same details, but it will all have the same general idea. Some people believe that that means that the Bible contradicts itself."

"I didn't think it contradicted, but what do you mean by gifts?"

"We have, as children of God, come together to use our abilities, our gifts, to accomplish His goals together. For example, Miss Mabel has many gifts. One is that she is a great cook. She makes these pies so people will buy them, and money goes to help the children. Now, she doesn't like to be around all those people, so there are others who come get the pies and sell them. It's a team effort with one goal in mind. It's the same for all of us."

"When do you get a gift?" I asked, thinking I didn't have any gifts I was contributing with.

Hunter stopped slicing and smiled at me before continuing. "They come when you need them most"

"What is your gift?" I asked but immediately felt stupid for asking. The mind-reading thing between his brothers and being able to sway animals were clearly amazing gifts.

"I was saved for a purpose, but now…now I'm not so sure what that purpose is. It's possible that…but then again…" he mumbled.

I changed my question. "Does it work in the opposite way? I mean Lucifer and his followers. Do they come together with gifts to accomplish their goals?"

"Yes."

"So you said that Seth is important. Is that what you mean, that he possesses some sort of gift that will benefit their side?"

"Yes."

"That's bad, isn't it?" My eyes lifted up to gaze at his down-turned lips.

"I don't know what it means yet. But we will figure it out. Davior isn't that smart, and he keeps getting too close to me." A soft chuckle escaped his lips.

I thought about Seth's ability to persuade people, and he didn't have to use special powers to do it. *What would that mean now that he's part of some devil cult?* I then thought about my mother and wondered if she knew what was happening and if she knew where I was.

I stared at the strawberry in my hand, biting the outside of my bottom lip. *Should I ask him how much he knows about me? Should I just assume he knows?* This was my chance to finally let all my secrets out. "How much, I mean from what you heard me tell Davior, do you know about my past?"

Hunter didn't answer, and the acid in my stomach swished around. I glanced across the table. My eyes passed his empty seat, catching a glimpse of burning red eyes peering out from the timberline.

"Hunter?" I whispered with my heart thrashing against my ribs, unable to remove my stare from the unmoving glow.

Seth? I thought as the eyes vanished. *Now I'm seeing things too.* I shook my head.

"I'm here," Hunter said behind me, causing me to jolt in my seat. "I'm sorry. I didn't mean to—"

"It's okay. I just didn't realize you had left, and then…" *It was just my imagination. If it had been Seth, he would not have just been waiting out there. He would have come and taken me.*

"And then I came up behind you," he finished. "Here. Let me take those. She's ready for them." He took the bowl, replacing it with more whole strawberries, and then left for a moment.

He didn't hear my question. With the acid still churning, I thought, *Maybe I should just assume he knows everything. Why do I need it verbalized?*

Hunter returned, sitting back in his chair.

"Why did Seth look the way he did? I mean with the red eyes. And, well, he acted differently too."

"Seth believes that you are his, and he also believes that by giving Davior what he wants, you will marry him willingly. He doesn't want to force you, but he will if it's necessary. He vowed to help Davior and is now going through some"—he thought for a moment—"changes. Seth felt possessive of you before my brother got to him, and now it's amplified, although, at the moment, Seth is not in control and is being controlled by Davior, but that will only last a short time. I'm not sure Davior will be able to keep that control over him much longer." He looked out into the field. "Davior has also given him other reasons to be even more possessive of you."

"And that would be?"

"Davior told Seth we have brainwashed you into staying with us and have turned you against him. You are a prisoner of our influences, and he is the only one who can save you." He let out a dry laugh. "He thinks you'll see him as your knight in shining armor, sweeping you off your feet, and you'll marry him on the spot."

Even with the sweet smell of the strawberries in the air, I smelled something fowl lingering in his words, and I twisted my face in disgust. "Yeah, like that would ever happen," I called out, just in case Seth was listening.

Hunter glanced at me with a pleasing grin before getting back to his work. "Davior is also doing all this for his own benefit as well. You know how he feels about you," Hunter said, picking up another strawberry, not looking up. "They don't keep to any rules, so once Davior gets what he wants out of Seth, he'll figure a way to get you for himself. He's unsure of many things, so I can't see clearly what he's thinking, but I know that he doesn't plan to hand you over to Seth willingly."

I didn't speak. Minutes seemed to pass between us while I absorbed his words.

I'm nothing. Why does he want me?

Hunter hesitantly spoke again. "There's one more reason. Davior told Seth that there is another man who is attempting to claim you. I think this, more than anything else, has caused Seth to be even more unstable. And now that we've met, he knows it's true."

"Oh," was all I could manage to say. *He knows it's true? Hunter wants to claim me? He wants me?* I felt short of breath as the blood raced throughout my limbs.

"So you can see why you need to be careful. You need to say near the house or near me at all times. Neither can enter the house. It's protected."

I liked the "near me" part. I expected the voice to chime in, the one saying I was making it all up, reading into something that wasn't there, but it stayed silent and still.

"Seth is going through a transition period for the next month, so we should be fine. Davior won't let him leave without supervision, and it would do him no good to bring him around you right now. It could ruin the work they have already done."

"Wait, what do you mean by transition period? Did Davior go through some strange ritual to be accepted into this cult? Is that how he learned to use black magic, and now Seth will be learning it as well?" If that were true, it would explain how he'd played those illusions on me.

"You'll have to be ready to face him," he said, ignoring my question but prompting a more serious one. He sighed. "There will be much for you to do before then, before he faces you again."

"Who? Seth? I have to face him?" I looked down at my red-stained hands, and the memory of Seth's fingers around my neck flashed before me.

"You'll have to face him, Jess," he said, looking over at my reaction, "just like you did with Davior."

I shivered, letting the knife slide between my fingers along with the partially sliced strawberry and pieces. I heard the knife hit the ground twice before it became silent. I could see a vision of Seth standing out in the blinding darkness, his blood-red eyes burning at me, waiting for the opportunity to take me captive. He was bigger, much bigger, pacing with rapid breath, and I was paralyzed in fear. He was like a wild, rabid animal, ready to attack.

Transition period.

I pictured his arms crushing me against his body as I stared at the cut bleeding from where the knife had passed through my fingers. It was interesting I didn't feel any pain.

"You won't be alone. But we might have to give the impression you are alone with him in order to keep Seth from instantly being out of control. We have to give him the chance to speak to you, for you to finally tell him," Hunter assured me.

"But why? I don't want to talk to him. I never made any promises to marry Seth. Those were my mother's promises. I told him that I never wanted to marry him, that I didn't want any part of this scheme or hers. I just wanted them to leave me alone, let me live my life. I only agreed to save my father, and when he died—"

There it was, all out there as the tears blurred my vision. Hunter pulled me up into his arms.

"Jess. Jess, please don't worry." He held me snug against his chest. "You'll be ready. You'll be completely safe. I won't let anyone hurt you again."

"I'm sorry I lied to you, all of you." I sobbed harder.

"Nothing to be sorry for. You'll see. Everything will work out."

"If you say so, I trust you." I gathered myself together, wondering who would keep him safe. Seth was not only bigger in size, but he had lots of connections, including his new friends.

"You can trust me, but even more, you can trust God." He pressed his lips against the top of my head.

"Have you two sliced the rest of those strawberries yet?" Miss Mabel called from inside the house, loud and clear.

"We are just about done," Hunter called backed as we both unlocked our arms and Hunter went back to his chair.

The strawberry juice made its way into the cut and stung a bit. "Ouch." I licked the cut.

"What's wrong?"

"I've got a little cut, just a scratch. No big deal," I said, especially considering what was coming, what I was going to have to do. "What is this magic they are involved in? What can they do with it?"

"It's not magic," he said.

"I saw it. The way the sun darkened in the middle of the day, the way they glided on the surface like ghosts."

"You know what? I'm going to finish these. Go wash up, and then I want you to read Revelation. It's time for you to know what we are dealing with."

I shrugged, staring into his beautiful, soft face, letting go of all the worry. Not wanting to lose myself in a book—that was surely a change for me. I was in a real-life fairy tale I never wanted to end, well, except for the whole Davior and Seth thing.

Although by now, in a fairytale, I would have thought the two main characters who cared for each other would have a least kissed. I liked where my thoughts were going.

Maybe I should just kiss him. Now there's an idea, I thought as I remembered how soft his lips felt moving along my cheekbone not so long ago before being interrupted.

I huffed as all those thoughts rushed through my mind like a raging river, with Hunter's face still keeping my gaze. The table was the only thing stopping me from carrying out the thought of taking the aggressive approach, my strongest feeling, the only feeling I wanted to have, and I wondered if the table could hold me.

I laughed loudly.

Hunter raised one eyebrow. I shook my head. After all, I was only human and a silly little girl.

"Go on," he said, sounding a little like Miss Mabel.

A Vision of Things to Come

The darkness closed in around me quickly. I hadn't paid attention to the time, and it was getting darker as I squinted to read the words on the page. Suddenly, a light appeared above me, but instead of looking up to see who was providing the light, I continued to read. I'm not sure how long I continued to read, but I read the last few paragraphs of Revelation out loud.

"'I am the Alpha and the Omega, the First and the Last, the Beginning and the End. Blessed are those who wash their robes, that they may have the right to the tree of life and may go through the gates into the city. Outside are the dogs, those who practice magic arts, the sexually immoral, the murderers, the idolaters and everyone who loves and practices falsehood.

"'I, God's Son, have sent my angel to give you this testimony for the churches. I am the Root and the Offspring of David, and the bright Morning Star.

"'The Spirit and the bride say, "Come!" And let him who hears say, "Come!" Whoever is thirsty, let him come; and whoever wishes, let him take the free gift of the water of life. I warn everyone who hears the words of the prophecy of this book: If anyone adds anything to them, God will add to him the plagues described in this book. And if anyone takes words away from this book of prophecy, God will take away from him his share in the tree of life and in the holy city, which are described in this book. He who testifies to these things says, "Yes, I am coming soon." Amen. Come, Lord. The grace of the Lord be with God's people. Amen.'"

I went back to the words "Outside are the dogs." Seth had become one of those dogs.

With little movement, I glanced over to the long, round hook that held a lantern glowing brightly in the vast darkness surrounding me.

I thought about all I had read, and there were many things I didn't understand. However, the theme of the chapter was simple and pointed to the future. A war was coming, a bloody battle of good against evil, God's army against Lucifer's army. I knew the Bible was written thousands of years before, but some of the things I read were actually happening, every day, and all over the world. The poor, starving countries, diseases like AIDS and cancer taking millions of lives, and the fighting over Israel—could it all just be a coincidence? *I watched the news, I read the papers, I had—*

I felt movement under me, and realized it was just Hunter, his arms encircling my waist. His chest rose and fell softly against my back in a deep, peaceful sleep. I supposed he wasn't going to allow me to stay up by myself without his knowing, even though I had promised not to leave the porch. A smiled formed along my lips, and I nestled down into his embrace, and he tightened his hold. I traced his arm with my finger, sweeping it up and then back down, his skin smooth and soothing to touch. I placed my cheek against his heart to listen to the melancholy rhythm.

Why couldn't my world stay just like this? I didn't have to go, I didn't have to ever leave here.

You're putting everyone in danger, Jessica. You're being selfish. There went the voice again, and I closed my eyes to shut it out. I had no desire to fight or make sense of the words that felt inserted into my head. Whether I was going crazy or being played like a puppet, I decided it would be best to ignore it. I was happy in the moment, and there was no other place on earth I wanted to be more than right where I was. I drifted off to sleep, falling into white, fluffy clouds surrounded by a brilliant blue sky; however, it didn't last long before the clouds turned black and covered up the sky.

The smell of hot cement and black tar lifted into the air, making it hard to breathe. Every breath felt restricted and burned in my chest. I let out a cough before realizing I was in Los Angeles, the smog capitol of the world. The intense, orange-tinted sun peered through a brown haze of smoke and beamed down on a stage. The platform, decorated in red and blue streamers, balloons, and banners, had been adorned with microphones. Television cameras focused on the center of the stage.

I stood several yards from the stage, along with thousands of people in front of me. Standing on my toes, I was able to see over their heads and get a clear view of the stage. We all waited for a person to appear and address the crowd. Out of the corner of my eye, I saw someone run by. People were talking all around me, although none I could clearly hear, as I looked to see who had just run in front of me. Then I caught sight of a little girl making her way out of the crowd. She was wearing a pretty, blue, silk dress with white ruffles on the bottom. She had big, white ribbons tied into a bow behind her back. She wore black, shiny shoes and carried a purse that matched her dress. From behind, she had curly, blonde hair.

Is it May? What is May doing here? I made my way through the loud, chatty crowd, pushing when necessary. "Excuse me," I yelled over the noise, hearing the grunting and irritation I caused.

But I didn't care; I was getting closer to May.

"May! May!" I screamed, but she didn't turn around.

The little girl began to skip, quickening her pace and still not hearing me call her name. I watched her reach the end of the crowd and toward a park on the other side of the gathering.

I kept my eyes on her as I moved through the crowd. I watched her skip through the park, past the swings, and into a thick line of purple bushes and disappear. I had surpassed the crowd, but May was gone. *Should I go after her?*

A loud noise caught my ear. It was coming from above, a helicopter flying extremely low and moving right toward me. The air whirled around and kicked up everything in its path, but when I looked up, there wasn't anything but the brown sky. The crowd cheered, looking toward the stage.

I forgot about May and headed back into the crowd and toward the stage. She was gone and out of danger, I hoped. *But this is just a dream, right?* I needed to see why everyone was gathered and the reason I was there. *Dream or not, don't take any chances.*

The air changed as I moved farther into the crowd. It was stagnant and smelly, like the bog on the other side of the fast-moving river, the bog Miss Mabel said kept people from going into that part of the swamp.

I passed one woman who began to stare at me. I noticed she had thick makeup on. The mascara was running down her cheeks, and her lipstick was covering her chin. Her eyes were a strange color—topaz. I looked away from her quickly and continued walking toward the stage.

A knot rose up in my throat.

I was finally close enough see the stage, but I wasn't able to make out the features of the person standing there. He was speaking, but I didn't hear any words. It didn't make sense. Another person in the crowd began to stare at me, like the woman had, only this time, it was a middle-aged man. Surrounding his eyes were black circles, and they sunk into his face. He looked very sick. He held out his arms, showing me his long, deep cuts from the elbow down to his hands. They looked like giant claw marks from some kind of animal attack, and it was recent, as the brilliant, red blood still oozed from his wounds.

I gasped and looked away, feeling nauseated. I couldn't catch my breath and noticed that others looked the same as I spun around and looked at each one. They were all staring at me, and I was the in the center of a forming circle. Someone else was approaching me from behind. I could hear hard breathing and footsteps that shook the ground and moved closer. The people around me changed. At least I thought they were people. They all looked like smeared wet paint, bright and colorful, with just an outline of who they were.

I was panicked and frozen in fear.

The person approaching stopped. I could feel his hot breath on my neck. It wasn't just hot, but scorching, and smelled like sulfur. A burning sensation traveled through me as I cried out and fell to the ground. The ground sizzled, burning through my clothes. The crowd cheered around me. I looked up, but the light burned like fire, so I closed them tightly.

Where is Hunter? He said he would never leave me.

I wanted to call out to him. *He must be close.* I shielded my eyes to open them and called out, but no sound came out. The crowd cheered louder with each attempt. The sweat dripped down my forehead and down the curvature of my back. I wiped my forehead with the back of my hand, but it didn't feel like sweat; it felt thick and sticky. I looked down at my hand, and it was covered in blood, my blood. I felt dizzy and put both palms of my hands on the hot, sizzling ground.

Just a dream. It's just a dream.

The person behind me shifted to stand in front of me, shading me from the bright glow. I looked up and couldn't make him out at first. He looked so different. His eyes were dark and shadowed, digging into his skull. He was speaking with authority over me, and it ignited the crowd even more. I saw a demon with his blood-red eyes, peeling skin, deformed face, but it was still Seth.

He raised his hands, motioning to the crowd. The little girl in the blue dress joined his side. Her face was also dark and deformed. It was not May. She laughed at my surprise, revealing her black tongue and missing teeth. Seth motioned again, and the crowd cheered. A tall man wearing a black, hooded cloak handed Seth something shiny. He held it up for all to see. They went crazy.

Seth pulled me up with a fistful of hair as I struggled to get free from him, kicking up my feet and swinging my arms, but it was no use. He was too big and too strong to fight. He held the small, silver dagger to my throat.

"I love you, Jessica," he whispered in my ear.

I screamed.

"Jessie. Jessie. Wake up. Wake up."

Hunter's voice floated in the air faintly as I felt the cold blade across my throat and felt my body being shaken.

I pushed someone's hands off me and ran for the porch steps, breathing hard and unevenly. I felt the urge to vomit but swallowed it back down. I would have run farther if I didn't hear Hunter's stern voice.

"Jess!"

I stopped at the edge of the porch. *He's out there.*

I paced back and forth, from one end of the porch to the other. It was still night, and rain poured down, creating a thunderous echo. The air felt damp but dry in my throat. I tasted the lingering sulfur. Tears streamed down my cheeks, and I shook all over. I positioned my hand on my heart, which was beating so fast I thought something could be wrong. Flashes of light, without thunder, lit up the sky over and over. I stopped pacing, looking out near the thickest part of the trees as multiple flashes made it look like daylight.

"Breathe, Jessie. Breathe." Hunter leaped to my side, not letting me push him away that time.

"He tried to kill me," I said, staring out at the trees, not really talking to Hunter but to myself. He was out there. I knew he was.

I struggled in Hunter's arms. I couldn't shake the feeling.

"It's okay. It was just a dream," Hunter said, stroking my hair with one hand and holding me close with the other.

"All those people wanted him to kill me. They wanted him to tear me apart." I knew it was a dream, but I also knew I was being warned.

"You said they aren't involved in a cult," I said and then thought about what I had read in Revelations about the burning sulfur, the smoke of torment, and a mark of some kind. "Think, Jessica," I said out loud and closed my eyes. "The faces, they all had a symbol on their foreheads."

The mark of the beast.

"Just a dream," he whispered. He stroked my cheek.

My pulse slowed, but not my mind. *He's not only going to kill you but everyone around you.*

The tears flowed uncontrollably at the voice—it was right. Hunter put enough space between us to wipe my face.

"But it was so real," I spoke more calmly.

"Was I there?" he asked gently, continually wiping the tears from my cheeks.

"No."

"Well then you know for sure that it was a dream." He moved my chin to bring my face up to his. "I wasn't kidding when I said I wouldn't leave you."

Hunter looked into my face and traced his finger along my jawbone.

I forgot the dream.

The light from the lantern burned dim, but I could see his face was filled with concern. My body relaxed against him as his other arm holding me pulled me even closer. The tears completely gone, he cradled my face in his hand.

"Better?"

Could he see how much I needed him? I never needed anyone before, not like this; I never wanted to need anyone until now. How was it that it all changed so quickly?

I simply nodded and sighed heavily. "What time is it?"

"It's close to sunrise. You should get some sleep in your bed."

I clung to him, and he circled his other arm around me and pulled me tight.

"No," I whispered, thinking of what I might dream about next or what might be waiting for me.

"Honey, you have to sleep," he softly whispered, touching his lips to my hair. The word *honey* sent a thrill throughout me.

"I'll leave a note for Miss Mabel to let us sleep in. She won't mind." He lifted me in his arms, and I wrapped my arms around his neck and placed my cheek against his chest. I might not have known what love was before or even had seen it. But I knew I loved him. I knew that no matter what was about to happen, I would always and eternally love him.

I hugged him even tighter.

He laid me in the bed, tucked me in, and leaned in to kiss my forehead as he had done before. I couldn't see him in the dark, but I could tell he was turning to leave me. I felt moisture rising in my eyes, my heart hurting.

How can he leave me here alone?

Of course, I was silly. His bed was only six feet away from mine. However, it felt like miles, and the dream felt more like inches.

I felt the bed move. Hunter was next to me, with his arm out to wrap around me.

"I'm probably being a little overprotective and will get an earful later, but I think it's best if I stay close to you."

"I was thinking the same thing," I whispered back with a little quiver in my voice.

He must have realized I was crying again, as his hand went up to wipe my tears again. *What he must think of me. I hate this new pathetic me. I should look him in the eyes and tell him that I'm just fine and I can take care of myself.*

The other voice said, *You should walk out the door and save everyone you love from destruction.*

The voice was right again, but I suddenly felt very sleepy, relaxed by the rise and fall of his chest.

"Jess?" he whispered, whirling a strand of hair in his finger.

"Yes?" I asked in a yawn, now letting sleep come, feeling safe once again.

"Never mind." He sighed and yawned himself. "No more dreams," he whispered softly.

"No more dreams," I echoed.

We woke up late, like Hunter had suggested. Everyone else was already up and out of the house by the time we woke. Hunter hadn't moved. He was still holding me as I popped my head up to see his face. Of course he was awake.

"How long have you been awake?" I asked.

"Not long." He smiled at me, tucking my hair behind my ear. "How do you feel?"

"Good, I guess."

"That must have been some dream. You were really upset."

"It felt so real." Thinking about the hot breath on my neck, I reached back to feel it. It felt normal.

"What?" He sat up to look at the back of my neck.

"Just something in the dream. It felt like it was burned," I answered, and then examined the palms of my hands.

He looked at the back of my neck, lifting up my hair, which caused me to giggle. He caressed the back of my neck with the tips of his fingers, sending those familiar tingles all over.

"Looks and feels normal to me," he said and then cleared his throat.

Does he really not know what he's doing to me? I turned to face him with half smile planted on my face.

"What?" He laughed. His eyes were almost sinister, sort of a different look for him.

"If you have to ask, then I shouldn't tell you," I said and went to get up, but he grabbed my hand and pulled me back to him.

"Sorry." He laughed nervously. "You're not making things easy for me."

"And what does that mean exactly?"

"I think it means we need to get dressed. The ladies from the church will be here soon to pick up the pies. I'm sure you don't want them to see you sitting here with me in your clothes from yesterday," Hunter teased.

The dream was too real not to mean anything. Hunter wanted me to read that particular chapter for a reason. Davior was not just in some devil cult. *Could he be the devil?* I laughed at my ridiculous thought. It wasn't like the devil walked around in plain sight...*or does he?*

Regardless of what the dream meant, I believed it was a sign of things to come. I was sure of it. What I wasn't sure of was what Hunter meant by me not making thing easy for him.

If he cares about me in a boy-girl way, then why doesn't he just tell me how he feels? Is there a reason we can't be together?

Molly came to mind.

All Dressed Up

It was just before noon when I exited the washroom, ready for our visitors. Hunter jumped in after, and while I waited for him, I continued to read.

I opened my Bible to the first chapter, Genesis, the creation of it all. I knew about Adam and Eve, well, the basic story anyway. I couldn't understand how they could be tempted into believing the serpent. They had paradise, God walking with them, and they wanted more.

Eve wanted the power.

That wouldn't have been my trigger; power over others had never sounded appealing to me. My mother, on the other hand, had been exactly like Eve in that way. She had wanted more than anything to have status, control, and any man she could get it from. She'd twist them into doing what she had wanted. My father had often hesitated at her nonsense requests or requests he hadn't felt right about doing and then he would ultimately give into her, following her down the darker path.

And now Seth. It was clear which path he would have chosen. It would have been him picking the fruit instead of the other way around. I couldn't blame him completely for the way he had been brought up. Most of it had been pounded into him since the day he was born, to succeed above all others at any costs. Meeting my mother had just reinforced the same mental training except for also encouraging him to believe he could rule the world someday. She had worked on building his ego to believe there wasn't another man alive who could compare. It had worked beautifully, and he believed it.

And if Davior is the devil…but how could he be the one and only devil if Hunter is his brother? Demons, they are demons. The blood left my face, and I felt light headed. Hunter was back at my side, dropping the towel he was using to dry his hair.

"You're so pale," he said, putting his extremely warm hands on my face. "Are you dizzy?"

I nodded. I also felt sick, but I didn't share that with him.

"Don't get up," he ordered, moving toward the kitchen and pulling out a plate from of the oven. "You probably need to eat." He smiled gently. "You didn't eat much last night."

"Have they turned into demons? Davior and Seth?"

He tried to feed me, scooping up the dry eggs onto the fork, but I grabbed the fork.

"I can do that," I said.

"You didn't seem to mind last night." He smirked.

"Oh. Well, I was sort of in a trance, so that doesn't count. You haven't answered my question."

He made me take a bite, but the food tasted old and dry.

"Better?" he asked before leaping up.

I nodded. "Okay, so now…"

We both heard cars coming down the path. Hunter stared out the screen door, combing his fingers through his long hair, and then bound it with a rubber band before pulling his boots on.

"Company time," he said with a heavy sigh. "They brought lunch, so don't worry about breakfast."

"I'm okay now," I said, glad I didn't have to finish the plate of food.

"Be good," he whispered in my ear, his lips slightly touching it. Then he inhaled a long, steady breath and sighed.

"You didn't answer my question, and I don't know what you mean about being good," I said.

In a superior tone, he answered, "I know." And with that, he darted out the door, dragging me behind him.

Two cars pulled up along the side of the shack. I knew both.

I was surprised to see Pastor James pull up in his red, beat-up pickup. He wasn't due out until next month, and he'd never brought anyone with him before. A man stepped out of the truck. He was tall and slim with blue eyes and long, straight, light brown hair that was tied in back. With just in a glance, I might have thought he was Hunter, only slightly older.

The other car I knew to be Miss C and Miss B. The three ladies filed out of the van. Miss Caroline immediately whisked me up into an embrace, giving Hunter no choice but to let go of my hand. My eyes stayed on the new person with Pastor James.

"Oh, it's so good to see you!" Miss Caroline sang.

"It hasn't been that long," I started to say before Miss Betsy grabbed me next.

They both seemed happier than usual to see me.

"You look very pretty today," Miss Betsy sang as she hugged me, looking over at Hunter.

He smiled at her with a weird expression. *What's going on?* I watched Hunter turn his eyes back on the person with Pastor James.

Molly stepped out in her usual way. She stumbled on the bottom of her dress and almost fell to the ground. She looked up sharply in confusion Hunter hadn't jump to her aid. However, his eyes stayed on the stranger. I was amazed at how quickly she recovered before hitting the ground. She patted down her ruffled-up, long dress before noticing Hunter's fingers were laced with mine.

I felt awkward, the way she pretended not to notice.

"Hello, Jessica," Molly said dryly. "I hope you are well."

"I'm good. Thanks." I tried to sound friendly. After all, I didn't dislike her, not really. I might have been jealous of her relationship with Hunter and the way she treated May. I had thoughts of drowning her. *Maybe I do dislike her.*

The crease in her forehead deepened, as it pained her to even speak to me. It was then her expression changed, as she noticed Hunter's attention was elsewhere. Her eyes narrowed, sending me the nonverbal message she wasn't going to give him up without a fight.

Hunter's attention changed and caught part of Molly's disdained look. I tightened my grip on his hand, hoping he would understand my gesture. I could handle it.

Molly changed her expression very quickly.

"Hello, Hunter," she said in a melancholy tone.

She watched his hand let go of mine and then move around my waist as he gently pulled me closer to his side. *That wasn't what I meant my by hand squeeze.*

"Hello, Molly. It's nice to see you." His tone wasn't rude, but it wasn't friendly either.

She looked away from his glare, but her skin began to look red, like a bad sunburn. I couldn't tell if it was because she was embarrassed or really mad.

I grimaced at him so he knew I disapproved of his tone. I could handle her looks of disapproval, but he didn't waver. He leaned to my ear but no words came out.

"We have something for you, Jessica." Miss Betsy interrupted.

Miss Caroline grabbed my arm and once again pulled me from Hunter. She took out a garment bag and tossed it into my arms before she grabbed out two more bags.

"Hunter, shoo. You have other things to attend to." She motioned him away from us as she hurried me into the house.

Hunter tried to follow us, and then Miss Betsy said in a pretend soft voice, "She'll be safe with us. Go."

How would they know to keep me safe? I'd be the one keeping them safe!

Everyone around me knew more than I did, leaving me stewing in frustration. *Why haven't I asked more questions? Why didn't I press Hunter to answer more questions?*

The screen door opened, and I looked back at Hunter, standing where Miss Betsy stopped him. Pastor James and the other man moved alongside him, and they all turned to walk into the woods.

I felt an uncertain achy feeling. He wasn't supposed to leave me.

"Lunch first and then a makeover," Miss Caroline said, holding a picnic basket in her other hand. She pulled out little sack lunches.

"What about the guys and Miss Mabel?" I asked. "Should I get them?" I started to bolt out the door.

"No, no. They have already been taken care of, my dear. No worries." Miss Caroline flashed me a big-toothed smile and handed me lunch.

I went straight for the swing, hoping I could see Hunter out near the tree line. No such luck.

May followed behind me, sitting next to me in the swing. Molly came out next and sat on the step with Josephine.

"I didn't see Joseph when we pulled up," Molly said to Josephine.

"No. He's been…well, gone for a few days," she answered.

"Where did he go?" Molly pursued.

"Where he usually goes." Josephine said, and the two looked over at me, and Molly grinned. She liked knowing the secrets being kept from me. "Still pouting, I'm sure."

May spoke with her mouth full, "I've wanted to ask you something, but I'm not sure how to ask."

"You can ask me anything, May. You should know that by now," I said.

She shrugged her shoulders.

"You and Hunter have been spending a lot of time together."

Molly stopped talking and listened for May's question. I know if I were her, I wouldn't have liked hearing "a lot of time together." By the look on her face, I'd bet on it.

"Well, do you love him?" She looked up at me, and I felt a hot flow of blood rush to my cheeks.

How do I answer that? He is my Prince Charming, and I am finally giving in. It still doesn't mean he feels the same or that a relationship is possible between us. There is so much more going on than just this little world here. I'm still not even sure I'm staying.

I might have told her I loved him if it were just us, but with Molly leering at me, waiting to hear my answer, I didn't want to reply and be the cause of more uncomfortable moments between Molly and me.

May put her small hand in my lap. "I'm glad. He's been alone for too long," she said.

I didn't have to answer to make Molly furious. Her eyes met mine with the same look as before, only instead of just her anger, I felt her sadness as well.

"Okay. Are we ready?" Miss Caroline sang, motioning for us to go inside the shack. We filed into the room, with Molly lingering behind. "I have something for all the girls."

"And we can't have anyone peeking." Miss Betsy giggled, shutting the front door and pulling the curtains over the windows.

Molly stood in a corner, not really participating in the excitement flowing out of the ladies.

Miss C pulled out the three long garment bags. I had seen plenty of those. She laid two on a bed and hung one up on the door jam. She slowly unzipped the bag. I giggled when she gasped. It was a little, over-the-top expression.

The first dress was for Josephine, and it had turquoise with white roses throughout. The bottom had a thick eyelet lace around the hem. I looked over at her, thinking she wasn't the sort to get all girly. Her eyes grew large and sparkly.

"For me?" Josephine managed to utter softly.

Miss C nodded, and then Josephine jumped up and hugged the ladies, especially Molly.

"You're welcome." Molly smiled.

Evidently, the hostility just shot my way.

"You'll look very pretty in it. We have shoes and ribbons to match too," Molly said and showed her the big bag filled with all kinds of hair trimmings and makeup stuff.

My mother had been the queen of pretty dresses and frilly things, all the things I never cared much for. I really didn't want them dressing me up like some poor girl who needed to feel pretty. I had closets full of dresses, some I never wore. Some were from rare designers that my mother paid an insane amount of money for. Yet, I knew these ladies didn't have much.

Who was I to take that away from them? If I protested them dressing me up, how would May and Josephine feel? I decided to let go of my stubbornness and enjoyed the day with them.

The next dress pulled out of the garment bag was pink with white roses, and it screamed May. A white, sleeveless jacket hung over the embroidered details. The dress looked like May—frilly, pink, and beautiful. Of course, she completely loved it and hugged everyone around the room. She took it off the hanger and started to put it on, and then Josephine hoisted hers in the air and over her head.

"I saved yours for last, Jessica." Miss C unzipped it very slowly and pulled off the bag.

I stared at it for a moment. One thing I noticed about all the dresses, they were handmade—beautiful, but handmade. My dress was made from a silk-like, thin material and not frilly or lacey like the others. The white, embroidered roses along the bottom were of such fine, intricate detail, I knew it took some time to do. I felt touched someone would do something like this for me.

"I didn't think you were into the girly, lacey things like the other two. You can wear this just about anytime, anywhere," Miss B said and smiled. "Do you like it?"

"I…I love it. It's beautiful," I answered, holding back the tears.

"Okay. Now everyone needs to put them on to make sure they fit, and then I have another surprise," Miss B said. "Jessica, you can use the washroom to change if it makes you more comfortable. The other two are fine out here."

That's what I did. I took off the clothes I was wearing and neatly folded them and then slipped on the dress. It was light and flowing and felt natural against my skin. Of course, my hair didn't match, since I had it tied up into a wild-looking knot.

I stepped out of the bathroom, and the ladies, except Molly, clapped their hands in excitement.

"Didn't I tell you?" Miss C said to Miss B.

"Yes, yes, but we definitely need to do something with her hair," Miss B said with a little bit of concern.

The other two girls looked just beautiful. Even Josephine twirled around. She was so different when Joseph wasn't near her.

Molly jumped up. "I'll do May and Josephine's hair," she said, digging through the bag she had brought.

"Perfect." Miss C made her way to me along with Miss B. "Jessica, you need to stay still unless you want Betsy yanking out your hair." She winked over at her, and she stuck her tongue out playfully.

I sat in the chair they placed in front of me. I wasn't happy about all this fuss. It just reminded me of my mother, whom I would have rather *not* thought about. The ladies talked among themselves as if I wasn't there. I focused my thoughts on everyone else and how much they were enjoying all the pampering.

"You know, I didn't think you really could do it, but you did," one of the ladies said to the other.

The chatter had been so loud and for so long I couldn't tell who was speaking to whom. I had heard Molly giggle with the girls from time to time, so I felt glad she was enjoying herself too, although I could do without the dagger glances in between.

"Of course, she's beautiful. God gets the credit for the foundation to work with. I just polished it up." I looked up, and it was Miss Betsy. She motioned for me to stand up.

"Give us a twirl."

Both ladies were clapping their hands joined by May's and Josephine's clapping.

I looked over at the girls, and they looked like china dolls. They were beautiful.

My mind interjected, *Why? We don't go anywhere. Why get us all dressed up?*.

From the dimness in the room, I could tell the sun had fallen behind the tall tree line, which meant it was about five o'clock or so. Just then, a knock fell on the door. The ladies fell over themselves in a panic.

"One moment please," one of them called.

Molly made it over to the door and was about to open it. Something made her put her hands in front of her and her head down.

Miss Caroline hurried me out the back door. She could see the confusion on my face.

"It's okay, dear." She got me out before anyone entered. "Ah, Cinderella!" she exclaimed, admiring her work, and then we went around to the side of the house.

She stood me in front of the red maple tree out of everyone's sight, just to the left of the house. Such an elaborate plan, and I felt silly standing there. She told me to stay, and she left.

It wasn't a second later Hunter stormed around the corner of the porch. He looked frantic at first, scanning the area with his eyes, and then he saw me and stopped. His eyes lit up, and the panic subsided.

I took a shy step toward him, looking down. I felt so impractical all dressed up, a thick covering smeared over my face, my hair up in a loose bun with stray curls dangling down. I was ready to explain to him how they really wanted to do it and I didn't feel right telling them no.

I glanced up, and there he was, close enough to touch. I quickly looked back down, looking at my feet. I had on thin, white, jute sandals with gemstones tucked around in a pattern to look like a rose.

He touched my face and lifted up my chin. I couldn't miss his tender, loving expression. I looked up at him with puppy dog eyes. He chuckled.

"You are radiant."

"I feel silly," I added, fidgeting with the dress.

"You were a pretty good sport to let them work on you," he said and encircled his arm around me.

"I would have broken their hearts if I had refused. I couldn't have that on my conscience." I was starting to get over the initial embarrassment, his embrace feeling more natural.

"I'm glad you let them, although you are beautiful in whatever you wear and your hair is just as lovely after a good night's sleep." He twirled around one of curls dangling along my face.

Someone cleared their throat, and we noticed we were no longer alone, with many eyes on us. Hunter read my face and turned around to see everyone watching us. The ladies were absolutely giddy, and Miss Mabel joined them. I could see her approval all over her face. Pastor James just gazed, and Hunter must have shot him a look because he looked away and blushed.

The new person stood there without emotion. Hunter placed one arm around my waist and led me to him.

"Jessica, this is…John Fox."

"Hello," I said.

John smiled slightly and nodded in a very graceful way.

"He would like to talk to you for a few minutes," Hunter said, staring into John's eyes.

The look caused my nerves to go into overtime.

"It's okay," Hunter whispered. "You're actually safer with John than anyone else, including me. He just wants to ask you few questions."

Questions? Told you it's time to leave. The voice spoke up so loud, I was sure everyone else heard it, but if they had, they pretended not to. I did think of Davior that time. *Could he be in my head? Pushing my thoughts like Hunter said?*

"Let's go for a walk, Jessica," John said, taking my elbow gently, and we disappeared into the woods.

"Tell me, Jessica, how did you find your way here?" His voice was deep but soft.

I thought about everything at once and all I'd experienced since I'd been there. I didn't want to tell any more lies, so I told him the whole story, starting with my father and his beliefs. I told him about my mother and our deals and about Seth. I hesitated when it came to the light, unsure if that was real or not. But I told him anyway. I told him of my meeting with Davior and the dreams, as we walked among the deep-green trees.

John listened carefully to everything I said and then asked, "A light led you to a postcard in the sand, and then the same light led you off the road and here?" He stopping walking.

"No. I had already wandered into the forest and gotten lost. That was when I saw the light. I was ready to give up and try to make my way back to the road, but then I saw the light."

"You're father, was he your natural father?"

That is a strange question to ask me. Would I have given my life for a step-father?

"Of course he was. If it hadn't been for the attack, he would have taken me away a long time ago, a special place where she couldn't touch me," I said, remembering the scene Davior had showed me. I believed she wanted him dead and had planned the whole thing.

He paused for a moment, looking into my eyes. The nervous feeling subsided as his face softened and we started to walk again.

"Thank you, Jessica. I have enjoyed talking with you, and I appreciate your honesty ," John said as we were coming out of the trees, and Hunter sprinted toward us.

"Jessica, can I have a moment with my son?" John asked.

I nodded and walked over to May, standing on the front steps.

Hunter's father? How is that possible? John couldn't have been more than few years older, ten years maybe, but that would be stretching it.

Everyone chatted on the porch, but I watched the two men in conversation. Hunter didn't look too happy and kept glancing over at me.

You still have time to leave. No one would notice. He knows you're putting his son in danger.

"Be quiet," I said, and everyone looked at me. "Sorry, I was talking to myself."

"Look, they're coming back. I hope we can go," Josephine said.

"Go where?" I asked at the same time everyone exited the porch and ran toward them. I followed.

"You know what needs to be done. Don't make the situation worse," John said, putting his hand on Hunter's shoulder.

"Yes, sir. I know."

"James, time to go," John called out. "I'll see everyone tonight." He smiled big and winked at me. "My wife will be delighted to meet you."

Miss Caroline and Miss Betsy high-fived each other at John's announcement, and Josephine jumped up and down with excitement.

Pastor James hugged Hunter and then hugged me. "See you tonight."

Hunter nodded.

The ladies started for their car, pausing to give me and Hunter a big squeeze. "Have fun tonight," Miss Caroline sang while Miss Betsy tried to hush her.

Molly walked over to us, limping, another feeble attempt to draw Hunter's attention away from me. I had to give her credit. It had worked before.

Hunter didn't move.

Molly stared in disbelief. If I could read her mind, tally all the looks she gave me today, I would bet she was plotting my demise. Hopefully, that was just my overactive imagination at work.

As our visitors left, the five of us watched everyone drive away. Molly looked out the back window, bewildered.

"She's sure not happy with me. I feel sorry for her," I said.

"That's my fault, and I'm sorry," he said through his tight lip. "She knows I've never had those types of feelings for her. She shouldn't be taking it out on you." He sighed and faced me. "I didn't like the way she was looking at you."

"It's hard to resist your charm. It's not entirely her fault either," I said.

He gave me a troubled smile but then changed his tone in one big breath.

"So, are you up for a little party?" He smiled, changing the topic from Molly.

"Ah, was that what this was all about?" I motioned to my dress and hair.

"Why are you so suspicious?" he asked.

I laughed. "Suspicious would mean that I have some sort of clue to what's going on. I've got nothing!" I added.

"Good," he chimed.

Enchanted Ball

Hunter led me back to the house.

"Now it's my turn," he said as he stepped into the washroom.

It wasn't long after he stepped through the doorway, wearing a black suit with a white, button-up dress shirt underneath. His eyes twinkled at me as he winked and did a quick spin on his heels. He put male models around the world to shame.

"You are breathtaking," I managed to say as the words seemed to linger in the air and made my heart thump loudly.

Could it even be possible that someone like him could be in love with me? Once again, the gatherings of insecurity were coming to an order, all sitting around the table of doubt. However, the strong voice, the one telling me to leave, stayed quiet.

Hunter's hand reached out for mine. I could feel his pulse racing through his wrists.

"No. You're the one who's breathtaking," he said, looking at me and then quickly away. "Ready?" he asked, clearing his voice.

"Yes," I said, trying to breathe normally. "Where are the others?"

"Oh, they left already. It's just us."

Hunter held my hand and led me out the back screen door. We didn't walk far before I saw a white horse standing proud with white beads laced in its mane and attached to his harness. The harness was attached to an old buggy with four large wooden wheels. Now it was official; Cinderella was going to the ball with her Prince Charming.

And he is very charming.

The coming night consisted of soft rays of light holding on to the day as the darkness pushed it back, forcing some stars to twinkle. The air smelled like fresh cut roses and felt soft against my cheek. The horse led the buggy across our lazy creek and then followed the snakelike bend, heading south. We stayed close to the creek but in front of the tree line. I watched the stars get brighter, clearer, as the sun completely disappeared. The dark shadows of the swamp that haunted me in my dreams now felt welcoming and peaceful. Little lights danced around us, but this time, I knew for sure they were fireflies.

Maybe I was in another one of those dreams, and if I was, let me sleep forever. Afraid to speak, I glanced over at Hunter. He looked nervous, scanning the area around us. I tried to be inconspicuous as I slowly slid my body closer to his. I felt his body relax a little, but he didn't remove his eyes from ahead of the horse.

Then the carriage stopped. We hadn't traveled far, so I was confused about where the party was. The party couldn't be in the middle of the marsh, the place Miss Mabel said people were kept out of by the smell, although there were no sour or decaying odors, just the sweet perfume of flowers.

Hunter helped me down from the seat and then whisked me up in his arms. He looked at my shoes, and I understood. The ground looked very gooey, but he seemed to know where to step without losing a shoe himself. He carried me through a set of dark, moss-covered trees.

"Close your eyes," Hunter whispered.

I did without question as he continued forward. I felt a tingling feeling similar to when a hand or foot goes numb, except it felt lovely all over my body. But it didn't last long.

"Okay. Open them," he said, setting me down on the hard path.

A beautiful house, all lit up, sat in the middle of the swamp. I looked down at my feet, noticing the cobblestone path. I followed it with my eyes as it wound up toward the front of the house.

Hunter tried to read my thoughts, his eyes not leaving my face. *Did he not think I would be impressed?* The front of the house reminded me of the old, colonial-style houses with white, round pillars and grand entrances. On one side, a huge glass dome, that looked like a fancy greenhouse, was filled with people. I could hear music and people laughing, escaping out into the air.

"It's stunning. Why out here in the middle of the swamp?" I asked.

"It's more like a compound with a fancy exterior. At any one time, it can house around fifty people. But there is more to it than just what you see ," he said.

"Really? But why out here? Who stays here?"

"I'll answer all your questions. I promise." He held both my hands. "But if I don't get you in there soon, someone might send out a search party." He chuckled, his eyes no longer scanning for danger. "You're safe here. I want you to have fun tonight. Don't worry about anything." He reached out to touch my cheek.

My legs wobbled slightly at his touch. He looked past me, toward the house, and nodded before moving forward.

Someone was watching us.

We entered into a luxurious ballroom bigger than anything I had ever seen or imagined. Everything in the room seemed to sparkle, from the flower vase on each round, laced table, to crystal chandeliers dangling above. Curved glass windows surrounded the entire ceiling, allowing millions of stars to beam down on the marble floor.

There were many small conversations going on all over the room, creating a soft buzzing noise which bounced off the windows. Someone played a piano soft and low so it wouldn't distract from the conversations. My mother would have called this cocktail hour, where everyone was supposed to mingle. It was at those parties I would stand in a corner or on the bottom step of the staircase, trying *not* to be seen.

We crossed over the threshold of double-wide doors, and the music stopped. The soft buzz got even softer until it ceased all together and all eyes were on me. I cowered back behind Hunter, and he tightened his grip on my hand, letting a low chuckle escape from his lips.

"There's no need to be scared, Jessie. They've all come here to meet you," he said, smiling and pulling me back next to his side.

"Why?" I whispered.

Hunter didn't have time to answer, as people were introducing themselves and talking to me like they'd known me forever. There was a lot of, "Nice to meet you," and, "I've heard so much about you," but other than that, it was all a blur.

My eyes were fixed elsewhere. A woman, slender, tall, and blonde, with radiant, flowing hair was approaching.

Hunter's mother, I guessed based on her similar look, but she looked so young, the same as his father, not near old enough to have grown sons.

My mother would hate her.

The woman moved toward me as she glided gracefully across the floor, keeping her eyes locked on me. She carried an approving smile on her lips, but it didn't calm my mental strain. Her dress elegantly glistened like the rest of the room and flowed from her shoulders all the way down to the floor.

What will she think of me? I felt underdressed next to her.

Hunter followed my eyes and smiled. The pianist started another low melody, and the crowd went back to mini conversations around the room.

"Hello, Mother," Hunter sang, still not releasing my hand but swinging his other arm around her in a hug.

People, meanwhile, still chatted away at me.

"Love your dress."

"He is quite the catch," another whispered.

"It's been awhile, son." His mother's small hand stroked his face and moved along his hair.

"I know. I'm sorry."

"I hear it's for good reason, so I forgive you." She kissed his cheek and leaned in to Hunter's ear. "Although, you should try to speak to Joseph, if he hasn't left already. He's still quite upset."

"Later."

"I know you don't mean to, son, but you can't drop everyone else in your life. You need to keep a balance," she said in a whisper.

How could he when he stayed near me all the time? No wonder Joseph hated me. I took Hunter away from him.

"Your father has good reasons for his suspicions, son. Don't push it. Give him time."

Even though it wasn't meant for me to hear, I knew she meant me.

"I know," he mumbled.

His mother knows you're trouble. Find your moment to sneak away before they throw you out. Cross over the cobblestone path. They won't follow you.

I took a few steps away from Hunter and looked out through the glass walls and past the lights that lined the path. I expected to see red, glowing eyes but saw nothing.

"Mother, this is my Jessica."

Hunter changed the conversation, pulling me away from the window. He announced it proudly, which made my cheeks feel hot.

"Jessica, this is Annabel, my mother."

"I'm honored to meet you," I said in sort of a curtsy position. After all, she did look like royalty.

Hunter snickered at my gesture, but his mother shot him a look that said, "Behave."

I quickly stood upright and offered my hand instead. She took it with both her hands. They were warm and soft, like the look in her eyes. "No, child. It's my honor."

She doesn't hate me. That's a relief.

"We will have another time to chat and get to know one another later. Enjoy the rest of the party."

"Thank you," I said, and she left us to join John in the middle of the ballroom.

The music stopped as I watched other instruments being brought up to the stage, and a short man stood at the microphone. A large semicircle formed along the dance floor. All were watching the man at the microphone as they quieted down.

"We'd like to start the evening off with a slow dance," he said, turning to the band with his hands positioned high in the air. Down his hands went, and the music began to play.

John and Annabel didn't move at first. John looked just as handsome as she did beautiful. They looked at each other with a love I envied. John then walked to the center of the circle and twirled her around before securely locking her to his body. They kissed softly before they started to navigate across the dance floor. Her eyes never left him as they kept in step with each other around the room.

They danced brilliantly, leaving everyone breathless with their hearts pounding and their faces flushed. The music stopped, and John lifted Annabel in the air, his hands on her hips, and then brought her back down, where she wrapped her arms around his neck.

The audience clapped loudly and cheered.

The music began again, only now it was a much faster tempo. The man on the stage flung his arms around, trying to keep up. I found it funny. He looked like a bird flapping its wings to take flight.

I felt someone pulling me out toward the dance floor, and it wasn't Hunter.

"May I?" his father asked.

Hunter nodded as he took his mother's hand.

Nervously, I let John lead me out to the dance floor. He whirled me around, having perfect control over my movements. I noticed others were beginning to join the dance floor. I wasn't a very good dancer, but it didn't matter. John was a good lead. I almost felt like a rag doll being tossed around since I couldn't feel the floor beneath my feet. It was so exhilarating. I smiled so much my face hurt.

If John disliked me or didn't trust me, it didn't show.

Hunter must have been a good student. I watched him lead his mother across the dance floor. However, they seemed to be in conversation most of the time. It must have been good and not about Joseph, because he couldn't stop smiling and laughing with her.

The music changed again, back to the softer, calmer melody. John twirled me out of his arms and across the floor. I thought I was going to fall until a familiar person caught me in his arms. John and Annabel joined each other in a tight embrace.

Hunter tightened his arms around my waist, pulling me close to his chest. I rested my cheek against his chest and closed my eyes, my arms intertwined around his neck, his cheek against my hair. We swayed slowly, our hearts beating to the same rhythm. His hand was wide on the small of my back, sending brilliant shivers throughout my body.

I liked this kind of dancing too. Nothing else existed around me, and my thoughts were silent—all of them. The sound of his heart beat in my ears. His protective arms around me seemed too good to be true. And then the music changed back to an upbeat tune. Hunter didn't change his sway, nor did I, as everyone danced around us.

"Excuse me," I heard someone say.

We both looked up. It was Pastor James.

"May I?" He cleared his throat.

"Of course," Hunter said, offering my hand with a half smile.

We both caught a glimpse of Joseph standing in the corner of the room, and I urged Hunter to go to him. I hoped they could work out their issues. I hoped Joseph would change the way he felt about me.

Pastor James wasn't a very good dancer, but he was a great storyteller, and it kept me from watching Hunter and Joseph.

"It was our first time hunting without adults. Neither Hunter nor I enjoyed the whole hunting thing, but it was a part of our culture that we went out at a certain age and brought back our first kill. If we didn't, the other boys would have not let us live it down, and the elders would have punished us in some way not pleasant. It was also a disgrace to the family if you didn't. So there was a lot pressure not to come back empty handed.

"We had been out most of the day, and still, not one of us had caught anything. We saw rabbits, squirrels, and some deer, but we just couldn't point the arrow and shoot a living thing. We ran across an old log. If we brought back a snake, that would be good enough, and we both didn't care for them as much as other animals. We looked inside, hoping to find one curled up, but instead, we found two raccoons, and they weren't moving. At first, we thought they were sleeping, but after making some loud noises and shaking the log, we realized they were dead. Not really looking too closely, we took two long sticks to pick up the raccoons and put them in our cloth sacks. We tied the bags closed. We were so relieved we didn't have to kill anything and had completed our task.

"We walked to the elders, who were starting to get worried about how long we were gone, and plopped our bags proudly at their feet. It was something to get a raccoon. Most boys went for the easy catch, like rabbits, squirrels, or even large swamp rats, but raccoons—they were fighters.

"The elders knew how we both felt about hunting, so they beamed. They were so proud, especially John. He was one proud father." He paused. "Oh yeah, by the way, I'm Hunter's older brother. I'm sure he hasn't told you yet." He looked over at him. "He knows you know now." He smiled.

"I only know of Davior." I paused but I was not surprised. "Okay. Continue the story."

"Oh yeah. Well, the elders opened my bag first and grabbed the skin of the animal and plopped it down and then Hunter's. If we had looked closer, we would have noticed that they weren't raccoons exactly," James said.

"What were they?"

"Hats. Raccoon hats." He laughed.

I laughed loudly too. Hunter started to make his way back to me, some anxiety on his face. Concerned his brother was embarrassing him, I assumed.

"Wait, that's not the best part. The best part is the hats were ours."

We both laughed loudly, and tears filled my eyes. Others turned to look at us, but it just made me laugh harder until Hunter joined us.

"Ha, ha, ha. Okay, brother. You've had your dance." Hunter faked a chuckle.

The music changed again, soft with a steady beat.

"So now I'm completely embarrassed," he mumbled, wrapping one arm around my waist, and the other holding my hand rested on his chest.

"Really? Your own hats?" I said, wiping the tears away.

"I was young. James should be more embarrassed since he's older." He looked away at James with a smirk.

They shared a mind-to-mind conversation, I assumed, remembering Hunter told me his older brother could communicate through thoughts.

I had never heard of such a thing. The twin thing, I had heard of, but I didn't think they could actually read specific thoughts. Maybe I had misunderstood.

"Well, I think it's an adorable story, and I haven't laughed that hard since…" I held him close to me, catching him off guard. "Never," I whispered. "It felt good, really good."

"Oh, well, in that case, I'm sure you'll hear all kinds of adorable things about me. Besides, I like hearing you laugh, even if it's at my expense." He twirled me around at one of the faster parts of the song, bringing me back to him.

"Did you speak to Joseph?" I asked.

"He's not being reasonable," he snapped, and then changed his tone. "I don't want to think about him tonight." His nose touched my ear.

A low grunt escaped his lips as he felt someone other than me tapping his shoulder.

"My turn." A tall boy with reddish-brown hair and freckles stood before us.

"Paul, Jessica. Jessica, Paul," Hunter said in defeat, giving over my hand.

"Charmed." He lifted my hand and kissed it.

Hunter raised his eyebrow at him.

"Shall we, my lady?" he asked, and off we went.

I must have danced with half a dozen boys before falling back into the comfort of Hunter's arms. I couldn't help but wonder if we were being kept apart on purpose.

"I need some air," I managed to say, completely out of breath.

"Let's step out to the courtyard," Hunter suggested nervously.

I caught Molly staring from the corner of the room, her eyes following us out the door. She looked sad and angry, trying to catch Hunter's attention, but it was no use. She was invisible to him.

Out in the courtyard, Hunter sat me down on a large marble bench. "I'll be right back." He started to walk off and then turned to me. "Now don't wander off. Stay right where you are," he said with more concern in his voice, scanning the area with his eyes as he spoke, before heading back inside.

My eyes adjusted to the light of the courtyard, and then I was able to see the beauty. I was surrounded by angels made of marble, each different from the other. In the middle of the courtyard, a garden of tall, purple, pink, and white wildflowers grew, and along the outline of the court, an outer path with tall, wide, cylinder-shaped fire pits burned, lighting up the entire area. The path was made of polished stone and reflected the soft glow of lights coming from inside. The air smelled clean and fresh, like after a rainstorm on a summer day. I took a big, long, cleansing breath.

I was alone in the majesty of it all except for the music, which was soft and faint as it glided in the air, and I felt completely safe.

Hunter entered the courtyard, walking slowly with a cup in each hand. His eyes once again looked past me, purposely not on me, as he handed me a cup.

"Thanks." I took a sip, wrapping both hands around the cup.

He sat next to me, placing both his hands in his lap, looking even more uneasy than before.

"How are you feeling now?" he asked, a quiver in his tone.

"Better. I've never done so much dancing before."

I smiled in his direction, but his eyes were turned down, looking at his shoes.

It was the first time I had ever danced because I wanted to. At the parties my mother had, I was forced to dance with old, smelly men. Once, Seth tried to dance with me, but I intentionally kept stepping on his feet. I pretended it was an accident over and over again. I stepped hard, and eventually, he decided it wasn't worth having swollen feet and hobbling for the next few days after. I had been a pretty good actress when it came to deceiving Seth.

As we sat in silence, I wished for something more to say. We sat for the longest time, listening to the music change from slow to fast, from fast to slow. I could tell that he was thinking about something, perhaps something John might have said to him.

Suddenly, Hunter was on his feet and pulled me into his arms. The cup fell to ground, bouncing a few times before settling in one spot. The music was playing once again, soft, slow, and lovely, like in a white, fluffy cloud dream, and he held me like he had when we danced. He swayed slowly, holding one of my hands against his chest, the other on the small of my back.

He pulled me back slightly. Our eyes locked into each other. I felt a rush of hot blood move to my face, feeling the sting in my cheeks. His eyes flashed over every inch of it, and his right arm moved from around my waist, and then his fingertips touched the outline of my face. Our chests pounded together, almost at the same tempo, and it echoed in my ears. I no longer heard any other sounds. I closed my eyes, hoping this would be it, my first kiss. He moved in closer, brushing his lips against my eyes, each one, and then moving slowly down my cheek. My body felt uncontrollably anxious as his lips were near my ear.

He whispered, "No matter what happens now, I want you to know that I care about you deeply." He continued across to my nose and kissed it.

He pulled back again. I opened my eyes, afraid he was going to stop, afraid he was coming to his senses. His face showed he was unsure of what he was going to do. If it was my approval he wanted, he should have known he had it.

He's too good for you. You know that.

The voice was right.

My eyes wandered past Hunter, and I felt a wave of disappointment come over my face. I didn't mean for it, I didn't plan it, but it was obvious; I wasn't good enough for him, and I knew it.

His hand moved to my chin, directing me back to his face. My eyes filled with tears. One moment, I was on the highest mountaintop, looking at endless possibilities, and the next, I was at the bottom of a ravine, so deep there was no light.

I turned my back to him, and he grasped on to to my hand.

I whispered, "I'm not good enough for you. I should leave before anyone gets hurt." My voiced was choked.

Finally, you've come to your senses. I heard the voice and squeezed my eyes shut. *Get out of my head.*

Hunter pulled my hand and turned me back around. And with a big smile on his face, he pressed his lips to mine. I felt my body relax into his. His kiss, although hard at first, turned soft and gentle over and over again. I returned the kiss, not able to tell his lips apart from mine as they melded together. A thousand, no, a trillion little shocks rang throughout my body, and I melted into him.

The moment wasn't quite perfect, as the strange voice boomed in my head.

You're putting everyone in danger.

I pressed harder against his lips, defying the voice growing louder until I noticed the music had stopped and we were being watched.

Someone in the shadows cleared his throat. The sound pulled us apart, and Hunter dropped his arms to his side and quickly turned with a smirk on his face.

John stood in the shadows. "Jessica, would you mind playing something for us?" It sounded more like a command than a request.

I'm not very good, I thought, gaining control of my erratically beating heart, but I nodded my head at his request.

"Lovely," John said, glaring at Hunter. "I'd like a few words with you in my office."

"Yes, sir," Hunter answered, and John disappeared back into the darkness.

"I'm sorry…I shouldn't have done that…but it has nothing to do with you not being good enough, and no one is in danger here except you. And as long as I live—" Hunter tried to say more, but I grabbed his shirt and pulled him to me. There was no reason for him to be apologetic. I kissed him that time, lacing my arms around his neck, feeling his arms pull me in closer.

The voice kept trying to squeeze back in, but it was no use. I heard a cry rattle my mind, and then it was gone.

"I think they are all waiting for you to play." He smiled, breathless, his nose touching mine.

"I'm sorry your father doesn't approve." I dropped my hand down to my side.

"It's complicated. I won't be long. I really want to hear you play." He took both my hands and squeezed.

"Don't rush. I'm really not very good, and I'd rather you not hear me," I said.

"I doubt that." He laughed.

Hunter leaned into my ear. "Play something special for me?" he whispered, sending another wave of sensations tickling the back of my head.

How could I not? I was his in every sense of the word. He could have asked me anything at that very moment, and I would have done it—almost anything.

"Okay, but first, I want to know what's going on with you and your dad," I demanded.

"They're waiting on us," he said, but I didn't budge. "I told you, it's complicated, and that's all I can tell you. I want to tell you more, but I can't." Then his eyes caught someone watching us in the shadows, and it wasn't John.

"Molly?" I whispered, looking at the tall, thin shadow staring in our direction.

"Can we go inside now?" he asked.

I nodded hesitantly. *Is this all about Molly?*

We walked into the room just as the announcer spoke my name. Hunter squeezed my hand and then released me to find his father. I walked forward, keeping my eyes focused on the floor. It would not be a good time to fall flat on my face in front of all those watchful eyes. I wondered if Molly saw us kissing as she stood in the darkness. She would enjoy watching me strike the ground. I know I would have if the shoe was on the other foot.

The man leading the band helped me up the steps and to the piano. The keys were bright ivory and shined up at me. I felt like it was talking to me, saying, "Hello, friend." It had been a long time, and how I had missed the touch and the sounds it made.

There was unfamiliar sheet music in front of me, and at the risk of fumbling over notes and chords, I decided to play one of my favorites, one I knew well with its faraway sound that carried me through all the sadness and disappointments of my reality and into my own world of hopeful possibilities.

Without speaking, I started to play.

My hands moved over the keys like the dance I had witnessed between John and Annabel. I drifted into my imagination and danced along with it, but not alone like before. Hunter was by my side. We danced under the white blooms of cherry trees, their white petals floating all around us. We were locked in each other's eyes, twirling around until we both fell down to the ground, laughing. He touched my face and then softly, tenderly kissed me. An explosion of white roses fell from the sky and covered us, all so soft, so lovely, followed by another kiss, lasting longer, with more passion than before.

And then the music was over.

Tears streamed down my face, but not from sadness. They were tears of release, emotions that were old, emotions that were new, emotions that were beyond words.

I didn't hear applause until I looked up and saw just about everyone had a tear in their eye, even Molly, who quickly wiped them when she noticed me looking at her. Then everyone applauded loudly.

The announcer offered his hand as I stood up.

"Brilliant. Just brilliant." He applauded. "Promise me you'll play for us again soon?"

I nodded.

The man started to help me down the stairs, but Hunter stood ready to claim me with his eyes glistening.

"You are amazing," he said, choking back the tears in his throat.

Another song began to play. He wiped my tears and swung me around into his embrace.

"I have to ask. You told me when you play, you imagine you are somewhere else. Where were you this time when you played?" His face was turned to the side, leaning his cheek to my forehead as we danced.

"With you," I whispered.

"Why were you crying?" he asked, sounding a little concerned, holding me closer.

"I guess I'm not very good at hiding my emotions. I was happy." I giggled a little, feeling embarrassed.

"So you weren't thinking about what you told me earlier?" he asked.

"What?" I asked, really not remembering anything before the kiss.

"That silly talk about you not being good enough, putting everyone in danger," he said.

"No," I answered, even though I still thought it. *Unfortunately enough for him, I'd rather be selfish at the moment.*

"Good," he said. "Because if you did leave, I would go after you, and then my whole family would be involved, and—"

"Okay, okay. I get the point." I laughed.

Then I had no choice but to stay. I then heard a sound like teeth grinding behind a door. I looked at Hunter, but it wasn't coming from him, and then to my right to see Molly heading in our direction with her nose turned upward.

"May I?" she cooed, not taking her cold eyes off me.

Hunter held me tighter, not at all being courteous.

"Of course." I handed him over similarly to how he had all night to various takers.

It was a strange feeling. I could feel him watching me walk away. I reached the edge of the dance floor and turned around to watch Molly draw him closer, but he kept pushing her back to arm's length. I thought about stepping out into the courtyard again but was whisked away by another man I had yet to meet.

I still kept watch over Hunter and Molly. Hunter's face was so stern, and he tried to watch me, but Molly did her best to stop him. He had a look of pain in his eyes and was in need of rescue. She, on the other hand, chatted away and laughed at her own words.

"I'm Jordan, by the way," he said, trying to get my attention. "She's in her own little world, you know."

And that did it. "What do you mean?" I asked, looking at Jordan.

"Oh, you didn't know? Interesting." He stopped speaking.

"You might be surprised at how much I don't know." I looked away, back at Hunter.

His gazed locked with mine.

"Oh, don't worry. You'll know everything soon enough. At least I think John will get over his…well, protectiveness. You just being here is a sign, and besides, you don't look—"

"What about Molly?" I interrupted. I already got the impression his father didn't approve; it only confirmed he feared the danger I was putting his son in, but with Molly, I was dying to find out what her deal was.

"Oh, sorry," he said. "Well, in our culture, usually, our parents pick out our future mates."

Oh no. I knew where it was going instantly. *Why didn't he tell me when he knew what I was going through?* For the first time, I was mad at him. *How could he not tell me?*

Jordan watched me grind my top teeth along my bottom teeth, and then he looked over at Hunter and shrugged his shoulders.

"Go ahead, continue," I said.

"His parents picked out Molly, but Hunter knew all along she wasn't the girl he was supposed to be with. After many years, our parents realized forcing people to love one another is the same as God forcing us to love Him. God wanted us to choose Him, so, in that respect, Hunter was free to choose a girl he loved. It's been a long time, Jess. We joked he would be like Paul, from the Bible, who believed it was better to stay celibate and devote his life to God rather than marry. Of course, that wasn't really funny. Paul had a great ministry. It just didn't seem right for him." He looked over at Hunter almost apologetically.

From the corner of my eye, I could see Hunter trying to wiggle away from Molly.

"I assume Molly felt differently," I said.

"Pretty obvious, isn't it?" He laughed and then became serious. "Although she's worse now. At least before, there was a chance for her. Now she realizes the truth, but it doesn't mean she'll give up easily."

"What truth?"

"I think our dance is over." Jordan smiled and kissed my hand, which Hunter snatched out of his hands.

They looked at each other for a moment, and Jordan smiled. They exchanged a quick hug while Jordan whispered something in his ear, and Hunter nodded before he took off into the crowd.

"I'm sorry." He sighed. "I should have told you sooner. I really thought after she saw me with you, she'd understand. I really didn't think she'd take it out on you, and I'm so sorry for that. Are you angry with me?" he asked, his lips pressed to my hair.

Yes, I am mad, I thought, *but how am I any different?* I kept Seth from him, and I knew, I knew all along he'd go to any measure to hurt anyone who kept me from him. *And still can.*

"No." I huffed and snuggled into his embrace.

He didn't say another word, just held me close.

I was glad that there hadn't been much conversation. I'd much rather be right there, with him holding me like I was the most important person in the room. I didn't want any more interruptions, no more questions. I hadn't wanted the night to end. Nothing could have been more perfect except for the looks John continued to shoot over toward Hunter. Hunter hadn't behaved the way John wanted him to. We were like two beings clinging to each other like it was the last moment of our lives, neither wanting to part with the other.

"Good night." I heard in a giggle.

I recognized that giggle as May's.

It was funny how everyone in our small little house were there and in the same room, and I never really noticed them. If it hadn't been for Molly's stares, Joseph sulking, meeting Hunter's mother, dancing with John, and the many other dance interruptions, the only person who had existed was Hunter, my handsome, protective prince, who took me to the ball and slipped on the glass slipper, which fit perfectly. And the best part—I didn't turn into a pumpkin at midnight.

All was well and good, at least for the time being.

Lights Out

May continued to stare in our direction, standing at the double doors and tapping her small, black, shiny shoe against the floor.

"My mother has suggested we stay here tonight at the compound," Hunter said, still swaying softly to a rhythm of our own.

I yawned, watching May yawn, and then I couldn't stop. I didn't want the night to end, and I didn't want him to stop holding me, but reality was setting in, and I wouldn't be standing much longer.

"Shall we?" he asked.

"Is everyone staying?" I yawned, thinking there were more than fifty people at the party.

"The compound goes back for miles, and there are other houses on the reservation. Although, this house is the biggest. My father likes to design and build, so the house continues to get bigger."

"Reservation?" I asked, fighting to keep my eyes open.

"Questions tomorrow." He smiled and kissed my hand. "There's May."

May waited for us to reach her at the entrance, and then she grabbed my other hand. She didn't look nearly as sleepy as I felt.

Hunter led us up a golden grand staircase. Large painted portraits of people lined the wall. I recognized some, but I must have been so tired my eyes were playing tricks on me. I could have sworn I saw one of Hunter as a young boy in a black-and-white photo. It must have been an ancestor who resembled him standing in front of a small, stone hut.

We climbed up the steps to the second floor. There must have been three more floors above us. The house seemed even bigger than it looked from outside.

May and I followed him to a room, where he opened the door.

"May, this room is for you," Hunter said as May wandered in with big eyes.

"Wow," she said. "I knew all along I shouldn't have stayed away from that smelly old bog. I would have been here a long time ago."

"Let's just say it's not easy to find," Hunter said, still holding the door knob in his hand.

"Thank you, Hunter." She jumped into his arms and hugged him, and he hugged her back, lifting her slightly off the floor.

"Don't thank me. Thank Annabel, but in the morning, of course. She decorated it just for you. She also lined the closet over there with clothes and other items you might need," he said.

Us staying wasn't a last-minute thing. Why?

He started to leave. Noticing that I wasn't following, he stopped and reached out for my hand.

"Your room is next door." He smiled sheepishly.

"My own room? Really?" May gleamed.

I wasn't happy. The thought of being in a room by myself didn't give me comfort at all. I didn't want to be alone anymore. I had enough of that in my old, rotten life.

I hesitated as he led me down the hall, walking very slowly. More pictures hung on the wall. These were paintings of wild horses in yellow meadows. I stopped at one I recognized, one that looked like the tiny shack with the lazy river on one side, the garden towering over the back, and the tall trees on the other side. But the roses surrounding the porch were missing. My hand went to reach out and touch where the roses would have been.

"My mother painted that before Miss Mabel moved into it. She is the one who added the roses. She said it reminded her of her mother," Hunter said, opening another door across from the painting. "This is your room," he said.

"Thanks," I said, still lingering on the painting before turning around.

"The rooms are all connected by an inner door, so if you want privacy, make sure to lock it," he said as he entered the room, and I followed. I saw my bag on top of the bed. "My mother stocked the room with clothes for you to have, but I grabbed your bag just in case. She tends to go overboard." He smiled, feeling a little uncomfortable all of a sudden.

I did too. I knew, just as well as he did, we could not sleep in the same room.

"I'm just on the other side of May. You're in one of the safest places I know of on earth, so don't go having one of those crazy dreams of yours, and no leaving the house without me." He smiled, trying to break the tension.

"I'll try," I finally managed to say in a low, mumbling voice.

A smile crossed over his face and then quickly faded.

"Sleep well," he said with his hands in his pockets as he leaned toward me and kissed my cheek. He turned and walked out, shutting the door behind him.

I quickly opened the door to May's room. Her smile filled the room.

"Can I come in?" I asked.

"Sure." She beamed. "Isn't this just the greatest?"

She was acting a little more like her age as she climbed up onto the bed and began to jump up and down before she fell back down and fluffed up the pillow under her head.

"I could never do that on those cots without falling straight to the floor." She giggled.

"So you've never been here before?" I asked. "You've never wandered into this part of the swamp?"

She yawned big. "I was told to stay away from this area. Besides, it smelled horrible, and if I had come close, everyone would have known I disobeyed." She yawned again. "Annabel said I can come over as much as I want. Did you know they have a pool and a big screen they watch movies on? I don't even know what a movie is." She laughed. "But it sounds great."

"Depends on the movie, I guess," I said, laughing at her excitement.

I sniffed at the air to find it was sweet with fresh cut flowers around the room. "Doesn't smell bad now."

"Nope, it sure doesn't. I think the smell is just to keep people out of here. It's a secrete place."

She was funny to watch. She really wanted to tell me all kinds of other things as she squished her soft feather pillow around her cheek. Her eyes were disappearing behind her heavy eyelids. She mumbled as she drifted off to sleep.

"I love you, Jess," she said with one last yawn.

I leaned over to kiss her cheek and cover her up.

"I love you too. Good night, May," I whispered into her ear.

I wondered why she was kept from this place. Joseph knew and was staying here after he disappeared, and Josephine knew he was here, so why not May? Yet another question to add to the list of questions hovering in my thoughts. I stood to leave when I saw Hunter open his adjoining door to May's room. He nodded and crawled into bed.

I shut the connecting door to dress for bed. I found a soft cotton nightgown and slipped it over my head. It flowed down to feet. I then opened the connecting door slowly. I peeked to see if he still faced my direction, but with his light off, it was too dark to tell. The open doors gave me little comfort.

I inched into the giant, feathery bed. It was so big we all could have slept on it, and comfortably too. Even though I fought earlier to keep my eyes open, the questions I hadn't asked earlier were burning in my thoughts, moving in a circular pattern.

Will Seth try to kill me? Is Molly the reason John wants Hunter to "not make the situation worse," or is he talking about Seth or Davior or the danger I brought with me? After all, Davior is John's son too. Davior is John and Annabel's son. Why didn't that click with me until just now?

No longer at the brink of sleep, I thought about the piano. There had been many nights, nights I would have an argument with my mother and the detail of her demands would ramble in my mind and I couldn't sleep. I would walk to my father's room and play my fingers along his skin, remembering every tune each white and black key made. Playing helped to unravel the knotted-up thoughts in my mind. My mother would have heard if I played on the real piano. But I wasn't in my mother's house, and the ballroom downstairs, located on the opposite side of the bedrooms, seemed far enough away that I assumed no one would hear.

Hunter said I was safe in the house. I thought about it for some time and then finally I made up my mind.

Everything and everyone lay very quiet as I tiptoed down the staircase. It took me several minutes to get to the ballroom, far enough away from sleeping people, already in their happy dreams. I would have felt terrible if I woke anyone up. I shut the big, oak doors and all the other doors that led out, even the windows, so the sound wouldn't escape out into the courtyard. The light from the moon glowed enough for me to see my way around the room, although it appeared darker around the piano. I noticed a round light-dimmer switch on the back wall behind the piano and slowly turned it. A light for just the stage beamed down on the piano.

I walked along the piano, caressing the long body of the piano with one finger. It was absolutely stunning, like everything else I had seen so far. I sat on the soft bench, feeling like it was made just for me. My hands gently glided over the keys, not making a sound at first. I took a deep breath and began to play.

My fingers traveled along the white and black keys, softly in the beginning. I let my imagination take me wherever it wanted to go. I let the music decide which notes would come next as it guided my fingers. I might have been playing terribly with no real plan, no notes to follow, taking me on a rollercoaster ride for one, and I wouldn't have cared. The melody in my head played soft and lovely, taking me to beautiful places, places I read about, places I wanted to go. Then I imagined what heaven might look like: a tall, white, embossed entrance gate, a path made of gold bricks and Hunter standing in front of me wearing a white tuxedo, holding a red rose, waiting for me.

The music flowed from my fingertips, and in my fantasy world, people gathered all around me, laughing and happy, peaceful and magical. I felt calm, safe, and loved. But my world began to betray me, and the music changed to something ugly. I started to think about the other place, the place described as eternal fire. The dream I had with the twisted faces and people with bloody scratches on their arms, dancing in a circle of fire all around me, people wanting to kill me, Seth trying to kill me; it had all been so real. The burning pain all over again, burning in my soul, and watching those I loved burn too.

Once again, the tune and surroundings changed, and my mother stepped into the vision and stood next to the piano, drumming her long, boney fingers with her perfectly manicured nails against the side. I couldn't stop myself from playing; it was the only way to make it all go away. Tears once again flowed down my cheeks.

I am safe here and happy, and I have more than I could have ever imagined. I thought about the fairy tale stories my father read to me, the princes battling the dragons and evil witches. *Hunter is that prince, and he would stand between me and the darkness, not allowing them to take me.* The music started to soften, and then I pulled back and stopped playing.

I sat at the piano, taking in long breaths. My eyes felt extremely tired and swollen. I thought about all the characters I had read about in the Bible. Almost all of them had some sort of battle, something they needed to rise above so that God could use them, although I thought I had suffered a lot, something worse was coming.

I shut the fall board over the keys and folded my arms on top. I reached over for the light switch above the piano.

"Lights out," I mumbled, staring into the moonlit room with shadows all around me. I closed my eyes, laying my head on top of my arms. I yawned.

A New World

I hadn't noticed the heavy drapery covering the windows, so when I finally woke up and pulled the curtains back, the sun was already up in the sky. I peeked in May's room, and she was already gone, so then I tiptoed to Hunter's connecting door, which was cracked open, and he was gone as well. I tried to remember if I had made it upstairs on my own or if someone found me curled up next to the piano and brought me to my room. However, I was more concerned about my next step than my past steps.

I went back to my room and wondered if I should dress first or slip on the robe before heading down the staircase. I looked for a clock with no luck. I peeked out the door to the hallway, where the bathroom was located. A note was taped on the door in front of me—"Towels are in the closet "—and it was in May's handwriting.

I looked through the drawers and pulled out an outfit I liked. I hoped it would make a good impression on Hunter's mother if I wore the clothes she selected. However, it wasn't a great sacrifice on my part, and I struggled to pick just one. They were all more than acceptable.

I quietly entered the bathroom, tiptoeing across the cherry wood floor. The décor was more of a Victorian style in that room. Crown molding outlined the room, and the walls were painted a dark green. I grabbed out a towel from the cherry cabinets and turned the brass knob to hot, and the water flowed from the shower head.

"Running hot water!" I gasped with excitement.

The hot water steam filled the air. Before I stepped into the tub, I felt its soothing, relaxing effects. It had been a long time since I had enjoyed a shower, and who knew when the next would come. I slipped into the hot, running water and stood in the middle of the stream.

The water seemed to have an endless supply, but my hands were beginning to wrinkle, so it was time to get out. I stepped out and dried myself with the fluffy, red towel and used the hair dryer laid out. I hadn't realized how much I missed having electricity and running water, although I would not have complained at the shack.

After getting dressed, I took my time going down the staircase. I heard voices as they floated up, and I followed the source. The nerves in my stomach flip-flopped, and my hands felt sticky.

What should I expect? John and his disapproving looks?

At the bottom of the stairs, I continued to follow the low rumblings of conversations until I stood at the threshold of an average-size kitchen. It was much smaller than my mother's, and instead of it being one room like hers, this kitchen opened to a dining area with a long, rectangular table, big enough for twenty or more people. I had expected to see servants, but if they had any, I didn't see them. Just his parents, busy preparing breakfast, while May, along with a few men I had met at the party, sat at the table.

Hunter saw me first and rushed to my side.

"Who said chivalry is dead? I bet he pulls her chair out too," someone teased.

"Where are Miss Mabel, Josephine, and Joseph?" I asked, sitting in the chair Hunter pulled out for me, followed by thunderous laugher. "Thank you," I said over their expressed amusement.

I could almost guess why Joseph wouldn't have stayed.

"My pleasure," he whispered in my ear, touching his cheek to mine.

I blushed, noticing everyone's eyes were on us.

May giggled. "They didn't stay. Josephine wanted to, but Joseph made her leave, and Miss Mabel is more comfortable in her own house."

"Oh."

Breakfast was handed out the moment I sat down. If it wasn't for the steam rising into the air from the hot, blueberry muffins, I might have thought they had been waiting on me. Muffins weren't the only food on the table. There were waffles with a thick, strawberry sauce on top, pancakes with chocolate sauce and whipped cream, crispy country potatoes, and veggie-and-meat omelets folded perfectly, not to mention the different kinds of juices in glass pitchers in the middle of the table.

"I didn't know what everyone likes, so I made pretty much everything," Annabel said in a joyful laugh.

Once everything was out on the table, John and Annabel sat down. Hunter pulled out the chair next to me and sat down too.

"Hunter, would you say the blessing, please?" his father asked.

He nodded and reached out his hands. I placed mine in his, and everyone else did the same until we formed a complete circle and bowed our heads.

"Heavenly Father, thank you for this beautiful day you have given us. Thank you for friends and family that you have continued to bless. Thank you, Father, for bringing Jessica into my life, and I pray for your guidance along with patience and understanding." He paused for a moment, squeezing my hand. "And thank you for providing this wonderful feast to nourish our bodies for your glory. I thank you in your Son's holy name. Amen."

Even though we had been a little family at Miss Mabel's, this felt so much like a real family, a mom and a dad sitting and eating together, stories being shared, and everyone having a great time. Most of stories being told seemed to revolve around Hunter. I assumed it was for my benefit.

I wondered if it was all too good to be true. All of this could be one big a dream. Maybe when Seth had tried to strangle me, I had gone unconscious and was in a coma like my dad. In dreams, anything was possible, and it would explain so much. Even with impending doom lurking over me, I'd choose this world over my own and stay in a coma forever. I wondered if my dad had dreams before he died, and if he had, were they happy, and was that the reason he never woke? I decided if he had dreamed they would have been happy. It made me feel better, and there was no sense in thinking otherwise.

My eyes moved to John, who seemed much more relaxed and jovial than before. I didn't see any disapproving stares across the breakfast table aimed at Hunter.

"Thank you. That was wonderful." I rose to help Annabel gather dirty plates.

"No, dear. You're our guest." She smiled, placing her hand on my shoulder and then taking the plates from my hand.

"Hunter, I need to speak with you and Jessica in the study," his father said softly.

A collaboration of snickers filled the room before John stared down each one in an unspoken "Zip it."

"Yes, sir," Hunter replied respectfully. "This way." He took my hand.

"Don't be mad," he said, turning toward me.

"Why would I be mad?" I grinned, raising an eyebrow.

I had no idea what he was talking about, unless it was about Molly, and I had already forgiven him for that. If anyone should be mad, it would be him at me. Molly wasn't near as dangerous as Seth.

"Well I…I heard you play last night."

"I'm sorry. I didn't mean to wake anyone. I thought it was far—" I started to explain.

"No, you didn't wake me. I watched you do a lot of tossing back and forth before you actually got up. At first, I thought you were having one of those dreams of yours, but then I watched you leave, so, of course, I followed you," Hunter said nervously.

"I didn't wake you? Did anyone else hear me?"

He shook his head. I felt relieved.

"I couldn't sleep. Playing the piano seems to help calm my mind."

"You were pretty out of it after." He chuckled. "I'm pretty sure the drool is still there."

"Oh." I was horrified.

"I'm kidding." He smirked. "So what happened? You were playing beautifully, something sweet and tranquil, and then"—he paused—"then it changed into…"

"A nightmare?" I filled in, staring blankly at the rose-colored wall behind him.

"I wouldn't say that," he said. "It was still amazing, the notes you were able to create. I could see you in a tranquil world with sunshine all around, and then the black, dark clouds covered up the sun before my eyes and left you lost in it."

"I was thinking about that nightmare when the music changed, the nightmare I had that night we were on the porch swing, the one where Seth tried to kill me. There was something new this time. My mother was there. It just felt so real. I still think it's a warning." I talked as if I strayed right into the dream again. "I fought back toward the end though. I didn't quite get there," I said, coming out of the trance.

"You play with such emotion. I didn't want you to know I was there, and I fought not to go to you when you were clearly upset. I knew those weren't happy tears." The corners of his lips turned down slightly. "So you're not mad?"

I thought about it for a few moments before I answered, just for my own amusement.

"You did tell me you weren't going to leave me, so I guess I deserve what I get when I go wandering off." I placed my hand on his face and then quickly pulled it back when I saw John coming round the corner.

Hunter leaned to my ear. "I guess that's true, but really, it is okay for you to be alone here in this house. You're safe, and I know that." He smiled widely. "That doesn't mean I want you to be without me."

And with that, we followed John into the office.

The office reminded me of my father's, large with books lining the walls from top to bottom with an oversized reading chair right next to a pop-out window overlooking a courtyard with an in-ground pool. I noticed behind the oak desk was an old chest identical to the one my father had, down to the same kind of gold key stuck in the lock.

That's strange, I thought and then continued to look around the room.

"Hunter tells me you are quite the reader, Jessica," he said, catching me eyeballing all the books perched several feet above us.

"I love to read. I used to read at least four to five hours a day. I suppose I got that from my father. I used to read to him often," I said and then asked, "Have you read all these books?"

"Yes. So has Hunter. This is actually his collection of books."

Another thing we had in common, more personal than just the arranged-marriage thing.

"You are free to come in here anytime you like and help yourself to any of the books. I'm sure Hunter would agree," John said.

"So, we must get down to business. First of all, Jessica," he said softly and with adoration in his voice, something I didn't expect, "we need to consider your safety. Obviously you will need more protection than living at Miss Mabel's, so Annabel and I would like for you to consider staying here with us."

My first thought was, *Does John just mean me alone? Will Hunter go back to Miss Mabel's and be done of his obligation?* I felt the voice squeezing its way through the shut door.

"Just me?" I managed to ask. "Isn't everyone at the shack in danger? Seth will hurt anyone who—"

Both John and Hunter chuckled.

"You don't need to worry about them," Hunter answered.

"He'll be coming after you too," I said softly, feeling my emotions burning in my chest.

"I already told you I wasn't going to leave you, and I meant it," Hunter said firmly.

"May will be staying here as well. I'm not sure we could keep her out if we sent her home." John chuckled. "You're free to stay in the room you were in, or you may pick another. There are many rooms in this house to choose from, and at the moment, most of them are empty," he said and then looked at Hunter. "Maybe one on the opposite side of the house."

Hunter fidgeted, looking embarrassed. John didn't approve of me for his son, or so I saw it that way. But at least he was letting Hunter stay here with me.

"So, Jessie," John said, "what do you think?"

I glanced at Hunter, but he was no help. His face downcast, and a reddish tint on his cheek. I thought about everyone's safety, and if they said I was safer by staying, then everyone was safer. I also thought about the party, the close dances and the kiss. *The kiss.* Just the thought sent another pleasing tingle down to my toes.

They want me here so they can keep their son safe. That is a good enough reason to stay.

I nodded my head.

"Good. Now that we've got that settled, we have another matter to consider," John said, clearing his voice to get his son's attention.

Hunter looked up rather sheepishly at his father.

"You know my feelings, Hunter; however, your mother sees things…well, differently. So…" John paused, again clearing his throat, which looked painful.

Was that John's way of giving us his blessing? Although he did say he felt differently than his wife. My heart leaped anyway. His mother was on my side, and that filled me with hope.

"There are some rules you both must follow, as for spending time together."

"Dad!"

"Son."

He raised his eyes, and Hunter got quiet.

"As for spending time together, you need to have a chaperone at all times." Hunter shifted uncomfortably in his chair. "May has already volunteered. She's assured me you both have been pretty well behaved; however, I still want it said." He looked over at Hunter. "There is a complication. Seth isn't going to take this well. Soon, he will have gone through the transformation period…"

There's that word again. He's not a butterfly…

"…And will then filter back into his life, if they haven't started it yet. He's already very strong and powerful, and I'm not just talking physical strength. James has seen that Davior will have spies throughout the forest for any openings they can get. Jessica, you're safe here, but no wandering off into the swamp. I've already talked to May about it as well. Our reservation is quite large, so you'll have plenty to do to fill your time." John turned to Hunter. "Son, most of the families have left, so the compound is our responsibility to maintain for the time being. We've got lots of work to do in the meantime."

He looked at Hunter sternly. "He won't let her go without a fight, son. We will have to be on guard around the clock. Hunter, you know this, but, Jessica, you need to know too. Lucifer is always calculating, always scheming. You have to be on your toes. You are safe here, but as soon as you step off the cobblestone path, you become in danger. You will see the cobblestone path outlines our entire compound. Think of it as an invisible wall, only at any time, you can cross over it. Davior and those of his kind cannot."

*What does he mean by invisible wall? Hunter carried me...*I then remembered the weird tingling sensation I had felt as he moved us through it.

I started to feel anxious and I wanted to leave the room, but John wasn't done talking to Hunter. I couldn't just get up and leave. *This is getting really weird.* I went over all the weird things, all the off comments, my questions about what Seth was turning into and what Davior really was.

I had stepped into a whole new world. My little thoughts were not far-fetched or my imagination. *How do I deal with all this?* I felt the blood drain out of my face, and my hands went clammy.

"Jessica, are you all right?" John asked me.

"I'm fine," I said, shaking my head and half listening to what John was saying. "What were you saying about Davior?"

Now the question was, why? *If that light was my father and he led me here, why?*

"Davior has been appointed Seth's steward," John then said to Hunter.

John stood up and walked over to the front of his desk and leaned on the corner, looking at me alone.

"There are many things that are uncertain right now, and Davior will use anything and everything to try to get you off these grounds, Jessie. He's made a deal with his...boss." John paused. "If you ever need to question something you think or feel, please feel free to talk to me about it. Hopefully, your stay is only for a short while, unless you want to stay longer, of course. I don't want you to feel like a prisoner here."

I nodded again.

I didn't mind staying at all, but I had to think of Miss Mabel. She needed us to help with the garden, the chores, and I felt bad her and Josephine would have to do it all. "What about the garden and harvest time?"

"We've got some folks who will be stopping by to help Miss Mable with the daily work, and you are free to visit her and the twins as long as Hunter or James is with you. You'll have to be cautious, and no wandering about," John said, still looking sternly at me.

"Why wasn't May allowed to come here before now?" I asked.

"The little house was meant to bring up children who were left as orphans on the compound. We wanted them to develop a strong understanding of what it means to work hard and help out others. Miss Mabel, an orphan herself, is the one who started it all when she was just a young girl herself. Of course, now, there is no reason to continue it, now that May is here," John said, standing up and leaving me with more questions. But before I could ask why, he turned to Hunter. "Hunter, there is one more thing I would like to talk to you about alone. If you would excuse us for a moment, Jessica. I believe that May is by the pool, waiting for you. There is a swimsuit up in your room."

"Thank you." I then sighed heavily.

Hunter stood up as I left the room, forging a smile and encouraging me to go, and then John shut the door. I lingered at the closed door, but I couldn't hear one word, not even a whisper through the thick wood. I gave up and wondered which of the three they were talking about: me, Molly, Seth, or Davior.

I walked up the grand staircase to my room. A light-blue, one-piece swimsuit with a ruffle around the middle laid out on the bed next to a terrycloth wrap, which covered me from head to toe. I then went down to the sparkling blue pool reflecting up at me. May was already having the time of her life splashing around.

"Jess, come on. Get in," she called to me.

The crystal-clear water splashed up against the sides of the pool, causing the water to shimmer. A reflection of the sky in the water caught my attention as it sloshed back and forth. The border around the pool was light blue marble tile with golden lines woven throughout. There were more angel statues surrounding the outline of the sun-bathing area.

"Are you coming in, or do I have to come get you? It's not deep." She stood up.

Although I wasn't frightened, I was relieved to see the pool wasn't deep. I sat on the edge of the pool and dangled my feet in the water.

"Are you scared?" She looked concerned.

"I might have been if I couldn't touch. I never learned how to swim." I smiled, kicking water toward her, but that wasn't why I had been scared the day at the river; it had been more about being dragged under by the current.

She splashed back, and we were in a full water fight. Water flew all around us, and I jumped in to get closer to her until we were both laughing. I inhaled water up my nose and started to cough uncontrollably. I was still laughing, but she stopped so I could catch my breath.

Another splash came up from behind me. I was still choking, but not as much, as Hunter came to my protection and pounded May with water. Of course, she loved it. I joined back into the fight but took May's side, and we both were splashing him until he gave up, waving his hands above his head. Soon after, the entire family was at the pool.

"Volleyball," Annabel called. "Girls against boys." She tossed the ball to John as he jumped in.

"You've been just dying to say that, Mom," a voiced jumped in.

"Yes, well, it's nice to not be the only female for once." Annabel smiled.

"Jordan," John chimed in, "you play with the girls."

Another brother. I should have known.

"I'm already here," Hunter called back, standing next to me.

"I don't want anyone hurt. You"— John pointed at Hunter— "this side."

"Fine." He pouted but kissed my cheek before he moved.

Annabel set up the net and then jumped in.

I wasn't sure how to play. I had seen it on TV, but never actually played.

Jordan stood next to me. "When the ball comes to you, send it straight up so I can spike it over the net."

"I'll try," I said, unsure of what he wanted me to do.

"Zero to zero," Annabel said as she hit the ball.

John returned the ball, and it headed in my direction. I held my breath, closed my eyes, and then pushed the ball straight up. Jordan stepped in and spiked it down on James. James hit the ball, but it went out of bounds.

"Yeah!" Jordan called out and hugged me.

Hunter twitched, and I was pretty sure it wasn't because we got a point.

The game continued just like that. Jordan and I were the score makers for our team. We won the first game, and then John told James and Jordan to change places. James would do the exact same thing. The ball would head for me, I pushed it up in the air, and James smacked it hard down on the other side. James also followed in Jordan's high-fives and hugs, lifting me in out of the water. I had noticed Hunter grinding his teeth a few times at his brothers. However, it seemed more like teasing and good fun than actual anger.

Somewhere in between games, we stopped and ate lunch poolside. I sat next to May, and she talked up a storm to Jordan, who sat on her other side. She enjoyed having someone new to talk to, and he enjoyed her nonstop chatter. He'd try to interject where he could, not such an easy thing to do when she barely took a breath.

The last game we played, the boys won, as they began to show me no mercy. We were all laughing, and my team went under the net to congratulate the other team. Hunter grabbed me up before one of his brothers could and hugged me tight. I giggled before he set my feet back on the bottom of the pool. I felt that same rush of feelings, the one that begs, "Kiss me," as I leaned into him.

Someone cleared their throat, and we both looked in the same direction. James tossed me a towel and then one to Hunter. We both caught them before they hit the water.

"So what did your father want to talk to you about?" I asked, drying off.

"Oh, it was nothing. He wanted to know if you knew about Molly. I told him Jordan already spilled those beans." He continued, "Molly was acting pretty strange last night, and he was just concerned. It's pretty obvious she is very upset."

"Obviously," I echoed.

"John's afraid she might try to get at you somehow, so we've told everyone it might be in her best interest not to come around here for a while."

We started to walk toward our rooms.

"Because of me. I'm not an infant. I can handle her," I said, thinking about her thin frame.

"I don't want you to deal with her. My family and I will keep a close eye on her. She won't be able to get close to you, just in case she snaps. It's amazing what some people will do in the name of love or, in her case, obsession."

"Molly has shot me some daggers. Good thing looks can't kill." Her look was unnerving, but I understood the pain she felt. "I do feel sorry for her in a way." My tone changed. "I mean, if my parents would have brought you to me and then you didn't want me…" I couldn't believe I had said that out loud.

"Well that wouldn't have happened," he said sarcastically.

Did he mean there was no way his parents would have matched us up, or did he mean that he wouldn't have wanted me?

"You know what I mean," he said. I looked over at his face, hoping more clarification would surface.

He said nothing more as we continued to walk. Something unrevealed occupied his thoughts.

What is it? I wanted to ask, but maybe it was better not to. Another question too: *Why do his mother and father look so young? And they keep talking about Hunter being alone for so long. Would he tell me if I asked? Could he tell me?* Hunter is good at skirting around a question, so I guess if he didn't want to answer, he'd come up with something else. So why not ask?

"How old are you, really?"

"Here we are." Hunter leaned against the frame of my door, his arms folded against his chest.

"So…you're not going to tell me? I thought you were going to start answering my questions?" I asked, moving closer to him.

"Does it matter?" he asked, tilting his head sideways with a smirk.

"No. I guess not." I leaned on the opposite side of doorway and stared at the painting on the wall once again. I sighed loudly.

"You know things are different. You've asked me questions, but really you knew the answers. I thought it would be easier on you to discover some things for yourself."

He was right about one thing, the weird stuff wasn't feeling as weird as it had at first. *I'm becoming one of them.*

After a moment of uneasy silence, I turned to go into the room.

"Oh, so I see how it is." He caught my arm and pulled me into him.

My heart skipped a few beats as his arms encircled my waist and he hugged me tight to him. I felt the water being squeezed from our suits and down my legs. The water felt cold, and a wave of shivers caused my entire body to quiver.

"You're cold," Hunter said and wrapped the damp towel he had around my shoulders along with his arms.

"I should change," I said, twisting out of his hold.

It didn't feel natural to want out of his arms, but I was done with him being evasive. I wanted answers, concrete answers to at least one of my questions as I stood in a growing puddle of pool water. The way he looked at me, they way he touched me, the way he protected me—there was no doubt in my mind about how he felt about me. And I wanted an answer.

Hunter's hand reached for mine, not letting me get away.

"Remember how I told you about the Cherokee, about the Trail of Tears," he said softly, looking down at my hand.

"Yes," I answered, confused.

"The legend about what happened after and what God had done for them?" he said a little more seriously, bringing his eyes up to meet mine.

I thought about it for moment. The Cherokee were forced off their land, and many died on the journey to the new settlements. The legend, which I had liked, had been about how God saved the people to fight against Lucifer in the battle between good and evil.

He's out of his mind if he thinks I believe he was one of them. I shook my head.

"I was twelve when it happened," he said, "playing a game with my brothers in the field."

"You don't look Native American to me. If you don't want to tell me…"

He just had to be joking.

I thought I would be okay with whatever he told me, but this was crazy. I'd believe a fountain-of-youth story easier than dead Indians. I tried to go into my room, but Hunter continued not letting my hand go.

"My grandfather fell in love with a missionary, and they were married. My mother is only half Cherokee, and I took on more of the white-man's look," he said, trying to lighten the moment.

I remembered he said they were immortal but they could marry and have families of their own. That they aged, but slower.

"Jess," Hunter said sternly, "I still remember the feeling like I wanted to die before God took mercy on us." He paused. " God gave us this gift of life, to be able to help mankind and to offset the plans Lucifer has for this world."

"So if you're all part of this and you lived so long ago, how do you live in the world without people knowing? A wife would know if her husband wasn't aging normally, wouldn't she?" *Okay, I'll play along. But why would Hunter lie? Why make up such a story?*

"James, for example, will appear to grow older in the church, and when the time comes when he can't fake it anymore, he will have to leave and start a new congregation or other mission work. It's pretty easy to fake aging with some hair color, wigs; and it's amazing what we can do with make-up these days. Jordan has recently left his mission work and will be staying here until his next calling. We hold on to knowing in the end, Lucifer will be defeated. But until that time, he'll continue to recruit, and we'll continue to help people and lead them away from the darkness and toward the light until the day we ride into the final battle," he concluded.

"The same battle as in Revelation? Come on," I said, only I half believed him. It should have made perfect sense. It should have all clicked right then and there, but the voice came back, knocking the door down with one big push.

See. He's lying to you. It's time to leave this place, Jessica. Continue with the plan to leave here. There is a wonderful life outside of this new prison full of deceivers.

I put my hands up to my ears to block out the voice and repeated with the one I knew was mine, *Leave me alone.*

I needed time. My head felt like exploding. A thousand thoughts swarming and colliding into each other made my knees weak, and I clung to the door. I couldn't process any more information, not at the same time.

"You've given me a lot to think about, but I need to take a shower before this chlorine leaves a permanent smell in my hair," I said.

My mind was trying to put all the puzzle pieces I'd been collecting since the day I arrived in the swamp into one clear picture. I couldn't do that with him just staring at me.

"I'm sorry." He hugged me close. "I was a little insensitive to just blurt that out. John warned me this would be hard for you to understand at first," he said as I gently put my hands on his chest to push him away.

"I…I don't know what to think. Just give me some time to sort it out, please," I said, sounding a little rude, but I needed him to go.

That's a first.

Hunter looked crushed. I walked into the room and looked at him before shutting the door and trying to smile. I sat on the edge of the bed, trying to recollect all of the of the story in more detail. It didn't help.

May skipped in through the side door, coming from her room. I could see Hunter's door was shut across the other side of May's room.

"What's wrong?" May asked.

"Nothing. I'm fine. I'm a little worn out. It's been a busy couple of days," I said, "and I didn't sleep well last night."

"Oh, but I slept wonderfully, better than I ever have," she said. "Maybe you'll sleep better tonight."

"I hope so. You really like it here, don't you May?"

"I do, and everyone is so nice. I especially like Miss Annabel. She let me braid her hair. It was so soft." She jumped on my bed.

The pit in my stomach felt like a giant hole. If Hunter was telling me the truth, and I knew deep down he wasn't capable of lying, they would all outlive me. I guess that wasn't so bad. I wondered if May would also outlive me. Was she also part of all of it too? I wouldn't ask her. She might not know.

Then both of us heard a soft knock at the door.

"Jessica." The voice was Annabel's. "May I come in?"

"Yes, of course," I said, standing up.

"May, would you excuse us for a moment?" Annabel asked.

"Sure. I'll get ready for dinner." She bounded into her room, shutting the connecting door.

"Sit, please. It seems my son has shared our story with you," she said, and I nodded.

"So it's all true," I said. "I already knew he was telling the truth, I just didn't want to believe it."

"That's a hard story to swallow. I'm sure you have some questions. Hunter thought you might feel better talking to me about it. But if you would rather be alone to your thoughts, I understand."

I thought about what I would ask her. *Does it really matter? When my lifetime is up, Hunter will still have to continue with his life. It seems, from that perspective, I get the better end of the deal, unless there is a way…but how could there be? Although, if the war is close, maybe I won't die.* I liked that thought better.

"I knew something was different at the shack, and I pretended it was in my imagination. There has also been so much to take in at once, but sitting here with you…no, it's still a weird concept to accept."

I chucked, and Annabel joined in. "Seeing an angel standing before you is pretty weird too."

"I need time to process it all, but I think I'm going to be okay," I said, and she reached for my hand. A thought popped into my head as she started to leave. "I do have a question though. How long do you think it will be before the war begins? The one between God and Lucifer?"

Annabel wasn't ready for that question. She hesitated.

"Honestly, we don't know for sure. Most of the signs are there, but we've thought that once before."

"Who?"

"A man in Germany. He had potential to be the antichrist, but he got too power hungry, too self-absorbed, and the people started to see the evil. At first, he was debonair. The people loved him. But then, he changed. No, the one who will start it all, the people will love him, and he will rule all nations. There will be a time of false peace and prosperity with this ruler. He will gain their trust. He will make people believe it's for their own good as the government slowly moves in and takes freedom from them. He will start in the most powerful nation before gaining control over the world. It will only be God's true followers who will see him for what he really is." She sighed.

"By control over the world, you mean The United Nations?"

The wheels in my head started to turn, like two gears fitting tightly together.

"That's what we think," she answered. "Of course, this is all man's interpretation of Scripture, so take it as such," she said. "We need to keep focused on the present and our individual calling until then." She paused. "Anything else you want to talk about?"

"No. I think I'll turn in."

"I can have Hunter bring up your dinner if you would like."

"I'm still full from lunch," I said, rubbing my stomach with a smile.

Annabel stood up gracefully and kissed the top of my head. She was quickly becoming the mother I had always dreamed of.

"Good night, Jessica." She smiled.

"Night, and thank you," I said quickly.

"My door is always open if you need to talk woman to woman." She laughed as she shut the door.

As soon as the door was closed, I lay back on the bed. What she said about the antichrist described Seth perfectly—not only what he had done, but his future goals. *Do they think he's the antichrist? Is that the transformation he is going through? Oh my gosh, this isn't good.* I curled up into a ball in the middle of the bed. *Somehow, I ended up here, on a reservation with Cherokee Indians who fight against demons, and since there are no coincidences, what reason would God have to send me here? Why me? What makes me so special?*

I grabbed the pillow and stuffed it under my head.

My eyes grew heavy as I thought about my new world and what gift God would give me to battle with. *He sent me here for a reason. But what?*

A House Full of Boys

A few weeks flew by in a wink of an eye, and I had spent some of my time getting accustomed to the house and grounds. Annabel took me and May from room to room, letting us pick out pieces we liked for our own rooms. She wanted us to make it our own, which we did. Annabel also pulled out an array of paints for us to choose from, and then the three of us painted. Annabel, the gifted artist, had done a mural of a farm with horses along a white fence for May.

When it came to me, I found country cottage pictures tucked in a room used for storage. They consisted of white houses and picket fences covered in some kind of flowering vines. They were too pretty to be stored away. I picked out a soft green to paint my walls, and Annabel created a mural for me as well. The style was a little different from the other paintings, but it was beautiful all the same. The mural was set in a wild, overflowing garden with two white Roman pillars covered with white and red roses growing on a vine. They wound around the pillar and joined across the top, with larger roses dangling down. The smooth stone path disappeared farther into the garden as the low, purple and yellow wildflowers grew thicker.

Besides decorating, I used some of the time to read. I was now on Psalms. I hadn't known the Bible contained poetry, and beautiful poetry too. My favorite was from Psalm 18: 16-19.

> He reached down from on high and took hold of me; he drew me out of deep waters. He rescued me from my powerful enemy, from my foes, who were too strong for me. They confronted me in the day of my disaster, but the Lord was my support. He brought me out into a spacious place; he rescued me because he delighted in me.

Hunter spent time with his father and brothers during the day. Mostly, they worked around the compound, but because it was so large, I'd go almost all day without seeing them. When I would ask what they had been doing all day, Hunter's answer was always the same: "Just guy stuff." My suspicion was John and Annabel were keeping Hunter and me from spending too much time together. However, Hunter was always back by dinnertime, leaving us a few hours together to walk the grounds before bed. We talked about various things, past and present. We kept the topic off Davior, Seth, or anything unpleasant. May trailed behind or in front of us in her own world, until she would begin to complain about how late we were keeping her up. It was then followed by an uncomfortable good night with May's watchful eye. We knew our time together was over for the day, and the only kisses given rested on my cheeks or the top of my head.

Although I was living in a strange world, it was more normal than my life before, and everyone who came and went seemed like regular people to me. Nothing was shocking or unusual. I could really forget the whole weird story and just live a normal life. If it weren't for the following week, when we hadn't seen much of the men, I wouldn't have worried at all. Annabel explained they were traveling farther from home. When I asked where, she just answered, "Oh, here and there." I just prayed they were safe until I saw them again and hugged Hunter a little tighter.

"You're not dressed!" May said, scowling at me until she saw the look on my face and softened her tone. "Why do you look so sad?"

"I haven't seen Hunter all week," I said, giving her a big hug.

She looked at me with a big smile.

"Well, you'd better get dressed. We are having a bonfire tonight! Doesn't that sound like so much fun?" She twirled around. "Hunter will be there." She giggled. "They'll all be there."

I smiled at her excitement and at my own. "Okay. I will."

And with that, she pulled on me until I got up, and then she pushed me into the bathroom.

Family events just seemed to keep Hunter and me apart even more. I was excited I would get to see him after not seeing him all week, but I would much rather take our quiet walk in one of the gardens. Maybe I would get kissed again. It seemed so long ago, more of a distant memory. A bonfire with everyone around didn't sound all that great to me.

If he loves you, he would fight for you instead of letting his family run his life. You don't have a chance against them. "Leave me alone," I said out loud. "I'm not leaving, you should give up."

Instead of a shower, I filled the deep, long tub with warm water and added a splash of strawberry bubble bath. The bubbles overflowed from the tub as I slipped into it. I was tired. It was my fault for staying up so late again, overanalyzing John's motives and everything else. Nighttime seemed to be the only time to mull things over. I drifted into a trance, nothing particular, just soft music playing in my head, and a vision of a swan or two swimming in a pond. Concentrating on the music and picture kept voices and other such thoughts from barging in.

Knock! Knock! Knock!

I jumped up at the sound, slipping on the ceramic tub, and then bumped my head on the edge of it. I made some kind of painful sound, and the door flew open. Thankfully, the tub was slippery enough I slid back down into the water and was covered in bubbles.

"Oh, Jess, I'm so sorry. I didn't mean to…you've just been in here so long. You didn't sleep well…" Hunter was in a panic, looking over my head, where my hand clung.

Then he found the bump with his hand.

"Ouch." I squirmed.

He bent down like he was going to lift me up.

"Uh…that's probably not a good idea. I'm not wearing a bathing suit under all these bubbles." He looked confused at first but quickly caught on, blushed, and then turned his back to me.

"Oh right! I'll go get Annabel," he said, starting to leave.

"No! I'm fine. Hand me a towel, please," I ordered.

I think I was less embarrassed with him there than the thought of his mother carrying me naked.

"I really think you should—" he protested.

"Hunter, please?"

He handed me the towel with his back facing me. I stood up slowly, feeling a little dizzy, but not from the bump.

I wrapped the large towel around me.

"Okay. I'm decent," I said, wrapping a smaller towel around my hair.

"I don't think I can agree with that." His smile was quite sinister.

"What?" I sounded irritated.

"You are anything but decent," he said, sweeping me up and carrying me back to my room.

"Ha ha."

He laid me down on the bed and removed the towel on my head, allowing my wet hair to spill out over the pillow, so he could examine my injuries, which I knew were minor, and he sighed.

"Did you know that on average, three hundred people a year drown in bathtubs?" Hunter said, spouting off information he'd read somewhere. I think it helped him not be so nervous in odd situations.

"That's not very many, considering how big the population is," I answered with a small smile.

"Yes, I know, but I don't know what I would do if I lost you because you fell asleep in the tub." He laughed.

"It would be so much better for another reason," I said sarcastically. "Demons annihilating my existence or Molly strangling me." I couldn't escape those thoughts. I did think of another reason, of a natural cause, but I kept that one to myself.

"That's not funny."

"You're still not ready?" May huffed in through the door and then pulled Hunter out the door.

She shut and locked the door and then stared at me for an explanation.

"I slipped in the tub and hit my head. Hunter ran in, but I was completely covered in bubbles, I swear." I showed her the bump to confirm my story.

"Well, all right," she said. "Now get dressed!" she ordered in a pouty sort of way.

"Yes, ma'am," I said as May walked to her side door, one hand on her hip and the other on the door knob.

"Ten minutes, and I'm coming in," she said before shutting the door.

I was done in less time and bounced into her room wearing another cute outfit Hunter's mom picked out for me. I hated the clothes my own mother had bought for me, but Annabel's taste in clothes—it was as if she knew me perfectly.

I twirled for May. The yellow summer dress was hemmed just below my knees, and it jetted out on the bottom when I twirled. The top of the dress was lined with little daisy buttons around a v-neck, and it had short sleeves.

"I love it." She glowed. "Let's go."

She pulled me downstairs into the game room, a big, open area with soft, white couches around a glass coffee table and a huge brick fireplace in the corner, where another small table with a chess set sat.

"Oh, Jessica, let me see your head." Annabel came over to me quickly.

"I'm fine really." I mouthed a sarcastic, *Thanks*, in Hunter's direction. He mouthed back, *Welcome*, smiling from ear to ear as Annabel searched my head for the bump.

I shrieked when she touched it.

"Hunter, go get some ice," she called to him. "It's not bad, but we should try to bring down the swelling."

Hunter was back in a second with some ice wrapped in a soft towel. I reached for it, but he wouldn't let me have it. He led me over to a soft chair and forced me to sit. He then slid in behind me and held the towel to my head very gently. His body felt good next to mine as I relaxed against him, feeling his chest rise and fall along with my breaths.

A large television hung on the wall like a picture frame, and it was on. All the men, except for Hunter, were glued to. It was on one of those network news channels that had continuous breaking news scrolling along the bottom of the screen. I wasn't watching, but I heard something that made me look up. Just then the television went off.

May pulled out a board game from the cabinet under the television.

"Hey, May, what do you got there?" James looked at the box. "Monopoly. I haven't played that in years. I'm in."

"That means I'd better play too, since James cheats." Jordan jumped toward them. "I'll be the banker," Jordan called.

"Oh yeah, I'm the one who cheats," James called back.

"That's right." Jordan smiled. "At least you can admit it."

They sounded like little boys as they looked in our direction.

"I should help Annabel in the kitchen." I started to get up, but Hunter pulled me back down with the towel still on my bump.

"I'm sure she would love the help, Jessica." John smiled at me.

I went to get up again, and Hunter didn't pull me back down, with John staring in his direction.

"You and I have a chess game to finish, son." He winked at me.

I didn't look back as I left the room, even though I felt multiple eyes on my back.

As if she already knew I was coming, Annabel said, "Jessica, would you mind chopping up those veggies over there?"

At the kitchen island, there was already a prep station ready to be worked at and two tall chairs.

"Sure," I said, sitting in the chair. "So, what is this bonfire tonight that May is so excited about?"

"Oh, it's just our away to keep in contact with our friends and share information or happy tidings. With some of the families traveling, it can get quite lonesome here. The chapel has been in the process of a remodel, so those who live near here, we haven't seen since the ball," she said, as if I knew about a chapel.

"Ouch." I sliced my finger, my fault for getting distracted.

"Here," Annabel handed me a napkin and then started rifling through a small drawer. "I always have these on hand." She smiled, pulling out a Band-Aid.

She took the napkin from me and wrapped my now-barely-bleeding finger.

"All better," she said.

We heard May laughing and accusing someone of cheating. We looked at each other and laughed.

"It's so nice to have girls in the house," she said and touched my arm. "It's been just me with these boys for so long. I love my boys, but sometimes I wished I would have had a little girl." She headed toward a cabinet and pulled out a skillet. "I've been meaning to ask, do you like the clothes I picked out? I really didn't know what is in fashion these days for girls. I ordered them online, so if you don't like them…"

"I love them. I wondered how you could have picked such beautiful and practical clothes, ones I would have picked out if I would have been allowed to buy my own clothes." I felt rather ashamed I hadn't thanked her. "Thank you so much for the clothes. I should have told you before now."

Annabel turned to me, carrying the skillet. "You've had a lot to think about these last few weeks. Please don't worry about offending me."

She put the pan below the cutting board, and I scraped the vegetables into it with the back of the knife.

I sat there very quietly. I wanted to ask her a question, but I wasn't sure how to bring it up.

"You are such a cheater!" We heard James yell out from the other room and then laugher.

"So what's next?" I chuckled, scooping the rest of the vegetables with my hand.

She pulled up a chair next to me and placed a new cutting board in front of me and then in front of her. She pulled out small pieces of dough from a bowl, rolled them into a ball, and flattened them with a tiny rolling pin. She then dipped a small scoop into a meat mixture from another bowl and placed it in the center of the dough. She then folded the dough and pressed down the sides to seal in the meat. They were then ready to go on a greased cookie sheet and into the oven. I made a few before Davior popped into my head. When I had first met him, I got the impression he thought his name was a joke. *That might not be a good topic. It's got to hurt knowing her son is fighting on the wrong side.*

"So, Jess, what's your mother like?" she said first.

Talk about a hurtful topic.

She put her hand over mine, noticing I shifted in my seat a few times.

"John told me things, but he's much more into the mechanics of things and less into the emotions. You don't have to talk about her if you don't want to," she said, sounding a little disappointed.

It was her moment to bond with me on a different level, and I was shutting her out. At least it felt like I was.

"No. It's okay," I said, realizing I wanted to bond with her in the same way. "I just didn't know what you already knew," I said, trying to play off my initial reaction.

I started with my earliest memory of her and worked my way up through the years. I found it hard talking about my father and how she used him to get what she needed out of me. Annabel listened carefully, almost jotting down notes in her mind. I left out my recovered memory about what I saw that night of my father's attack, the one Davior dug out from the vault.

Annabel and I finished stuffing the little, round dumplings, and there were a lot of them.

"It's hard to believe a mother can be so cruel." She said. "Let's get these in the oven."

She grabbed a few trays, and I grabbed a few trays, and we walked over to the oven.

"I have forgiven her," I said after we put all the trays in. "At least for the things she's done in the past."

At least for the things I knew were true. The memory Davior forced me to remember I hadn't been completely convinced it was true. Davior could have made it seem worse than it was. He could have made me see something other than what really happened to make me want to chose revenge.

However, I believed my father intended to take me away from her.

We popped the little pastries in the oven, and Annabel put one arm around me and gave me a squeeze.

"That's very mature of you," she said almost proudly, which gave me a different kind of feeling, a true mother's love.

"Please don't hesitate to treat me as a mother. You know, someone to talk to, confide in. We can do each other's hair," she teased with a silly look, and we both laughed. She kissed my forehead. "Would you like to tell May and the boys dinner will be ready in ten minutes?"

"Can I ask you one question first?"

"You can ask me anything, Jess," she said with her arm around my shoulders.

"Davior," I said and then looked at her face. Her expression didn't change, so I continued. "He said something when I first met him, something about you having a sense of humor or something like that."

"He's always hated his name." She shook her head. "I thought it was quite original."

"Why would that be comical?"

"It's not." She turned and went over to the sink to wash the heads of lettuce sitting out on counter. "One day, my mother was reading a story. It was the story about King David. After all these years, I'm not sure why I heard it or even where in the story the two are close together. Anyway, I heard the name Davior. It was David and Savior jumbled together. From then on, I said if I had any male children, one of them would be Davior."

The correlation of Davior thinking it was some sort of joke wasn't obvious to me, but I was trying to figure it out on my own. Annabel noticed my eyebrows drawn together.

"Because of the path he has chosen, he finds it funny David was a man after God's own heart and, well, you know who the Savior is."

"Oh," I said. It made sense.

"I still have hope he'll change his allegiance. I don't believe the light he once had inside is gone completely."

"I'm so sorry." I just stood there.

"All right now, no gloomy face, okay? Go." She smiled and pointed toward the game room.

I nodded, smiling.

I felt bad for Annabel to have lost her son and for him to have lost connection with his family. But it felt good to talk and spend time with her, even though some of it was sad. How I wished my mother would have been like her.

I walked into the room, and May held up her money for me to see.

"I won! I won!" May jumped up and hugged me.

The two brothers winked at me.

"Of course you won. You're the smart one," James said.

The attention now was on the two men playing chess. They didn't look up at all the commotion. Jordan whispered in my ear. I nodded. I walked over behind Hunter and kissed him softly on the cheek. Hunter, surprised, looked up and smiled.

"Checkmate!" John yelled loudly.

James and Jordan roared.

I stood back for a second, enjoying the way his skin felt on my lips, before Hunter whisked me up quickly, not minding every eye focused on him.

"So I guess you're not mad at me for barging in on your bath." He smiled.

I shook my head. "Embarrassed is more accurate." The words seem to escape my lips as his eyes glistened at me.

We both noticed everyone had left the room and we were alone for the first time in weeks. Hunter placed his hand on my face, tracing one finger from the top of my eyelid down to the bottom of my neck, pulling me closer with his other hand; and then, so softly, he kissed my lips, and I kissed him back. His hand released my face and enclosed around me tightly, his lips not leaving mine. My hands wrapped around his neck, pulling him to me. My heart raged for more of his sweet breath, the touch of his skin against mine. I pulled back to catch my breath, but also just in case we were being watched.

"Sorry," he said, only this time, his face wasn't downcast, nor did he look sorry he kissed me.

"Hey, we're waiting for you two!" Jordan called.

Hunter sighed. "I guess I'm forgiven yet again." He smiled breathlessly.

"For now," I teased in a whisper. "I guess I don't have to worry about drowning in bathtubs either."

The Bonfire

After dinner, the family sat around the game room, talking and laughing. Hunter told some childhood stories about his brothers, since they had embarrassed him earlier. John and Annabel told the story of how they were the product of an arranged marriage. We all talked until dark swept into the room, and May hovered at the window to point out the first evening star.

John and James left our conversation earlier to prepare for the evening.

"See! It's time! It's time!" May jumped up and down.

"Okay, okay. Calm down. We're going." Jordan laughed as she took his hand and pulled him out of the room.

Annabel, Hunter, and I followed. We were in another courtyard, one I must have missed in my strolls around the grounds. The fire was already in full motion, with shooting flames reaching out for the dark-gray sky. The fire pit alone was at least twenty feet wide with wooden benches horseshoed around it, enough for two hundred or more. Off to the side of the campfire sat a table with large sticks, marshmallows, chocolate, and graham crackers, along with other snacks, and May noticed right away.

Hunter joined up with his brothers once we got down to the fire. He kissed my hand before he disappeared with them.

May was overexcited and clapping her hands. I imagined steam shooting out her ears. The more I watched May there on the compound, the more I understood why she was taken to the shack. Although she was still young, May was well grounded and quite mature. I laughed seeing her act like a child. I knew what it meant to grow up quickly. I might have been twenty physically, but I had turned into an adult the moment my father faded into his own world, forcing me to be the responsible adult.

My mother knew nothing of responsibility if it hadn't concerned her.

The air surrounded me, feeling like early fall, still warm during the daytime but a quick cool down once the sun had gone. I gave up trying to gauge time and just let the season speak to me. I was glad for the cool air because the fire blazed and put out some massive heat.

I sat on the bench farthest from the flames, but May stood closer with a stick in her hand. I watched her catch the marshmallow on fire and whirl it in the air. When she finally blew it out, the marshmallow was black.

My eyes were then drawn to the color of the flames. Some were red, some orange, and some even blue, shooting up wisps of smoke, hypnotic as the flame twisted and weaved in harmony, and the red, glowing embers peaked through the blackened wood with still some fire left in them. I thought about a song I had heard played on a flute. It had been haunting but beautiful at the same time, a lot like the swamp was. The flames came alive as I recalled the melody. I began to hum the melody out loud, in a trance, as I stared into the flames, tapping my hand against my leg to keep up with the beat. I imagined I was dancing in the fire, but no harm was coming to me. I couldn't feel the heat, just the soft touch as each flame shot me up into the sky and then cradled me and twirled me back down toward the ground.

I felt someone grab my arm, and it all stopped.

"S'more?" May offered.

"What?" I laughed, shaking myself out of the daydream.

"Do you want one? It's a toasted marshmallow and chocolate sandwich. I made this one for you," she said. "I didn't burn this one."

"Thanks, May." I took a bite. It was very gooey but good and sweet.

"What were you just doing?" she asked.

"Oh, I suppose I'm just letting my imagination run away with me," I said and hugged her.

"Well, you looked ghostly." She giggled.

The flames were inviting me to join them. The thought mulled over, and then I began to see our guests arrive, and we both stared at the entrance to see Miss Mabel entering the courtyard. Both May and I jump up and ran over to her.

"Well, don't you two look just lovely." She beamed.

I wanted to tell her I would come over to help her, that I would stay with her if she needed me, but she saw it all over my face.

"You need to be here, where you are completely safe. Don't go wandering off. You hear me?" She kissed my head. "We all have our purpose here in this life. Mine has been to look after young ones and teach them morals, hard work, and God's ways. My time is coming to an end, and soon, very soon, I'll receive my reward in heaven," Miss Mabel said in her singsong voice. "So you do as you're told, young lady. Keep yourself out of harm's way".

"Yes, Miss Mabel."

"Mabel," John called to her.

"Excuse me, ladies, I'm being summoned." She winked and left us.

I heard a commotion coming from inside the house. Hunter and Miss Caroline were arguing. I knew it was wrong, but I moved in closer to the glass door to eavesdrop. Miss Betsy saw me and hurried outside toward me.

"Hello, dear." She hugged me. "Come sit with me," she said as she placed her hand around my shoulders, glaring behind us. "Are you enjoying your time here?"

"Yes. Annabel is taking very good care of us," I answered, trying to look behind too.

"Oh, she is just a doll," Miss Betsy continued, "and she has the best parties."

At the bonfire, all the seats were taken except for a few in front. I sat down next to Miss Betsy, who held on to my hand.

Miss Caroline soon followed out the door and then sat next to her. She looked flushed and smiled over at me before whispering something into Miss Betsy's ear.

I looked around for Hunter. I still didn't see him, or his brothers, for that matter. I did see a shadow directly in front of me on the other side of the flames. I looked hard. No one else seemed to notice the slender frame. Then it moved around the fire. It was Molly, her eyes reflecting the flames, red, hot, and burning me.

Maybe we should talk woman to woman. I could tell her I'm sorry things didn't work out for her. As I started to stand, looking at Molly, Miss Betsy saw what I was about to do and gently sat me back down.

"That's not such a good idea, dear," she whispered into my ear.

Molly watched me as she stepped into the shadows but not out of my sight. Her eyes drifted away from me. I followed her new direction to find Hunter staring at her from across the flames, his face hard and angry.

I went to get up again, but Miss Betsy pulled me back down.

"Just wait, dear." She patted me on the leg.

I grunted.

John stepped out in front of the large crowd.

Hunter walked out with his brothers, one on each side of him, with their arms around his shoulders. They stopped, and each hugged him and went to go sit with the crowd.

Hunter made his way to me.

He sat down, not meeting my eyes. His feet tapped along the ground, and then he shifted in his seat. I placed my hand on top of his, and he laced his fingers in mine and then pulled my hand up to his lips with a gentle kiss, his eyes fixed on John.

"Welcome, friends. Thank you for being with us on this very special night." Hunter rocked on his heels. "God has truly blessed us all. He has taken us from the deepest and darkest hour to raise us up with his own hands, chosen to fight with him in that final hour to defeat the evil of this world. Praise be to God," John cheered.

Everyone said amen.

"We have been honored to walk among the weak, to share with them the hope that is only in the risen Savior. You have allowed God to use you to snatch the souls of people from the very darkness and bring them into the light, so when the day comes they depart this world, they stand before the gates of heaven instead of being fed to the hounds of hell," he continued on with his pep talk, and the people clapped and cheered, and then his tone changed to a more serious topic.

"Our enemy is on the move. We need to be more watchful than ever. The time is near, my friends. Our time is coming to show God what we are made of. It's time our faith be tested in ways unimaginable, and we need to stay firm." He stared out into the darkness. "Even in our darkest hour, God knows our pain, and he wants to comfort us. We need to lean on him and not let the evil sweep us away." He paused for a moment with a long sigh and stared into the darkness. "Praise be to God forever."

Everyone echoed, "Praise God."

"Now, friends, let us rejoice in tonight, for God has blessed us once again," John said, although there was something not rejoicing in his tone—more of a sound of defeat.

I could feel the pulse in Hunter's wrists quicken, his eyes focused on John.

"Let me first tell you a story about a young man. He was our great grandfather of long ago," John said, now sitting in the chair in front of the fire, his hands up in the air.

I was already at the edge of my seat, ready for his next words to pour out.

"A young man wandered along a river, his heart filled with love for a girl in his village. All the other young men had tried to get her attention, but she showed no interest in any of them. He wandered for hours, thinking of how he could stand out in the crowd of suitors. How could he make her see he was her one true love? He wasn't tall like some of the other boys, who could reach up high for the best fruit on the trees and leave baskets of treats at her feet. He wasn't strong, so he couldn't hunt the buffalo to offer her parents. He wasn't even the most handsome or sought after, as some of the other boys. He had nothing special to compete against them. He got down on one knee and prayed to God. He asked God to send him a sign, a thought, something that would help him win the girl he loved with all his heart, something that would stake his claim on her so the other boys would flee. Just then, an object hit him hard on his knee, sending a sensation throughout his body. He didn't remember kneeling in the stream." John paused and reached down.

"He looked down at a long stick, and a vision of music flooded his mind. God had given him the answer, and with God's directions, he hollowed out the stick with a hot stone and dug out five holes, all the time recalling the image God had placed in his head. Once he was done, he blew into the stick. The most beautiful music came out.

"The young man was out in the woods for hours. He listened to this heart as he composed a song just for her. That night, he played her song outside of her hut, and she fell in love with him. That song became their song and would follow them into the afterlife, binding them eternally," John concluded and stood up.

Everyone seemed to have a tear in their eye, including me.

What a beautiful story.

I then noticed the short stick Hunter clung to in his other hand. John looked over at Hunter, and he stood up and faced the crowd.

Hunter began to play.

The sound was beautiful and faraway. With each breath in and out, a new, haunting, old sound filled the air and floated in the sky as it escaped out of each hole of the flute. I closed my eyes, letting it flow into my soul, dancing and caressing my heart. I felt his soul and my soul folding together like no other feeling I could describe. No one else was around, just the two of us together in a world I created just for us. It was magical until the music stopped.

No one made a sound. Hunter's eyes were on me, and tears swelled in my eyes. He reached his hand out toward me, and I did the same as our hands joined.

"No." We both heard a small voice stepping out from the shadows and turned toward it. "No, no," Molly continued to say, but the intruder's voice drowned her out and screamed at me over and over.

No, no, no. You stupid girl.

The voice stabbed at my inner ear, and I placed my hands over the top. "Go away," I screamed back, not caring if everyone thought I was losing my mind. Maybe I was crazy.

You know you aren't good enough for him. Leave now. Run. Run.

"No," I cried and fell to my knees.

Molly was no longer my immediate issue, blurred out by the shaking of my body.

"Jessie, what's wrong," Hunter asked, dropping down next to me.

My temples pounded beneath the tips of my fingers, and I pressed hard, hoping it would help. It didn't, and the sharp tone continued to explode inside. I didn't care anymore if he thought I was crazy.

"The voice in my head," I said, locking down on my teeth. "It's awful."

"Davior!"

"What?" I asked through my pressed lips, crouching into a ball.

"James," Hunter hollered with an edge to his voice.

"Yes, I'm on it. Hang in there, Jessie," James said before running off into the trees past Molly, who just stared at me with a look of enjoyment across her face.

Then, just as quickly as it came, the voice was gone, and so was Molly.

"Is the voice gone?" Hunter asked, putting his arms around me, feeling my body shake under his arms.

"Yes," I said with tears in my voice. "I'm sorry I didn't tell you. I wasn't sure it was him. I mean, I knew it wasn't me, but..."

"You couldn't have known. He was taking some of what you told him and using it against you, making you think it could have been your own thoughts. I should have seen what he was doing," he soothed. "James ran him off, and now you know it wasn't your voice, it would do him no good to continue it."

"That's good." I rubbed the spot between my eyes. "Don't blame yourself. Until now, most of the time I heard that voice was when you were gone. How could you have known?" Then I realized something else was ruined, the reason Molly interrupted and Davior screamed. The commotion hadn't stopped the eyes of our guests watching us, and they were all too quiet.

"Just in case, next time you hear strange voices, I want to be the first to know."

I nodded my head in agreement against his strong chest.

"So, where were we?" He spoke softly.

Hunter reached into his pocket and pulled out a beaded ring, covered with tiny, turquoise gemstones. "Jessica, the song I played was for you, your song, like the song the young man played for his love. I love you, and I will love you all the days of my life." He held the ring out, his hand shaking while he slipped it on my finger. "Will you marry me?"

Everything went silent, even the crackling of the fire, the crowd, the birds, the wind—all held their breath, awaiting my answer. I felt overwhelmed as I stared at the dark brown gemstone ring. Everything was happening so fast.

I looked into Hunter's nervous face, and I couldn't help but smile. He looked so much like a little boy, waiting for my answer. I looked back down at the ring. Why was I hesitating? I loved him. I loved him more than my own life. He was so much more than a friend or even a boyfriend. My emotions got the best of me as I lunged for him in a long kiss, knocking him off his balance.

We heard a loud, painful cry that pulled us away from each other once again, only this time it wasn't in my head.

"Molly?" I said under my breath.

"I told them she shouldn't have been here tonight," he said, not caring about the sorrowful cry in the darkness and guiding my face back to meet his. "Was that a yes?" he asked in a nervous chuckle.

"Yes," I said softly. "I love you."

John jumped up and put his arms around both of us. "Annabel and I are pleased at this union, and you have our blessing," John said, looking at Annabel.

"Finally," someone called out, and the crowd cheered.

He said "our" blessing, but he meant Annabel's blessing.

John turned so only we could see his serious face.

"It's your decision to set the date, but there are certain things that must be done first. You are to be married, unless…"

Hunter cleared his voice, and John got the meaning and changed the topic.

John then whispered, "I must go and find Molly. I'll take your brothers with me. You stay here and play for our guests."

"Yes, sir," he said, looking at me.

"I would love to hear you play more, although, not my song."

He nodded. "I'll only play that one for you from now on." His lips brushed against mine before he began to play.

The evening continued on as if nothing bad had happened at all. After Hunter played a few more melodies, people began to socialize. There were plenty of snacks and s'mores. I warned May of an unpleasant stomachache to follow if she didn't slow down. She just gave me a big, chocolate-toothed smile. Hunter stayed by my side, sneaking in soft kisses and tight embraces where he could.

Miss Mabel caught us at one of those moments. "I'm so happy for you both." She hugged us. "God brought you here, and we know why now. Everything else will work out. If you trust the good Lord, He will see you through."

"Are you leaving?" I asked.

"Yes. It's time to get back. Josephine wanted to come, but you know Joseph. I don't want to leave them too long. Good night, my loves." She kissed us both and was gone.

Hunter pulled me from the crowd, through the house, to the garden on the other side of house.

My head was still spinning. *I'm engaged. And not to just someone, but someone I want, someone I love more than I could ever imagine.*

"We need to talk," he said. "I want you to just listen to me first, please." He sounded serious.

"First of all, I didn't want to propose to you this way. It's just part of our traditions, and I didn't want to take it away from my family. In our traditions, I shouldn't have even kissed you before now."

Oh no. What's this about?

He read my worried expression. "No." He smiled. "I want to marry you…I would marry you right at this moment if I could. There are certain matters that are out of my hands, and our engagement might be longer than we both want."

I know he wants me, that's enough for now. I'll wait as long as I have to.

"I warned you to let me finish, my love," he said softly.

Say that last part again. I nodded and took a deep breath.

"There is one thing you should know before you agree to marry me," he said, taking both my hands in his and raising them to rest on his chest.

His heart was fiercely pounding.

"When God saved us and blessed us with this life, he also gave us all the glories of the life he created. As you already know,

I'll age, but much slower than you will. The older I get, the less I age."

Unless the war comes first. I nodded my head.

"The elders in our faith have tried to decipher codes from scrolls God left us. The one man who knew how to read them vanished years ago. He took some of the scrolls and hid them, so we only have fragments. In the scrolls, there were prophecies made about our people. One of them was about the last days of earth as we know it. In the last days, our women will no longer be able to bear our children. The sign of this would be the last child born would have special gifts. One was that he or she would be able to communicate with animals. We believe it's May. No woman in our tribe has given birth in more than six years." He paused, looking at me sadly.

"But you can communicate with animals."

"No, I can't actually speak to them. May can have actual dialogue with them, and they with her."

That explained the crane, although I never actually heard her speak, since she spoke in a whisper. "You said gifts. What are the others?"

"Uh…" A funny look came over his face. "Um…the child would be able to change the hearts of men who have turned to the darkness back to the light and would also have healing powers. We take these things for what they are, humans trying to understand the mind of God. The facts that she does communicate with animals and that women have stopped having children, it just seems to make sense."

"Wow. Our May. I knew she was special."

Looking at me, rather frustrated, he said, "Jess, by marrying me, you'll never be able to…I mean, we won't be able to have children together." He swallowed hard.

I sat there for a moment. In all the times I dreamed of my future and what I wanted it to be, I had never considered children. *Uh, that's sort of weird for a woman to not think about children, isn't it?*

"It doesn't matter to me. As long as I have God and you, I'm complete."

My hands reached out for his face. It felt hot but began to cool at my touch.

"You don't seem too sad about it," he said.

I noticed even though he was relieved by my reply, he seemed almost sad.

"Does it bother you? I mean not to have children?" I asked.

"Yes. I think to have a child is one of the greatest gifts God gave to his people." He looked very dreamy. "God has blessed me with you, and I have no right to ask for more." He pulled me to him. "So you really do want to marry me?"

I wrapped my arms around his neck. "Unless you have something more to toss at me to try to scare me away?" I teased.

"Oh, well, just the end-of-the-world stuff. You seem to be adjusting well to that already."

"That works for me too, because then I don't die before you." I paused, seeing his expression change. "I know God is in control and everything will work out in the end. I'm actually luckier than the other humans," I said halfheartedly and smiled.

Hunter looked at me funny. "And why is that?"

"For one thing, I get to live here, where they can't go, and since I know you all age slow, you don't have to stage your deaths. When I go, I'll have you all around me."

"I guess that's a different way to look at it," he said, and then his face turned sad again. "Only, you are very young, my sweet girl, and there is no need to talk about death."

"Sorry, you're right." I nuzzled against his chest. "We should focus on the time we have together and let God handle the rest."

"Well, we still have to be watchful and obedient. God does handle every situation, and if we listen close enough, He'll guide us through it. Just because He knows the decisions we make and the situations we put ourselves in doesn't mean He wanted us to take that route. Always remember that," he said little more seriously.

"So don't purposely seek out dangerous situations. Got it."

"Exactly!" He smiled and then kissed me softly, lingering.

"Hunter, um…sorry." It was Jordan coming around the corner.

Hunter looked up at him. "I need to talk to you." He looked at me. "Sorry, Jess."

I looked at Hunter. "Go. I'm fine."

James came around the corner, followed by John.

"I'll meet you in the study in five minutes," Hunter said, taking my hand.

"No. It's fine. Go," I said.

"Yes. Take her back to where the guests are, to Annabel," John agreed with Hunter.

Hunter led me back to the party.

"I thought you said I was safe here? Why couldn't I—?"

"Something has changed, Jess, and until I know what's going on, stay near my mother."

I pouted.

"Please, Jess, don't fight me on this. Promise me."

"Okay," I agreed.

I saw Annabel across the courtyard, and she started walking toward us.

"I'll be back soon." He kissed my cheek and ran toward the office.

"Do you know what's going on?" Annabel asked.

"Molly?" I guessed.

"I'm not sure. She was pretty upset. Come on, dear. Let's have a cup of tea." She led me into the house.

We walked to another part of the house, a greenhouse type room, filled with roses, daffodils, tulips, and carnations, just to name a few. The ceiling reached up tall, and I noticed a shelf that went around the entire room lined up with books. White wicker chairs were clumped together in small areas around the room. The smell of the flowers perfumed the air, and then I realized it smelled like Annabel. The white, elegant French doors opened to a veranda that spilled out of the room. Right away, it was my favorite room.

She left for a moment and then was back with a tea set. We sat down on the soft pillows out on the veranda.

"This is my room. John has his study, and this one is mine. Do you like it?" she asked.

"It's beyond words. I can't believe I missed seeing this room all these months," I answered, sipping my tea.

"Then it's yours too. Feel free anytime. After all, you will be my daughter-in-law soon enough." She smiled. "It seems like everything is moving fast. I know." She sighed. "It happened the same way for me. Only I was nineteen, practically a child still, and scared out of my mind, but then I saw John standing in front of me. We were married two months after we met, and I thank God every day for this life."

"There's something I have been wondering." I wasn't sure how to ask it.

"Like I said before, you can ask me anything, Jessie." She poured me a second cup.

"Well, everyone has said how happy they are for Hunter and he's been alone for so long. What about James and Jordan? I haven't met a wife or seen anyone."

"Oh, well, Jordan's wife died over six years ago. She died in childbirth. There was nothing the doctors could do."

"Oh, I'm sorry."

"She's with the Lord, and they'll be reunited soon enough." She paused. "James was married, oh, seventy years or so. You lose track when you've been around as long as we have." She laughed. "They had enjoyed many years together, but they weren't able to have children. His wife had a rare tumor when she was young, and to save her life, they removed her ovaries. They both loved children and spent a lot of time at the shack with Miss Mabel."

Maybe Hunter and I could live there too? But then I remembered there would be no more children, and I felt a little sad.

"Recently, he started thinking about remarrying, but I think he changed his mind."

I wondered if it had to do with me. I remembered how he sort of flirted with me until Hunter just about attacked him.

"How are you feeling?" Annabel asked, placing her hand on my knee.

"I'm not sure," I said. "Everything is moving pretty fast."

"You two have been flirting with each other since the day you met." She laughed.

I guess we have. And I was too busy, too worried about how he felt to notice he had treated me differently since the first day.

"I guess that's true." But then I thought about the way John had looked at the bonfire. He didn't seem very happy about the announcement, more like he was being forced. "But I didn't think John wanted…" I paused, thinking I shouldn't say anything.

"We have a lot of old traditions. The reasons behind them are mostly for a good reason," she said, leaning back in her chair. "John wanted Hunter to wait even longer, but with the rules and a chaperone following you both around, it was clear to me you belong to each other; therefore, everything else will work out. John means well and wants what's best for both of you. There is a matter not quite cleared up, and John had wanted to tie up loose ends before giving his approval."

Molly, I thought. *He wanted to give her time to accept it.*

Annabel poured another splash of hot water into her cup and mine.

"So, should we include your mother in the planning?" Annabel asked straightforwardly.

I hadn't thought much about it yet. *Wedding.* The thought echoed through my mind. Just that word alone use to leave a bad taste in my mouth, but now the taste was different, sweet and delightful. But the thought of my mother brought another taste to my mouth, one I shouldn't even try to describe. *What would she think of me marrying Hunter? She would be impressed by the fine paintings and lavish details of this house. Would she think I was marrying better than she had planned and give her blessings? No, she wouldn't.* It wasn't money that drove my mother; it was power, and Seth was well on his way to obtaining it, only I wondered if it was the kind she was hoping for.

"I don't think that would be a good idea," I finally answered, staring at the fine features in the tile floor. "Anyway, I thought regular people couldn't come here?"

"We can bring her here without her knowing exactly where she is."

"I appreciate the offer, but—"

"She wouldn't be able to hurt you here. I wouldn't allow it. No one would allow it. She should be here, at least for the wedding. No matter what, she is your mother, the woman who carried you in her womb for nine months." She placed her hand back on my knee. "Pray about it, Jess, please."

"Okay." I sulked down in my seat. "I'll pray about it."

Dear God, Please say no.

She patted my knee and got up, carrying the tray. "Oh, by the way, the boys are not allowed in here, so if you need a place to think or just get a moment to yourself, just shut the door." She winked. "Shall we go tell our guests good night? It's getting late."

Annabel gave me even more to think about. I almost felt guiltily I didn't want my mother to be part of my life at all. I might have forgiven her for those things I knew had happened, but what if she had planned my father's attack? What if she had planned for him to be killed and not just injured? I didn't know how I would react face to face. Could I forgive something so horrible?

God forgave all of David's sins, and he had a man killed. David was a good example of how far God's forgiveness would stretch, and although I hadn't sinned like him, I was forgiven and had no right not to forgive. *Easier to say it than to do it.*

Then I started to think more about me.

Shouldn't my wedding day be about me for a change, not her?

I could see her turning everything into a party that somehow helped her or made her look good. She would complain about everything I wanted. I pictured her pulling out her wedding dress and holding it up to me, the one her mother and her mother before her wore. I had hated the tight-fitting dress, and it smelled musty. How many times had I protested? I felt the pain moving inside me. The dormant volcano once again sparked inside. *If I forgave her, why am I feeling like this? Why am I bringing the past up?* I thought and then answered, *because I know what she's capable of.*

I sat there for a long moment in the soft chair, staring out into the shadows of the garden.

"Jess," I heard someone whisper softly.

I looked around the room but didn't see anyone. I got up anyway and stood at the open doorway to the garden. I was sure Annabel was wondering what had happened to me. I stretched, wiping my face, and looked up into the night sky, the stars beaming down.

Hunter's arms went around my waist, pulling me into his warm body. He whispered close to my ear, sending chills down my spine, "You are going to get me in so much trouble for coming in here," he said in an uneasy tone.

I found it funny he was truly afraid of being caught, and not of demons or Seth or even my mother, but of his mother. *Interesting.*

I leaned into him, letting him support my body, still looking up at the sky. His head moved down to rest his cheek to mine. It felt nice, soft and cool against my chapped skin. Finally, he wasn't turning away, finally the wait, the wonder of how he felt about me, was over.

He loved me, and I loved him.

"Is everything all right?" he asked, stroking his cheek against mine.

"Your mom thinks I should invite my mother to help with the wedding plans and be a part of the wedding. I don't think I can do that." I turned toward him, snuggling into his embrace, his cheek resting on top of my hair.

"She can't hurt you anymore, and she has no power over any of us. It's totally up to you. I'm not sure I agree with the timing, but you do need to face her, Jess."

It surprised me to hear him say that, and I looked up into his beautiful face, confused.

"But then she'll know I'm alive. She'll be in our lives. She's a horrible, terrible person. She will make everyone miserable, and I don't know what will come out of her mouth. She's…" I blurted out, and I pulled away from him to gather control. In a softer tone, I said, "I said I forgive her, but maybe I really haven't."

"Seth knows where you are," Hunter said, reminding me.

"That's true," I said, wondering if he would share his new-found friends with her too.

"Just because you forgive someone doesn't mean it doesn't still hurt. You need to confront her about…" He paused. "I'm sorry. I know you don't want to talk about it."

I didn't know what to say. I knew he knew, but I still couldn't get the words out. Somehow, saying it out loud made it more real. I wasn't ready. He pulled me back to him. "You're worrying too much, honey. We have time to talk about it. It would be different here. She would be different. Let's not talk about it anymore tonight. Okay?" he pleaded, working his fingers into mine.

"First, can we please leave before she catches me in here?" Hunter let out a huff.

I chuckled through my tears, and we left the room. Mission accomplished; Hunter didn't get caught.

Everyone had cleared out by the time we returned to the courtyard. James and Jordan were putting out the fire. They looked like little kids in the middle of the street on a hot summer day, dumping water on each other instead of the fire. John went over to help since they seemed to be having problems. He carried a bigger bucket. He got close and lifted it over their heads without them knowing it and drenched the two. Both boys looked at each other and, with the same thought, picked up John. We followed them as they carried him toward the pool, with him protesting the entire time, and then they all went flying into the pool.

Everyone roared in laughter. The three in the pool looked at each other and then at Hunter.

"Oh no." He backed away, but they were already climbing out of the pool.

"I thought you weren't afraid to take the plunge, little brother," James teased.

"Ha ha." He darted out of his reach, only to be caught by John.

They all grabbed a piece of him and jumped into the pool.

May, Annabel, and I laughed at the silly boys.

"Come, ladies. Let's retire for the evening," Annabel said, putting her arm around both of us.

Both May and I yawned. It had been one busy, crazy, unexpected day. I glanced back at the young man watching me. I felt a little sad I wouldn't see him until morning, but it wouldn't be long before... My heart thumped wildly again.

As I was getting ready for bed, I thought about how Hunter played the song he wrote for just me. I had never written anything before, but I wanted to try. If it was terrible, I would never have to play it for him. I already played a melody in my mind every time I saw him and thought about him. Now to compose it. Of course, if I left my room, he'd follow me, so I needed a plan.

Talk to Annabel in the morning, she'll know what to do.

I heard a soft knock at the door. I opened it slowly.

"I just wanted to say good night." He touched my hand, curling his fingers into mine and bringing my hand up to his lips. "Sleep well."

His face moved toward mine, and with a gentle, soft kiss, barely touching my lips, he whispered, "I love you."

How much I wanted him to lie next to me so I could listen to his heart beat, feeling his chest rise and fall, taking my mind off of everything but him.

I didn't want to think about my mother, yet she took center stage. How fitting that my happiest day ever would be clouded with thoughts of my mother. She would have loved that.

"I love you."

Our foreheads bent together.

We both noticed May watching. I giggled. She waved to Hunter, and he smiled and said good night to her too before shutting the door.

"I'm so tired!" she exclaimed. "Can I sleep with you tonight?" she asked.

"I thought you liked your own room," I said, remembering her excitement of having her own room.

"I do, but..."

She didn't have to explain. Molly's painful cry echoed throughout all of our minds.

"Sure. Climb in. Which side do you want?" I asked.

"This one okay?" She took the side closer to Hunter's room.

Of course she would. I wasn't the only who felt safer when he was near. "Perfect. Good night, May."

"Night, Jess. Love you." She yawned.

I meant to say it back, but she was already snoring. I guess it was a good thing we all slept in the same room for a long time. The snoring had become comforting.

My New Secret

May was still asleep and curled up with a pillow in her arms when I snuck out of bed. The night, still holding on to the dark, shadowy world, would soon give way to the light of a new day. A few birds squawked, some soft and cheerful, with a few loud, high-pitched sounds coming from farther in the swamp. The air felt cool and wet and smelled like a fresh new day.

I hoped Annabel was already up, and I quietly slipped on my robe and slippers. She mentioned to me in passing she was up before the rooster crowed at dawn. Of course, I had never heard a rooster crow anywhere for that matter. I assumed it was a metaphor meaning early. Anyway, I wanted her to myself with no one else to hear our conversation; after all, it was going to be a secret, my big surprise.

"My, you're up bright and early." Annabel smiled, watching me enter the room. She then folded up the newspaper and placed it in a basket on the long table. "Would you like some coffee?"

"Yes please," I answered. "Is anyone else up yet?" I asked, looking around for signs of tall, masculine figures.

"No. Just us."

"There is something I would like to do, but I'm not sure how. I thought maybe you could help me."

Her eyes lit up as she sat next to me, setting the coffee in front of me.

"I want to try to compose a song. I've never done it before, so I don't know if it will be any good, but I want to try. The problem is, how can I work on it without Hunter knowing or seeing me work on the music?" I asked and sipped the hot, cream-filled coffee that was just the way I liked it.

"We have a small piano sitting in a storage room. No one would know if we moved it into my room," Annabel suggested.

"But wouldn't someone suspect something if they heard the music?"

"No, dear. Those doors are solid oak and are built specially to keep noise from escaping. You will have to make sure you shut and lock all the doors and windows when you play. Even though Hunter knows he is not supposed to be in there, if he knows you're in there, I'm not sure he'll keep to the rules." She smiled, raising one eyebrow. She knew he was in there the day before. "We can cover the front of the piano with plants and flowers, so if anyone glanced in there by chance with the doors open, no one would know it was there. I'll take care of the arrangement. You can start tomorrow if you wish."

"What about Hunter letting me out of his sight?" I asked, knowing there was no longer any reason he had to stay away from me or be purposely kept busy.

"I'll take care of that too. For the daytime hours, I have a list of projects I've put off lately. This would be a good time to start checking them off." She paused in thought. "For the evening hours, you'll need some alone time, maybe a book to read on those nights when you can't sleep." She winked.

"Thanks." I got up and hugged her.

The sound coming from the staircase sounded like a herd of wild animals, big ones, heading in our direction. But it was only Hunter who stood at the doorway, breathing hard.

"Oh, there you are," he said, trying not to sound worried. He swung me around and kissed my cheek. "You're up early," he said, trying to disguise the worry in his tone.

"Girl talk," Annabel said. "Hunter, I need to talk to you after breakfast for just a few minutes."

"Am I in trouble?" he asked, looking at me with a quizzical look.

"Not yet."

"Good girl," Annabel approved.

Breakfast tasted wonderful, and everyone talked about the night before and teased their little brother.

"I told you he wouldn't pass out," Jordan argued with James.

"He was this close," he said, making his fingers form sort of a pinch but still open.

"Nah. He did better than we did." Jordan, who was sitting on the other side of Hunter, nudged his shoulder.

"That's right," Hunter joined in. "James, you passed out. How did I forget that?" He looked at Jordan, and they both looked at James.

"It was almost a century ago." Jordan laughed.

"Yeah, well, you try being the first one to have to do that." James looked a little embarrassed, looking up at me.

"That had to be very hard to do," I offered, "especially in front of a crowd."

"No. Hunter is the only one who had to do it in front of the tribe. We did it with our family present only," Jordan said, clearing off some of the plates. "I thought for sure he'd pass out,".

"Oh." I thought for a moment. "Why was that exactly? Why did he have to do it in front of everyone?"

Hunter pushed back his chair to look at me. "Their soon-to-be wives knew nothing of our real life. James and Jordan lived off in the world. They found love there but could never tell their wives about this place or our history. Our family traveled to where they were living to meet the ladies and carry out our traditions. So it was just family they played for, but in tradition, it is supposed to be before the entire tribe."

"We had to play in front of their family members too. My mother-in-law just about attacked me after I played," James interrupted.

We laughed. I understood. The music was so alluring.

"But how is it that I am allowed to know? Don't get me wrong, I am completely happy about it, but why am I so different?"

John answered, "Jessica, no one…not since we have been immortal has anyone ever just stumbled onto this land. At first, we were worried you were part of some scheme Davior was part of to get inside our borders. Then, after you faced him and turned to God, it was clear you weren't part of any scheme. God sent you to us, to my son. But we don't know why. That is why I've asked you both to wait on setting a date."

My dad was planning to take me somewhere, somewhere my mother could never find me. Could it have been here? I thought about the painting of the chief in my father's office and the crosses that looked almost identical to the one hanging above the mantel in the shack. *If my dad was one of them, could that mean…* I stayed quiet until May pulled on my shirt.

"Will you come in the pool with me? Please!"

I held her face in my hands. "How can I refuse you?" I hopped up, leaving Hunter still staring at his father.

"Oh, wait. With all this commotion… It's Sunday, isn't it?" Annabel questioned. "James?"

"Yes, it is. Sorry, May. After lunch." James said, and May nodded. "We reopen the church today," he said, looking over at me. "That's what we've been working on and finally finished on Friday."

"What time does it start?" I asked, looking down at my robe and slippers.

Hunter jumped up. "We've got thirty minutes to be in the sanctuary."

Everyone scattered to get dressed. Hunter, May, and I jogged up the stairs.

"So where is this church?" I asked.

"You've only seen a fraction of the grounds, my love." He smiled. "We've been doing some remodeling, which is why we haven't gone."

"I know. Annabel told me. At least I know what you guys have been doing all these weeks?" I asked.

"That and a few other things. Twenty-five minutes and counting," he said before leaving me at my door.

I had so many dresses to choose from. Normally, I would stay clear of anything pink. My mother had tried to cram pink into everything I owned. However, there was an appealing light pink dress that seemed to speak to me. I pulled it out, along with a pair of pink and white heels.

I've never been in a church before, except for that one time. I hope this is okay to wear.

I stepped into the dress, pulling it up. I couldn't quite zip it all the way up, so I left it and would ask May to help me before we walked out. I sat at the vanity to fix my hair. I didn't wear it up often, but it would be much quicker. There were all kinds of things in the drawers: ribbons, combs, scrunches, clips, bobby pins, and other things I'd never seen before. I piled my hair up on top and fastened it down with a stick comb which had white flowers and pink sparkles all over it.

As I looked in the mirror, I thought of how much older I looked with my hair up. I saw my mother's face in the reflection and quickly turned around to find no one was there. I went over to May's room. She had already left.

I heard a knock.

"Ready?" Hunter asked through the door.

"Um…yes, but…" I paused. "May left, and I can't seem to zip my dress all the way."

"Can I help?" I looked in the mirror to see how far it went on my own.

Past the bra strap…but I guess it's okay.

"Jess?" he called again.

"Come in," I said. "I guess it's fine."

I turned around before he entered with my back to him. I could feel his hand on the back of my neck. He gently moved his fingertips up and down, sending chills down my spine. I couldn't move.

"Please," I whispered, not really wanting him to stop.

I felt his hand fumble for the zipper and slowly but deliberately touch my skin until it was all the way, and then he pressed his lips on the base of my neck and lingered there for a moment.

"Are you trying to drive me out of my skin, and just before going to church?" I huffed, placing my hand on my heart, and turned to him.

"Sorry. I couldn't help myself." He smiled, slightly blushing. "You are very hard to resist, and beautiful, as usual."

"And you are very handsome," I said, straightening his tie.

I looked into his eyes, leaning into him, and kissed him softly and slowly. He blushed again.

"Ready?" he held out his arm.

We walked down the stairs and through the back door. We walked for about ten minutes, along the cobblestone path, before reaching a white church. The building was another large structure adorned with stained glass windows on all sides. There were familiar faces walking up the steps, once again congratulating us.

Hunter and I walked up the stairs and through the heavy-timber double doors. I tried to sit in the back and out of sight, but James ushered us to the front of the church, where the rest of the family sat. A man I had not met led the music.

We stood and sang "Amazing Grace," and I knew the first verse. I didn't realize there were other verses to the song. As I sang, I following along in the book Hunter held up for me. I felt tears swelling up. It was such a beautiful song. *God really did give us amazing grace.*

It seemed like every song picked touched my soul in some way, like it was meant for me at that exact moment in my life. I kept dabbing my eyes. Powerful emotions, one right after another, flowed through me. *Why am I crying?* But I kept singing, getting louder when it came to the repeated choruses, and I didn't care how I sounded. I was singing praises to God and I loved it. We sang four more songs before sitting as John took center stage.

"Good morning," he addressed the congregation.

Everyone echoed him.

"It's a beautiful day that God has created for us. Amen."

John opened his Bible and began his sermon.

The sermon focused on John the Baptist and how his life was created to pave the way for Christ. He talked about the obedience John had in listening to what God had told him to do and how following his example kept us in a closer relationship with God himself. "Christ was baptized by an ordinary man, an imperfect man. Why? So that we too can follow His example." James asked me once about being baptized and yet I didn't follow through. *It's time I did, I wanted to.*

After the sermon, we sang a few more songs, and then we were dismissed.

"James, can you take Jess back to the house? I need to talk to Dad for a minute."

"My lady." James offered his arm as my questioning look caught Hunter's eyes.

"I'll be just behind you," Hunter said to me.

James and I started our walk back.

"James, how is it that you are here and not at your church?" I asked as we walked out together.

"Oh, well, it was time to move on anyway," he said.

"Why? You hadn't been there very long." It was something I remembered from a previous conversation.

"I'm needed here right now, and that's okay with me. Dad said I can preach here from time to time if I want to."

"I was thinking about the sermon today. How does the whole baptism thing go?" I was trying not to sound too anxious but like it was more for informational purposes.

"The first thing you should do is make a public profession in front of the congregation. After that, you follow through in believer's baptism."

"What is a public profession?"

"You are just letting others know you are a fellow believer in Christ. We then take a little walk over to the stream behind the church and submerge you under the water." He laughed, looking at me. "Are you all right? You look a little pale."

"You hold them under the water?"

"Dunked is more like it. Jess, no one would let you drown." He laughed.

"I know. It's just…" I tried to think of an excuse for my fear, but I couldn't think of one. "I think I…I'd like to be baptized," I said quickly, like pulling off a Band-Aid.

"Of course you can. I can let my dad—"

I interrupted him. "Would you do it?"

James looked at me, surprised but happy, maybe more like honored, I would ask him. "If that's what you want," he said.

I nodded.

"I'm supposed to lead the service in a few weeks, unless you want to do it sooner." James was already thinking about a sermon.

"No. A few weeks is good. Just let me know for sure which Sunday so I can…prepare."

"Okay," he agreed.

"Don't tell Hunter though," I said.

James looked at me, surprised.

"I want to surprise him."

"Oh, sure. No problem. He'll be very happy," James said and led me into the house, where May stood in front of us with her swimsuit already on.

"You're going to turn into a fish." I teased.

"After lunch, May," James said with a fatherly voice.

She huffed and walked toward the kitchen to see when that would be. I followed after her. Annabel would probably need help anyway.

The afternoon was filled with pool time. After we played a few rounds of volleyball, we sat around the pool. I listened to the guys argue about which man suffered more in the Bible. It was funny watching them all huddled at one end of the pool. Annabel came over and started asking me questions about my favorite flowers and colors, with May adding in her suggestions

I still couldn't grasp the fact I was going to be married. I also didn't anticipate I would plummet into one of my musical daydreams and be able to stay there forever, but I had done it. Every silly little girl's dream landed just where I was. The king and queen, the prince, the dark evil outside the gates, it was real. I was glad my plans were not the ones God had planned for me. I was glad His plan was better and bigger than the one I tried to do on my own. I wanted to share that with others, the ones who scoffed at God like I had done and tell them God's plans are better. I wondered if I would get that chance, but with the evil that waited to snatch me, I'd only put everyone at risk. If I left, I knew Hunter would follow; they all would follow, and the bloodshed would be my fault.

It was more important than before to stay, no matter how long. Of course, that's what I wanted all along.

A few weeks dashed by. James and Jordan left half days to help out with some missionary churches up the coast. I wasn't exactly sure where they went, but they were always back by mid afternoon for some game or deep conversations neither I nor May were privileged to hear. Hunter was not left out of those meetings, which gave me some time to work on my project, but it never seemed enough time, and I hadn't made much progress on my song. I would stare at blank note paper Annabel had dug out for me to use.

I also spent time with Annabel in the gardens, hoping for inspiration. She had done almost all the work herself and took care of every garden on the grounds. John would help on occasion for heavy lifting, but she really had done most of it alone before May and I had come along.

Hunter made trips out to Miss Mabel's and the orphanage, where Miss C. and Miss B. were, twice a week to check on their supplies and needs. He was never gone long and would bring back a basket full of fruits and vegetables.

Anytime Hunter left, I would sneak into Annabel's special room to work on the composition. There were a few late nights when I couldn't sleep, so I'd sneak down, trying my best not to wake anyone. Although Hunter always managed to follow me down and hide behind a fake tree in the hall. I would go into the room anyway and work for a few hours. When I had finished, he would still be there and quietly follow me back up. I felt bad he was so worried about me, so I limited my nightly runs and composed more during the daytime. Hunter seemed much more anxious in the evening hours than during the day.

I remembered how Davior had said the best part of the day was the night. *Demons come out at night*, I thought and then laughed. *That's so cliché.*

A few Sundays went by, and I heard James going over his sermon notes in the game room, and as I passed by, he looked up from the notebook and winked. I had been anxious about this day ever since I'd mentioned I had wanted to be baptized. I wanted to be baptized; however, his little wink only made me more fretful, and it sent my heart into a panic. I took some deep, casual breaths as I sat down at the table for breakfast so Hunter wouldn't notice.

We all ate and headed out for church. Along way, new faces joined our walk, and I was introduced as Hunter's fiancé. I loved hearing it. *The future Mrs. Hunter Fox.* I smiled and shook their hands.

We got to the church and sat in our normal spots. James got up and began after the music, but I didn't hear the sermon at all. I did, however, watch every move James made across the stage. Then the moment had come. James asked if anyone would like to come forward to join the fellowship. Everyone looked around in sort of an amused sort of way. *Of course they all were believers, all baptized, so why would he ask such a question?* He then looked right at me as I stared back. I felt like a deer caught in headlights, and I couldn't move. He kept his eyes on me until everyone was looking at me, which made the situation worse. I finally stood and began to walk forward. I kept my head down but could see smiling faces from the corner of my eye.

"Jessica, do you know Christ as your personal savior?" James asked me.

"Yes."

"Will you follow Christ and be baptized by submersion?"

I hesitated. Hunter slipped his hand into mine. I felt a sense of comfort Hunter followed me and stood at my side. The most important decision of my life, and he was there to share it with me.

"Yes," I said confidently.

"Amen," James called out, and the congregation confirmed. "Let's sing 'Praise Be to the Lord' as we walk out to the river."

Everyone exited out of the church, singing as loud as they could until we got to river. The water flowed gently, and I shouldn't have hesitated. I put one toe in and shivered. The water was extremely cold, ice cold. James waited, holding out his hand for me, his teeth chattering.

I can't go through with it. I can't step out there. It's too cold. I was making excuses while James turned into a popsicle, his lips matching the color of the sky.

"It's not that bad," James said with his whole body trembling.

I still wasn't convinced. Hunter jumped in, and his teeth began chattering too.

"I'll freeze with you." He smiled, holding out his hand to me. "The water is barely moving." He knew the other reason I hesitated.

With no more excuses left, I stepped out into the water.

James held me securely by the waist, but Hunter stood right next to me, holding my other hand.

I'm safer than anyone could be, safer than I deserve.

"I baptize you, Jessica, my sister, in the name of the Father, the Son, and the Holy Spirit, dead to sin and risen to a new life in Christ."

The three of us wore blue lips and shivered uncontrollably. James dismissed the congregation in one quick word.

"The pool is nice and warm," Hunter said, smiling.

The three of us took off in a run toward the house and then to the pool and jumped in.

It felt nice and warmed up my body quickly. I pulled off the wet dress to reveal my swimsuit underneath. James had swim trunks on under his slacks. We both looked at Hunter, still wearing his dress shirt and tan slacks, and laughed.

"Oh, so this was planned." He smiled, pulling me to him.

"Sorry, bro, she swore me to secrecy." James splashed at him.

I stood and faced Hunter. "I'm sorry, but I wanted to surprise you."

"I'm very proud of you." He pulled my wet hair back and kissed me.

"All right, all right. Break it up." Jordan jumped in, clothes and all, and splashed next to us.

We all roared with laughter.

Molly Returns

I wasn't making much progress on my piece of music, and I complained to Annabel as we weeded one of the gardens.

"How about I arrange a little girls-only PJ party in garden room, and then Hunter will know you're with me and May. You can spend as much time as you want." She pulled out a clump of weeds and tossed it into bucket.

"That might help, as long as he doesn't hide behind the fake plant and wait for me to leave."

"He does that?"

"Yep," I said, placing cut tulips into a vase and arranging some baby's breath around them, "every time."

"I'll have John make the rounds and send him to bed if he's in the hallway. When do you want to do it?"

"Tonight?" I asked. "With them being gone all day at Miss Mabel's, he'll be pretty tired already. Maybe once John sends him up, he'll just fall right to sleep and not worry so much."

"Okay. Sounds good. I'll mention it after dinner." She smiled, looking at the vase. "Nice arrangement."

"Thanks, Annabel."

"You can go put them on the table. We'll need to start getting dinner ready pretty soon." She looked at her hands and legs, covered in dirt. "After I clean up."

We both laughed.

After dinner, we planned for our girls' party. May was in on it too. We made her promise not to tell, and she promised by crossing her heart.

We all walked into the room together and shut the doors and windows.

"So what's it going to be tonight, May?" Annabel asked.

"Checkers." She set the box down on the round table. "Jordan taught me how to play yesterday, and I need to practice so I can beat him."

"Sounds like a good reason to me." Annabel laughed.

I sat at the small piano with my clean sheet of paper and sharpened pencil. I composed a few notes, but none written in any sort of pattern. So that was where I started, a beginning to tie it all in.

May and Annabel stayed in the room, playing games, while I composed, and it didn't seem to matter they were there. I managed to finally find the melody I was searching for and forgot they were in the same room with me. I'd play a few notes and then write them down and then scribble some notes I thought might work and then play them together. Hours had passed before I realized I was alone.

I arched my back and stretched up my arms before I went back to work. Music told a story, and if I couldn't tell our story just right, I would give up this silly notion I could compose. I took a deep breath and began to play what I had so far.

The melody started out in confusion, as I was lost in the woods. It was cold and gloomy, and I didn't know which way to go. Then the tune became softer, lighter, as I saw the light streaming down, and then it circled around me. As it lifted me, the music built up. It inspired me to want a new life, one with God.

Bang! Bang! Bang!

I jumped out of my seat.

Bang! Bang! Bang! came from outside the window.

With my heart racing, I cautiously walked over to the window.

Molly.

Her face was swollen, with dark circles surrounding her eyes.

"You have to come. Something has happened. You have to come," she said. Her voice was wild, frantic.

"What? What's happened?"

"You have to come. You have to. He's going to kill him," she said again.

"Wait," I said. "What's going on, Molly?"

"If you don't come now, he'll kill him. You know he will. You know him better than anyone," she said again.

Seth.

"Okay. Let me go get hel—" I started to say, but she cut me off.

"There's no time! No, no. He'll kill him. Don't you understand me? You need to come now," she said, grabbing my shirt through the window, her fist twisting my clothes.

"Who is he going to kill?"

"Hunter. Seth is going to kill him." She paused, looking angry at my delayed reaction. "Well, fine, if you won't help him," she said, letting me go. "I'm not going to let that Seth kill him. At least I'm willing to fight for his life."

"What? Molly," I called, climbing out the window.

Darkness surrounded me. Even the shadows of the night disappeared by the covered moonlight, and no stars were shining, not one. I chased after Molly, catching only glimpses of her red garment flowing behind her. She ran so fast once we passed over the cobblestone path, she vanished.

Oh no, I ran through the barrier! I thought, still running in last direction I had seen Molly. Out of breath, I stopped to looked around the forest I stood in. The ground felt soggy, and my bare feet sank down into it. A light appeared and filled the area. At first it frighten me, but then I saw the moon was peeking through thick clouds. Molly appeared through the trees, calm and with a smirk on her face.

"I guess you're not as smart as everyone thinks you are."

"Molly? What's going on? Where is Hunter?" I shook my head in disbelief.

"Seth's going to kill him." She mocked being scared. "Stupid girl, if I knew it was going to be this easy, I would have done it way sooner."

"So where is Hunter?"

"Oh, I'm sure he's sleeping in his bed, secretly dreaming of me, of course. That's what you wanted, right?"

"So this is a joke?"

"No, it's not," she said, her eyes blazing. "Ever since you have come into our lives, you have made everything very difficult for me. Hunter is mine! I'm not letting you come in here and take him from me. That song he played belonged to me, not you."

She moved inches from me and lashed out her hand at my cheek. My cheek stung and felt wet. The feeling I had, the sorrow I felt for her broken heart, faded into the pain I felt as she paced in front of me.

"Hunter looked at me in a way he never had before." Tears filled her eyes and began to run down her cheek. "He was furious with me for how I was treating *you!*" She twisted her hands together. "So I ran. I ran until my feet started to bleed."

I looked down at her feet. They were bare and bloodstained.

"I fell to my knees, and I cursed God for allowing this to happen. He's not a fair or just God!" She raised her hands up, and her tone changed.

She continued to talk with her back to me. I squatted down and picked up a thick tree branch and hid it behind my back. I wasn't going to go down easy, if her plan was to kill me.

"I knew I had to take matters into my own hands. It was the only way," she said under her breath, as if she were talking to herself. "I knew they were looking for you. We all knew. The best part was I didn't have to go far to find them." She chuckled.

I wondered if Molly had met Seth. They were a perfect match with their two faces.

"Apparently, they have spies everywhere."

She stopped. Whatever it was in her head made her angrier as she moved closer, and then too close. I swung at her with the branch, and as it connected with her, the force knocked her into the thick, black mud.

Molly looked up in disbelief, wiping her bleeding cheek. "Who do you think you are? You already have a man. Why would you come and take mine? I wanted to like you, Jessica. I really did." She laughed. "But that time has passed." She stood up.

I stood ready with my stick for another round. But another figure moved through the trees. I was praying it was Hunter and his brothers coming to my rescue.

Well, I had one thing right.

Davior walked out from the darkness and into the moonlit clearing. His eyes were fixed on me, staring at me the same way he always had, in admiration. He looked at Molly, covered in mud, her cheek bleeding, and then to me, positioned like a baseball player ready to bat.

"I'm impressed," he said and crossed his arms against his chest.

"Okay. So I got her here. Remember, you promised me I can go back to my life without anyone knowing I helped you," Molly blurted out.

"Go," he said, not allowing his eye contact with me to be broken.

I stared right back, still holding my stick. Davior noticed the deep scratch on my face, and his mouth turned down.

"You said she wouldn't be able to return. I have your word," Molly demanded.

Davior laughed loudly, and it echoed through the trees. He turned his fierce eyes on her. "I said go!" Davior said, pointing in her direction. "Before you can't."

Molly was stunned and stumbled backward before she found her footing and then vanished.

Davior turned back to me, regaining his smooth demeanor. "It's been so long since we last spoke, Jessica. I've missed you."

Someone came up behind me, taking the stick from my hand with force. Davior's hand came up and caressed my stinging cheek, and the bleeding stopped.

"She doesn't like you very much. I'm sorry I had to resort to that. She was pretty upset when I found her in our part of the woods and ready to sell her soul to the devil to get you out of the picture. Of course, I've been trying to get to you since the day Hunter ripped me away from your beautiful face."

He grabbed my hand to bring it up to his lips and noticed the ring I wore.

"Ah. My great grandmother's. So you agreed." He tossed my hand down, looking betrayed.

"What do you want from me?" I demanded.

"It's not about me anymore," he said softly. "I have a higher purpose for you."

"Seth?"

"Yes. He's quite angry with you. He believes you belong to him, and he's not letting you go. He would rather see you dead, but now…now he wants to see Hunter dead as well."

"But he can't die."

"Oh, did he tell you that?" He sounded amused.

"Well no, but I thought he was immortal."

"We don't die from age, but we can be killed, I assure you," he said. "It's just too bad though. My brother and I might not agree, but I hate to think he's going to be killed over this."

"Why? Why doesn't he just kill *me*? Why Hunter?" I asked with tears forming.

"Really, it's the only way. About now, Hunter knows you are missing. I can see he's frantically searching and blaming himself for not keeping a better watch over you. Very careless of him, I might add. It was like he wanted me to take you away. He knew I was near, watching, waiting."

I knew who Davior served, someone higher than Seth, and I knew he was a liar, but what he saw through Hunter's thoughts I knew to be true.

"So how is it that you can read his thoughts? Doesn't it work both ways? He'll know where I'm at."

"He's too angry, too focused on only you. I seem to be unnoticed. He's been very unfocused lately." He smirked. "Oh, my poor mother. He's destroying the house she so carefully decorated." He chuckled. "And Molly…too bad she's a terrible actress. No one believes her."

"Why kill Hunter? I'll go willingly," I said. "I'll do whatever you want."

"Because he will look for you day and night. He'll try to kill Seth first, but we'll be ready," he said with confidence that terrified me. "It's not about Hunter or any of my family, really. This is all about what Seth wants, so he'll serve my master. However, I know my entire family will do whatever Hunter wants. He's always been the favorite. Right now, he wants you, and they will rally to his side like they always do," he said in a very carless way. "A battle is unavoidable at this stage. You should have come willingly before you got my family involved. Honestly, I tried, Jessica. If you would have just listened to my instructions, to the little voice inside your head, it could have been avoided."

"It wasn't so little."

"And yet you still didn't listen." He wiggled his finger at me. "Oh well. What's done is done."

Davior was playing on my guilt. I tried to remember he didn't care at all about his family.

"Where is Seth?" I asked in a whisper, wondering if he was there, waiting beyond the trees.

"Well, he's a pretty busy guy these days. Lots of people to meet and all. I'm sure it won't be long." Davior offered his hand out to me. "I have more than adequate accommodations for you until then."

"What if I don't want to go?"

Davior raised his hand, and two more men came out of the clearing.

"I'd prefer you go the easy way. I don't want to see you hurt any more than you have been," he said, reaching out to stroke my cheek again.

I flinched away.

He offered his hand again.

What choice do I have? I prayed for God to keep Hunter safe as Davior led me out of the forest and into the unknown darkness before me.

Into the Dark of Darkest Places

I never enjoyed scary movies, mostly because I lived in one and my mind had not required a movie to create dark images. They had already existed, scratching at the windows, wrestling in the trees, creaky doors opening, and my favorite, footsteps in the shadows getting closer. I remember the countless people walking along the sandy shores of the beach, looking up at me, a pale, thin girl staring motionless at them. How many of them thought of me as a phantom trapped in the immense, pallid house on the hill?

Seth had loved horror films.

On weekends, he had spent a majority of his time at my mother's house. The time was supposed to be used to connect with me and persuade me to accept the fate I had no choice in. However, I would escape to reading in my father's office, while he watched vampire-slasher-killer-type movies. He had tried to get me to watch them with him or would try to convince me to watch just one part. I'd look up and be nauseated from seeing all the blood or, worse, someone being slashed to pieces. Seth would then proceed to explain how unreal it all really was, giving his own play by play of how it should have been done to make it more believable. I didn't know what was worse, the details he used or the pleasure he had received from watching me turn white as a ghost.

At least in those days, the days before I left, I knew what to expect, how to act, how to hide, but there was so much more on the line and there was nowhere to hide. Neither one of us were the same people. I belonged in another world, not the one I started out from, but the one I ended up in, the world of good, forgiveness, and love; and he belonged in the other world, the one filled with evil, hate, and all-consuming power.

Feeling Davior tighten his grip on my hand, I knew we were somewhere in the middle of both worlds.

With the ramblings only in my mind, I walked in silence. Two men walked in front of us, one to my right and one to the left of Davior, and two more walked behind us. I was completely surrounded. Davior wasn't taking any chances, as he continued to hold my hand tightly and occasionally ran his index finger across the top. I wanted to pull it from him and run; however, I was no match for all of them. I'd never get away and would end up with another scar on the opposite cheek.

"Would you like to know why John wants you to wait?" He was practically gloating about having information I would obviously want.

"I don't trust the words you say, so you can keep it to yourself," I snapped.

"Jessica, I have no intention of lying to you."

His voice softened, sounding more like Hunter's voice when he spoke in a normal tone. And the way he acted toward Molly after he noticed the mark she left on my cheek would have been similar to Hunter's reaction. Except I don't think Hunter could kill anyone. When Davior looked at Molly, even she saw the rage building and left before he killed her. I believe he would have if she had pressed him longer.

Maybe he can be saved from this fate. Maybe he still has some good left inside his soul.

The forest floor felt soft under my feet with tiny granules sinking in between my toes like sand, and it was very different from the swamp.

Am I still in the swamp?

The moon hovered directly above us, full and bright with ribbons of light pushing through to the thin path between the trees. The shadows moved around us, peeking out through the tall cypress leaves with no noises—no rustling, no animals crying, no birds chirping, and, even stranger, no crickets or beetles. Except for my footsteps touching the ground beneath me, a dead silence filled the air.

We continued down the path, moving forward, and then I noticed the corridor ahead disappeared into a set of dim, bulky trees and bushes. On closer approach, the trees and bushes looked more like soaring barriers, a wall that did not look passable.

Is this were we will stop?

"You'll need to wear this." Davior held out a long coat. "It's going to get very hot, my dear. This will keep your skin from getting scorched."

As much as I didn't want to cooperate, the thought of my skin sizzling wouldn't do anyone any good. So I reluctantly plunged my arms through the sleeves and zipped it up. He also threw down two black boots for my bare feet, and I shoved my feet into them.

Davior, taking the first step into the bushes, reached for my arm and pulled me along with him and right through the wall. I felt despair as we left the light of the moon into an unknown world of blackness, which surrounded me like a dark cloth. I held out my hand to my nose, and I couldn't see it. Tightness constricted my chest from rising and falling due to the hot and thick air sticking to my throat, so I couldn't swallow.

There is nothing here. I'm walking through a void with not even the sound of my feet against the ground.

I gripped Davior's hand.

"I'm here," he whispered in my ear. "You're safe as long as you stay close to me."

I winced at his words and the touch of his lips on my ear but I held on to him with both hands. I was forced to trust him. The only person I felt safe with seemed worlds away.

Oh, why did I not listen to him? How many times did he remind me not to leave the cobblestone boundary without him? How many times did he tell me to be watchful? I should have known Molly's plan. I should have known she would try to trick me. I've put him and his family in danger. I know he will come after me, but at what cost? And it was my fault once again.

Through the complete darkness, a red, glowing light appeared, growing larger as we moved forward, just like looking through a telescope and focusing the knob to bring the picture in closer. An outline of a tall mountain began to take shape, and a glowing light appeared, an entrance into another unknown. I heard faint moaning and stifled cries as we moved closer, and then we passed into the red glow.

"Ah. Home at last." Davior took a deep breath.

The air smelled of thick sulfur with clouds of smoke sparking like lighting above us. I choked with every breath. Everything was shadowed with a red tint, even the clouds of smoke that billowed up in gray puffs. Tall, pointed mounds of dirt stuck up from the ground, and some dangled down from the cavern walls like icicles. Fire roared all around me, and I tasted the salty sweat of my skin.

There were people—at least I thought they were people—with thick collars around their necks attached to chains that bound them to their work. They were all thin and malnourished looking, with bruises and scrapes all over their bodies. The chains were covered with thistles and thorn shapes digging into their skin every time they brushed against it.

A group of people moved toward us while Davior spoke another language to the men who had accompanied us on the journey. Not understanding what he was saying, I watched the group of people as they got closer until I realized they weren't people, not all of them. The larger figures were nonhuman, with horns and twisted faces, pushing and pulling long lines of people behind them. One of the creatures looked up as he passed and snarled out toward me. His three long, sharp limbs reached out toward me. I jumped back behind Davior. Davior raised one hand, and the creature went back to his work, pulling the chain.

"Sorry, Jessica. He thought you were one of them." He pointed to the people chained together. "They are being taken past the gate."

At first, they looked like regular people, and then one of them turned it's head to face me. It had more than one face.

I gasped. "What are they?" I asked, frightened, still behind Davior.

"Those are the two-faced liars. Those are the people who lived in your world, the ones who claimed to be God's followers, but in secret, they lived sinful and lustful lives. They are the ones willing to go against God, seek out Lucifer, but then cover up their dirty little lie and sit in church. Isn't there a saying there is a special place in hell for those kinds of people?" Davior asked.

I had heard it, but I didn't answer.

"They do serve their purpose though" he said.

I thought of Molly and what she had done.

"Am I in hell?" I asked with a hard swallow.

"Now, now, Jessica. You have to be dead to get in there. Think of this as more of an outside gate or processing area, where souls are collected and sorted. It's also for those of us who are living and serving our master until our time comes to live above ground."

"So then, at the compound, was I outside the gates of heaven?" I asked.

"Not quite." He laughed loudly.

"I'm glad you find me entertaining," I said, trying to hold back the fear brewing inside. I couldn't let him see it.

He laughed again.

I watched all the warped, pained faces working and suffering. Some were high above, working on thin ledges. I watched one fall into the pit below. Others were scattered throughout the cavern and staring in my direction. Moaning and cries mingled with the crackling of the fire.

What a horrible, horrible place.

Sweat dripped into my eyes, which had been already burning from the sulfur and the heat radiating in the air. I tried to wipe the ash off my skin, but it only smeared into a black mess.

"I'm sorry. I'm not being a very good host." He sounded upset with himself. "Come this way."

I followed Davior to a bridge. The bridge was a thin wedge in between two sheer cliffs, and below it, a hot, flowing lake moved rapidly and struck the sides of the cliff, sending lava splashing straight up into the air. The canyon of flowing lava went on for miles and miles. I swallowed hard, pushing some of the ash accumulating in my mouth down into my throat, and stayed close to Davior.

We got to the other side of the bridge before I noticed it was the only bridge, within my sight, that crossed the ravine. I also saw for the first time a big house all by itself.

One way in. One way out. I'm trapped!

The house sat propped up on stilts with sheer cliffs and a lava moat on all sides of it. If it weren't for the sheer look of the house, a mansion outside the gates of hell, my mind would have scrambled out of control. The building just happened to be quite stunning, with details oddly familiar, only I couldn't put my finger on why. Davior led me up the steep steps, and he stopped.

"Make yourself at home here. Seth designed this house for you, to make your stay comfortable; however, I added a few touches of my own, ones I hope will please you." His eyes lingered on my reaction before he continued.

I stared blankly at him, but I was shaking inside.

Davior opened the door to a grand room with a high ceiling and a golden staircase that went on forever. Davior pulled back a curtain from a window.

"Even the view is for you."

"I don't plan to stay here long," I said, walking over to the open window in shock. I saw no fire, smoke, or ash, but an appealing country garden of roses and tulips. I could even smell their soothing fragrances.

"The kitchen is fully stocked. Seth said you would prefer to cook your own meals, but if you would like, we have someone who can cook for you." He walked over to the entrance of the kitchen and leaned against the wall. "I've also been known to be an excellent cook."

He grinned at me, but I didn't reply.

I'm not staying here. I'm not staying here. I would find away to escape.

Davior turned back around and went to the door, and then hesitated, his back to me. "No one can enter through the blackness, especially any of my family, without me knowing about it, and they know that. You also cannot leave unless you are escorted out by Seth or myself—no one else. Jessica, please don't cause any further harm to yourself by trying to leave here. I really don't like seeing you in pain." His voice was soft and then changed to be more stern. "It will be awhile before Seth joins you, so try to make yourself comfortable." He paused and sighed. "I will be coming by daily so you won't be alone. If there is something you want, something I can bring—"

"My freedom?" I said with tears running off my chin.

His body stiffened. "I'll be back soon. Try to rest now. It's been a long journey. Good night, Jessica." He walked through the door and shut it.

I ran to the door and reopened it.

Davior was gone.

In disbelief, I walked out onto the front porch, and a white bunny hopped across the green, thick-bladed grass and then through the purple bushes on the outskirts of the yard. I stepped out cautiously onto the grass, feeling the suppleness seep between my toes. I took another step, cautiously wondering what would happen next, and nothing happened. No arms punched through, trying to grab me. No black, swampy, glassy water sucked my foot down under. I was slightly impressed with Seth's attention to details, or Davior's, in their make-believe world.

I continued to step forward, quickening with each one that didn't hit an invisible wall or a cliff plunging several feet to my doom, until I was running. I ran fast and hard until I could no longer breathe and had to stop. I bent over, trying to catch my breath, and when I looked back behind me, there was the house.

I hadn't run anywhere.

A feeling, a sensation, rose up inside, causing my heart to beat hard and fast against my chest with a stabbing pain, one that journeyed throughout my skeleton and shook me to the very core of my foundation. I was trapped. The burning traveled into my heart, constricting its rhythm and making it hard to breathe.

How am I going to get out of here?

My heart and soul were breaking, my body reacting to the emotional pain. With tears flowing without restraint, I dropped to my knees and prayed. I prayed for God to show me the answer. I prayed for Hunter's family and their safety. I prayed for Hunter and for God to give him guidance not to do anything crazy.

Time at the entrance to hell felt like it stood still. I slept when I felt completely exhausted, I ate when I felt hungry, and I tolerated Davior's company. Even though I lived in the dark of darkest places imaginable, the sun shined brightly in the middle of the sky in my fake world. No nighttime came, no bright stars, no brilliantly shining moon, no storms; not even the colors of the leaves on the trees changed. I was left wondering how many days had passed and if Hunter was okay. And I wondered if I would ever see him again.

I took comfort in the only thing they could never take away from me. My relationship with God. I was soothed by prayer and felt connected with God in a new way and I leaned on his strength to get me through the valley I couldn't escape. I remembered another scripture I had read in Psalms chapter three and recited it out loud from memory twice a day.

O Lord, how many are my foes! How many rise up against me! Many are saying of me, "God will not deliver him." But you are a shield around me, O Lord; you bestow glory on me and lift up my head. To the Lord I cry aloud, and he answers me from his holy hill. I lie down and sleep; I wake again, because the Lord sustains me. I will not fear the tens of thousands drawn up against me on every side. Arise, O Lord! Deliver me, O my God! Strike all my enemies on the jaw; break the teeth of the wicked. From the Lord comes deliverance. May your blessing be on your people, Amen.

God would use me for his purpose, and I prayed I would be ready when the time came.

The house holding me prisoner was beautiful enough to be on the cover of *Better Homes and Gardens*. The inside decor spoke more of my mother's taste than my own. It made sense Seth would have mixed the two. My dream home would be more along the lines of a simple cottage covered in flowery vines and honeysuckle. One of my favorite cottages I had seen in a magazine was Anne Hathaway's family cottage. Annabel had told me how Shakespeare had written some of his sonnets on the very porch of that cottage. I closed my eyes and pictured the cottage. Tunes began to fill my head.

Davior said if I wanted something, just ask.

Davior came and I asked him for a piano, and soon enough, one was placed on a platform overhang overlooking a window video of a garden. Although I had played random music when he was around, I worked on finishing my song for Hunter when I was alone. Unfortunately, I wasn't alone often.

Davior walked into the room, and I quickly stashed my papers behind the music books.

"I thought you might like this." Davior showed me a book by one of my favorite authors.

I slammed shut the fallboard over the keys and stood up quickly, moving toward him. "Just because you've been nice to me doesn't change anything. You are holding me prisoner here," I said, reaching out for the book in his hands. "You can bring as many flowers and plants in here as you want. You can change the scenery a hundred times to please me, but I know what lurks around me, and I know what you are keeping me from."

A happy life.

"You're not giving me much of a chance to make you happy, Jessica." His voice was sincere.

"Keeping me a prisoner is not a good way of going about it." I thumbed through the book and then looked up when he didn't reply back.

A look came over Davior's face. An angry expression spread across his face, but it wasn't at me. Without a word, he hurried out of the room and out of the house, leaving me standing alone.

That was odd.

He returned after a minute or so, a look of confusion plastered all over his face, carrying a tray of food. "I'll be back later." He set the tray down and left in a hurry.

I wondered if it was Hunter, if he was close and reading Davior's thoughts.

That's not good either. They'll kill him.

I shook off the thought and sat back down in front of the piano. If anything happened to me, I wanted Hunter to hear it or, at the very least, see the notes I had written for just him. I didn't know how I would do that, but somehow, I would get the message to him. I was willing to do anything in my power to keep him safe and alive, and if that meant a show, a pretense, to make them think I'd changed sides, so be it.

God is always in control. I'll admit I didn't know the reason or the outcome, but a plan had started forming. It wouldn't be easy, and I didn't know if I could pull it off, but I also didn't believe I had come up with it on my own.

Seth's Rise to Power

He didn't just walk right in. Davior did.

"Seth is outside and would like for you to join him on the porch," he said, not looking into my eyes but staring off in the distance, past me.

I took a deep breath and started to walk toward the door. I knew what I needed to do and said a short prayer in my mind.

Lord, give me the strength to be convincing.

Davior grabbed my arm as I passed him, moving his face to my ear. I felt his cool cheek brush mine, and I shivered. He whispered, "Do not anger him any more than he already is."

I walked out onto the porch, not sure what I was going to find. I kept seeing those hot, red eyes staring at me from the bottom of the stairs the night Davior made me remember my father's attack.

Seth stared out. His back faced me. He seemed bigger than I remembered. His shoulders were broader, his body was stout, and he almost touched the rafters with the top of his head. His breathing was hard and fast, and I couldn't tell if that meant he was angry or something else.

"Seth," I whispered.

He didn't move but took in a deep breath at my voice. He was absorbing my presence, letting it soothe him, something he had done once before, after trying to kiss me, and I pushed him across the room. He was so angry and wanted to hurt me, but he was able to control it and walked away, sulking.

Seth spoke softly, with a deep, raspy voice. "I've been worried since you left. Your mother is absolutely beside herself." He paused, still with his back to me. "I looked everywhere. I investigated every location you had pinned on those maps in your father's office. My father helped with all his connections, until he passed on a few months back." His voice cracked.

I took some satisfaction in knowing that. *I wonder if he's down there, in the pit of hell for what he did.*

"I'm sorry," I said, although I didn't mean it. *Shame on me, I shouldn't want revenge; besides, I don't know for sure if he tried to kill him.*

"No matter. Now it's all mine." He shook his head. "No. It's all ours," he corrected and turned to me.

Once again, I shivered at the sound of "ours." I had never belonged to him, although if I wanted my plan to work, I had to play along; I had to play more than nice. I swallowed hard.

The man before me was still Seth but older and ragged. His eyes were black and sunken into his face. Besides his larger physical appearance, he also looked tired and worn down.

I swallowed down my fear and hoped I still had a certain amount of power over him.

"Don't be afraid of me, Jess." He walked toward me, noticing my facial expression. "I'm still undergoing changes, and I look… well, different here than I do up top. It's only underground I take this shape. It's a small price to pay for all that has been given to me."

"What has been given to you, exactly?"

"You, for one."

"That doesn't explain why you look the way you do."

"No." He laughed. "I've been given immortality. I've denounced God and now worship the real king of this world. You'll see, Jess, they can do the same for you."

I would never denounce God! I thought as he continued to speak.

"You never believed in all that God crap anyway. Lucifer is the real king, and he can grant you whatever you seek. His only requirement is you join him," Seth said with excitement, not thinking for one moment I might not agree.

"You're a demon," I stated, not at all surprised, but the fact he was immortal sank deep into my fears.

"Such an ugly word. I prefer the *devil's associate*." He took a few steps toward me. "Don't be scared."

"I'm not scared," I said, covering the chill in my tone; however, I was terrified as he took my hands, looking down.

"I'm still the same…" he started to say but didn't finish.

Before I knew it, my head was lying against the porch deck, with broken wood around me. I could taste iron in my mouth, wet and sticky. Davior jumped out in front of me, furious.

"Seth!" He held out one arm against his chest, holding him back from me.

Seth wanted to kill me, I could see it in his eyes as he took on a demon body, busting through the roof of the porch, breaking anything and everything in his reach. His face swelled up, and the purple veins in his neck protruded as the red blood pumped through them.

"What is that on her finger?" Seth screamed. "We already talked about this, Seth. Remember?" He spoke to him as though he were a child having a tantrum. "She cannot take it off as of yet. It's not her fault. Remember who did this to her."

I was grateful I wasn't dead yet, but he was turning that anger toward Hunter. I couldn't let that happen. I picked myself up and ran past Davior, throwing my arms around Seth's neck, pressing my lips to his. I didn't know if it would work or if he would kill me on the spot. It was a chance I was willing to take. And in my reasoning, I knew Seth well, and if he was still in there somewhere, he wouldn't refuse me. I could always get him to do what I wanted, by womanly persuasion.

Seth's kiss felt opposite of what I felt with Hunter, and it turned and wrenched my stomach as he pulled me closer, lifting me up from the ground, pressing even harder onto my lips that burned with blood. He began to relax as my feet touched back down, and I put my hand on his face as he released me.

Showtime…

"I'm so happy to see you," I said. The tears should have given me away, but he didn't seem to notice. I pulled at the ring, but it wasn't coming off.

Seth smiled wide, with a touch of surprise on his face. It pleased him. I saw his teeth were black like coal, and I couldn't help but wince and look away.

"I know. I'm sorry," he said. "But really, I am quite handsome up top," he said again, touching my cheek with the large scar.

He looked over at Davior.

"Molly, sir. She was quite upset with Jessica."

"Did you kill her?" Seth asked.

"No. I wasn't to harm her, remember?" Davior spoke calmly. "If it hadn't been for her, Jessica would not be here."

Davior left out he almost had killed her.

Seth grunted. "But her mouth is bleeding too," he said, looking at my swollen lip he had just created by smacking me across the porch.

"She tripped," Davior answered, and that was the end of that.

Making Seth angry was bad, and I knew that now. Only, I had forgotten about the ring. My beautiful gemstone ring reminded me of what waited for me, or did if I made it out of there alive.

Lord, give me strength.

We all walked into the house. I tried to tug off the ring again, but it wouldn't come off.

"It will stay on your finger until you accept another's proposal or if you die. I think death is more likely," Davior whispered so Seth wouldn't hear him. "Think of the ring as a binding contract. Once the contract is broken, it no longer applies and it will disappear forever. Seth already knows, but his emotional state is a bit unstable at the moment. I tried to keep him away longer, but he wouldn't hear of it," Davior said. He handed me a pair of white gloves to wear. "He could forget again."

"Why don't you look like him?" I said, grabbing the gloves from his hands.

He bent in toward me and whispered. "Let's just say I work here, but they don't own my soul. I'm already immortal, with my own set of abilities, and because I'm not much of a fighter, there is no need to take on the ugliness of demons."

I wonder if that's not the only reason. Maybe the light inside hasn't gone out. I wanted to believe it. I wanted to believe he'd come back to his family.

"It must be hard for you to take orders from him," I said sarcastically, slipping the gloves over my hand, and then I paused for moment and looked up at him. "Thanks," I forced past my lips.

"I see what you're doing." Davior smiled slyly, placing his hands in his pockets. "You're a pretty good little actress, aren't you? Well I can be quite the actor as well."

"I don't know what you're talking about," I said dryly, and I ran after Seth, who was already several feet in front of us.

I needed to get out of there as soon as possible. I was feeling confident my plan would work after the kiss scene. At least the first step seemed achievable: to get out.

Seth was standing by the piano, looking at the scrap pieces of paper with my composition notes.

Crap. I forgot to hide them.

"Did you write something?" He smiled.

"Yes," I whispered, thinking quickly on how I could use this for my benefit.

"I don't remember you writing your own music. Would you play it for me?" He sat on the bench and then patted the seat next to him.

I couldn't play for him. An idea raced through my mind. I grabbed the papers, trying to look playful. "Well, I've had a lot of alone time here, all by myself. However, this song is special, and don't you think it should be revealed at one of my mother's gatherings? You know, all of your friends and associates." I wasn't lying about playing it for a special occasion.

"Oh. Did you write it for me?" he asked, grinning from ear to ear, and I looked away from the rotting teeth, not intentionally.

"Sorry," he said, noticing my look of disgust.

It bothered him to look the way he did, and I could use it.

"I guess you just have to wait and see." I forced a smile and changed my tone. "How is my mother?"

"Yes, well, about your mother. She's strong, as usual. Everything has gone according to plan as far as everyone else is concerned. Now that I have you back…" He looked down at his watch.

"Sir, you should be leaving soon," Davior said, stepping between Seth and me.

"Is there somewhere you need to be other than here?" I asked, looking past Davior and at Seth.

"I was only to stay a few minutes. I wasn't even supposed to see you yet, but I had to. Jess, I've missed you so much." He pushed Davior aside and hugged me.

"Please don't leave me here," I whispered desperately. "I don't want to be alone, not here." I hugged him and buried my head in his chest.

This was it. Was I convincing enough?

"Davior said I shouldn't. Don't you like it here?" He stroked my hair.

"It's nice, but I don't like being here all alone. If I would be in your way, I could go visit my mother. It's been such a long time."

The idea was floating in his mind, but he was struggling with the reasons Davior gave him not to take me out of this place, the consequences. I needed to seal the deal. I pulled up and looked at him. Then I looked down.

"I want to kiss you, but I have to admit it's sort of difficult." I tried to look shy.

The one thing he always tried to steal from me was a kiss, and I was offering it willingly. It was a deal he couldn't pass up.

"Davior," he called, releasing his grip, "Jessica is coming with me."

My heart skipped. *It's working.*

"Seth, we talked about it. It's not wise to—" Davior was cut off.

I shot Davior a look, one of pleasure.

"She's coming. You will be coming as well. She'll need a companion when I am working," Seth ordered again.

"Yes, sir," Davior said through his teeth, looking right at me.

I looked away quickly from his stare with a thin smile on my lips.

"You'd better pack some clothes. We have to leave in ten minutes." Seth beamed at me.

I beamed back, and that time, it was genuine. I would be in the world again, and the first step was complete.

I wasn't fond of the clothing, the same stuff my mother made me wear, so I just grabbed a few things and tossed them into a large blue bag Davior brought up to me.

"I know what you're doing." He smiled. "It's very becoming on you, lying."

"I don't know what you're talking about." I shoved more clothes in.

"He still can't come close to you with me around." He tapped his head with his index finger. "And if he tries, he'll be dead before he can even lay eyes on you. Just keep that in mind."

"I still don't know what you're talking about. Please take this down. I'm ready," I ordered, handing him my bag.

"Yes, my lady." He spoke slowly and moved to stand right next to me, brushing his arm against me. His smile was thin and nervous.

I must be on the right path.

I figured out quickly Seth was the master over Davior, at least for now. And I could manipulate Seth with no problem. Even the monster within gave in quickly to my attempt to persuade him. Davior had no choice but to follow his orders. That was good. That was very, very good.

Seth opened the door, and fire once again leaped up, along with sulfuric air, and soot danced around. Seth placed a cloth over my head, and I let him carry me out of the holding area, through the darkness, and into a clearing, where a helicopter waited for us. Davior followed close behind.

We landed in an air field, where we boarded a small plane and then landed to get on a helicopter. The final stop was on the roof of a building, where men in long, black coats hurried us into a glass elevator. No one spoke. Seth turned to me and actually took my breath away when he smiled at me. He wasn't kidding. He was quite debonair, and his smile was beautifully bright. It didn't change the way I felt about him or the way I felt about Hunter, but he *was* handsome.

Seth touched my hand softly and laced his fingers into mine as we stepped out of the elevator. Cameras were flashing all around me, and the men in the black suits stepped out in front of me to shield me from their sight.

"Is this the fiancée we've all heard about?" one called out, aiming the camera in my direction.

"When is the wedding date?" another called.

Seth kept moving forward until we reached the back of a platform away from the media. I thought about the nightmare I had had and trembled.

"Davior, there are two chairs reserved in the front row." Seth took my hand and stroked his cheek with it. "Wish me luck."

"What's going on?" I asked.

"A lot of things have happened since you've been gone, and today is a big moment for me. All that time I spent with my father and working in his offices, well, my dream has finally come true, Jess. I'm so glad to have you with me today. It wouldn't have been the same without you here." He kissed my hand and motioned for Davior to take me.

"What's going on?" I whispered to Davior.

"You'll see." He smiled, taking my hand in his, but I quickly jerked it back, and he laughed.

Davior led me out to the front of the stadium. Red and blue streamers blew in the light wind. There were thousands of people gathered behind our chairs. I couldn't tell where we were as I looked around for landmarks. Davior motioned for me to sit. I did as a man came out from behind the curtain.

"Welcome, Californians!" he called, and the people cheered.

"I know you are all here to congratulate the youngest governor in the history of California, so, without further delay, Seth Mackenzie Worthington the third," the man said.

The crowd was so loud. I put my fingers to my ears.

How can these people be so blind? A governor, the first step in his plans.

I couldn't believe he had pulled it off. *I bet my mother is happy.* I glanced around at the stage for any sign of her; this was her big moment too.

I caught Seth's eyes on me as he took the stage, but no sign of my mother.

"Thank you. Thank you so much for all of your support. I couldn't have made it this far if it hadn't been the support of my friends and family."

The crowd cheered louder.

Worrying about growing old and Hunter outliving me was becoming less of a concern. The war between God and Lucifer was coming. Seth would be governor and then a senator, if he was still on the same course he had talked about.

Would it be the United Nations next? Of course, would it matter now? Would I ever see Hunter again? I felt my ring under the gloves and rubbed my index finger along it. *I wonder where he is. Does he know I am out of that horrible place?*

Seth continued to talk to his supporters. He talked about things he had planned to change, and other political topics. He actually believed what he was saying as the teleprompter kept in step with his movements. Everything he said sparked the crowd, gaining their trust and confidence. I wondered if Davior had written his speech.

After a while, my eyes were beginning to gloss over, and Davior nudged me and chuckled.

Seth then addressed the crowd, "Before I leave you today, there is one more person I would like to thank, my future mother-in-law, Evelyn."

He called her out, and she walked out onto the platform.

Although I knew she'd be here, I gasped at the sight of her and wished Annabel was sitting next to me—the person who treated me more like a daughter than my own mother.

Seth whispered in her ear, and she looked down right at me. She smiled, but it was halfhearted. I could tell I was ruining her moment, as Seth then reached out for my hand to join him too. If it hadn't been for Davior, I would have blown it right there. I wouldn't have moved. I actually thought about making a run for it, but if I had, the media would have slowed me down. They loved a good scandal.

Davior pulled on my elbow and then led me up to Seth. I saw him look back quickly past the crowd, with the distracted look he'd worn before, and then he released me to Seth.

Could it be Hunter or one of his brothers?

"And this is my beautiful fiancée, Jessica, for those of you who have not been introduced." He played it off like I had been always by his side. The crowd cheered.

I thought about Hunter as I stepped slowly toward the platform with the cameras rolling. I prayed he would see through my pretense. He had to. I needed to keep up the charade until the right time for my escape. Although another thought occurred to me: *Even if I could escape, would I find my way back? And if I found my way back, would I be able to cross over the cobblestone path?*

I hoped Hunter had a plan of his own and somehow, some way, we'd meet somewhere in the middle, where no one got hurt.

Seth pulled me up onto the platform, wrapping his arm around my waist. Cameras flashed like crazy. My body began to shake, and I thought about the last time I had eaten or had anything to drink, and then everything went black.

The Diversion

I woke in familiar surroundings, but there was no comfort in that, as I was back in my original prison: my mother's house, on my mother's leather couch.

"Oh goodness. My poor darling." It was my mother's voice, echoing from another room.

We weren't alone, and she played concerned mother with convincing emotions. Davior explained the lie to her about me being kidnapped and brainwashed.

Why wouldn't Seth have told her where I was before now?

I couldn't tell for sure if she was buying it or not, but I'd know soon enough. I sat up and combed at my hair with my fingers.

Davior entered the room moments later, carrying a tray of food. "You need to eat something." He set it down in front of me on the clear glass table.

"I'm fine," I snapped, irritated at what he'd just told my mother.

"You need to drink too. I'm thinking you're dehydrated and that's why you passed out."

Davior looked over his shoulder, like someone had said something to him, but no one was there. He seemed agitated for a moment and then sat down next me.

"Is something wrong?" I asked, wearing a smirk across my face.

"No. Eat!" he said, annoyed at my question or at something else.

"Fine." I grabbed a finger sandwich and stuffed it into my mouth.

I was already starting to feel my old self creeping back into my body. I detested everything around me: the sight of the fancy furniture, the familiar smell of my mother's perfume, and most of all, the clicking of her footsteps as she paced in the kitchen.

She's waiting for him to leave so she can tear into me without witnesses.

"After you eat, you need to go upstairs and get dressed. Seth's reception is tonight, and he has requested you play the song he thinks is for him in front of everyone. You have four dresses you may choose from, and I've already laid them out in your room." He stood up and left the room.

My mother came in next. "Jessica, you look absolutely horrible! How did you get that scar on your cheek?" She pointed to my cheek, sounding very annoyed. "That's what happens when you run away from home."

I didn't run away. I am not a child, I thought, but kept quiet.

She didn't believe Davior's story. That was good. I'd rather her believe the truth, it was all me. There was no reason for her to be mad at Hunter and his family.

"You look just dreadful. Maybe we can cover that scar with some makeup. I'll get someone over here now." She tapped her foot and picked up the phone. "We don't have much time to talk now, but we'll converse later." She scowled at me. "Go up to your room and get dressed. I'll be up in a minute. Susan, yes, I need you here in five minutes," she said to the person on the other end of the phone, motioning me with her other hand to go.

I felt like I had never left at all, and despair filled me. No second step, no part two of the plan was forming; instead, a blanket of doubt and emptiness surrounded me with every step up the staircase to my familiar prison. To end up in this house, and in the same situation, should I have even left? *Yes, of course.* I had found a love that surpassed all understanding, a love that would be with me always and I would never turn away from, because I was always His. The love I felt for God and He felt for me. No one could ever take that away from me, no matter what they forced me to do. I prayed for His guidance and once again for those I had come to love. Whatever God wanted to happen, I would embrace.

We entered the reception arena, which was bigger than I had anticipated with every news station, magazine reporter, and newspaper outlet covering the event. Seth moved me from one section of people to another, keeping me close by his side. He introduced me as his fiancée to everyone who approached us; however, Seth had never actually asked me to marry him, and I was grateful I could still feel my beaded engagement ring beneath the white lace gloves. My eyes started to swell with liquid, and I felt hollow inside. With no new plan sprouting and with so many people there, I would never be able to escape without being noticed.

Seth appeared to be very charming and intelligent in his new state, moving from room to room very smoothly, with eager faces to meet him. Everyone around him was a fool, in my opinion, not able to see his sudden burst of anger or rolling eyes when someone would talk about contributing to the poor or elderly.

I can see him for what he really is.

Most of the guests were not overly interested in me as I stepped behind Seth, trying to stay in his shadow. I was back to being invisible, which had been the way I liked it.

Someone clinked a glass. It was time for Seth to make a speech, and we were rushed to another larger area with a platform.

Davior slithered to my side as Seth took center stage. "Nice party, isn't it?" he cooed.

"Yes, it is," I said involuntarily.

"Jessica, please don't continue to be mad at me." He turned me to look into his eyes, and I started to feel faint.

"Don't do that!" I shouted, shaking myself out of it.

"Sorry. I wasn't trying to." He swallowed hard. " Jessica," he said, pleading with me, "just be careful, please."

"Why?" I asked softly, not wanting anyone to overhear.

Davior looked at me, puzzled.

"I know what's going on here. Why bother with me? Why am I even here?" I continued to whisper.

"You should know the answer to that. Seth is willing to do whatever it takes to keep you with him, including joining our family and our cause." Davior was moving toward my ear. "But there could be another option for you. You could join me, and I will keep you safe from any harm. I can keep you free of Seth." His lip touched my ear. "I know you care for me."

I bit down on my teeth and resisted the urge to punch him. *How dare he act like he's looking after me, that he cares about me, when all along, he has been the one who has put me in this situation to begin with?*

I turned away from him, but he pulled me back, looking at me differently, not with the same glare as before, inches from my face.

"Jessica, darling," Seth called loudly from across the room, and everyone's eyes were on me and Davior.

Davior quickly jumped back, releasing his watch.

"Would you mind playing for us?" Seth asked me softly.

I walked down the aisle toward the stage and stepped up to the piano and then sat on the bench. My hands blocked from view, I took off the gloves and then stroked my ring while taking a deep breath. I then said a quick prayer and whispered so softly even I couldn't hear it.

"I love you."

I then began to play.

The music I composed for Hunter was actually a duet. I took the soft, haunting melody of the river cane flute, my song, and intertwined it in the notes I wrote for him. I prayed if Hunter could hear it, he would know. He would always know my heart belonged to him forever, no matter what happened. As I played, I reminisced on all my memories of him: the first time I saw him, standing in the dark shadow in the shack; the first time he smiled at me, jumping over the porch railing and handing me a rose; us arguing about shapes in the clouds in the soft meadow; him lifting me down from his shoulders in the cornfield; us standing on the porch, looking up at the stars with his arms wrapped around me; our first kiss in the courtyard; and lastly, the night he played my song and asked me to marry him.

The music stopped, and tears streamed down uncontrollably as I rested my hands in my lap. I was glad my mother had asked for waterproof makeup, or I would have looked like the women in my dark dream, the ones with black mascara smeared on their faces.

Seth clapped loudly and unexpectedly pulled me off the bench into a hug. I hadn't put the gloves back on, so I hid my hand. He kissed me hard, breaking open the cut on my lip. The crowd cheered.

Musicians stepped up to the stage, and music began to play as Seth carried me down to the dance floor and clumsily danced me around. It was nothing like the soft sway of dancing with Hunter or the precise steps with John, and I was thankful when others started to cut in. Davior seemed a little concerned by it, other men dancing with me, but Seth attended to other concerns and called Davior to him. Something else was going on, and they both disappeared behind the stage.

Is this my chance? I felt lost in my search for answers. *If I don't act now, while I'm free from their sight, when will I get the chance again?*

An old man swept his arm around my waist and began to dance. He smelled of Old Spice and vodka. His steps were clumsy, and he kept stepping on top of my feet. I was glad when another stepped in to take his place.

"You look beautiful tonight." I knew that voice. I pulled away to look at his face.

"James! Oh, James!" I hugged him, and tears began to fall, but he pulled me back.

"Careful. You don't want to draw attention to us," he said, wiping my tears.

I knew that, but then I started to panic. "He'll kill you. You... you shouldn't be here. It's not safe for you. Go, I'll distract him so you can get far away before he knows you're here."

"Yes, okay," James said like he was talking to someone else. "Yes. I'll tell her."

"Who are you talking to?"

"Hunter said to tell you to stop worrying. You're the one to be saved. Really, we don't have much time for this, Hunter," James argued with himself.

"He can hear me?" I asked, feeling excited and alive for the first time in a long time.

" I'm allowing him to read my thoughts, but it's rather annoying. Yes, yes, you love her. Can we get her out yet?" He paused for a moment.

I closed my eyes and imagined Hunter saying he loved me, standing right there next to me. It was so hard not to be giddy.

"I guess you'll have to endure my dancing for a little while longer."

"Where is he?" I whispered, my eyes scanning the crowd.

I wondered if people would notice. Somehow, they would see I was glowing, different, happier, but no one seemed to care.

"You remember Hunter telling you about how he and Davior can read each other's thoughts," he said.

I nodded.

"So you can understand he has to stay farther away from where Davior is, or else he'll know we're here." He paused, listening to the voice in his head. "Hunter is just close enough to distract Davior, to get him far enough away to get you out of here."

"So how it is that you can hear him?"

"Being the oldest, I can tune into all of my brothers, but I can also choose to tune them out. My gift. Davior can detect me if he's really close, but he can only read my mind if I allow him to,"

James said, sounding anxious. "I've been testing the perimeters for weeks now."

"So that's why I would see Davior's facial expression get angry and he would leave." I laughed thinking about it.

He nodded but then frowned. He was now looking at my face.

"I saw how you got this." He touched my bleeding lip from the hard kiss Seth had planted on me. "But how'd you get this?" he touch the scar that apparently even makeup couldn't hide. He rolled his eyes.

Hunter was badgering him.

I hesitated. *How can I blame her? I don't want them to go after her. She has a fate worse than death waiting for her when her time does come.* I looked up at James. He had those same soft, caring eyes that belonged to my love.

"It was Molly," I said so low I almost didn't think he heard me.

"I know," he said. "We'll deal with her later, bro. Focus," James said calmly. James looked back at me.

"I shouldn't have told you," I said. "I'm sorry."

"You don't have anything to apologize for, Jess. Hunter wanted me to tell you that, but I'll second that." He smiled.

Someone tapped on his shoulder. *Oh no,* I thought, and I held James tighter to me. I think he enjoyed it.

"It's just Jordan." James laughed softly.

"May I?"

James handed me over reluctantly. I didn't want to let James go either. In some small way, Hunter was there too.

"Well, young lady, you have made things very interesting since the day you met my brother." He twirled me around the dance floor.

"I'm sorry," I said, looking down.

"No, no, no." He held my head up. "I love it. I haven't seen this much excitement in years." He was being sincere.

"Oh, well, that's my world, filled with drama. You should meet my mother while you're here," I teased.

"Oh, I already did. I danced with her just a few minutes ago. She's quite fascinating. Evil, but fascinating."

James was back, tapping him on the shoulder.

"Hey, I didn't get much time—"

James cut Jordan off. "It's time," James said, with a long, black jacket in his hand.

Both boys escorted me into the non-dancing crowd. James slipped the jacket on me, pulling the hood over my head and zipping me up. I saw across from me, someone dressed just like me. She looked up and smiled. It was Annabel. I knew immediately what they were doing. She was a decoy.

"But what if she gets hurt? I can't let anyone get hurt because of me. It's my fault all this happened. If Seth finds out it's not me, he'll kill her," I said, shaking my head as I unzipped the jacket and tried to shimmy it off, but James pulled it back on and looked into my eyes.

"Annabel will be perfectly safe with John. It's just a diversion to get you far enough away," James said.

I was still shaking my head, almost hysterical.

"Look, Jessie, if you don't follow our plan, my brother will not go along either. He will crash this party. We are family, and we stick together, so either we do this quietly, or it will be open war in front of all these people, who could also get hurt," James said sternly.

I understood exactly what I must do: follow their plan.

To Kill or Not to Kill

Jordan, James, and I walked quietly out of the crowd. Not one person looked in our direction as Annabel stepped out onto the dance floor. I took one final look back before exiting the hall to see Seth standing back on the stage. However, Davior was nowhere in sight. James would know if Davior knew something, so there was no need for me to worry, at least about that, as we stepped out of the building.

It was a beautiful California evening as the winds blew the smog off to the east. The sky gleamed a brilliant purple, red, and yellow, and the sun began to set behind the ocean, the silhouette of the waves crashing against the cliffs and the loud, pounding surf echoing through the canyon into the air. James opened the door to a blue Infiniti parked just outside the reception hall, and we climbed into the backseat while Jordan stepped into the driver's seat.

"Safety first." Jordan grabbed his seat belt and fastened it.

James did the same and looked to see I hadn't.

"Yes, I know," he said under his breath and reached over to fasten mine. "Let's get out of here."

Jordan adjusted his mirrors and fumbled with the radio for a moment. "Life Is a Highway" blared on the radio. "Cool," he said and floored the gas pedal.

Moments later, a phone rang, and James pulled a phone out of his pocket and handed it to me.

"Hello?" I said, looking strangely at James.

"Jess," he said, relieved.

It was Hunter, and tears started to fall once again. "I'm so sorry. I should have known better. I shouldn't have followed her." I rambled on until he stopped me.

"No, honey, it's not your fault. Shh. You're in good hands now. You're safe. Don't worry, please," he pleaded with me in a cracked voice.

"I miss you," I said, pulling myself together.

"I miss you so much," he said back. "I wanted to come get you myself, but…" He paused.

"I know. I'm glad you didn't." I continued trying to sound brave. "Davior is going after you, isn't he?"

"I can handle Davior. Don't worry so much," he said calmly.

"Davior was using me so they could get Seth to do what they wanted."

"Jess?" he said softly.

I took a deep breath. "Yes."

"I know all of Davior's plans, so let my family and I take care of this. There's more than you know, and I promise to tell you later. Right now, you need to get some rest. Okay?" he said, trying to calm me.

"I love you," I whispered.

"I know." He paused again. "I love you too," he said, and then phone went dead.

"What happened?" I looked at James for an answer.

"Cell phones are great, but these hills seemed to cut off the connection. Hunter's fine. He said you should try to sleep now. You look like you haven't slept in days." James pulled off his jacket and folded it to look like a pillow.

"I can't remember the last night I slept well, and I'm feeling nauseated watching the blurred scenery anyway," I said, looking at Jordan in the rearview mirror, referring to the fact Jordan was going as fast as the car would let him go.

"Hey, I've been given strict orders to get you home ASAP, and since we can't fly…" Jordan looked into the rearview mirror.

"Just make sure we get there in one piece," James said.

"I'm an excellent driver. See? No hands." Jordan laughed back.

"Hunter's going to drown you for that one." James snorted.

"Bring it on, bro. I'm up for it," Jordan jeered.

I enjoyed the little spat between them. I felt like I was already home and Hunter was just in the next room. I laid my head on the bundled jacket and tried to sleep.

The hot sun on my arm woke me. I was disorientated at first as I yawned and stretched, looking out the window, and then I realized who I was with and felt relieved.

"Where are we?" I asked, rubbing the sleep out of my eyes.

"Alabama," Jordan said, looking back. "We're close now. Just a few more hours."

My stomach growled loudly.

He laughed. "We'll stop at the next station. We need to fill up the gas tank anyway."

I looked over at James in a peaceful sleep.

"That whole mind thing takes a lot out of him. Hunter and I agreed he needed at least a few hours of sleep, although he should wake up now."

"No. Don't wake him yet. Wait until we stop," I said, looking into the mirror at Jordan.

He agreed.

Jordan slowed closer to the speed limit as we approached a town. I stared out the window, amazed at how fast time had flown by. The trees didn't have any leaves on them, so I assumed it was late fall, maybe early winter. It hadn't felt overly cold in California, but that could have just been one of those summerlike days that happen in the concrete city even in the dead of winter.

I couldn't wait to be home with my new family and back to planning a wedding, my wedding, although the words Davior had said about knowing the reason John wanted us to wait dangled in my mind.

I should have let him tell me.

The car stopped. "James," Jordan called loudly, slamming his door shut after getting out.

James's eyes popped open wide, and he gasped.

"Jess, you okay?" He looked around to see Jordan helping me out. "Yes. She's right here," he answered back. I assumed it was Hunter's voice in his head. "Sorry. Jordan just scared me to death. Nothing unusual."

Jordan handed me some money.

"What do you want to eat?" he asked James.

"I'll go in with her. I need some aspirin," James said, rubbing the spot between his eyes with his fingers.

"It's like a hangover," Jordan said loudly and then laughed.

Jordan just loved to tease everyone, especially his brothers. James nodded. "I'm fine. Let's go."

We walked in to the store. No one was there except us and the cashier, who couldn't have been more than fifteen. He stared at me from behind the counter.

James noticed and laughed. "Seems like you've got him in awe."

"He's just wondering which one of you beat me up."

"Not funny, Jess." He paused for moment, looking rather curious.

"What?" I asked.

"I'm not hearing him. Hunter's not responding to my thoughts." He looked at my concerned face. "I'm sure he just moved out of my range. We're traveling in opposite directions until we get you to the Georgia border, and then he'll head for home. He knew we were close. It just took me off guard for him not to comment on some guy checking you out." He chuckled.

"You heard him in the car just a few minutes ago, right?" I asked.

"Actually, no. I was trying to respond before he asked. But now that I think about it, he hasn't said anything since I fell asleep. Everything is fine, Jess. Don't worry," James said, trying to lighten my worry, but he couldn't hide the worried look on his face

He took out the cell phone, but we were out of service range. *Isn't that just the way it always is?* "Do your headaches block… What's the word? Transmission?" I asked.

"I…I don't know," James said, now looking at Jordan, who walked in on the conversation.

Jordan looked serious, but that quickly turned to excitement.

"We need to get her out of here and fast," James said.

I wasn't sure I understood, but I hustled out the door, and Jordan threw money at the cashier. "Keep the change, and have a nice day," Jordan said with a smile.

We all jumped into the car, and Jordan floored the gas pedal.

"Okay. What just happened?" I asked.

"There's going to be a fight after all. I knew I could count on him." Jordan howled like a wolf.

"Jordan!" James scolded, and then spoke to me. "Jess, if I can't hear Hunter, he can't hear me and the phone is not working. He warned us that if for any reason he couldn't know what was going on, he was coming for you." James was still rubbing his head.

I opened the aspirin bottle and handed him two tablets. It took a few minutes to piece it together, and then I remembered Davior was following him.

"But if Davior is behind him, shouldn't we be able to reach the grounds before him, even if Hunter catches up to us?" I didn't see the urgency.

"If Hunter changed course and got close enough to Davior, he would have known we had you and where we were going. We can hope he's out in the middle of nowhere with no phone connection, or else."

"Or else what?" I asked.

"It's not just Davior and Seth we'll have to deal with."

"Oh." I sulked into the back seat.

"Come on and get us," Jordan hollered out the window and then found another song he liked on the radio, "Eye of the Tiger." "I need a radio in my room." He beat the steering wheel to the rhythm.

"I'll put it on my list." James shook his head at him.

We drove along the snakelike road for miles. I tried not to look out the window at the blurred trees, which made me a bit queasy.

Then, suddenly… "Jordan, stop!" James called out.

Jordan began to apply pressure to the brakes, but it was too late, and we smashed into a fat tree trunk lying across the road. We didn't hit as hard as we would have if Jordan hadn't slammed on the breaks, causing the car to spin and hit on the side of the car instead of a direct, head-on hit. My head hit the passenger side window. James scrambled out of the car and pulled me out.

"Jess, are you okay?" James touched the small cut on my forehead.

"I'm fine," I said, trying to stand, but I felt a bit wobbly from the spinning.

"She's okay. It's just a scratch," he said to Jordan

"The log was placed here." Jordan smiled as he began to pace the tree-lined road. "Come out, come out, wherever you are."

The air was still, and no noise could be heard. The sky that was bright with sunlight began to darken, and I knew what was coming, just like before.

"Come on, you cowards," Jordan called. "I can smell your stench so I know you're there."

I could see the tops of the trees swaying like someone or something moved through them and in our direction. The sky changed into a gray mist, and a thick fog rolled down and surrounded us. Seth climbed out of the trees first, in his demon form, and he was exceedingly angry. His face was a bright red, veins in his neck bulging out, and his teeth were jagged, covered in black soot.

"Trying to steal her from me again?" Seth asked in a deep, huffing voice.

"Seth, let me handle this," Davior said, walking out behind him and then standing in front of Seth.

"My brothers, you don't have to be involved in any of this. Why fight over this girl? Is she worth dying for?" Davior spoke calmly, looking at me. "Just hand her over, and we'll be gone."

"James, did you hear someone call us brothers? I don't see a brother standing before me." Jordan danced around and looked right at Davior. "I see a worm, a little worm who follows his master's orders. Why don't you go back to the hot, stinky hole you crawled out of?"

"It's not about her. It's about you trying to control—" James said but was cut off.

"Then I guess you've made your decision and you leave me no choice," Davior said and then smiled.

"Bring it on, little worm." Jordan sneered at him, walking toward him.

"I think I'm going to enjoy this." Davior expressed his amusement as he lifted his arms.

Ten creatures stepped out of the trees. They were bigger and scarier than Seth. He at least resembled a human. These were monsters, and they gnashed their sharp teeth, looking at Jordan and James.

Oh no. How can they fight against monsters? That was not good. James bent down to me.

"When the fight starts, run." He pointed in the direction we had come from. He shook my frozen body. "Jess, are you all right?"

"They are monsters. How are you going to fight against them?" I said, breathing hard, watching Davior strut in front of the large beasts towering over him.

"Jess, I know you're scared and it understandable, but we have fought them before. Hunter can't be far behind." He stood up and walked over to joined Jordan. "Oh, and Jess," James called

Twisted Roots | 361

out over the low growls, "you are a part of our family now, which makes you important to all of us. Don't listen to the lies."

But they are outnumbered. How could I not be worried?

I watched in fear, as the disfigured demons circled Jordan and James.

"No," I screamed out, but no one heard me. Just as I was about to get up and run to Davior to stop this, another person jumped into the middle with them. It was John. *John will reason with him. Davior won't fight his own dad, would he?*

"Son, do you really want to fight us?" John asked calmly.

"You're not giving me a choice, old man," Davior said, joining his army. "You shouldn't be involved in this."

"Jessica is part of our family. You can change, Davior. I can feel the conflict inside you. You still can—"John started to say, but Davior cut him off.

"I can what, come back home? Travel to the missions? As appealing as that sounds, I think I'll pass," Davior said.

"So be it," John said as he waved his hand.

More men jumped into the middle of the circle, outnumbering the demons. Seth stepped up next to Davior. He was bigger than before and angrier—fuming at me. Even with more men, they still looked outnumbered against the hefty, monstrous demons.

Two of the monsters had a set of blood-stained spiral horns that ended in sharp points like a spear. There were others with long, pointed tails that curved from their backs, and they held them in front, jabbing them toward the men who stood in front of them. They all made a deep huffing sound and scuffed their feet at the challengers. Both the men and the demons hunched into attack mode, staring at their competitors until Davior took the first step forward.

The fighting began, and I should have run. Instead, I stayed frozen, watching the men fight off the demons. John kicked one squarely in the chest and knocked him back as another came forward, only to do it again to another. James was able to knock one down by sweeping his legs in front of him. Jordan was trying to get his arms around a monster. The demon shook his body, trying to get him off, and in the process, he crushed the smaller monsters under his feet. All the men had their own style, and they seemed to be doing well. Davior was in the circle but was directing the demons and not in the actual fight himself, but I no longer could see Seth.

Run, you fool.

I got up and ran as fast as my legs would go, back away from the fight and in the direction we had come from. I ran along the side of the road in hopes to see a car flying toward me. I would know who it was.

"Where do you think you're going?" he asked in an unpleasant tone, filled with rage vibrating in his throat.

I could feel the ground shake with every step he took. He was gaining on me fast, so I ran into the trees. He was bigger, and it would be harder for him to weave in and out like I could. At least that way, I had a chance, maybe not much of one, since he was crunching down on some of the smaller trees as he stepped, but I had to try something.

Staying close to the road and watching for any sign of Hunter's car was only allowing Seth to gain on me. I went farther into the brush, making my way through the thick, brown bushes, scraping up my arms and legs. My plan must have worked. I was no longer feeling the ground quiver beneath my feet. I stopped to catch my breath, my head bent down to my knees. I looked back but couldn't see Seth.

A sigh of relief passed over my lips. *But where is the road?* I had gone too far in.

I wasn't going to panic. So I picked a direction and started walking. I then heard a car in the opposite direction of where I was heading.

Hunter! My heart raced as I turned and ran toward the sound of the approaching, screeching tires.

I tripped over the bushes and ran through the branches to make it to the road as fast as I could, but when I got there, no car was in sight. I was also no farther from the fight. I found myself right back where I had started.

Breathing heavily, feeling the tightness in my chest, I watched the men continue to battle, seeing three demons lying outside the fight, motionless. Some of the men were hurt, with scratches and blood from their mouths and face, but none had fallen yet.

"Please, Lord, let none die," I said softly but out loud, still gasping for air.

I felt a midsized earthquake shake under my feet. I thought about running, but it was too late, and I had nowhere to go.

"How could you?" Seth's voice boomed from behind me. "I loved you! I could have given you anything, anything, and this how to you repay me? I'd rather you be dead than with him," Seth said as he moved toward me.

This is no time to give up.

My eyes scanned the ground for a weapon, anything I could use. A thick wooden post lay a few feet from me, and I went for it, picking it up and grasping it firmly with both hands. I stood firm, facing Seth, waving the post back and forth in the air. I swung out with all my strength as he moved in closer and I hit him in the chest, but it made no impact.

Seth was amused by my attempt. He reached out and grabbed the post, twisting it out of my hands. He toyed with it a moment. I thought he was going to swing at me, but instead, he crumbled it into dust. He laughed and moved closer while I was stepping back.

"There is still a chance for us, Jessie. No one else needs to get hurt," Seth said, looking over at the group in combat, drawing my eyes there.

I watched the men fighting and more demons joining in. Something else in the road caught my attention, something shiny and sharp.

Seth's manner began to calm, and he was changing, shrinking, and looking more like a real person again and not the monster who fed on anger and rage.

"Marry me, Jessie." He paused, reaching his hand out to mine. "And I'll spare your friends. I'll even spare...him," he said, not wanting to say Hunter's name.

I looked over at the battle, watched another demon fall outside of the circle. It would be better for Seth to just kill me than to give up. All those men fighting were all ready to give their lives to save me. Hunter would give his life to save me. The time to fight back had come, and if that meant Seth killing me, so be it.

I'll die wearing his ring to heaven, I thought happily and then narrowed my eyes on Seth.

"No," I said under my breath at first. My eyes glared into his. "No! I will never marry you! I'd rather be dead than marry you!"

I watched his face instantly change back into the hideous monster. I ran for the object in the road. I was almost there when I felt him grab at my arm. He didn't quite have me, and I slipped out of his hold. He sent me tumbling on the black, rocky asphalt.

I overlooked the burning of my gouged skin and looked around for the sharp bright-red, painted-metal stake, the kind used to string barbwire to keep the animals from getting on the road. I reached for it when Seth stepped on my arm. I heard an awful crunch. Seth reached down for me, grabbing me by the neck.

"Let her go." I heard a familiar booming voice. "Now!" he commanded.

Seth's smile widened before he turned around. His hands were still on my neck as he turned, pulling me along with his motion. I felt like a rag doll, limp and motionless in his grip. He then dropped me down onto my knees. I gasped for air, noticing one arm was not working the way I wanted it to.

"So we meet again," Seth said, staring at Hunter as he began to pace. "This is a domestic issue that concerns me and my fiancée."

"That's where you're mistaken, Seth. She has never accepted your proposal." Hunter looked down at my broken and torn-up body. "However, she has agreed to marry me."

Our eyes locked, and I could see the pain and anger building up inside Hunter. Something strange was happening to him. His chest widened with each deep breath in, and he was getting taller.

Seth reached down and grabbed a handful of my hair and then lifted me off the ground. I cried out, still watching Hunter's anger change him.

"Well then, I guess it's too bad neither of you will live to fulfill your vows." Seth chuckled.

And that was all Hunter needed and he lunged for Seth. Seth dropped me and I landed on my broken arm, causing the bone to pierce through the skin. I quickly tore the bottom of my dress and wrapped it around the injury. The pain was intense, but I wasn't going to give into it. I dug deep into my soul, into my strength. I needed to help.

If I could just get to that stake...

Now there were two battles going on.

John, James, Jordan, and other members of the tribe were fighting the demons and Davior. Not only were they immortal men, but they were strong and doing well as I watched another two demons fly into the air and fall onto the ground. Seconds later, there was a puff of smoke, and the dead disappeared. Davior yelled something, and more demons crawled out of the trees.

Hunter and Seth were circling each other, like in a wrestling match.

"I'm going to enjoy crushing you," Seth yelled.

Seth was in his full monster form, but Hunter looked different too. He didn't look monstrous, like Seth. Actually, he didn't look much different than he had before, only he was larger, much larger, and just about as tall as Seth. They were better matched, except Hunter's rage made him stronger.

"Do you see me scared, Seth?" Hunter asked in a mocking tone.

"Jessica is mine!" Seth yelled, sending vibrations through the air.

Instead of responding verbally, Hunter laughed and smiled brilliantly in my direction. I couldn't help but smile back. The pain vanished for a second as his love for me filled me like a drug.

Seth charged for Hunter, knocking Hunter across the road. Hunter landed hard but bounced up quickly and laughed.

"Is that all you got?"

Seth then went over to the car and lifted it up over his head, his breaths faster and furious. With one loud grunt, he flung the car in Hunter's direction.

"Look out," I couldn't help but yell.

The car flew through the air, twisting and turning, missing Hunter by inches, as he dodged the car and screamed back behind him. "Incoming."

The car landed on its side, tearing up the black road and kicking up sparks. It was heading toward the other fight going on. The men and Davior heard Hunter and scattered, but the demons hadn't moved, and the car smashed half of them instantly.

"Well, that worked out well, didn't it, Seth?" Hunter asked.

Seth grunted loudly in frustration and lunged for Hunter again, only, Hunter was ready for him. He was able to turn Seth around into a head lock, his arm wrapped around his neck. Seth was choking. Hunter's eyes were wild. He then picked up Seth and slammed him down on the road, causing the road to split down the middle.

Seth laughed, standing up and brushing off the little bits of asphalt on his clothes. Meanwhile, I went for the stake. My adrenalin kicked into high gear. I could do it. I dragged my body along the ground and reached out, touching it with my fingertips, keeping my eyes on the fight. Seth, with both hands, pushed Hunter, sending him in the air, clear across through the trees.

Hunter moved slowly, not recovering from the blow as quickly as before.

"It's now or never," I said to myself, seeing my only opportunity to fight back with Seth's eyes on Hunter.

"Oh, come on," Seth said. "I barely pushed you." He laughed, watching Hunter wipe the blood from his forehead.

I forced my legs to stand, gathering all the strength I had inside to move forward—all the pain I felt all those years, visions of my mother, visions of Seth's father and what he did to mine, the life taken from me, and him trying to kill Hunter.

I let out a loud, deep grunt of my own. Seth turned, and I jabbed the stake into his right shoulder, piercing all the way through. He screamed as I backed away from him. I had aimed for his heart. I had meant to kill him, not just maim.

Seth grabbed the weapon and pulled it out in one long tug as he screamed, dropping the stake to the ground.

"It's too bad, Jess," he said in a dark, raspy voice, absorbing the pain he felt. "Now you'll have to die." He walked slowly toward me.

I couldn't outrun him, so there was no point in trying. He reached out with one hand and squeezed it around my neck, lifting me up so only my toes dangled on the ground.

I heard a loud growl, and once again, I was dropped to the ground.

Hunter charged Seth, knocking him into several large, thick trees. Seth wasn't moving. Hunter ran toward him again, picked him up, lifted him above his head, and threw him across to the other side of the trees.

Davior called the demons to protect Seth as Hunter was going for him again.

"Hunter," I heard John call several times, getting closer each time to where I was.

My eyes began to close as I laid my head against the asphalt. I could hear John at my side and felt my sticky blood seeping through the cloth. My head throbbed in pain.

"Jess. Jess, can you hear me?" I heard another voice, one frantic and desperate.

I tried to open my eyes, but they felt so heavy. I tasted the thick iron in my mouth and coughed. I felt pain again as someone touched my arm, a burning and then cool as I felt something being poured on it, and then back to burning as it was rewrapped into some kind of splint.

I tried to sit up, but I couldn't.

"Don't move please, honey," Hunter said, pleading with me, cradling me in his arms.

"Okay. That should help and stop the bleeding," John said to Hunter with one last pull on my arm.

I whimpered.

"I know it hurts." I could hear the tears in his voice. He stroked my face with the back of his hand.

"When we get you home, we'll give you something for the pain," John encouraged me. "James, call Mike and tell him what's happened. We'll be home in less than an hour."

Hunter carried me into the car, and I rested in his lap. The pain was terrible, but not as terrible as feeling I would never be there again, in his arms.

"You're going to be just fine," Hunter said in his worried voice, his lips resting on my hair. "Focus on something other than the pain." He thought a moment and then began to hum a lullaby.

The lullaby was my song. I closed my eyes and stepped up to the piano. I wore a long, white gown that spilled out over the bench. The intricate, small sequins around the bottom glistened. My hair twisted up softly. Curls dangled in front of my face and along the back. I wore my locket, along with diamond earrings that glistened off the keys. I started to play Hunter's song.

We danced under a white gazebo with white flowers covering the structure and dangling down. He twirled me around, with his gaze only on me. Then he pulled me in a tight embrace. His eyes slanted to my lips, which he was tracing with his finger. My heart, filled with love, beat along with the melody. His lips were inches from mine as he drew closer.

Everything was so soft and lovely as I began to fade into it.

New Beginnings

I started off in this life miserable. From the time of birth until the time I ran away, I had hated everyone and everything in my life, except for my father. I had felt like someone who was delivered to the wrong family, perhaps switched at birth or something like that, and my real family would come along and find me and I would finally be where I belonged.

Finally, it happened.

I awoke from a very deep sleep, feeling groggy and a bit unsure if I had really experienced the events in the last year. I almost expected to wake up in my old room, hearing my mother chastising me for something.

My eyes scanned the room, and the wildflower garden mural Annabel had painted welcomed me home.

"Good afternoon," he whispered gently into my ear, sending those wonderful sensations throughout my body.

I turned to face him, his lips inches from mine. He slowly inched toward me, touching my lips softly with his, his eyes never moving from mine. The tingles of excitement, the passion I almost forgot in that horrible, dark place, raged up inside as my heartbeat and breath quickened. He kissed me softly again, taking deeper breaths, trying to control himself. I couldn't believe how lucky I was as my pulse raced and I needed more. I needed him closer as I pressed my lips harder against his. A sharp pain from my lip registered in my brain, but I didn't care as I pressed even harder. My hand moved to his face. He pulled back slightly with a brilliant smile on his face.

"Careful," he said, touching my lip.

I ignored his request and went to raise my arms around his neck, and it was then I remembered my arm being broken. Covered in a thick plaster, my arm wasn't going to move easily.

I still had the same thought and one working arm. "It's been too long. I don't care. I've missed you so much." My hand went around his neck and pulled his face closer to me, pressing my lips against his. I could feel his heart rapidly beating against my chest as his kisses felt hot and wild. He pulled me closer before he stopped.

"Jess," he said, his breath still hot, trying to calm his pulse. He sat on the edge of the bed.

"Sorry," I said, a little frustrated, but I really didn't mean it, and he knew it.

He propped a pillow up against the backboard and leaned against it.

"Nothing to be sorry about, my love, except your lip is bleeding again." He casually leaned over and grabbed a tissue from a box on the nightstand next to the bed.

I took in a heavy sigh and sat up, only to see static flying all around in the air. "Maybe that's not such a good idea." I slid closer to him and laid my cheek against his chest. "How long was I gone?"

"Two months." He sighed. "I thought I was going to go crazy, but all that is past us now, and you're safe again." He stroked my cheek with the back of his index finger.

Everything started to come back to me, the night Molly tricked me, the long walk through the darkness and into the fire, the mansion outside the gates of hell, the dance with James, and then…

"Was anyone hurt?"

"A few scratches. Besides you, everyone's fine." He spoke calmly.

"I'm so sorry. If I hadn't followed Molly—" I tried to sit up again, with tears falling, but Hunter held me to his chest.

"Shh. It's not your fault. Molly fooled all of us. We should have kept a better watch over you." He held me tighter to him.

I raised my head to look at him, and he leaned down and kissed my tears. I stared into his eyes with the same passion that flooded me before. The feeling consumed me, and I kissed him again, with my hand reaching up to comb through his hair. He returned the same passionate kiss until I rolled him down on top of me.

"She's awake! She's awake!" I heard May calling from the doorway to downstairs.

Although I wasn't happy about being interrupted, it was so good to hear her little voice.

Hunter sat up quickly, trying to breathe again, smiling, looking down at me. His face was flushed and his hair frazzled, and he looked like he was wearing bright red lipstick. I sat up next to him, dabbing my bloody lip. I didn't feel as dizzy as before.

"You might want to look in the mirror." I said.

He knew exactly what I meant and ran into the bathroom before everyone was standing over me. Miss Caroline, Miss Betsy, and Miss Mabel were the first to enter, followed by Josephine, Jordan, James, John, Annabel, and May, who jumped on the bed, throwing her arms around me to give me a giant kiss. There was one other person who entered whom I had not met yet, and there was no sign of Joseph.

"How are you feeling?" John asked first.

"Good," I answered. "So how long do I have to wear this?"

John looked at the person I didn't recognize.

"Hi, Jessie. We haven't met formally, but I'm Mike."

"Mike is one of our doctors," John added. "He travels to and from the mission fields, so he's not always here."

"The thing is, Jessie, I've never seen this sort of thing before." Mike hadn't even finished, and I was thinking bad thoughts.

"See. Compound fractures like the one you have normally can take three months to be at eighty percent and eighteen months to be fully healed, but your bones…well…" Mike hesitated.

Oh no. They won't heal. Something is wrong, rumbled through my mind.

Hunter saw I was thinking something bad, so he jumped in.

"You're healing much faster than a regular person would," Hunter interjected.

"Sorry. Yes, Jessie, you are healing very quickly, and we should be able to take the cast off in about three weeks or so," John said, looking at Hunter apologetically. Mike just stared at me, so dumbfounded he couldn't seem to speak.

"She's looking a little flushed," Hunter said, moving everyone out of the room. "She needs rest." He looked back and winked at me.

Hunter was making an excuse to get everyone out of the room, although I was very tired. I lay back down on the pillow.

I was thinking the same as they were. *Why me?*

"We'll talk later," John said to Hunter, walking out. "Door stays open." He smiled at Hunter.

"Yes, sir." He smiled back.

They all left, and it was just us again.

"You're going to get me in big trouble." He sat back in his spot, and I laid my head back on his chest.

"I'm not the only one to blame," I said as he twirled my hair around his finger.

"Which brings us to another topic," he said. "I think we should set a date. My mother is getting anxious."

I sat up to face him. "I thought your dad wanted us to wait?"

"He's okayed for us to set a date, just not too soon."

"What month are we in?" I asked.

"It's late December."

"Wow." I turned to him.

"So, what do you think?" He reached out to stroke my hair.

"I don't' know," I said, wondering if I should mention a date earlier than my twenty-first birthday and see what his reaction was.

"What do you think about June?" he asked.

"No. Not June," I said, thinking about my birthday and the wedding plans that were originally planned for me.

"Sorry. I forgot. Then how about July?"

"It seems so far away."

"There are lots of things that need to be done before then, my love." He paused. "It will be here before you know it."

"July it is," I said, giving in, but my mind was on other thoughts.

Hunter pulled me to his face and kissed me gently on the cheek. I looked up into his face. I wanted to kiss him again, like I did before, but he stopped me.

"Let's let your lip heal. It's been beat up enough." He laughed, touching it once again.

"Fine!" I pouted, laying my head down on his chest and yawning.

We didn't talk anymore as I fell asleep.

The next time I woke, Hunter wasn't next to me, and I sat up quickly in a panic.

"I'm here," he said, getting up from the chair in the room.

"You left me," I accused.

"No. I've been here the whole time. You thought I was overprotective before." Hunter smiled.

"But—"

I was referring to him being next to me, and he knew it.

"You know why." He blushed.

"Oh. I guess you're right," I said, sounding frustrated as I sat up.

"I'll get you something to eat." Hunter leaned down to kiss my forehead.

"I'm not hungry," I said, thinking about what John said. "Someone must know why I'm healing faster than a normal human, or at least have a guess."

"Your father isn't who you thought he was. We think he might be…" Hunter paused.

"What? You think he's what?"

"One of us," he quickly added, "but we don't know for sure. We planned to visit the grave before you were taken, but then…"

"I know," I said in shock.

"We're not directly related," he said quickly, smiling again. It hadn't even cross my mind.

"What? How do you know that if you don't know—"

"The day you cut your finger and Annabel dabbed the blood, well, John had Mike test it. That's why John didn't want me, well, to get too close to you before we knew. Of course, by that time, it was too late anyway." He chuckled.

"I guess you wouldn't have chuckled if we were related," I said, my mind trying to work out what he was telling me. "You think my father was…like you?"

"It's possible."

I didn't know exactly what that meant; however, the thought tickled me enormously. The thought I belonged to this world all along gave me a feeling of entitlement.

"There is something else you should know too," Hunter said rather hesitantly. "We can't seem to trace your mother's heritage either."

"Oh, but you don't think…" I started to say.

"We don't know. It's just that in tracking your father's background, we found out your mother's background is just as covered up. It could be because of the political influences your mother's parents were involved in, but we can only guess. Honestly, it doesn't really matter, but John would like to know for sure who they really are."

"I'd like to know for sure too," I said, thinking of what it all could mean. *Have I started to age slowly? Would I be like him?*

"Doesn't matter, Jess. You are with me now, and your past is your past. I know what you're thinking." He smiled. "But it doesn't matter to me if you age slower or you age like everyone else. I love you for you, and nothing would change that. We'll be married in July, and I already have the perfect place for us to honeymoon."

"Oh really?" I asked, taking my mind away from the topic at hand.

"Yep," he said, standing up. "You need to eat something. I'll be right back."

"No. You can't go without telling me," I said as he got to the door.

"I guess you'll just have to wait and see," he called as he walked down the hallway.

I could hear him walking down the grand staircase toward the kitchen.

There were so many thoughts running through my mind, so many possibilities. They were all amazing and happy thoughts. The words my father spoke to me so many years ago flooded my mind, as he seemed to be speaking to me at that very moment.

There are magical places that exist in this world, places that the master architect created to balance good and evil in this world. The time will come when you will leave this house and go into another life that awaits you, a life you deserve, a life with a greater purpose.

"Now it's time to find out exactly what you meant, Dad," I said.

I wondered about the journals in the old wooden chest, just like the one in John's office.

Could the papers inside contain the answers everyone is searching for? I hope Hunter is ready for our next adventure.

Epilogue

Seth sat back in his fine, black, leather chair. Scotch on the rocks, his new drink of choice, was now an empty glass in his hand. He shook the ice around and around, until the ice began to spin fast, gliding around the rim of the glass. He then slammed the glass down on the old wooden desk without breaking it. He reached over for the bottle of scotch, which was empty, and slammed the empty bottle down too, only that time, he sent millions of tiny pieces of glass flying through the air.

Jessie's picture was staring at him, her eyes piercing through him as he recalled the screams flowing from her mouth.

"I couldn't control myself," he whispered to her, touching the face of the picture to stroke her cheek. "I didn't mean…"

The vision of her dying and his tight grip on her throat seemed too much for him to take. After all, he did love her and never meant to hurt her.

He reached again for the scotch, forgetting that it was empty and now shattered around the room. Another bottle sat in a drawer next to his feet, the bottom drawer, the same one his father had hid his bottles in. He reached down, listening to the rain pound again at the double-paned, bulletproof glass that surrounded his office. He heard something else but chose to ignore it. No one besides him ever worked past ten. He glanced at the clock, which read 2:15 a.m.

Seth found it humorous, the thought of a thief sneaking in. Actually, he would have enjoyed killing someone he cared nothing about, someone on whom he could take out all his frustration and anger. Maybe it would help. The thought began to fester as he stared at the door, forgetting the scotch sitting in the drawer waiting for him.

The door started to open, and a smile crept over Seth's face until…

"It's just you." Seth pulled another bottle out of the drawer. He pushed it shut and then began to pour the scotch into the glass.

"Sorry," Davior said slowly, "sir."

Seth spun around his chair to look out into the starry night, clicking the ice in the glass as he drank.

"Sir?" Davior asked, but Seth remained silent.

"Seth?"

"Did I...did I kill her?" Seth knew it in his mind, but he needed to hear it.

"No, she's not..." Davior said as Seth quickly spun around in his chair, staring Davior in the eyes.

"What? What did you say?" Seth asked, leaning across the table, his eyes wide.

"Jessica is not dead but is recovering at a faster rate than a normal human," Davior said with some amusement in his own tone.

Seth fell down hard in his chair in shock. He picked up the photo and stared at her portrait once again. That time, the picture did not move or scowl at him. He poured himself another round and downed it quickly.

"There is something going on, something to do with Jessica, but I'm not able to figure it out yet. I'm not sure they even know, but I do have my sources—" Davior was still speaking when Seth interrupted.

"Forget about her," Seth said in a low mumble, setting the picture back down on the desk.

"Seth, what are you saying?" Davior asked.

"I'm saying we have a lot of work to do, and I suggest we move forward." He glanced at Davior's strange expression but continued. "There is still a matter of finding me a wife. That should be the next order of business, someone smart and savvy to our way of thinking, don't you think, Davior?" he asked.

"Seth, are you sure? There is still a way we could—"

"Let her be happy, at least for a little while. Let him know what it means to have her love, and then, when the time comes, when the final battle begins"—Seth's eyes began to fill with rage—"Hunter is *mine!*"

1